The
Dragon Lord's
Daughters

Also by Bertrice Small
in Large Print:

Rosamund

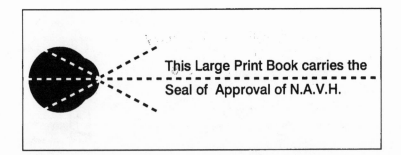

This Large Print Book carries the
Seal of Approval of N.A.V.H.

The Dragon Lord's Daughters

Bertrice Small

Thorndike Press • Waterville, Maine

Published in 2004 by arrangement with Kensington Books, an imprint of Kensington Publishing Corp.

Thorndike Press® Large Print Romance.

The tree indicium is a trademark of Thorndike Press.

The text of this Large Print edition is unabridged.
Other aspects of the book may vary from the original edition.

Set in 16 pt. Plantin by Elena Picard.

Printed in the United States on permanent paper.

Library of Congress Cataloging-in-Publication Data

Small, Bertrice.
    The dragon lord's daughters / Bertrice Small.
      p. cm.
    ISBN 0-7862-6523-X (lg. print : hc : alk. paper)
    1. Great Britain — History — To 1066 — Fiction.
2. Nobility — Fiction. 3. Sisters — Fiction. 4. Britons — Fiction. 5. Large type books. I. Title.
    PS3569.M28D73 2004
    813'.54—dc22   2004041276

For Sophia Patricia Small,
when she is old enough

As the Founder/CEO of NAVH, the only national health agency solely devoted to those who, although not totally blind, have an eye disease which could lead to serious visual impairment, I am pleased to recognize Thorndike Press* as one of the leading publishers in the large print field.

Founded in 1954 in San Francisco to prepare large print textbooks for partially seeing children, NAVH became the pioneer and standard setting agency in the preparation of large type.

Today, those publishers who meet our standards carry the prestigious "Seal of Approval" indicating high quality large print. We are delighted that Thorndike Press is one of the publishers whose titles meet these standards. We are also pleased to recognize the significant contribution Thorndike Press is making in this important and growing field.

Lorraine H. Marchi, L.H.D.
Founder/CEO
NAVH

* Thorndike Press encompasses the following imprints: Thorndike, Wheeler, Walker and Large Print Press.

Prologue

Ancient Britain before the Dark Ages

The Enchanter looked directly at Lord Ector. "Arthur may not marry the girl," he said.

"But why?" Lord Ector protested. "Her father and I have made an agreement that Lynior and Arthur will wed at Beltaine. She is already ripening with his child. It is a good match for a nameless foundling. Lynior is her father's only child."

"You should have consulted me first before you made any life-altering decisions for the lad," the Enchanter said quietly.

"Consulted you? You have not been back here since the night you brought Arthur to my wife and me as a newborn infant," Lord Ector said. "We don't even know who you are, but since you appeared in our hall in a puff of smoke we assumed you came from the Fair Folk, and it would have been dangerous for us to refuse an emissary of the Fair Folk."

"I am Merlin," the Enchanter said quietly.

"The king's Merlin?" Lord Ector was

impressed, and perhaps just a little afraid. Merlin, half fairy, half human, was known to be a most powerful sorcerer.

The Enchanter nodded. "I was in Uther Pendragon's service once, but the king died thirteen years ago, Ector of Gwynedd. Since then Britain has been at war with itself, as you must surely know. The lesser kings cannot agree on a High King. Now I have called a council to be held in London at the time of the Winter Solstice, which the Christians call Christ's Mass. The new king will be chosen then by my hand, and you must be there with your fosterling, Arthur, and your son, Cai. You cannot refuse me."

"Nay, I cannot," Lord Ector said, "but why do you forbid Arthur his marriage to Lynior? What difference should it make to you?"

"Come to London at the Solstice, and you will see," Merlin replied quietly.

Lord Ector sighed. "Lynior's father will be very displeased, especially considering his daughter's condition."

"Tell him that Arthur will, at the proper time, recognize his child, and that neither his daughter nor his grandson will suffer for it. I will personally see that the maiden is given a husband of good family who will cherish her and her child. Tell him that Merlin the Enchanter has made this promise."

"I will," Lord Ector said, nodding, and then he blinked hard, for Merlin was gone. Shaking his head Ector of Gwynedd wondered just what this was all about. Well, they would know at Christ's Mass, and not a moment before. Now he had the painful task of telling Arthur that he could not wed with Lynior; and the more difficult task of telling Lynior's father. He sighed, and then calling for a servant, sent for his wife.

Maeve came, and he told her of Merlin's visit. "Are you certain you were not dreaming?" Maeve demanded of him. "You imbibed a great quantity of new mead with your supper, husband." She gave him a small fond smile.

Ector sighed again, and drew his wife down into his lap. "I was not dreaming, lass," he told her. Her plump weight on his knees somehow gave him comfort. She was a good woman, and they had been wed for over twenty years now.

"So it was old Merlin himself," Maeve said. "Ohh, I wish I had been here! And he has plans for our lad, does he? I wonder what they are. 'Tis unfortunate about Lynior, but if the Enchanter says he will make it right, then he will. You must tell Lord Evan as soon as possible."

"And Arthur?"

Maeve shook her head. "Tell Evan first that he may tell his daughter as we tell Arthur. I see no reason why they should not remain friends. They have a child in common. I will come with you to Evan for he has a hot temper like our own Cai, and he prizes Lynior greatly especially as she is his only child."

But strangely Lord Evan was not angry. "From the moment I gave my consent to the match," he said, "I have been troubled each night with terrible dreams. Now I understand why. This marriage was not to be."

"The Enchanter says he will personally choose a good husband for Lynior. One who will cherish her, and her child," Lord Ector told his old friend.

"If I cannot have Arthur then I want no other," Lynior said, entering her father's hall. "I do not need a husband to be happy. I will raise my son alone, teaching him to be the good and honorable man his father is. Does Arthur know?"

"Not yet," Maeve told the young woman who was to have been her daughter-in-law. "Merlin says Arthur will acknowledge his child."

"It is a son, I carry," Lynior said calmly. "I intend naming him Gwydre. Arthur's fate must be very great that Merlin himself is involved."

"It was Merlin who brought Arthur to us all those years ago," Lord Ector said, "though we did not know it at the time who he was. But when a man appears in your hall in a rumble of thunder and a puff of smoke, you do not argue with him or ask his name."

"You will go to London at the Solstice?" Lord Evan asked.

"Merlin has commanded it. The High King will be chosen then, he says. I am to bring Arthur, and Cai will accompany us as well," Ector replied.

"You'll not leave me behind," Maeve said sharply.

The two men laughed, and Lord Ector said, "Nay, wife, I will not leave you behind. You shall come with us, and see the new king crowned."

So Lord Ector and his family traveled from their keep in the north of Wales to London in time for the Solstice. The closer they got to the ancient city the more crowded the roads became. It seemed that everyone in Britain was gathering to see the new High King chosen by the great Enchanter, Merlin. Ector and his party were fortunate to find a single room to share in a small inn within the city. The men-at-arms who had traveled with them had to content themselves sleeping with their horses in the stables.

On the day of the choosing, Cai, Arthur's older foster brother, discovered that he had not brought his sword with him, and he wished to wear it to the council. A warrior was not properly dressed without a sword. "Go find me a sword," he told the younger boy.

"Where am I to find you a sword?" Arthur demanded. "I have no money. Do you think someone will just give me the loan of a weapon because I ask it?"

Cai cuffed the boy irritably. " 'Tis your fault in the first place," he scolded Arthur.

"You are in training to be my squire. What kind of a squire forgets his master's sword? If we were going into battle I should certainly be at a disadvantage, shouldn't I?"

"But you aren't," Arthur argued. "We're just going to stand among the crowd and see the new High King chosen from among the twelve lesser kings, Cai."

Cai knocked his younger companion to the ground with a hard blow, and then standing over him growled, "Find me a sword, youngling, or I'll give you such a beating that you'll not walk for a month!"

Arthur scrambled to his feet, and stumbled from the inn's courtyard, his head throbbing from the blow. Cai had a foul temper, and it was no use arguing with him when he got like this. He wasn't going to find a sword for his elder, but he could at least keep out of the range of his fists

14

until it was time to leave for the choosing. He hadn't wanted to come to London. But they had told him he was not to wed with Lynior after all, and he was instead to come to see the new High King chosen. He didn't understand why that was so important, or what seeing the new High King chosen had to do with his marriage to Lynior. But there was to be no marriage now, and no one would explain to him why. His foster father had said bluntly that he didn't know himself. It had just been ordained by a higher authority.

Suddenly a bent old man, leaning heavily on his staff, his black cloak covering him from head to foot, sidled up to Arthur and said, "You seek a sword, young master, do you not?"

"How did you know?" the young man said, surprised.

"Go into yon courtyard," the old man said, pointing with a bony finger, "and you will find what it is you seek." Then he hobbled off down the street, seeming to disappear before Arthur's very eyes into the mists of the morning.

For a long moment the lad debated, but then he decided that nothing ventured, nothing gained. And wouldn't Cai be surprised if Arthur did return with a sword for him? Striding into the grassy courtyard he saw a large boulder, and thrusting forth

15

from it was a great sword with a bejeweled hilt. Upon the stone were carved the words "Who Pulls This Sword From This Stone, Is Britain's Rightful High King," but the boy did not see the words. He saw only the sword. Cai was going to be very surprised. He chuckled. Reaching out Arthur drew the weapon from the rock.

"Now you will come with me, Arthur, son of Uther Pendragon, High King of all of Britain," a strong authoritative voice said, and the old man with the staff stepped from the shadows of the courtyard.

Arthur turned. "Who are you? And who did you say I am?"

"You are the only son of Uther Pendragon, and his wife, Igraine, who was once wife to Gorlois, Duke of Cornwall," the old man said.

"Nay, old sir, you are mistaken. I am Arthur, younger son of Lord Ector of Wales," Arthur responded politely.

"You are Ector's fosterling, Arthur Pendragon. I brought you to him myself the night you were born. He knew not who I was," the old man replied.

"Who are you?" Arthur asked, curious now.

"I am Merlin the Enchanter," was the answer, "and 'twas I who placed the sword in the stone, and put a spell upon it so that only the rightful king of all of Britain might take it. All the lords of this land have been here before you to attempt to draw this sword forth from the stone. All have failed. 'Tis you, Arthur Pendragon, who is Britain's rightful High King. Now, put the sword back into the stone from whence you drew it, and wait for me while I go to gather the lesser kings. You will then take the sword from the stone a final time before witnesses, and be proclaimed High King."

"Is this why I could not wed with Lynior, Merlin?" the young man asked.

Merlin nodded. "You have your fate to follow, my lord, as Lynior has hers. She will give you a son in the spring, and from him will a line of Pendragons be born down through the centuries."

"Lynior's son cannot be king after me?" He didn't understand.

Merlin shook his head. "None will follow you, Arthur Pendragon, though you will have one other son. I cannot prevent his birth though I would if I could, for he will be a curse. Nay, Lynior's son must remain unknown to all but a few that the Pendragon line continue. You have half sisters, Arthur. The daughters of Gorlois. Morgause, Elaine, and Morgan. They are magical creatures who will seek to revenge their father on you and yours. To keep Lynior's son safe you must keep him hidden even as I kept you hidden with Ector all these years so that you might live to follow in your father's footsteps."

Arthur nodded slowly. "I understand," he said, feeling as if the stone that housed the sword was now upon his shoulders. He knew suddenly, and with great insight, that his boyhood was over; that the life ahead of him would be filled with adventure, passion, pleasure and pain. There would be great successes, and equally great disappointments. "You will stay with me, and guide me, Merlin, won't you?"

"I will remain with Your Majesty as long as I can," the Enchanter said, a small smile touching his wintery features.

"And no matter what happens my blood will flow down through the centuries?"

"Forever and ever, my lord. You have my promise," Merlin answered quietly.

Arthur thrust the sword back into the stone. "Fetch the lesser kings then that I may prove myself their High King."

"Yes, my lord," Merlin replied, and he hurried off.

And so Arthur drew the sword from the stone in the grassy courtyard a second time, before all the lesser kings of Britain, and was proclaimed High King, though there were some who were not happy. His reign was a great one as Merlin had predicted, but the daughters of Gorlois, his half sisters, were a constant thorn in his side. The eldest of them, Morgan Le Fay, a powerful enchantress, seduced Arthur who had never met her, and conceived a child by him. Their son, Mordred, eventually became the downfall of his father's kingdom.

But in the mountains of north Wales, Lynior, daughter of Evan, raised Arthur's eldest son, Gwydre, in secret, protected by Merlin's sorcery even after the ancient Enchanter disappeared. And through Gwydre, and his wife, Eres, daughter of Odgar, who was the son of Aedd, King of Ireland, the line of Pendragon continued down through the centuries unscathed.

Part One

Averil

Chapter 1

"I shall marry a great lord," Averil Pendragon told her sisters as they sat together in their father's hall. Her golden head nodded emphatically with her pronouncement.

"You shall marry the man our father chooses for you," her sister Maia said.

"And he shall be a great lord," Averil repeated.

"Perhaps," Maia said. "But he could as easily be an old merchant to whom father owes a great debt, and wishes to pacify; or mayhap a knight father wishes to bind to our service. Your dower will be small, Averil, for though you are the eldest of us, you are still naught but a concubine's daughter. My brother Brynn and I are the true heirs," Maia concluded loftily with a satisfied smile.

"But I am the most beautiful of us all," Averil shot back. "Everyone says I am the fairest of our father's daughters. My beauty shall not be wasted on some merchant or simple knight. I may be the daughter of a concubine, but our father loves my mother, and so my value is great."

"You are the most beautiful of us all!" their youngest sister, Junia, said with a sigh. "You are both very beautiful, and I am so plain."

"You are not plain, Junia," Maia said. "You are simply young."

"Aye, I am," Junia replied. "You have such rich red hair, Maia. And you, Averil, are descended from the Fair Folk, and have hair like spun gold. My dark hair is so common." She sighed.

"But your features are exquisite," Averil remarked. "You have the most perfect little nose, and a sweet mouth, Junia. As for your hair, it has the blue-green shine of a raven's wing. It is hardly common, sister."

"But I am a concubine's daughter, too," Junia wailed. "And the youngest! What sort of dower will I have by the time I am old enough to wed? Father will probably have to match me with the old merchant." She began to cry.

"Now see what you have done with your proud boasting!" Averil snapped at Maia. "You have made the baby weep, and if we cannot stop her we will be punished."

"What about your boasting about being the most beautiful and marrying a great lord?" Maia demanded to know. Reaching out, she pulled Junia from her stool, and into the comfort of her arms. "There, there, chick, do not fret. Father loves us all equally, and we will all have grand dowers and great lords for husbands I am certain." She stroked her little sister's dark head.

"Really?" Junia sniffed softly.

"Of course, you goose!" Averil said impatiently. "We are the Dragon Lord's daughters, and descended from King Arthur himself. Even today our ancestor's memory is still strong. But because I am the eldest I shall be wed first, and I will be fifteen next month, sisters. I think it is time for me to be matched. Most girls are wed younger than fifteen. Da just doesn't want to let us go."

Junia's tears faded away. "I did hear our da speaking with the lady Argel about matches a few days ago," she said innocently.

Maia's arms dropped from about her sibling. "What did my mother and our father say?" she demanded to know.

"There were no names spoken," Junia replied.

"But what did they say?" Averil pressed her little sister. "They had to have said something that piqued your curiosity, Junia, else you should not have mentioned it."

"They said the time had come to consider marriages for you both. Father said he would follow the example of our prince, the Great Llywelyn, and seek among the Marcher lords for suitable husbands for you. That's all that I heard. I swear!"

"What did my mother reply?" Maia wanted to know.

"She agreed. Nothing more. You know your mother, Maia. She is so kind and soft-spoken. It is rare that she disagrees with our father. My mother says we are fortunate in her for another wife might not be so thoughtful of her husband's concubines, or allow them to live in the keep with the lady and her children," Junia finished.

"My mother says if the lady Argel had been able to bear her children sooner we might not be here at all," Averil remarked. Then she turned her attention again to the prospect of a husband. "We must listen more closely, sisters," she told them, "for we shall be told nothing before it is engraved in stone. We shall have to learn everything for ourselves."

The three heads nodded solemnly in agreement.

Several days later, however, Averil overheard something that displeased her greatly. Her father was considering making a match for Maia first because she was his legitimate daughter. Never before had Averil Pendragon known her sire to put one of his children above the other, no matter their birthright. And worse! He would make no overtures towards any family until Maia was fifteen, which was a whole year away. *I will be sixteen by then,* Averil considered, *and too old for a good match.* She sighed, and began to think what she could do, but she could think of nothing. She kept this knowledge from her sisters, but she did speak with her mother, Gorawen.

Gorawen was as beautiful as her daughter was. They shared the same pale golden hair, and fair skin. But Gorawen's eyes were silver in color, and Averil's were the light green of her father's. All of the Dragon Lord's daughters had green eyes. "You were right to come to me," Gorawen said. "Your father can wait no longer to match you with a husband. You are more than old enough, but if you must tarry until Maia is wed, who knows how old you may be. Certainly too old to attract a good match. I will not allow your beauty to be wasted on some insignificant family!"

"He has never before put her before me," Averil said, her tone irritable.

Gorawen laughed softly, and patted her daughter's hand. "He has always been more than fair with you all, and Argel too, but this is different, Averil. There is no avoiding the fact that both you and Junia were born on the wrong side of the blanket."

"So was our ancestor, Gwydre, the founder of this house," Averil muttered.

"I know," her mother replied, "but that was centuries ago, and Gwydre was a man. It is different for lasses, Daughter. My birth was true, but I was one of five daughters. There was no dowry for me for either a husband or the church. My father, Arian ap Tewydr, was more than willing to give me to Merin Pendragon as his concubine. He knew your father would treat me well, and I should be safe for the rest of my days. He made your father swear on his ancestor's name that the children born of our union would be well cared for, and you have been, Averil."

"Why did you have no other children, Mother?" Averil asked.

"I did not want to give your father a son when Argel had not. She is a good and patient woman, but even good and patient women have their limits. Ysbail gives us all enough difficulty."

"But Argel did give father a son," Averil said.

"But only after many years of marriage. That is why he took Ysbail for a second concubine, however she birthed Junia much to her annoyance, but then she is a foolish woman. If she had birthed a son he would have been overshadowed by a legitimate brother, for Argel managed at last to have the son, who is your father's heir. Ysbail would not have been happy to have any son of hers forced to take a lesser role."

"You both might have had more daughters," Averil said slyly.

"We might," her mother answered, "but we did not." Then she laughed. "I will tell you when you need to know, daughter."

"Will you speak with my father?" the girl asked.

"Eventually," Gorawen said. "Your birthday is not until the last day of April, my daughter. I do not want your father aware of what you heard, or that you were eavesdropping when he and Argel were discussing your fates. Let me handle this in my own way, and my own time. You will, I promise, be wed before Maia."

"I believe you, Mother, for you have never lied to me," Averil said.

"You must learn to cultivate patience, Daughter," Gorawen chided gently.

"I will try," Averil promised, and her mother smiled.

"Good. You want to show your father that you are ready to leave his keeping, and be a good wife to a husband," Gorawen said. "Your behavior must never shame us." Then Gorawen dismissed her only child, and considered how to deal with the situation with which Averil had presented her. The truth was that Merin Pendragon had kept his two eldest daughters too close for too long. Averil and Maia should have both been matched earlier, and their marriages ready to be celebrated. Her own child would be fifteen at the end of the month, and Maia would be fourteen on the fourteenth of May. She smiled to herself. Once the wheels were set in motion to match Averil and Maia she was certain that Ysbail would begin demanding equal treatment for her daughter. Junia would be but eleven on June second. There was time for Junia. First Averil, and then Maia. Maia's match would be the better one no matter, but Merin would see that Averil was given a good husband. Her daughter would have a good dower portion. She would not have to be a concubine like her mother, Gorawen thought, satisfied.

She arose, and calling her serving woman for her cloak, Gorawen went out into the spring day. The courtyard of the keep was quiet but for the poultry scratching about in the dirt. Several dogs slept in the sunshine, and by the kitchen garden, her destination, a fat tabby dozed amid the new greenery. She shooed him awake and away, and taking her knife from her robes began to cut some herbs. If she was to have her way about Averil she must get Merin into her bed. Of late, she noted, his manhood did not rise to the challenge of her womanhood as it once had. He was no longer a young man. He had wed Argel late, being thirty. He had been too busy in the service of Llywelyn ap Iowerth, called the Great Llywelyn, who was his overlord, and lord of almost all of Wales. It was Llywelyn who had finally sent him home, and told him to marry before it was too late.

So Merin Pendragon had returned to his keep. His parents were gone from the earth, and he realized the prince was right. He needed a wife. He had found a good match in Argel urch Owein, daughter of Owein ap Dafydd. Argel had been fifteen when they wed. But to her distress she could not seem to conceive a child. After four years Merin had brought Gorawen into his keep, and nine months later Averil had been born. A year later Argel had brought forth her first child, a daughter, Maia. But after that there was no sign of another child.

Gorawen knew well how to prevent conception, having been taught by her grandmother, a wisewoman. She had prevented another pregnancy in order that Argel might have time to conceive a son for their shared lord. After a while Merin grew impatient, and brought another concubine into their midst. Ysbail conceived immediately, and birthed Junia. Gorawen saw that her grandmother's potion was fed to Ysbail that she not birth a son; and she prayed to the gods both old and new for Merin's seed to take root in Argel's womb again, and that it be a son. Her prayers were finally answered in the summer that Averil was six, Maia five, and Junia three. Argel birthed a son on the first day of August. He was a healthy child who was called Brynn.

After that there were no more children born of Merin Pendragon's seed, and as the years went on the master of Dragon's Lair Keep began to lose interest in his women. Now and again, however, Gorawen could lure him to her bed, and help him to gain pleasure. It was usually when she wanted something badly, for Merin Pendragon was no fool, and she would not shame him. So when that evening she murmured an invitation in his ear he had smiled knowingly, and nodded.

Gorawen was awaiting her lord. She had had a tall oaken tub brought to her chamber, and filled with hot water. Now having undressed Merin she climbed into the tub with him, and began to bathe him. He grunted with pleasure as she scrubbed his back with a boar's bristle brush, and a rough cloth. She picked the nits from his graying head, and washed his locks thoroughly. "Where have you been sleeping?" she demanded. "You are flea bit on your back. You need a new mattress, my lord. I shall tell Argel."

"Do it yourself," he said. "She is morose of late, and can take no suggestion. She weeps at nothing. I do not understand it. She is not breeding, I know for certain."

"Perhaps her juices are drying up," Gorawen suggested. " 'Tis a sad time for a woman to know she may never again bear life in her womb."

"You and Argel are the best of friends, and make my life pleasant," he said. "You would think kindly of my lady." He pulled her wet, naked form against him, and kissed her heartily. "You're a good lass, Gorawen, mother of my eldest child."

She stood quietly in his embrace, and smiled. "You are good to me, and to our daughter, my lord. But come now, and let us get out of the tub. I have a fine treat for you." She smiled again, and climbed out of the water, quickly wrapping a drying cloth about herself, picking up the other to wipe the water off Merin's big body. He was yet a fine figure of a man. When they were both dry she led him to her bed, settling him, hurrying to bring a plate of sweetmeats and a cup of wine for his pleasure.

Merin Pendragon had a sweet tooth, and

33

reached at once for the plate. He popped a sweetmeat in his mouth, chewing appreciatively. "What are they?" he asked her.

"I dried plums last summer, and soaked them in sweet wine in a stone crock all winter. Then I rolled them up, dipped them in honey, and rolled them in crushed almonds. Do you like them, my lord?" She climbed into the bed next to him, and sipped from his cup.

"You're a clever wench, Gorawen," he told her, unaware that the wine the plums had been soaking in was imbued with a potent aphrodisiac she made from the herbs in her garden. He reached for her as he felt his passions begin to stir.

Gorawen melted into his arms. "My dear lord," she murmured, holding her face up to him for his kisses, tasting the wine and the plums on his breath. Her fingers began to caress the back of his neck gently, but in a way that had always pleased him greatly.

"What do you want of me?" he demanded, shifting her so that she now lay beneath him. He pulled the drying cloth open, and stared down at her big breasts.

"Later, Merin," she said softly, her tongue teasing his ear, her breath hot, and sending shivers down his spine.

He chuckled. "A very clever wench," he told her with emphasis. Then covering her body with his, and feeling his lust beginning to rage, he thrust into her, sighing gustily as she received him, wrapping her legs about his waist. Soon she was crying out to him with pleasure, and for the first time in a very long while Merin Pendragon felt like the inexhaustible youth he had once been. He groaned as her body shuddered with her pleasure not once, but twice. And at that second burst of satisfaction he loosed his own juices with a howl of gratification, finally falling away from Gorawen, his breath coming in quick pants.

They lay together recovering from the bout of Eros that had surprised even Gorawen. The plums were more successful than she had anticipated. At last recovered she said, "Now I will ask a favor of you, my lord."

He laughed aloud. "And I will grant it you, sweeting, as you have pleasured me mightily this night. What is it you will have of me?"

"I want you to find a husband for Averil. She will be fifteen at the end of the month. It is past time she was matched, wedded and bedded," Gorawen said.

"I have been thinking on it," he said. "For both Maia and Averil."

"Maia is your legitimate daughter, but she is the younger, my lord. She will be easier to match, but she should not be wed

35

before her elder sister. If they had not all been raised together without prejudice in your hall it might be a different thing. But you have treated all your children, both licit and illicit, in the same loving and kindly manner," Gorawen pointed out.

"Ahh," he said, "I see the difficulty here, sweeting. It takes time to make the kind of match that must be made for Maia, and if much more time passes, Averil will be considered too long in the tooth."

"Aye, she will. My lord, she is the most beautiful of your daughters. Use that beauty for a good match. Then the match you can make for Maia will be even better than you might have hoped for as she is the legitimate daughter. And little Junia will have an opportunity she might not if her sisters are married well, and better."

"A clever wench," he repeated for the third time that evening. "But who?"

"You have said you would follow the example of our prince and seek among the Marcher lords for sons-in-law. This may also prove useful when Brynn is of an age to take a wife. I know that the prince hopes to rid himself of this English king who is his overlord, but I wonder if that will ever happen. And we who live here in Wales must think of ourselves, and our children, first. What are the politics of great men to us?"

Merin Pendragon nodded. "You reason well, sweeting, though you be but a woman. The more we ally our family to the families of the Marcher lords the better off it will be for us. I will do as you have asked me, and find a husband for Averil first, but I will tell Argel of my decision before I do. She is my wife, and as loyal to me as are you."

"Of course you must speak with Argel, my lord! She is mistress in this house, and I respect her as I do you," Gorawen said sweetly. She lifted the plate of sweetmeats from the table by the bed. "Will you have another, my love?"

"Aye, I will!" he said smiling at her. "I vow, Gorawen, no one, not even my dear Argel, pleases me, or treats me as you do." He ate three more of the plum delicacies.

"I have been happier with you than with anyone else," Gorawen told him honestly.

He smiled warmly at her. Soon his lust was afire once more to his surprise, and he was putting her beneath him once again, and satisfying their shared desires with the enthusiasm of a man thirty years younger.

When afterwards he slept, replete with his pleasure, Gorawen arose, and took the plate of sweetmeats away. There was but one left upon the plate, but she did not want him to have it lest he associate the wine-soaked plums with his lust for her this night. It was the first time she had used such means to arouse him, and she was quite surprised by the success she had had. But he was content with her, and his own performance tonight. She smiled wickedly. He would not have the same success with Ysbail. The other concubine would have to suck his cock to a stand to bring them both any pleasure at all, and it would be quick. As for Argel, she no longer cared if her husband visited her bed. But because of this night Gorawen's daughter would be matched first. Merin would explain it all to Argel, and Argel would not argue. She never did.

Now Gorawen began to wonder who Averil's husband would be. There were several fine families among the Marcher lords who would do. A younger son? A favorite son born on the wrong side of the blanket? Gorawen considered what kind of dower Merin would provide for his eldest child. There would have to be just enough cattle, and sheep, to add to Averil's beauty to make her most desirable. Since she was favored by her father, the manner of her birth would not matter. But Gorawen knew she had extracted all she dared from Merin this night. Now let him make good on his promise, and then she would haggle with him over their daughter's dower.

The next afternoon she took Averil into

her herb garden ostensibly to teach her of things she must know, but also to tell her daughter of her small success with Merin Pendragon. "You may not tell anyone of what I have said to you," Gorawen warned Averil. "Your father has given me his pledge, and he will keep his word."

"Who do you think it will be, Mother?" Averil asked, excited.

Gorawen shook her head. "I have no idea, but you may trust your father will do his best by you. It will surely be a son from one of the Marcher families, for the Pendragon interests lie with them if we are to continue to survive."

"Maia said I should be given to an elderly merchant that father is indebted to, or perhaps some simple knight," Averil said, "but I know that will not be. The better my match, the better Maia's match will be."

"Aye." Gorawen nodded. Then she said, "Now, here is a secret remedy I shall teach you, daughter, so that if you desire to prevent conception of a child, you can."

"The priest says it is a woman's sole function to bear new life," Averil replied.

"The priest is an old fool and should know better since he and his hearth mate have birthed nine younglings they could not feed were it not for your da. Surely he has had some pleasure of his mate other than just children." Gorawen laughed knowingly.

"Teach me all you know, Mother," Averil said eagerly. "Some say you are a witch with all your knowledge of herbs and potions. I would learn all you are willing to share with me."

"Humph!" Gorawen sniffed. "Fools! I gained my wisdom in my father's house at my grandmother's knee. She thought that because I had no dower it might be an advantage to me wherever life would lead me. And it certainly has been." She bent her head and pointed.

"The seeds from the wild carrot, mashed into a paste and formed into a pellet that can be taken each day will prevent conception, Averil. It is not wise for a woman to have babies too quickly. Two years between each child is healthy."

"Why did you have no more children, Mother?" Averil asked.

"If I had borne a son before Argel it would have made all our lives difficult," Gorawen explained. "And your father did not need more daughters. Three was enough."

"You prevented Ysbail from having other children, didn't you?" Averil said with great certainty.

Gorawen smiled, but neither did she confirm or deny her daughter's suspicions.

40

"Here, this is sparagus. The best stalks are those with their heads turned downward towards the earth. They have two uses. Alleviating constipation, or stimulating romantic relations. You must add a little seasoning to them after boiling or they can cause the fibers of the stomach to be damaged. A pinch of salt is enough."

"Its uses are quite varied," Averil noted.

Gorawen laughed. "Yes," she agreed, "they are."

"How does it affect romantic relations?" Averil asked.

"You boil the stalks until they are just tender, with the salt, and then you serve them in a dish of melted butter," Gorawen said. "The sight of a woman slowly eating the sparagus, licking the stalks with her tongue, sucking upon the stumps, stimulates a manhood greatly. When you do this before your husband he will imagine you are licking his stalk, and sucking upon it."

"Ohh!" Averil exclaimed, and she blushed. "I never realized . . ." Her voice trailed off as she blushed once more.

"You will not discuss what I tell you or teach you with either of your sisters. Junia is too young for such knowledge, and as for Maia, it is up to her mother to enlighten her. Now, with regard to a husband's manhood, you must be absolutely certain it is clean before you touch it. Most men do not bathe regularly, but you must make certain that your husband does. Wash him yourself, which he will enjoy, or bathe with him, which is even more pleasurable," Gorawen said. "In the finest castles and keeps the hostess is responsible for bathing her guests of honor. That is how the daughters of the house learn. Here at Dragon's Lair, however, we have no guests. There is no reason for anyone to come here." She paused a moment to think, and then Gorawen continued. "Both you and Maia must learn the art of bathing a man. I will speak to Argel about it. I believe you should practice on your brother, Brynn."

"Wash Brynn?" Averil was scandalized. "That little heathen never bathes, Mother, and except in the summer when he swims in the stream I think water never touches his skin."

"Well," Gorawen said, rising from the garden, "you and Maia have to learn how to properly wash a male. Brynn and your father are the only men of rank at Dragon's Lair, and I do not think it proper that you wash Merin." Then, forgetting Averil entirely, she hurried off to find Argel and present her with this problem.

Argel was in the hall of the keep, working at her loom. She was weaving a tapestry depicting King Arthur's marriage to his wife, Guinevere. The other of Merin

Pendragon's concubines, Ysbail, was with her, sorting out threads by color for her embroidery frame. They looked up as Gorawen entered the hall.

"The girls must learn to bathe a man," Gorawen began. "Here, our Lord Merin is beginning to consider husbands for Averil and Maia, and they are lacking in the basic knowledge needed and known by the most common goodwife!"

"Marriages for Averil and Maia?" Ysbail screeched. "What of my daughter?"

"Junia is too young yet," Argel said, ending any argument. "First our lord will seek a match for Averil, for she is the eldest. It must be a very good match if Maia is to have an even better one. And these two marriages will determine what kind of matches can be made for Junia and Brynn."

"Of course," Ysbail said slowly. Then she added, "Our good lord had best work quickly, for Averil is really getting too old to match. I want to see Junia wed at thirteen."

"Averil's beauty will make up for her age," Gorawen said through gritted teeth.

"Averil is the perfect age to wed," Argel noted quietly. "But Gorawen is correct. The girls are well versed in housekeeping, but know little of common hospitality or courtesy towards a guest. This lack must be remedied quickly."

"We'll have to use Brynn," Gorawen said.

Argel and Ysbail burst out laughing.

"I know, I know," Gorawen said with a grin, "but we have no one else, do we?"

"Nay, we do not," Argel said, wiping the tears from her eyes. "We will begin this evening. I shall have the large oak tub set up in the hall, and they can begin to learn. Junia may also take part in these lessons. She is not too young for that."

"Poor Brynn," Ysbail said.

"He will survive," Argel said dryly. "And who knows what we will find beneath those several layers of dirt. They'll have to pick the nits from his head."

"There is much to learn," Gorawen said, "as our daughters will soon find out."

In early evening the tub was brought into the hall and set before a fireplace to be filled with hot water. Cloths for scrubbing, brushes, cloths for drying, and soap were placed on a small table that had been set at the tub's edge. Averil, Maia and Junia, long aprons over their chemises, were waiting for their brother to be brought into the hall. They looked at each other, and began to giggle as he was dragged in forcibly, howling with his outrage. At eight years of age, Brynn Pendragon was the image of his father. He was tall for a boy of nine, with long gangly limbs, and thick black hair.

Seeing the tub he struggled all the harder. "I'm not taking a bath!" he raged. "Bathing is for weaklings and Norman coxcombs!"

"Shut your gob!" his father roared at him, and he cuffed the boy sharply, stilling his outrage and struggles. "A proper chatelaine of the house always bathes her guests. Your sisters have had no experience in this art as we rarely receive visitors. You and I are the only men of rank here, and I don't intend on allowing my daughters to wash me. I am not yet that feeble. So 'tis you, my son, who will submit with good grace, or I'll beat the hide off of you. I am about to seek a husband for Averil and then Maia. Would you have them disgrace the name of Pendragon by being ill-mannered in matters of hospitality?"

Brynn said nothing, but he was still now. He had received one or two beatings from his father in recent years. It wasn't an experience he wanted to repeat.

"Do you never change your clothing?" Averil said as she came up to him, and began to peel his garments from the boy's frame. "Ewww! And you stink, little brother! For shame! You are a noble's son, and should have more care of your person." She handed the boy's clothing to

Maia and Junia, instructing them to toss them in the fire.

"That's my favorite sherte!" the boy protested.

"You could poison soup with it, you heathen," Averil scolded him.

Their father and his women chuckled, but made no move to stop her.

When the lad was brought naked Argel said, "He should stand in the tub, lasses, while he is thoroughly washed. Then he is to sit in the water while the nits are picked from his head prior to washing his hair."

The three girls set about to bathe their brother, scrubbing him vigorously until his skin was pink again.

"Do we wash all of him?" Maia inquired nervously.

"All!" the three mothers chorused.

Maia looked at her little brother's masculine apendage, then her eyes met Averil's.

"You do it," she said. "He is my brother."

"He is my brother, too," Averil noted, "but I'll do it today. You will have to do it tomorrow."

"Tomorrow?" Brynn yelped! "You're going to do this tomorrow, too?"

His mother laughed. "Every other day until the girls can bathe you properly. I'm sorry, Brynn, but they must learn. If we

46

had guests they would have already learned, but we are so isolated here in the Welshry, and only those with business at Dragon's Lair come to Dragon's Lair."

Averil took up the washing cloth, soaped it heavily and washed her brother's male member, pushing the foreskin on it up to wash beneath the skin. Her hands moved quickly and efficiently beneath him to soap his seed pouch. She splashed water on him, rinsing the foam away. "That wasn't so bad," she noted to Maia.

"A grown man's equipment will be bigger, lasses," their father warned them.

"Sit down," Maia instructed her brother, and when the boy had, the three girls began picking the nits from his head and hair.

He squealed as their fingers dug sharply into his scalp and pulled along the locks of his black hair. "Ouch! Have a care, sisters! Ouch!"

"Your hair is filthy, Brynn," Averil told him. "You are old enough to know you need to wash it, and yourself, regularly."

"Too much bathing is not good, the priest says," he told them. "He says it is a vanity to wash too much."

"Listen to the priest in matters concerning your soul, my son," Merin Pendragon advised, "but where the body is concerned, listen to your women. You'll get a lot farther with the lasses smelling like a rose than like a dung heap."

The three sisters were finally satisfied with their nitpicking, and poured a dish of water over Brynn's head. He gasped and sputtered, but they paid him no mind, instead lathering his head with the rich soap, rinsing it, washing and rinsing it a final time. Then they yanked him up, ordering him to step from the tub onto a cloth, which he did. The three girls then set about drying their brother off.

"Get in between his toes," Gorawen suggested.

Finally, Brynn Pendragon was cleaner than the day he had been born. "I smell like a flower," he grumbled.

Averil handed him a clean sherte. "You can roll in the pig byre on the morrow, little brother," she told him with a grin. "Then we shall have something worth washing the day after tomorrow."

"You'll have to catch me first," he warned her, glowering.

"Don't worry, Brynnie, we will," she answered him in dulcet tones.

"Go seek your bed, my son," Argel said quietly. "Your father and I would speak with your sisters now." She kissed the top of his dark damp head.

"Good night, Mother. Good night, aunts. Good night, Da," the boy said, and left the hall without further protest.

"That was well done, lasses," Argel praised them, "but your skills will need some refining. Your brother will be bathed every other day until I am satisfied that you are knowledgeable in this. You may go to your beds now. God protect you and give you sweet dreams this night."

The three sisters curtsied to the lady of the castle, and then each girl kissed her mother, and their father, before leaving the hall. They slept together in a large bed in a room at the top of the keep. Reaching their chamber they removed their skirts and tunics, washed their faces and hands, and cleaned their teeth with a cloth. They took turns brushing each other's hair out and plaiting their locks into a single braid for the night. Then they climbed into their bed, drawing the curtains about it, and pulling up the fur robe that kept them warm.

For a long time they were silent, and then Averil said, "Did you note our brother's manhood? It seemed small, though father did say a grown man's is larger."

"He isn't even nine yet," Maia defended her little brother. "It does get larger, my mother says, when he becomes a man. She wanted me to know that so I wouldn't be shocked when I had to bathe a man."

"How big does it get?" Junia wondered. "It seems to me a useless piece of flesh, dangling there between Brynn's legs. What use has it other than to pee?"

The two older girls giggled.

"My mother says when roused the manhood grows in length and thickness. It becomes as stiff as a piece of wood," Maia said.

"Why?" Junia demanded to know.

"Because, you goose, the man puts it into you, and makes a baby. If it were all flaccid he could not do it," Averil said.

"Where does he put it?" Junia asked, fascinated.

"We'll show you," Averil replied, making eye contact with Maia, who, leaning over, held her little sister down while Averil pushed up her chemise, and put a finger on Junia's hairless little slit. She pushed the fingertip past the two nether lips, saying, "It goes in there. Deep. I don't want to put my finger any farther lest I damage you, Sister."

Junia's eyes were wide with both surprise and shock as her older sister pulled her chemise back down again. "Where I pee?" she gasped.

"Nay, not there. There is an opening farther along. That is where the manhood is lodged, little one," Averil explained.

"Does it hurt?" Junia wondered.

"My mother says the first time it does, for the manhood shatters your maidenhead, which is hidden within you," Maia said. "But after that, she says, when the girl has been made a woman, there is pleasure if a man is skilled. She says our father is very skilled, and wishes the same happiness for all of us."

"I wonder who our husbands will be." Junia sighed.

"That is something you won't have to think about for a while," Maia told her. "Averil will be the first of us to wed, and it must be soon, for she is fifteen on the last day of this month. And then I will be wed, probably next year sometime if Da can find the right husband for me. But you aren't quite eleven, Junia. You have several more years before a husband will be chosen for you, and you are wed."

"I shall miss you both when you are gone!" Junia replied.

Averil laughed. "But you will have this bed all to yourself, and you know you have always wanted that. You are forever complaining that Maia and I crowd you, and kick."

"But I will be so very lonely," Junia responded. "I shall have no one to talk with before I go to sleep. Or to remind me to say my prayers. And I really like sleeping in the middle between you both."

"Well, you will have us both for a while, chick," Averil said, giving her little sister a kiss on the cheek. "Now, let us all settle down. I am fair exhausted from bathing our brother this evening."

"Gentle Mary, may you and your son, Jesu, watch over us this night," Maia said.

"May angels guard us through the dark hours," Junia replied.

"And bring us safely to another day so we may walk in the path that God has set out for us to walk in," Averil concluded. "Amen."

After a few moments of restlessness the three sisters slept.

Chapter 2

Godwine FitzHugh lay dying, his bastard son, Rhys, and his only legitimate heir, a six-year-old girl, by his side. "I trust you to look after Mary," he gasped. "You are all she has now." His gnarled hand clutched at his grown son.

"You know I will protect her, Father," Rhys said quietly.

"Have her pledge her fealty to the Mortimers, and you also," the dying man continued. He glared with dimming sight at the other man in the room. "Priest! You have heard my wishes. My son will have charge over my daughter, and over Everleigh. You must swear it before the Mortimers. Do you give me your promise?" His hands moved restlessly over the coverlet, plucking it nervously.

"I do, my lord," the priest replied.

Godwine FitzHugh turned his attention to his children again. "Find an heiress, Rhys, marry, and get children on her quickly. Make a good match for Mary."

"Aye, Father, I will do my best," Rhys

FitzHugh swore. But as he swore it he was thinking that obtaining a wife would probably be impossible. He had nothing to offer any woman. And an heiress? He almost laughed aloud. His father meant well. He had given him his own name, and raised him, for his mother had died at his birth. So had his half sister's mam. His father wed late in life, having spent his earlier years keeping the peace for the king here in the Marches between England and Wales. His own birth was the result of his father's youthful passion for Rhys's mother.

"Steal your bride, lad," his father whispered.

"What?" Surely he hadn't heard correctly. He looked questioningly at his sire.

The old man grinned, looking like a death's head as he did so. "Find a proper-tied lass, steal her and take her virginity," he repeated. "The family will have to agree to a match if you do that, my son. I know your birth is against you and for that I apologize."

"There is no honor in such an act," Rhys murmured to his sire.

"Don't be a fool, lad. You cannot afford to be honorable in this matter. You need a wife, and stealing one is the only way you will get a lass. Bride stealing is not really dishonorable, Rhys. It is done all the time."

His son laughed ruefully, and then he nodded. "I will have no other choice, I suppose, if I want legitimate sons," he said softly.

Again the death's head grin flashed briefly. Then Godwine held out his hand to his daughter. "Take my hand, Mary, and swear on the FitzHugh name that you will obey your brother until you are wed, and bring no shame upon our name."

The little girl took the cold, emaciated hand in her small plump one. "I promise, Father," she said solemnly. "And I shall never send Rhys from Everleigh no matter my husband. He shall always be bailiff here. I swear it on the Blessed Virgin's name."

"Good," her father replied. "Now give me a final kiss, my daughter, and leave me to die, for I shall not live to see the sunset this day."

Mary FitzHugh bent and kissed her sire's thin and chilly lips. "Godspeed you, my lord. I shall always pray to the Blessed Mother and our Lord Jesu for your good soul." She curtsied and then, turning, left the room.

"Priest! Shrive me and give me the last rites of Holy Mother Church. Then you will leave me with my son," Godwine FitzHugh commanded the cleric.

The priest did not argue, doing as he

was bid as Rhys FitzHugh knelt nearby, his dark head bent. Finished, the priest bade his master farewell, and exited the death chamber.

"Come and sit by my side," the lord of Everleigh manor said to his son. "Your presence comforts me."

Rhys FitzHugh brought a chair by the draped bed, and sat.

"I would have married your mother, you know," his father said, "but that she died giving you life. Her family was worthy of mine."

"I am content," Rhys assured the dying man.

"You should have inherited Everleigh," Godwine FitzHugh said regretfully.

"Aye," Rhys agreed, "but that was not the way my fate was to be played out. You have been a good father to me, my lord. I have no complaint."

"I can leave you naught, for what silver I have must be kept for Mary's dower. My lands are not so great, my son, that I could spare you the coin." It was said with true regret.

"Then I shall certainly have to steal an heiress bride," his son said with a small smile on his usually stern face.

"The Pendragon girl!" his father said suddenly. "In the Welshry. She probably has no lands, for there is a brother, but she has a good dower the rumor goes. Her father might spare some of his pastures for her. His own heir is just a bit older than Mary. The family claims descent from King Arthur. She would be a good match. Not so highborn as to be able to cause trouble with the king, or with the prince of the Welsh. Take her, breach her, and her sire will make the match. He dare not do otherwise." Then Godwine FitzHugh fell silent, and at last he drifted into a quiet sleep from which he did not arouse again.

Listening to his father's last few breaths, Rhys FitzHugh gazed through the chamber window. The sun was near to setting. Finally, he arose, and taking a small polished piece of metal he held it above his father's face. There was not the slightest hint of breath upon it. Godwine FitzHugh was dead. His son bent and gave his sire a final kiss upon his forehead. Then he went to call the serving women to help his sister prepare the old man's body for the grave. The lord of Everleigh would lie in state in his own hall the night, while his two children held vigil over him. His serfs and freedmen would be allowed until midday the next morning to pay their respects, and then Godwine FitzHugh would be buried.

The body was prepared in its shroud, and set upon its bier with tall footed iron candlesticks placed at each corner. Two kneelers with cushions were brought into the hall, and Rhys and his younger sister, Mary, knelt in prayer. As the night hours crept by, Rhys watched the child carefully, but her back was straight, and her shoulders did not slump with the weariness he knew the little girl must feel. Pride surged through him. His father had not had to tell him to watch over Mary. He had adored her from the moment of her birth.

The dawn came, and the servants came into the hall, rebuilding the fires that were almost out; bringing a meal. Rhys arose stiffly, shaking each of his legs in turn to ease them. He raised his sister to her feet. "Time to break our fast, little one," he told her.

"We cannot tarry," she said dutifully. "Our people will be coming. It would not be respectful to father to be eating when they arrive."

"Hawkins will not allow any in until we have taken some nourishment," he assured his sister, but he knew she was right. She already wore the mantle of Everleigh.

They ate, and then Mary stood at the entry to the hall with her brother, greeting by name each serf, each freedman and -woman who came to pay their father respect. At midday the coffin was nailed shut and removed from the bier to be taken to the manor church where the mass was said.

Then trailed by her brother, and the Everleigh folk, Mary FitzHugh followed her father's coffin to the family cemetery where he was buried. And when it was over she collapsed and was carried home by her devoted brother and put to bed where she slept until the following morning.

Two days later Edmund Mortimer, the overlord of the region, arrived with one of his sons, Roger, who was Rhys's friend. He was ushered into the hall of Everleigh and seated in the chair of honor. Mary Fitz-Hugh came to him, and kneeling placed her tiny hands in his, swearing her oath of loyalty to him, and through him, to the king. When she had finished, and been helped to her feet by her brother, Rhys then knelt and gave his pledge to Lord Mortimer as well.

"What provision has been made for you both?" Lord Mortimer asked.

"Fetch the priest," Rhys told a servant. Then he turned to Lord Mortimer. "Our father spoke to the priest of his intentions in the presence of my sister and me, my lord."

Father Kevyn came, and when asked by Lord Mortimer of Godwine FitzHugh's intentions said, "My late lord put his daughter into the care of her half brother whom he knew would give his life, if need be, for the demoiselle Mary. He is to care for her, make a match for her when she is old enough, and husband Everleigh as if it were his own. There is also some small silver for a dower."

"And for his loyal son?" Lord Mortimer asked.

The priest shook his head. "There was some advice given to Rhys FitzHugh, but nothing more."

Lord Mortimer nodded, understanding. If there had been no little sister Godwine FitzHugh would have probably left his estate to his bastard. But the girl was his legitimate heiress. She could not be overlooked. "What advice did your father give you, Rhys FitzHugh?" Lord Mortimer asked.

"He suggested I steal an heiress bride, my lord," Rhys answered honestly.

"And will you?" Lord Mortimer was smiling with amusement, but it was strangely good advice, for there was little else left for the young man.

"I must think on it, my lord," came the careful answer.

Lord Mortimer laughed. "It may be that your sire gave you excellent advice, young Rhys FitzHugh. How old are you now?"

"Five and twenty, my lord."

"You should not wait too long to take a mate. Your seed is at its best right now for making sons. Have you sired any children yet?" Lord Mortimer nodded to the servant who placed a goblet of wine in his hand.

"Under the circumstances I thought it wiser not to, my lord," Rhys answered.

"Ah, yes," Lord Mortimer agreed, drinking down his wine. Then he arose and turned to Mary. "Your brother will, I know, take the best of care of you, demoiselle, but should you ever need my counsel or aid, you have but to send to me." He took up her small hand and kissed it, bowing as he did so to the little girl.

"And when you need my aid, my lord," Mary answered him, "I will do my duty as your liege woman." She curtsied to him.

"I should expect no less of you, Mary FitzHugh," Lord Mortimer replied.

"I would remain to visit Rhys, Father," Roger Mortimer said.

Lord Mortimer nodded, and then he was gone from the hall.

"When are we going bride stealing?" Roger asked his friend with a grin.

"For God's good mercy, Rog, I have just buried my father," Rhys answered him.

"I shall leave you, brother," Mary said with a small smile. "I am learning to make soap today." She curtsied, and left the two men.

"My father is right," Roger Mortimer said. "You cannot wait too long. Certainly

61

your sire, God assoil him, would not want you to wait."

"He said I should steal the Pendragon girl in the Welshry," Rhys answered.

" 'Tis as good a choice as any," Roger agreed. "Her father's family claim their descent from King Arthur. Merin Pendragon has a son, but he's also got plenty of coin and cattle for a daughter. When shall we go?"

Rhys laughed. "I don't know if it is an honorable thing to do, Rog," he replied. "To steal a maiden so her father will be forced to make a marriage and settlement on the girl does not seem right to me."

"Bah! Bride stealing is done all the time. You haven't got a choice. I'll wager your old sire didn't even leave you so much as a silver piece. He left you with all the responsibility for your sibling, and Everleigh, and naught but a bleak future."

"I will remain as Mary's bailiff," Rhys said.

"Perhaps, but when Mary weds, Everleigh becomes her husband's property. He could have a poor relation who he will want to make bailiff here. Mary may want to please him. Then where will you be? A dowered bride is the answer to all your difficulties, Rhys. With her silver you can find a small piece of property for your own so when Mary weds one day, you and your wife will have your own home to go to and be happy," Roger Mortimer concluded.

"You have my life all settled, then," Rhys said with a smile. "Perhaps I should prefer to go crusading when Mary is grown and settled," he suggested.

"You'll be too old then," Roger said. "Crusading is difficult work."

"So I must steal an heiress bride," Rhys said.

"We'll go tomorrow to scout out Pendragon's keep and see if we can gain a glimpse of his daughter," Roger said enthusiastically.

"Nay, we will not. My father is only just buried. Mary and I need time to mourn in peace. A stolen girl will not bring peace into our hall. She will certainly wail, and weep until the matter is settled between her father and me."

"A week," Roger Mortimer said. "I will give you a week. And do not argue. Both my father, and yours, would agree." He grinned. "I wonder what she's like."

"Who?" Rhys replied.

"The Pendragon wench. For your sake I hope she is round and sweet."

Rhys laughed. "Mayhap she's too young to steal," he suggested mischievously.

"We'll steal her anyway," Roger responded. "If she's too young to breach she will be easier to train to your ways. You can win her over with sweetmeats and ribbons.

"If she's ready to be mated then you will have to charm her, and overcome her maidenly fears with kisses. Either way a girl can always be gotten around, Rhys."

"You sound so damned knowledgeable, Rog," came the reply, "but I don't see you wed yet."

"Mayhap the Pendragon girl will have a sister," Roger Mortimer said with a deep, wry chuckle.

"Come back in a week," Rhys FitzHugh told his friend. "But leave Mary and me to our small mourning now."

Roger Mortimer departed, returning exactly a week later with a dozen young men from his father's estates, all mounted upon good horseflesh. "I thought we should have company," he told the astounded Rhys. "It will be far more impressive to have a lord with a troop of men-at-arms at his back steal Pendragon's daughter than just two fellows on horseback," he explained.

"You're mad!" Rhys answered him, half laughing.

"Get your horse," Roger Mortimer responded. " 'Tis time to go bride stealing."

"I don't know," Rhys demured. "It seems so drastic a step, Rog."

"Your own father suggested it, and what other choice do you have?" his friend reminded him. "Perhaps some freedman's daughter? A step up for her, but a step down for you. Get your horse, Rhys, and let's get on with this matter. The sooner the deed is done, the sooner your future is secured."

"We could fail. What if the girl is well guarded?" Rhys considered.

"We'll never know unless we ride over into the Welshry and survey the situation for ourselves," Roger Mortimer replied sensibly.

Rhys FitzHugh nodded. "Let me speak to Mary first," he said.

"Hurry!" Roger answered him, grinning.

Rhys found his sister in the solar of their stone keep. "I have to go out," he said. "I may be gone a day or two, dearling. Rhawn will look after you, and you have Father Kevyn, too."

"I hope she's pretty, and amenable," Mary said sweetly.

"Who?" Rhys feigned innocence.

"Your heiress bride," Mary replied, giggling. "Do you think some handsome man will steal me one day, Brother?"

"He had best not," Rhys responded. "I should have to kill him if he did. You will be properly matched, Mary."

"Why is Pendragon's daughter not properly matched, then?" Mary wondered.

"They are Welsh, and half savage," Rhys

told his little sister. "Who knows why they do what they do."

"Why, then, would you steal a girl like that?" Mary said, curious.

"Because her family, while rich in cattle and other livestock, is not an important family. They may be angered by my actions, but they will not complain too loudly, and the girl will be decently matched. As for her brother, he is too young to fight me, I am told. He is not much older than you are, dearling. Now give me a kiss and let me go, for Roger and a troop of his father's men are waiting for me."

"Do the Welsh really eat children?" Mary asked him nervously.

"Nay." Rhys laughed. "Who told you that?"

"Rhawn says they do," Mary replied.

"Rhawn is an ignorant old crone," Rhys said. "If she tells you many more stories like that I shall have to beat her. You may tell her that I said so." He bent down and kissed his little sister's lips quickly. "Prepare the guest chamber for the bride while I am gone, Mary."

"I will, Rhys. God go with you and bring you home safe to Everleigh," Mary said. She kissed her brother's cheek and gave him a sweet smile.

The big dappled gray stallion he rode

was waiting eagerly for him in the courtyard of the keep. Rhys mounted it, and then looked to Roger Mortimer. "Do you know where we are going?" he asked his friend. "I surely don't."

"I know the way." Roger chuckled.

The first thing Rhys noticed as they rode away was that the horses hooves had been wrapped lightly to prevent the sound of their passing. None of the animals was a light color, and the men were garbed in sober hues that would not draw attention. While the countryside was scantily populated, a large party would always draw attention, but these men rode seemingly without weapons, nor could the thick leather vests they wore beneath their tunics and capes be seen. A sharp eye would have understood it was a raiding party, shutting their door quickly and praying it passed them by.

The first night they camped at twilight, for the days were growing longer with the onset of spring. They carried barley cakes, strips of dried beef, and flasks with water. They lit a small fire to deter the wild beasts, the men taking turns at the watch through the night. In the morning they rode out again. Merin Pendragon's keep was but a half day's journey farther. As the sun reached the midpoint in the heavens they stood looking at Dragon's Lair, which was set upon a low hill across the flower strewn field that lay at the foot of the hill upon which their horses were now standing. The field was dotted with fat cattle.

"Oh, she'll be very well dowered," Roger said softly. "There's a lushness and richness about this place unlike any other I've seen in the Welshry. Look about you, Rhys. The rest of it is mountainous and rough upland such as we have traveled through. How did this Pendragon gain such a fine land? Mayhap the fairy who was his ancestor gave it to him."

"I thought he was descended from King Arthur," Rhys replied.

"He is, but his ancestor's mother was part fairy, they say, and Merlin the sorcerer brought her to this place, and together they raised up this keep we see by means of magic. Then Merlin put a spell upon these lands that they would always be fertile, and that the Pendragons would thrive. That is how the story goes, I have been told."

"While I am willing to believe that Pendragon's family descends from King Arthur, I am loath to think there are any fairies in the family tree." Rhys laughed. " 'Tis a child's fable. There are no such things as fairies."

Roger chuckled. "Perhaps you are right," he replied, "but look there, in that stand of willows by the stream. Three maidens, and

68

one with golden hair that seems more magical than real. Do you think one of them is Pendragon's daughter?"

"Let us ride down and ask," Rhys suggested. Turning, he said to the men behind him, "Make yourselves discreet, lads. We don't want to frighten the little dears. Rog and I will ride down and introduce ourselves."

Together the two young men rode slowly down the rise, moving as they did closer and closer to the stream with its willow grove. The trio of lasses looked up as the riders moved their mounts at a leisurely pace across the little brook. The look was a wary one.

"Is this Dragon's Lair?" Rhys asked politely.

"Aye, it is," the tallest of the three said.

He noticed that she was easing the two younger girls behind her as she spoke. *Clever girl,* he thought to himself. "I am Rhys FitzHugh of Everleigh, and my companion is Roger Mortimer, Lord Mortimer's son. Will you not introduce yourself, demoiselle?"

"Have you business with my father?" Averil asked Rhys.

"You are Pendragon's daughter?" he answered her with the query. Jesu! She was beautiful! Obviously, his luck was about to change.

69

"I am," Averil said. Then she turned and said to her companions, "Run home, and tell the lady Argel that we have two guests."

As Maia and Junia turned to go, Roger Mortimer moved his stallion between them and their path, blocking their route. The two young girls looked up at him startled, and he saw fear coming into their eyes. "I will not harm you, demoiselles," he reassured them, "but it is not quite time for you to run home."

"What are you doing?" Averil demanded, seeing his actions.

"You are Pendragon's daughter," Rhys repeated, thinking she was very beautiful.

"Aye, I am Pendragon's daughter," she answered him impatiently. "My name is Averil." Why was he asking her the same question over and over again?

Rhys FitzHugh moved his horse as close to her as he could, and reaching down he wrapped a hard arm about her slender waist, quickly lifting a very surprised Averil up onto his mount before him. "You will come with me, then, Pendragon's daughter," he said. And turning his animal about he moved swiftly across the stream, then put his horse into a canter, calling as he did so, "Roger!"

Roger Mortimer grinned down at the two startled girls. "Now, lasses, you may run home and tell the Dragon Lord that Rhys FitzHugh of Everleigh Manor has taken his daughter. He may come to Everleigh to discuss marriage terms at his convenience, of course." Wheeling his own horse about, Roger Mortimer followed his friend.

Averil had at first been stunned by what had happened. Now, galvanized into action by the sight of the keep growing smaller behind her she shrieked aloud, causing Rhys's mount to rear up in his flight. She began to pound at her captor with her clenched fists. "Villian! Put me down this instant! How dare you lay hands on me! My father will punish you for this outrage! Put me down!"

Struggling to keep his startled horse under control while hanging onto this raging shrew was almost too much for him. The girl came close to falling to the ground although he doubted that she realized it. "Stop struggling, lady!" he commanded her in a stern voice, attempting to tighten his grip on her.

Averil looked directly at him, and reaching up, clawed at his face with both of her little hands.

"Oww!" he yelped as he felt her sharp fingernails breaking the skin. Yanking his animal to a sudden halt he quickly repositioned his captive, forcing her facedown

71

across his saddle before moving on again.

Averil howled in fury at this new outrage. "Are you trying to kill me, you monster?" she yelled at him. "Why are you doing this to me?"

He ignored her question as he gained the top of the hill again where Lord Mortimer's men were waiting for him and Roger. "Take the lady and tie her hands together, put her on the horse we brought, then bind her ankles so she may no longer injure herself or me," he ordered the nearest Mortimer man-at-arms as he tossed the girl from his saddle. His hand went to his face. The little bitch had blooded him!

Averil found herself on her rump in the grass. Faster than they might have anticipated she scrambled to her feet and attempted to run back down the hill. Rhys jumped from his own mount, tackling her almost immediately. He then hauled her kicking and screaming in her barbaric Welsh tongue back to where a gentle gelding was waiting saddled for her. Hoisting her onto the creature's back he grabbed both of her wrists in an iron grip. "Bind her!" he yelled, and was instantly obeyed, one man wrapping a strip of narrow leather about her wrists, while another tied her ankles together beneath the horse.

Averil screamed at the top of her lungs,

and was rewarded by having a slender piece of silk brought for the occasion being tied about her mouth to gag her. The girl's green eyes glared furiously at her captors, and the man tying her wrists crossed himself when he had finished, so fierce was the look she gave him.

"Best to hurry," Roger said. "Those two little lasses are running swiftly. Pendragon and his men will be upon us quickly. 'Tis best we put as much distance as we can between ourselves and them. If we can outrun them the rest of the day, we'll escape them tomorrow, I'm certain."

Rhys nodded, and remounting his stallion took the lead rein he was handed. Then they galloped off, heading for the English area of the Marches. Roger and the men followed. They did not stop for several hours. In late afternoon they heard the sound of a pursuing troop behind them, but those following were not yet in sight. The man they had sent ahead galloped up.

"Up ahead!" he said. "There is shelter. Hurry!"

"We'll hide," Roger Mortimer told the men-at-arms. "You go ahead and lead them astray for us, but for mercy's sake, don't get caught!"

"I'll leave two men with you, my lord. Your father would skin me alive if I didn't," the captain said, nodding at the two men by his side. Then, without waiting for an answer, the captain and the rest of the troop galloped speedily off.

The scout was one of the two men-at-arms. He brought them to the ruins of what had obviously been a religious house, and dismounting, the men led their horses, and their captive, into the half collapsed wreck of a farm building. Averil's leg bonds were released, and she was dragged, struggling, to a pile of moldering hay, and secreted beneath Rhys's dark cloak while he sat upon her to still her fruitless attempts at escape. And they waited.

They could hear the baying of hounds and the thunder of horses' hooves coming nearer and nearer. There were shouts, and the sounding of a horn. The horses with them stirred nervously, but were soothed by the three other men so they did not whinny to alert their pursuers. And then the sounds of pursuit moved on by them, and soon it was quiet once again.

"They're gone," Roger said.

"They're sure to return this way," Rhys replied. "I smell rain on the wind. It may be safer remaining here. I don't want to begin our journey again only to meet the lady's outraged father returning home, and have no place to hide her. Do you think your father's men can outrun the Welsh?"

"Aye. They'll have no trouble. Pendragon is unlikely to even catch sight of them except briefly. They'll be into the Englishry by nightfall, and I doubt the Welsh will follow them there. The Dragon Lord will accept his heiress has been bride-napped and will have to come to make a settlement."

"We're not at Everleigh yet," Rhys said wisely. "I would remain well hidden for now." He stood up, and as he did he realized his captive had ceased her struggles. He pulled his cloak off her. Averil had fainted. He bent to make certain that she was breathing, sighing with relief at the sight of the rapidly beating pulse in her slender throat.

"Nay, you didn't kill her." Roger chuckled. "She is a beauty, isn't she? What luck you have had, Rhys!"

"Aye, she's pretty enough," he admitted. What had he done? He had stolen this highborn girl from her family, and the possibility of a good match with some nobleman. He was a baseborn son, and would never be more than a bailiff. Her family would kill him for this, but the die was cast, and the girl did have the most kissable lips.

"Pretty? She is beautiful! Look at that hair! It's like spun gold. And her figure, slim, yet nicely rounded where it should be," Roger enthused. "Her features are very fine, not at all coarse. What a lovely little nose she has. It is straight without a hook on its end or a bump in its slim little bridge. I wonder what color her eyes are." He sighed. "Aye, you bagged yourself a truly fair maiden, Rhys."

They sat and waited until eventually, as the sun was sliding into the long May twilight, they heard the sounds of horses again passing them by, but this time going in the direction of Dragon's Lair. One of the men-at-arms had slipped out at the first sign of Pendragon's return, and hidden along the track to make certain of who it was riding by. Finally, when all had been quiet for several long minutes, he returned.

" 'Twas the Welsh, my lords," he confirmed. "And the lord of them all was swearing something fierce as they went by." The man chuckled.

"We'll wait a bit longer," Rhys said, "before I remove the lady's gag so she may eat and drink." They sat in silence again as the faint rumble of thunder could be heard heralding the approaching storm. Finally, Rhys bent and untied Averil's gag.

She glared up at him. "You have almost killed me," she snarled.

"Are you hungry or thirsty?" he asked her, ignoring her complaint.

"I have to pee," she snapped.

He flushed at her words. But then he

76

pulled her to her feet. "I'll have to go with you," he said. "For some reason I do not feel I can trust you."

"I cannot pee with you standing there watching," Averil told him. "Put me in that closed stall there. Untie my hands so I can hike my skirts. Then close me in. There is no means of escape there, and I will have my privacy. Or do you wish to embarrass me in some futile attempt to master me?"

"Lady," he told her, "I have only your best interests at heart."

Averil sniffed dismissively, and held out her hands to him. He untied them and did as she had bid him, leading her to the closed stall and closing the door behind her. He heard Roger snicker and glared across the glooming of the stable at him.

"I'm finished," he heard Averil call.

He opened the door and led her out. She moved slowly and stiffly, having been confined for the last several hours. When he had returned her to her place he moved to tie her wrists together again.

"How can I eat if I cannot use my hands?" she demanded of him.

"I do not trust you, lady," he told her bluntly. "I will feed you myself." He bound her hands together again.

"I shall be battered and bruised," Averil told him. "My da will kill you when he

77

catches up with you."

"Your father has come and gone. He will come to Everleigh sooner than later to make a marriage settlement with me for you, lady. I have stolen you, and you are now mine."

"I will never be yours, my lord! I should sooner enter a convent than be your wife!" Averil cried. She was furious, for she had never felt so helpless in all of her life.

"Before your father comes, lady, you and I will be well and truly mated. No convent will have you, for you will most certainly not be a virgin," Rhys said harshly. "Now still your foolish protests or I will consummate this union here this very night before these witnesses."

"You wouldn't dare!" Averil said, but then seeing the threatening look in his eyes she grew suddenly silent, and sat quietly.

"There is but soldier's rations," he half apologized, bringing her a barley cake, which he broke in small pieces and fed her.

"Wine?" Averil demanded.

"Water," he said, putting his horn flask to her lips.

"Can you not afford wine?" she replied scathingly.

"Do you want the water or not?" he asked through gritted teeth.

"Aye. I must remain alive so I can watch while my father kills you slowly for this

78

outrage you have perpetrated upon me," she said sweetly. Then she drank thirstily.

Roger Mortimer laughed aloud hearing her words. "She has spirit, Rhys. You will breed strong sons on her."

Averil shot him a look of pure venom, and Roger laughed again. "If you only had a sister, lady," he said.

"I have two," she snapped. " 'Twas my younger siblings with me when you kidnapped me. I am the eldest of Pendragon's three daughters and a son."

The May moon had begun to rise through the trees as the twilight deepened into night. The storm that had threatened them earlier had passed over without rain. Averil slept atop Rhys's cloak, curled into a protective ball. Roger had put his own cloak over her when she had fallen asleep. The five men took turns at the watch while the horses browsed in the grass behind the entrance of the half-standing structure where they sheltered, the moonlight silvering their hides.

When the morning came mist hung in the air, but the blue sky above promised a fair day for their ride. They arose before the sun, ate, drank and attended to their personal needs before starting out once more. By midday they had crossed the invisible border into the Englishry where they found Lord Mortimer's men waiting to escort them the rest of the way. They arrived at Everleigh in late afternoon. Rhys cut the bonds holding Averil, and lifted her from her horse.

"Welcome home, lady," he said. "This is Everleigh." He led her into the house.

"It is yours?" she asked, looking curiously about the hall where they now stood. *It could be worse,* she thought.

"Nay, it is my sister's. Mary is our father's legitimate heir. She is six, and I have charge over her. I am my father's bastard."

Averil began to laugh.

"You find that amusing, lady?" he said, half angrily.

"Nay, my lord. I find it an incredible coincidence," Averil answered him, regaining control over her emotions.

"A coincidence?" he said, his handsome face wearing a look of puzzlement. "What is coincidental about my birth, lady?"

"I, too, am my father's bastard," Averil told him.

"You are Pendragon's daughter? You said you were!" he cried.

"I am Pendragon's eldest daughter, born to his concubine Gorawen. Am I not, then, what you sought, my lord?"

"I sought the Pendragon heiress," he said slowly.

"That, my lord, would be my second

80

sister, Maia," Averil told him. "The little one with us was Junia, the youngest, who is the child of our father's other concubine, Ysbail. Oh, dear! You have indeed made an error, haven't you?" She smiled sweetly at him.

"I will send you back immediately!" Rhys said. This is what came of not following his own instincts, he thought to himself.

"You cannot send her back," Roger said, shaking his head.

"Why the hell not?" Rhys demanded.

Averil was giggling now.

"Because having stolen her you are bound to wed her lest you bring dishonor upon yourself, your family, upon her, and upon the Pendragon family," Roger said. He looked to Averil. "Are you in favor with your sire, lady? Will he come for you and settle a bride price on you?"

"My da loves all of his daughters equally well," Averil said. "As I am the eldest of his children I am probably his favorite. He will dower me when I wed, but I do not intend upon marrying with this buffoon who has kidnapped me! In fact, I shall help da to slaughter you, Rhys FitzHugh of Everleigh, and I shall enjoy every minute of your demise."

Rhys was struck dumb by the tangled situation, but Roger kept his head. He spoke up again saying, "Lady, you, too, have no choice in this matter. No other man will have you now, nor the church, either. You will be considered tainted goods."

"But why?" Averil wailed. "Nothing has happened but that this village idiot stole me away. I am as pure as I was before I ever laid eyes on either of you."

"Lady, your word would not be enough to convince another man. You are a woman. Women lie. And men, caught in impossible situations, lie as well. Neither my word as Rhys's best friend, nor his, will be accepted in this matter, I fear. You will have to wed one another or both be disgraced forever."

"Then I shall be disgraced forever!" Averil cried dramatically.

"But I cannot be, for my sister's sake," Rhys said slowly. "I will marry you, lady, even if you are not your father's heiress. Mary's good name must be protected."

"I will not marry you!" Averil shouted, and she hurled herself at him, pulling his dagger from his belt and striking at him.

Roger leapt forward and knocked the weapon from her hand, wrestling the girl away from Rhys who was now bleeding from his shoulder. "Be still you little Welsh savage!" he ordered her, calling for the servants with his next breath to attend their master. The servants ran into the hall, and seeing that Rhys was wounded set up a hue and cry. "Attend to his injury," Roger commanded them. "The blade did not go deep. He is not dying. Give him some wine. God's wounds, lady, you have blooded him twice now in the last day. Have mercy!"

Rhys, pale now, sat while his wound was treated and bound up by Rhawn, his sister's nursemaid. "Where is Mary?" he asked her faintly.

"Where this barbarian you have brought back with you cannot harm her," Rhawn said balefully, glaring at Averil.

"Do not set the evil eye on me, old crone!" Averil snapped. "I have not come willingly with this fool who is your master. And now he has ruined any chance of happiness I might have had by his impetuous actions."

"I will wed you," Rhys said, thinking she needed his reassurance.

"Did you not hear me?" Averil said. "I will not marry you."

"Aye, you will, daughter!" her father's voice said grimly. And Merin Pendragon entered the hall at Everleigh, his men at his back.

Chapter 3

The Dragon Lord was a big tall man with a strong air of command about him. He strode into the hall at Everleigh, and without being asked seated himself in the chair of authority at the high board. "Now, Rhys FitzHugh, you will explain yourself to me while I decide if I shall allow you to wed my daughter whom you have dishonored, or merely satisfy myself by killing you for the insult you have dealt to my family." His green eyes scanned the younger man curiously. "Is this manor yours?"

"Nay, my lord," Rhys answered honestly.

"Kill him, Da!" Averil said ruthlessly. "I tried, but only wounded him."

"To whom does this manor belong, Rhys FitzHugh?" the Dragon Lord asked, ignoring his eldest daughter. Women could be so damned emotional. Could she not see this was possibly an opportunity?

"Everleigh is the property of my little sister, Mary FitzHugh," Rhys replied.

"Then you are bastard born?" the Dragon Lord queried. His bastardy was not a problem, but his lack of lands could be, Merin Pendragon considered.

"Yes, my lord." Rhys was extremely uncomfortable. This was FitzHugh's hall, and yet here he stood like a beggar in his own home, feeling like a naughty boy before this Welshman. He glanced towards Roger Mortimer, but Rog was silent, and had that guilty look upon his face that always gave them away as boys.

"Are you your sister's guardian, Rhys FitzHugh?" the Dragon Lord wanted to know.

"I am, my lord," Rhys said. "On his deathbed my father told me that had my own mother not died with my birth he should have wed her. And when he finally did wed he lost another woman in childbirth. My sister, Mary, is six years old, my lord. Our father asked me to watch over her, and over Everleigh, and see her well matched one day. I will honor my father's wishes, but it is not difficult for me to do so. I love my little sister."

"So at least you have a place to live until the day comes that she weds, Rhys FitzHugh. When she does you will have to make certain that her marriage agreement includes keeping you on as Everleigh's bailiff else you find yourself homeless. If you do well, then no prospective husband should object to such an arrangement." He sighed. "Now what in the name of the Blessed Holy Mother induced you to bride-nap my daughter? I want the truth now!"

"I sought an heiress for myself, my lord. I am five and twenty years, and it was time I took a wife. Before he died my father suggested I find an heiress, and kidnap her so her family would be forced into letting me have her lest my behavior stain her honor."

"Did you not realize that I had three daughters, and only one of them true born?" the Dragon Lord asked the younger man.

"Nay, my lord, I did not," Rhys said, flushing and feeling the full weight of his stupidity now. "She said she was your daughter. She was the tallest, and I assumed this was she whom I sought."

Merin Pendragon burst out laughing, and he laughed until the tears were rolling down his ruddy face.

"There is nothing amusing in this, Da!" Averil burst out angrily.

"Aye, lass, there is," her father replied. "He seems an intelligent young man, yet he behaved stupidly, and now he must live with his error in judgment." The Dragon Lord turned to pierce Roger Mortimer with his glance. "And you, young Mortimer, were part of this? What will your father say when I complain to him, and I will."

"We meant no harm, my lord," Roger quickly said, "and Rhys did not hurt the girl. I swear it!"

"He tied and gagged me, Da! He starved me!" Averil complained. She sneezed. "I think he has given me an ague, forcing me to sleep in the ruins of a barn last night. I almost froze to death, Da."

"Your suffering is duly noted, daughter," Merin Pendragon remarked dryly. There was a hint of laughter in his voice. Then he said to Rhys, "You will have to wed her now, though she is not my heiress, young FitzHugh. If I had caught you before nightfall we might have salvaged Averil's good name, but you have had her with you overnight, and whatever either of you may say regarding the matter I must assume the absolute worst."

"My lord, my men were with us, and Roger, too. They will swear that nothing untowards took place," Rhys declared.

"It is not me you would have to convince," the Dragon Lord said. "Under the circumstances I should never be able to find another husband for my daughter, and I think you will agree that Averil is far too lovely to waste on the church. I am prepared to be generous despite all that has happened."

"Why would you be generous?" Rhys demanded to know, now suspicious. These

87

Welsh were a crafty people, and perhaps the wench was not as pure as she appeared.

"I should rather go into a convent than marry this buffoon!" Averil declared angrily. "Take me home, Da!"

"Be quiet, Averil," her father said softly. "This matter is not your concern."

"Not my concern? I should like to know why not! It is my life you are talking about. My life you are so casually deciding without any care for me at all! Would my mother approve of this, my lord father?"

"Your mother has the good sense to trust my judgment, daughter," the Dragon Lord told her. "Now, be silent." He cuffed her lightly, warningly. He loved her, but he would not be spoken to in such a manner before strangers.

"What ho! The hall!" came a voice, and they all turned to see Lord Mortimer entering with several of his men. "Merin! You Welsh devil, 'tis good to see you again."

The Dragon Lord arose from his chair, and coming around and down from the high board went forward, hand outstretched to meet his old friend. "Edmund, you English devil! I concur. Did you know that your son, and young FitzHugh, here, came over the border into the Welshry and stole my eldest daughter?"

"What?" Lord Mortimer feigned surprise. "I am shocked, Merin. Absolutely shocked!"

Roger Mortimer opened his mouth, and then closed it.

"Well, young Rhys, you shall have to wed the Dragon Lord's heiress if you are to salvage your honor, and hers," Lord Mortimer said.

"I did not steal the heiress, my lord," Rhys murmured. "It seems my lord Pendragon has three daughters, but only the middle one is true born."

"An unfortunate error on your part," Lord Mortimer replied, and he swallowed back the laughter that threatened to overwhelm him. How could he have forgotten that Pendragon had two rather toothsome concubines? And of course, they would have had children. "Nonetheless, the lady's honor must be restored, Rhys FitzHugh."

"Nothing happened to the lady, my lord Mortimer. Roger and the others will swear to it!" Rhys replied. "Will you not intercede for me in this matter?"

"No, no, my young friend," Lord Mortimer said. "You must do what is right, and there can be no argument."

"Let us seek Prince Llywelyn," the Dragon Lord said. "I will set forth this matter before him. I will offer my daughter and her dower to any who would have her.

If another will take her despite this misadventure, then I will accept him as husband to my eldest child. But if none steps forward, Rhys FitzHugh, you must wed Averil then and there. I can be no fairer than that."

"A most generous offer," Lord Mortimer agreed.

"Am I to then be sold off as if I were a heifer?" Averil spoke up.

"An unwed woman is indeed a commodity," her father replied. "If a man cannot have sons who can fight for him, then a daughter who can be married off in the most favorable alliance possible is the next best thing."

"Send me to a convent!" Averil cried dramatically.

"Why, child, you are far too lovely," Lord Mortimer said soothingly. " 'Twould be a crime against nature to incarcerate so fair a maid behind stone walls."

"Is it agreed then that we will take this matter to Prince Llywelyn?" the Dragon Lord asked.

"You will go with us, my lord?" Rhys asked Lord Mortimer.

"Aye, I think I had best lest you lead my son astray again," Edmund Mortimer said with a small grin.

"I think it is usually the other way about," Rhys replied meaningfully.

"Feed us, young FitzHugh, and then we will start out again," the Dragon Lord said. "Better we spend the night here at Everleigh, my lords, for the hour grows late," Rhys suggested hospitably. "Rhawn," he called. "Fetch your mistress and have her come to greet her guests."

"I am here, Rhys," Mary said, coming from the shadows. She was a pretty child, her dark brown hair fashioned into two plaits, and her bright eyes a clear blue. She wore a pale yellow tunic over her orange tawny gown. "I but waited until you had completed your business. You are welcome to Everleigh, my lords, and my lady." She curtsied prettily. "Come to table. The meal is about to be served. My lord Pendragon, you will sit on my right. Lord Mortimer on my left. Lady Averil will seat herself next to her father with my brother, and you, Roger Mortimer, will sit by your father."

Merin Pendragon was enchanted by the little girl. The child had beautiful manners, and even at this tender age knew her duty as chatelaine. Still, she was young yet. She could die, and then her brother would inherit Everleigh despite his birth. It was unlikely anyone would challenge him for it.

The meal was simple. The bread trenchers were filled with a tasty pottage of rabbit, onions, and carrots in a thick gravy. There was plenty of fresh bread, a crock of butter, and a small wheel of hard flavorful cheese. The pewter goblets were filled, and kept filled with an excellent ale with the hint of barley.

"You keep a good table, my lady Mary," Merin Pendragon approved.

"Rhawn, who both nursed me and kept my father's house, has taught me, my lord," Mary replied. "I still have much to learn."

When the meal was over Mary bid the gentlemen good night, and taking Averil by the hand said, "You will sleep with me tonight, my lady Averil." She led Averil up the staircase in the hall to an upper floor. "I have a fireplace in the solar," she said, "and it is kept alight most of the year. The men will be comfortable in the hall. There are several bed spaces. They are used to rougher accommodations than are we."

"Your brother made me sleep in a tumbledown stable last night," Averil said with badly concealed ill humor.

"If he did, it was probably the best place he could find," Mary responded calmly. "My brother is a good man, lady." They had reached the solar, and Mary turned, looking up at Averil. "Are you to be my brother's wife?" she asked.

Averil swallowed back the quick sharp retort that was on her tongue, saying instead, "I do not know. Such arrangements are the province of men; my father, your brother, and the Great Llywelyn, who is our prince."

"So I am told," Mary said, "but I wonder why it should be so."

"So do I," Averil answered her softly. Then she smiled down at the child.

"I have a little sister named Junia who is just a few years older than you are."

"Does she look like you? You are the most beautiful girl I have ever seen," Mary said frankly.

"Junia looks more like you," Averil answered her, "but that her eyes are green. We all have green eyes, my sisters and I. Maia has red hair, and Junia's is dark. Our brother's hair is dark too, and his eyes hazel colored. Only Brynn and Maia have the same mother. Our father has a wife, and two concubines."

"That is immoral!" Mary said, shocked.

"No," Averil answered her, not in the least offended. "It was of necessity. The lady Argel was barren for several years after her marriage to my father. So Da took my mother, who is called Gorawen, to his bed. I am my father's first child. Then the lady Argel produced my sister Maia. But after that there were no other children so Da took a second concubine, Ysbail. Junia was born from that union, but the lady Argel finally produced the desired son.

Your brother is bastard born."

"That is so," Mary replied. "I had not considered it. But our father did not wed with my mother for many years after Rhys was born, and his mam was long dead. Do you all live together?" Mary was fascinated.

"We do," Averil said. "We are content to do so."

"I have never heard of such a thing, but then, 'tis said that the Welsh are a barbaric people," Mary innocently responded.

"We are most certainly not barbaric!" Averil spoke up defensively. "Many men keep other women, and sire children on the wrong side of the blanket, Mary FitzHugh. Are you English then barbaric too?"

"I meant no offense," the little girl said apologetically.

"I know," Averil told her. "You but prate what you have heard others say. But you must be more guarded in your speech, Mary FitzHugh. You might insult someone without meaning to who might not take into account that you are but a child."

"I think I should like to have you as a sister," Mary said. "Did you do the embroidery on your tunic?"

"Aye, I did," Averil admitted.

"Could you teach me how to do such fine embroidery?" Mary asked.

"Perhaps, but tomorrow we leave for Aberffraw, and Prince Llywelyn's court, so this matter between my family and your brother may be decided," Averil said.

"When you are wed to my brother will you teach me?" Mary persisted.

"If I am wed to your brother, aye, I will," Averil promised. *But I should sooner remain a maid and wither away first,* she thought. Rhys FitzHugh was the most annoying man she had ever encountered. His surprise that he had not stolen Merin Pendragon's heiress and then his reluctant agreement to wed her to save her reputation was more than aggravating. She could but hope there was a man at Prince Llywelyn's court who would agree to take her. Anything would be better than this arrogant Englishman.

The next day they departed for Aberffraw. It was a long ride across northwestern England, and Wales' Mary FitzHugh was left behind, for her presence was not necessary. It was Midsummer's Eve when they reached Prince Llywelyn's court. They had crossed the Menai Strait to the Island of Anglesey, with their horses and baggage, utilizing several small local ferries. Around them the Irish Sea washed the beaches of the island, and an almost imperceptible mist rose and fell over the landscape.

There was nothing on the island that stood higher than a thousand feet. Here, Averil knew from the history her father had instilled in all of his children, the ancient druids had made their last stand before being massacred by a people called the Romans. Merin Pendragon knew all of this because the family from which he had descended had followed the old ways once. While they were now good Christian people, the old ways were not forgotten in his hall.

There was an almost magical air about Anglesey. The marshes and wetlands of the island were filled with waterfowl. In the lush green meadows fat cattle and sheep grazed. There were few dwellings along the path they traveled, but those paths were lined with tall hedges. Now and again they rode through a small forest, but most of the island was bare of woodlands.

Reaching Prince Llywelyn's court Averil found she was not particularly impressed. Her father's keep was more grand. She was surprised as the prince was married to King John's daughter, Joan. The prince's home was nothing more than a small castle of timber and some stone. About it clustered a small village with a church, and several cottages that did not appear particularly prosperous. The air about them was warm, and softer than any Averil had ever known. They were welcomed in the prince's hall, and Averil was given a place in the solar to sleep. The prince would hear their case immediately, for there would be festivities this night to celebrate midsummer.

Averil asked a serving woman for water to bathe her hands and her face. She rifled through her pack to draw out the clothing she would wear into the prince's hall. Her hair was full of dust, but there was not enough water to wash it. She brushed and brushed and brushed her long tresses into a semblance of respectability. Then, having removed her travel-strained garments, she bathed as best she could, put on a clean chemise, and dressed. Her gown with its long fitted sleeves was a dark green brocade with a round neckline that was embroidered in gold threads. Over it she wore a dark green sleeveless tunic that had been embroidered at its scooped neckline and along its hemline. Her long golden hair was adorned with a simple gold chaplet decorated with stylized flowers. On her feet she wore soft leather shoes. Her only jewelry was a thin gold chain with a round gold pendant upon which was a red enamel dragon, her family's insignia.

Satisfied that she was respectably clean and well-garbed, Averil joined her father, Lord Mortimer and their companions in the prince's hall. The meal was being served, and they found places below the high board where they might sit and eat.

Averil ate little, and was especially careful of her garments. She thought the variety of food being offered was very generous and impressive. Here, then, would be Joan of England's influence. She could learn from this visit, Averil considered as she watched the servants dashing about with their bowls and platters. When the meal had been concluded, the prince's majordomo called for silence.

"The lord Merin, of the ancient and honorable house of Pendragon, descendant of Arthur, King of the Britons, has come before the prince for a judgment in the matter of his daughter's honor. Come forward, Merin Pendragon, and speak your piece. All those connected with this matter will also show themselves now," the majordomo said.

Merin Pendragon bowed before his prince and his wife. "My lord," he began. "Several weeks ago my eldest daughter, here with me," and he drew Averil forward so she could be seen by all, "was taken from my lands by Rhys FitzHugh, the bailiff of the manor of Everleigh in the Englishry. His purpose was to steal a bride, and he thought that my daughter Averil was my heiress, but here he erred in judgment. Averil is my eldest child, but born to my concubine, Gorawen, true-born daughter of the house of Tewydr. This offspring of mine is dearest to my heart of all my children, my lord. I had only begun to consider a match for her, and given her great beauty it would have been a very good match, you will agree. It is right and proper that Rhys FitzHugh wed with her now, having stolen her from us. But while he has said he would, he yet demurs in his duty. So, my lord, I bring this matter before you. It has been agreed among us that your judgment will be accepted by all who come before you this day in my daughter's behalf. Lord Mortimer, Rhys FitzHugh's liege lord, has accompanied us with his own son, who was also party to helping his friend steal my daughter. Lord Mortimer will defer to you in this matter, my lord."

Prince Llywelyn looked down upon them. "Averil Pendragon, what have you to say in this matter?"

"My lord, I will accept your decision," Averil said so softly that they could barely hear her. She did not look directly at the prince, for it would not have been considered polite. She did, however, remember to bob a curtsey to the prince and his wife.

The prince nodded, impressed by both her beauty and her manners.

"If, my lord, another man would be willing to take her to wife, Rhys FitzHugh could be absolved of his crime."

"What dower will you give with the girl?" the prince asked.

"A herd of six young heifers, and a healthy bull. A flock of twenty-four ewe sheep with their lambs, and a breeding ram. She has a fine horse, a chest of linens, and pewter. Another of clothing in good repair. She comes with her own loom, for she is an excellent weaver. And I have set aside fifteen silver pennies, one for each year of her life. She excels in housewifery and does the finest embroidery I have ever seen. She is able to read and write her name. She can speak English and French as well as our own tongue."

"She has no land?" the prince said.

"Nay, my lord. My daughter, Maia, who is my true-born daughter, will have the only bit of land that I can spare from her brother's inheritance," Merin Pendragon said.

The prince nodded again. "The girl is well dowered despite her lack of land."

Averil looked about the hall. It had suddenly dawned on her that she was very far from home. Her gaze moved swiftly as she looked over the many men in the crowd. More men than women. Strange men. Rough-looking men. And who knew where their homes were. At least Rhys FitzHugh's home was within two days of Dragon's Lair, and her family. What had she done, being so damned stubborn and dramatic in her refusal to accept her fate and take Rhys FitzHugh for a husband? And how was she going to escape being snapped up and married to a complete stranger? She bit her lower lip in her vexation as she considered the possible courses open to her.

Joan of England leaned over and whispered something in her husband's ear.

The prince spoke once again. "Averil Pendragon, were you harmed in any way by Rhys FitzHugh?" His meaning was very clear and it was the single straw she needed to save herself. She snatched at it. A blush suffused her pale cheeks. Her golden head drooped, and she was perfectly silent. She dare not lie, but she knew what her silence would imply, and so she remained speechless.

The men in the hall looked at one another and nodded, some shaking their heads, murmuring regretfully. A man wanted a virgin for a wife no matter her dower portion. With this girl they could not be certain until the wedding night, and even if she was proved pure, no one would ever believe it under the circumstances described this evening.

"Nothing happened between us!" Rhys FitzHugh burst forth.

"Averil Pendragon, will you not speak to us?" the prince encouraged her in his most kindly tones. The poor lass was obviously very shamed.

Averil's golden head drooped even lower, and she turned as if to hide her face in her father's broad chest. Her slender frame appeared to tremble.

"Damn it, you wicked wench," Rhys cried, "tell them the truth!" He was furious as he realized what she was doing. She had decided to have him, but she would regret it.

Averil pressed closer to her father as if seeking his protection. Her shoulders shook visibly. Merin Pendragon forced his face to remain serious, but oh, how he wanted to laugh. Averil had obviously decided that after dragging them across Wales to Aberffraw she would, after all, have Rhys FitzHugh as her husband. He wondered what had caused her to change her mind. He put an arm about his daughter, reinforcing the very impression Averil wished to make. "My lord?" he pressed the prince.

Llywelyn the Great shook his grizzled head. "We can ask no other to take her under these circumstances, Merin Pendragon, despite her generous dower and her great beauty. Rhys FitzHugh, having stolen Averil Pendragon from her father's protection, you must wed her now if you are to restore her honor and yours. This is my decision." He turned and looked at

Lord Mortimer. "Edmund Mortimer, I know you for a man of honor. Will you see that your liegeman does his duty?"

"I will, my lord prince," the Englishman said quietly.

"Bring a priest forth, then. This couple shall be united forthwith," the prince ordered.

Oh, Holy Mary, Averil thought! She had only meant to make it impossible for another man to claim her. Now she was to be wed to Rhys FitzHugh immediately. There would be no escaping him or his ire. She peeped at him from beneath her dark lashes. He looked very angry. Would he beat her for this wicked trick she had played on him? Probably he would. Averil shuddered nervously, and seeing it Rhys smiled a slow, wicked smile, his eyes making contact with hers, and holding her in his thrall. *Now, you wicked little bitch,* the look said, *you will regret your perfidy this day.*

"Oh, please, my lord prince," Averil said in her sweetest tones. "Could we not return home to Dragon's Lair first? I would have my mother, my sisters and brother with me when I wed this man."

The Great Llywelyn appeared to consider, but Merin Pendragon spoke up first.

"My daughter is sentimental about our family, my prince, but I believe it best the marriage vows be said now. We will all return home to Dragon's Lair afterwards, and celebrate this union before Rhys FitzHugh may take his bride home to Everleigh. It would allow us time to bring his sister, the lady Mary, to our home to join in these joyous festivities."

"Then so be it!" Prince Llywelyn said in a jovial voice. "A Midsummer's Eve wedding before our own celebrations begin. Where is the priest?"

Averil turned to her father. "Da! Why are you doing this?"

"Do you think I do not know you, Averil?" he replied softly. "If I allow you to return home unwed you will find some excuse to avoid this marriage. And believe me, daughter, no other will have you now because of this misadventure."

"But it wasn't my fault, Da! And nothing happened! I swear on the Blessed Mother than I am still a maid," Averil told her sire.

"I believe you," the Dragon Lord replied, "but no one else will until the bloodied sheet is taken from your bed and hung for all to see."

"Oh, my God!" Averil gasped. "Oh, Da! Do not make me sleep with him tonight, I beg you! Not here in this strange place." Her green eyes filled with tears.

"I will speak with him, Averil. I'm sure Rhys FitzHugh is no more anxious for a coupling than you are. Not yet. But he will be, my daughter." He turned away from her, and reaching out, drew the subject of their conversation forward. "You will wed her tonight, but you may not have her until she is ready. Do you understand me, Rhys FitzHugh? For all her spirit she is inexperienced and young. She has not her mother to comfort her in this situation, and she is afraid though she would deny it."

"I am not a monster, my lord. This is not her fault. It is mine. My father meant well when he advised me to steal an heiress bride. But I could have ignored that advice. I could have refused to go with Roger when he came with his troop of men for me. I did not. I might have learned a bit more about the family whose daughter I meant to take." He smiled a brief, rueful smile. "Nay, 'tis my sin, not your daughter's. She might have saved us all the trouble of traveling half of Wales, however, but then, I was not eager, either. It is indeed my fault, for I should have known better."

"I may come to like you, Rhys FitzHugh," the Dragon Lord said, "and so I will give you this bit of advice, which you would be wise to take. Averil is headstrong, and she has a temper, but she is a good lass with a kind heart. She will try your patience, but she will be loyal to you. Treat

105

her with kindness and she will reward that patience."

Rhys FitzHugh nodded. "You have given me good counsel, my lord. I will try to heed it, but I suspect that your daughter will not make it easy for me."

Merin Pendragon chuckled. "Nay, she will not. But she is a prize worth winning like her mother, I assure you."

The priest arrived in the hall. He listened to the Great Llywelyn, his master, and then turned to the Dragon Lord and his party. "Let the bride and groom step forward," he said. "There is no blood impediment to this marriage?"

"None," Merin Pendragon said.

"The dower portion is agreed upon, and the parties are both willing?"

"The dower has been pledged before witnesses in this very hall, and aye, they are willing," Merin Pendragon replied.

"Then they shall be joined according to the rites of Holy Mother Church," the priest said. Then he looked out over the hall. "Be silent, all of you! This is a sacred and proper rite of the church. You may resume your pagan celebrations of midsummer when I have finished, but not a moment before!"

The hall grew quiet as the priest joined Averil Pendragon and Rhys FitzHugh in holy matrimony before her father, Edmund and Roger Mortimer, Llywelyn the Great, the prince of the Welsh, Joan of England and their court. Finally they knelt for a blessing, and then the priest departed as the hall once more grew noisy with revelers celebrating Midsummer's Eve.

Averil found herself alone briefly with her new husband. For once in her life she was struck dumb. She felt very foolish, but she simply didn't know what to say to him.

"You might have agreed to this several weeks ago, wife, instead of dragging me across Wales," Rhys finally said, breaking the heavy silence between them. "What made you change your mind, Averil?"

"I looked about the hall and decided there was no other as suitable as you, my lord," she told him, at last finding her voice.

He laughed. "Then I suppose the trip was worth it," he told her.

Averil flushed. "I'm sorry I'm not the heiress," she said sharply.

"So am I," he agreed dryly, "but your dower is quite good, and we'll manage."

"Why did you not breach me that first night?" she asked, curious.

"I was advised to, but it would not have been honorable," he told her quietly. "And as you have brought the subject up, I would have you know that I am a patient man, Averil. And this is neither the time nor the place for our cojoining. When we get home to Everleigh we will discuss the matter."

Unable to help herself Averil put her small hand on his big one, and looked up into his face. He was very handsome, she thought, but not in the pretty way that Roger Mortimer was. "Thank you," she said softly.

"You have green eyes," he noted with a small smile.

"All my sisters do, but Maia's have a hint of emerald in them, and Junia's are a dark green. Your eyes are silvery blue. They are very pretty," Averil said, and then she blushed again.

"Your father says you have a temper, but also a good heart," he told her.

She nodded. "I do."

"You are honest," he said with another smile. "I have seen your temper."

"I try to be fair, my lord," Averil answered him.

"Do you want to join the festivities?" he asked.

"Perhaps we might share a cup of wine," Averil suggested, "but I really am so very tired, my lord. I want nothing more than a good night's sleep in a real bed, or on a mattress before we must spend our days traveling home, and our nights on the hard earth."

"Agreed," he said.

He found a servant who brought them a large goblet of wine mixed with potent, honied mead to share. It was very strong, and to her embarrassment Averil found her head spinning. Her legs began to give way beneath her, but Rhys sensed it. Catching her up in his arms before she fell, he cradled his new wife, surprised by the feelings she aroused. Calling to a servant, he asked to be shown the way to the solar where Averil was staying. With the servant going before him he climbed a flight of narrow stairs. Averil's eyes were closed, and she was murmuring softly. She was indeed very lovely, Rhys thought. Perhaps he had not gotten such a bad bargain after all. And there was silver as well as kind in her dowry. Silver could buy him his own land, and more silver could be made breeding the sheep and cattle her father was giving him. Nay, it was not a bad bargain at all. If they could learn to get on, then all would be well.

Arriving in the solar he said to the serving woman sitting by the fireside sewing, "The lady is indisposed. Where am I to put her?"

"Ah," the woman said, "the Dragon Lord's child. Lay her upon that small cot by her pack, my lord. Is she all right?"

"Two sips of wine with mead," he told

the servant. "She is very tired. Our journey has been long, and tomorrow we must return home." He set his burden down where he had been instructed. Taking the little chaplet from her head, he laid it aside.

"Poor lass," the servant replied. "I will look after her, my lord."

Reaching into his pouch Rhys drew forth a coin. "Thank you," he said, pressing the large round copper into the woman's hand. Then he left.

When Averil finally awoke it was daylight again. The solar was filled with chattering women. Her gown had been eased, and her slippers had been removed from her feet. Her mouth felt very dry, but before she could even sit up a serving woman was at her side with a cup of clear water.

"Drink it all, child. There is a potion in it to restore your energy, which has been badly drained," the woman said, and cradling Averil's shoulders she helped her into a half-seated position, putting the cup to her lips.

"How long have I slept?" Averil wondered aloud.

"Why, all of last night, and into this morning," the servant said. "The first mass has already been said, and they are breaking their fast in the prince's great hall."

"I must get up!" Averil exclaimed. "We are leaving today."

"You should rest, lady," the woman responded. "You are very pale."

"I am always pale," Averil replied, and she drank the potion down.

"Are you of the Fair Folk, then?" the woman asked.

"They say I have an ancestress who was one of them," Averil told her.

The servant nodded. "Aye. Every few generations it is said the strain reappears in a son or a daughter, lady. Very well, I will help you."

Averil asked for a basin of water, and while she waited for it to be brought to her she removed her good gown and tunic, packing them away with her chaplet and shoes, changing into a tan gown and brown tunic, and a sturdier pair of leather shoes for riding.

She bathed quickly, scrubbing her teeth with a rough cloth, and wove her long golden hair into a thick, single plait. She set a sheer cream-colored veil over her head, fastening it down with a chaplet braided with brown silk and gold threads.

"I will bring your pack and your cloak to the hall, lady," the serving woman said.

Averil looked distressed. "I have no coin to reward you," she said regretfully.

"Your man did that last night, lady. He

111

was generous," the serving woman said, smiling. "Go along, now. When you need them, your possessions will be brought to you."

"Thank you," Averil replied, and she hurried off to the hall to find her father and the others. The others. Her husband. She was a married woman now. And he had been kind last night. She wondered if he would continue to be kind.

Her father found her first. "Hurry and eat, daughter," he said. "We want to be off Anglesey and onto the mainland before midday. Where is your husband?"

"I don't know," Averil said. "He brought me to the solar and left me last night."

Averil sat down at one of the tables below the high board. A servant slapped a hollowed-out trencher before her, and filled it with oat stirabout. Another servant gave her a piece of buttered bread, and set a cup before her.

"Wine, ale, or cider?" he said.

"Wine," Averil told him. The hair of the dog to calm her belly, and her nerves. She ate slowly. Her father had disappeared again, probably seeking the others.

"You slept well?" Rhys FitzHugh had seated himself by her side. "Wine," he told the attendant serving man.

"Yes, my lord, thank you," Averil replied.

"Good! When you have finished your meal we will ride."

"Did you have a good night, my lord?" Averil asked him.

He grinned. "Roger and I got very drunk," he began. "What happened after that I do not know, but I woke up on a hillock in a meadow outside the castle."

Averil reached out and drew a piece of grass from his dark brown hair. "I think, my lord, that my bed was more comfortable."

"As would mine have been if you were in it," he said softly.

"You promised!" she cried, flushing.

"And I will keep that promise, Averil," he assured her. "I have merely remarked that a man sleeps better with a woman by his side."

"I have never even kissed a man," she told him.

"Good!" he told her. "Then mine shall be the only lips you ever know."

"Do you want to kiss me?" she demanded to know. "You but touched my forehead with your lips after we had been wed yesterday."

"If you want to be kissed, Averil, I will kiss you," he said.

"If I must ask you then it is not worth it," she told him quickly. "I am finished with my meal." She stood up. "We had

113

best be going, my lord."

"You will ride by my side today, lady, so we may learn to know one another," he told her. "Come along now." And he took her hand in his, leading her off and out of the hall to where their party awaited them.

Chapter 4

It seemed that they rode for days although their return was actually no longer than their journey to Aberffraw had been. Each night they made camp, and Averil's bedding was set next to her husband's. Yet not once did he touch her, or even kiss her. And each day they rode side by side learning bit by bit about each other. Rhys spoke of his father with admiration, and how he loved Everleigh. He told Averil of how when he was eighteen his father had, to everyone's surprise, fallen in love with the daughter of a distant relation who had been orphaned and placed in his custody. They had wed, and nine months later Mary had been born. Her mother, however, a delicate creature, had not survived the childbirth.

"Was your stepmother good to you?" Averil asked him, curious.

"Always," Rhys answered. "When Rosellen was first brought to Everleigh it was thought that my father would match her with me, for we were close in age. She was sixteen. But Da loved her from the first sight he had of her, and she him. Their marriage was the right thing. And because she loved my father she was good to me even when she was carrying her own child. That child might have been a son and heir for my father. Still, Rosellen treated me with great kindness."

"Is that why you love Mary so much?" Averil said.

"Aye," he agreed, "but you will come to love Mary, too, for she is sweet by nature," Rhys responded.

"My sister Junia is sweet, but Maia is more determined than even I am. I suppose it comes from the pride she has in being our father's legitimate daughter although no one in our house has ever made a distinction between us. We are simply the Dragon Lord's daughters," Averil explained.

"And your mothers all get on with one another?" he queried her.

"My mother, Gorawen, and the lady Argel, are great friends. Da's second concubine, Ysbail, is a good woman, but inclined to be a bit prickly. She is very concerned that her daughter Junia not be slighted. But of course, Junia never is."

"You love your sisters," he remarked.

"Aye, and our little brother Brynn," Averil told him. "He is almost nine. He looks so much like Da that we sometimes have to laugh when we see them together.

He is very proud that he descends from King Arthur. He knows every bit of our family's history, and will tell you all about it whether you will or no."

"You will miss your family," he said quietly. It was a statement more than a question.

"Aye, but you will not forbid them Everleigh, my lord, will you?"

"Nay, they may come when it suits them," he replied.

"If your sister is the mistress of the manor, what am I to do?" Averil asked. "I am not used to being idle. Will we live in the manor house?"

"I have always lived there, but there is a bailiff's cottage, Averil, if you would prefer it," he told her. "It has not been lived in for many years. The last bailiff of Everleigh was a cousin of my father's. He had neither chick nor child. When he died I was sixteen. My father then made me the manor's bailiff, so the cottage is mine by right."

"If your sister and I can exist peacefully together then we shall live in the manor house," Averil said. "But if Mary is in charge, and she has Rhawn, then I shall spend my days making the cottage habitable again for us one day. For now I shall set my loom up in your hall. Will that be satisfactory, my lord?"

He nodded. "I think it a wise thing you

plan, Averil, for once Mary is wed we would do well to leave her with her husband though she should never ask us to go. Still, it will be several years before my sister is old enough to be married."

They had chattered back and forth as they rode each day, and Averil began to consider that she had made a good match even if Rhys FitzHugh was not a great lord. How Maia and Junia would tease her over her former boasting, *but then, see who they would have as husbands one day*, Averil thought. Maia, of course, would make the best match, being true born. And Ysbail would certainly see that Junia was not wed badly.

They finally arrived back at Dragon's Lair, and as they entered the hall of her father's keep Gorawen ran forward to embrace her only child.

"I am wed," Averil said softly.

"Has he been kind?" Gorawen asked anxiously.

"He has had no opportunity," Averil murmured.

"Thank heavens!" her mother exclaimed low. "There is much you need to know, my daughter. There are things I must teach you before you go to his bed. I shall tell him that he may not have you yet."

"I do not know if he even wants me, really," Averil said. "He has not even kissed me yet, Mother. While there was little occasion for coupling along our journey, surely he might have found a moment to steal a kiss, but he did not."

"Perhaps he is shy," Gorawen suggested with a small smile.

"He kidnapped me, Mother!" Averil said. "I hardly believe him to be shy."

"Do you talk with one another?" Gorawen was becoming just a little concerned.

"Aye. I have learned much of him, and he me," Averil answered her parent.

Gorawen nodded. "That is to the good," she said. "I think perhaps your husband is giving you a chance to adjust to your new situation in life. He has shown no animosity at having to wed you?"

"Honor was at stake, Mother," Averil responded. "And if I have learned one thing, Mother, it is that Rhys FitzHugh is honorable despite his behavior in the matter of obtaining my person."

"But he shows no anger towards you at having made the error he made?" Gorawen persisted. "Often a man will make a mistake where a woman is concerned, and then he will blame her for his blunder. Has this been the case with you and Rhys FitzHugh?"

"Nay," Averil said slowly. "I believe he has come to terms with what he has done. He speaks fairly to me, and has not censured me for his fault."

"Good, good!" Gorawen said, but she thought to herself that she would watch this new son they had obtained most carefully. Averil had not her experience where human nature was concerned.

Averil kissed her mother's cheek, and then turned to curtsey to her father's wife.

Argel took the girl by her shoulders and kissed her on both cheeks. "Welcome home, Averil," she said. "I am happy that all has worked out well for you."

"Thank you, lady," Averil replied sweetly. "Now, my sister Maia must have a husband of her own. But let him be near, lady, so we do not lose one another."

"And then my daughter must be matched," Ysbail said sharply.

"Junia has several years before she should wed," Merin Pendragon said.

"But he must be as fine a gentleman as is chosen for Maia," Ysbail persisted. "Not some poor bailiff such as Averil has wed, though I will admit he is handsome."

"Aye, aye!" the Dragon Lord said impatiently.

Now it was the sisters' turn to greet the returning Averil. They rushed her with little shrieks and giggles, hugging their eldest sibling.

"What is it like?" Maia demanded.

Averil shook her head at Maia. "The hall is hardly the place to speak on such things," she said, reluctant that her sisters know she was still a virgin.

"He is very handsome, as my mother says," Junia remarked.

"Is he?" Averil turned and looked at her husband. "Aye, I suppose he is."

"How could you not notice?" Junia said.

Averil grinned. "A man should never be told how beautiful he is, little one. They are vain enough about everything else."

"I wonder if my husband will be handsome," Junia replied.

"Your husband must be a man of some property, and good family," Maia told the youngest of the trio. "Handsome does not count. Wealth and family are the only important factors in a marriage. You are a descendant of the great Arthur, no matter you were born on the wrong side of the blanket, sister."

"But Averil said she would wed a great lord, and Rhys FitzHugh is hardly a great lord. He doesn't even have lands of his own," Junia noted.

"He is bailiff of a great manor," Maia replied quickly. She did not want Junia pointing out that their eldest sister, indeed the most beautiful of them all, had married badly and beneath her, though certainly through no fault of her own. Why, if Averil had not protected her two sisters that day, Maia thought, it might be her now wed to a bailiff. She shuddered delicately at the idea. Rhys FitzHugh was certainly not the man of her dreams. The man of her dreams was tall, dark and dangerously handsome with an air of mystery about him. She just didn't know who he was yet.

"Rhys tells me there is a stone bailiff's cottage if we wish it," Averil said. The truth of innocent Junia's words had not been lost on her.

"But you've lived in a keep all of your life," Junia said. "Will not a cottage seem small to you, sister?"

"Mayhap it is a big cottage," Maia suggested. She glared at Junia. Would the brat not be silent? Could she not comprehend the awful truth of the situation?

Averil laughed softly. "Perhaps he will become a great lord one day," she said, a twinkle in her light green eyes.

"Oh, sister, I am sorry!" Maia replied low.

"Do not be," Averil responded. "I have had the many weeks we rode across the land to Aberffraw and back to think on it. Rhys is an honorable man, and I believe he will be kind to me and the children I give him. He has a home, and a respected position. It is unlikely he will ever lose either. We are well matched, and another man might not have been as accepting of me despite the fine dowry Da has offered."

Maia nodded slowly. "You have gained some wisdom in these weeks away from us," she said. "Though we are but a year apart, you seem older to me now."

Averil laughed. "I do not know if it is wisdom, or the simple acceptance of the facts that stare me in the face now," she admitted ruefully. And then she laughed softly.

"Well," Junia put in, "if he cannot be a great lord, or a wealthy man, then it is certainly a good thing that he is handsome, isn't it?"

Her two elder sisters laughed, and Averil cupped the girl's face with her hand.

"Is that what you shall seek in a mate, Junia? A beautiful man?"

"I think it a more obtainable goal than a great lord," Junia murmured dryly.

Maia chuckled. "Clever puss! She may be right."

"I want a bath," Averil said. "My nose has become numb to my own stink, and that of the horses we rode. My bottom has turned to leather these past weeks!"

"Yes," the lady Argel said, overhearing. She turned to Rhys FitzHugh. "You, too, will certainly want a bath, my lord. I will have it made ready. Your wife will bathe you herself. I am happy to say that all of our daughters know how to properly conduct themselves with guests." She signaled to a servant.

Maia and Junia looked at Averil mischievously. Their eldest sister swallowed hard, but then she said, her voice smooth and calm, "Yes, my lord, it is a wife's duty to bathe her husband when he needs it. I shall go and oversee to the preparations so that all is done properly. My mother will bring you to me when all is in readiness." Then, with a brief nod of her head, she glided gracefully from the hall.

"You've done better than I would have thought, young FitzHugh," Lord Mortimer noted with a grin. Then turning to the lady Argel he said, "We will avail ourselves of your hospitality tonight, my lady, and I thank you."

"Of course, my lord Mortimer. You and your son are welcome. Would you like baths, too? Our daughters and I can see to it." Her mild brown eyes were twinkling.

Roger Mortimer looked most enthusiastic, but his father quickly said, "We shall wait until we return home, lady, if you can bear with our stink. And again, I thank you."

The lady Argel tilted her head graciously. "I must go see that the cook has enough for the supper. We were never certain when you would return. Gorawen, go help Averil. Ysbail, I will need your aid. Daughters, go to my solar and rest yourselves. We will leave the hall to the men for now."

"Those who call the Welsh barbarians have never visited your home, Merin Pendragon," Lord Mortimer said. "Your wife is most obviously a treasure. And your two women!" He smacked his lips lightly. "How you have managed to keep the peace between them, I do not know."

"Each has her place in my house and my heart," the Dragon Lord told his old friend. "They are assured of it, and thus coexist. If they did not they would go, for Argel is my wife, and she is a good woman."

"But Gorawen has most of your heart, my friend," Edmund Mortimer said wisely.

Merin Pendragon said nothing, but he did smile briefly.

Gorawen. His wife's mother, Rhys FitzHugh thought. He could see from where Averil had obtained her looks, but for her green eyes.

"Do you wish us to send for your sister, Rhys FitzHugh?" the Dragon Lord asked. "We will be celebrating your marriage to my daughter for the next few days."

"We shall celebrate at Everleigh as well," Rhys answered. "I think it best Mary remain on her own lands. It is a long trip for one so young, and there is no place to shelter but for that ruins. My sister is yet tender."

The Dragon Lord nodded. He understood. "My son and I shall accompany you and Averil back to Everleigh," he said. "It will be a fine adventure for Brynn. You have not met him yet. He is a good lad. And strong. Perhaps we might consider a match between your sister and my son one day."

Clever, Edmund Mortimer thought to himself. Then the Pendragons would have lands in both the Welshry and the Englishry. Old Merin is ambitious of a sudden.

"Mary is too young yet for me to consider matching her, my lord," Rhys replied.

"She would be lady of Dragon's Lair," Merin noted. "Her husband would have his own lands and cattle."

"My sister is lady of Everleigh. She has lands and cattle in her own right," Rhys replied. "When she is older we will speak on it, my lord, but I make you no promises."

"Well said, young FitzHugh," Lord Mortimer agreed approvingly. He was considering that little Mary might make a fine wife for his youngest son, John. A man had to look after his own, and he had not the influence or wealth of his more powerful Mortimer relations who lived at court.

Merin Pendragon knew his old friend Edmund Mortimer well enough that he understood he would have a rival for little Mary FitzHugh and her lands. But he felt no animosity towards the Englishman. The heiress was a choice bit. As long as one of them won her for their family, and not some stranger, Averil and her husband would be safe.

In the bathing room of the keep the servants were lugging buckets of boiling water and dumping them into the great round, gray stone tub. Gorawen poured a small vial of fragrance into the hot water. The scented steam rose up, wafting the smell of lavender about the chamber. In the hearth the fire burned hot. Averil had already pinned up her long golden hair, and divested herself of her garments save her chemisette.

"Will you help me, Mother?" she asked her parent.

"I think not," Gorawen said. "You have been well taught and are capable of washing a man by yourself. Because he is your husband you must get into the tub with him, Averil. You, too, need a bath. Besides, it may encourage Rhys FitzHugh to a greater familiarity of your person. Your marriage must be consummated sooner than later, my daughter, and I believe sooner would be best for both you and Rhys."

"But I thought there were certain things

that you wanted me to know, Mother," Averil protested softly. The idea of getting into a tub with Rhys FitzHugh was startling.

"Aye, there are. But when I consider what I can teach you, I know it is better that Rhys FitzHugh find you as pure a virgin as you really are. Once he has taken his first pleasure of you, and has no doubts as to your innocence, then I shall teach you the many delights a woman can share with her husband, and the pleasure she can give him. Rhys will not be unhappy in his wife, my daughter." She looked about the room. "The bath is ready. I will go and fetch Rhys. Warm the drying cloths on the rack by the fire, Averil. Have you already forgotten what you have learned?" Giving her daughter a pat of encouragement, Gorawen hurried from the bathing room.

Averil looked about her to be certain all was in perfect readiness. She hung the large clean cloths over the wooden rack by the fire as her mother had instructed her to do. She checked the temperature of the water with her hand. It was quite hot. She moved the little oak steps one more time. With a round tub it didn't really matter from which direction one entered it. Her brushes lay in orderly fashion upon the stone tub's rim. There was a clean washing cloth, and a bowl of soft soap. Everything was as it should be.

The door to the bathing room opened, and Rhys FitzHugh stepped through, a surprised look upon his handsome face as his gaze swept the chamber. "You have a room just for bathing?" he said, astounded.

"Don't you?" she asked him.

"Nay," he said. "We have an oak tub, or we bathe in the stream near the house."

"And yet you English infer that we Welsh are barbarians," Averil murmured.

"Not all Welsh houses have such rooms," he defended himself.

"Perhaps not, my lord, but this is how I have been raised. Please sit down on that stool now so I may remove your boots and clothing," Averil told him, sounding far braver than she actually was.

He obeyed, and she quickly pulled the muddy, well-worn boots from his feet. Her little nose wrinkling with disdain, she unrolled his foot coverings and dropped them onto the floor. Indicating that he should now stand she began to remove his garments. First his cotte, a calf-length tunic from which she shook the dust and laid carefully aside on a chair back. Beneath it he wore a chemise. It was laced up the front. Averil's slender fingers undid it quickly. For a moment she stopped. Beneath the open chemise his chest was broad and smooth, devoid of hair. When she took the garment from him he would be quite naked. She considered how to remove the chemise.

Making the decision for her, Rhys FitzHugh took Averil's two small hands and held them to his chest for a moment. "I think, wife, we must now become acquainted with one another," he said in a quiet voice. "Let your dainty hands explore, Averil. There is no wrong in it, and it would give me pleasure."

Averil felt her cheeks suffused with warmth. "My lord." Her voice was a whisper. "I am a virgin." She could not look at him.

Rhys FitzHugh tipped her face up so that their eyes finally met. "I know that," he said softly. Then, dipping his head, he brushed her lips with his just briefly.

Her little mouth made an "O" of surprise, and she gasped.

He smiled. "You have never been kissed," he said.

"Of course not!" The tone of her reply was indignant. "I was meant to be wife to a great lord, Rhys FitzHugh. I could not go to a great family with my honor besmirched."

"Then I am fortunate to be the recipient of your chastity," he replied dryly.

"Yes, you are!" she said indignantly. "And I am rewarded for my good behavior by being wed to a manor bailiff with naught to his name but a stone cottage! What in the name of Holy Mary made you steal me away other than you thought I was my father's heiress?" she demanded of him.

"I needed a wife," he said, "and my father told me before he died that a rich wife was a sight better than a poor wife."

"Then you have been cheated, too," she responded.

"Nay, I have not. You may not be your da's heiress, Averil, but you are well-propertied for a lass born on the wrong side of the blanket. And, you are extravagantly beautiful. You will be desired by many who see you, including some who are great lords, but you are my wife, and I know your own sense of honor will not allow you to betray me or the FitzHugh name. My father did give me his name, you know, and our children will be true born." He smiled down on her. "I like the feel of your hands on me, wife."

Averil blushed furiously once again. Rhys FitzHugh was a most infuriating man, she thought. She drew his chemise from him, saying as she did, "Get into the tub, my lord, before the water grows cold." Her eyes were everywhere but on him, now.

He could not refrain from chuckling. "Aren't you getting into the tub with me?"

he asked her mischievously, his eyebrows waggling wickedly at her.

"I can wash you quite well without getting into the tub," she said sharply.

"You can, but you won't," he told her. "I am your husband. I want you in that great stone tub with me." Then, before she might protest further, he picked her up in his brawny arms, mounted the two steps, and climbed into the tub.

Averil shrieked with her surprise. "Put me down!" she cried to him.

He complied, gently dumping her into the hot water with a grin. "I would be well washed, wife," he said.

Averil grabbed a scrubbing brush, and whacked him smartly on his dark head. "Why, so you shall, my lord husband!" she told him. She dipped her hand into the stone soap crock, and slapped the runny soap on his hair. "I won't bother picking the nits today," she said. "A good soaping should rid you of them." She had stepped up on the tub's little stool that sat beneath the hot water. Her fingers dug fiercely into his big head as she scrubbed his dark — and she was noticing — somewhat curly hair.

"Ouch! You shrew!" he yelped. "You will take my scalp off!"

"Your hair is filthy. Close your eyes!" She dipped a large scoop of water and dumped it over his head. Then she added more soap and began to scrub again.

"I'll smell like a field of flowers when you get through," he protested. "The bees won't be able to restrain themselves from me."

"A clean head will be a great improvement for you," she snapped. She began dipping water again, and rinsed his dark head until there was no more evidence of soap.

"God's mercy," he said, "but you have sweet little titties, wife."

"What?" Her cheeks grew hot again as she raised startled eyes to his face.

"The way your sheer little chemisette clings to them is quite provocative, Averil," he murmured, moving nearer.

She looked down, and gasped with her shock. Standing on the stool so she might wash his hair put her but waist deep in the water. The soft fabric of her garment clung to her flesh, molding it in a very sensual manner. Not only her breasts, but her torso as well.

Her pale skin grew beet red with embarrassment.

"Take it off," he said in a low, hard voice.

"What?" She could not have heard him correctly.

"Remove your chemisette, or I will rip it from you, Averil," he told her. "I want to

133

see you as you were made."

"It isn't right!" she cried low.

"I am your husband," he told her, his voice gentler now. Jesu! The sight of her beneath that wet fabric had roused him mightily. He had forgotten for a moment that she was so innocent despite the unorthodox household in which she had been raised. Merin Pendragon might keep a wife and two concubines, but Rhys FitzHugh had seen no evidence of licentiousness in his house.

"We may be naked for one another?" she questioned him.

"We may, and while your chemisette needed laundering, Averil, I would see you without it."

Averil slipped down into the water, and then drew the garment from her person, wringing it out and tossing it onto the bathing room's stone floor. "I must continue bathing you, and then bathe myself," she said. Her heart was beating very quickly now.

He nodded, appreciating her modesty. He would see her soon enough when she had to exit their bath. "Let me wash your hair first," he suggested.

"You?" She was surprised.

"Your tresses are beautiful, Averil, and in as much need of soap and water as were my unruly locks," he told her.

She hesitated a moment, but then said, "Very well, my lord." Then she stood quietly as he unpinned her long hair, rubbed in the soap, lathering it into suds, rinsing it, soaping and rinsing a second time. When he had finished Averil twisted her rope of golden hair free of water, and pinned it up once more.

"Now you smell like a field of flowers," he said with a small smile.

"Let me wash you now, my lord, as I have been taught," she replied. She took up another brush, soaped it, and began to scrub his back. Her hands moved swiftly, sliding beneath the warm water to wash with the cloth what she could not see. After she had laved water over his clean skin she turned him about, and washed his face, his neck and ears, his chest and his arms. "Now," she said as she finished, "you must do the rest."

"Will you not do it?" he asked. "Your mother said you knew well how to bathe a man, Averil."

"Would you have me handling the private parts belonging to our guests, my lord?" she countered.

"I am not a guest, Averil. I am your husband. Now finish your task, wife, or I shall have to tell your parents that I am displeased with you," he threatened. "And, Averil, from now on you will wash no other men. Only me."

She swallowed hard. Then taking up the soft cloth she soaped it again, and plunged it beneath the water. She swirled her cloth about his flat belly, moving down to his groin. She rubbed gently over his pubic mound, which was covered with thick wiry hair. Delicately she washed his manhood and the pouch of life beneath it. The manhood was large, and it was very hard. It seemed to have a life all its own as it throbbed in her hand. Averil swallow nervously again. "I believe I am done," she said, low. Then she began to wash herself.

"I want to take you here," he said in a rough voice, and his lips were pressing against the damp nape of her neck. He pulled the cloth from her hand, and soaping it began to rub it over her breasts. "You are so damned tempting, Averil. I am not sorry that I stole the wrong girl." His arm fastened about her waist, and he pressed himself against her body. "Did you ever think you would lose your virginity in a tub of warm water, my beautiful young wife?"

"You cannot!" she gasped. "You will shame me if you do this now!"

"How?" he demanded. The cloth had dropped away, and he was fondling her round little breast, squeezing the soft flesh, pinching the nipple lightly to make it pucker.

"There will be no bloody sheet for my da to fly. People will assume you had me when you first stole me. Or they will say I was no virgin at all, and speculate if I had a lover. Please, Rhys FitzHugh! Not here! Not now! If my virtue is questioned my sisters may suffer as well."

He groaned. For just the briefest moment he had forgotten that she was a virgin. She was so incredibly desirable. "Get out of the tub, Averil, and wrap yourself in a drying cloth," he said.

"But I must dry you, my lord," she protested.

"If you put one more finger on me, wife," he told her, "I cannot prevent myself from having you, here and now. If you want that bloody sheet displaying your innocence to fly from your father's tower in the morning, you will do what I tell you. Now!"

Averil scrambled from the tub, taking one of the large drying cloths and wrapping herself in it, her back to him, as she toweled herself free of water. Her body was tingling, especially her breasts. The blood coursing through her veins right now boiled, she was convinced. She had been but briefly kissed. Lightly fondled. But she knew she was more than ready to lie with this man. He might not have her love yet, or her trust, but he had certainly engaged her lusts.

"Come out, now, my lord husband," she finally told him. "I think you can trust me to dry you without further ado."

"Aye," he agreed as he climbed from the water. "I have managed to quiet my big boy, but not for very long, Averil. This union of ours must be consummated, you will agree." His manhood still looked very dangerous.

"I do," she admitted as she swiftly and efficiently dried him off. The conversation was perturbing, she considered. There had never been a man in her life before but for her father, her brother, the keep's servants and men-at-arms. No one had ever looked at her with desire. Averil was the Dragon Lord's eldest daughter. She was untouchable until Rhys FitzHugh had stolen her away, and ruined her chances of a rich marriage. She should be angry at this man, and she was. Yet he excited her, and the teasing glimpses he had given her of what lay ahead in their marriage bed were tempting.

He took the drying cloth from her and wiped his face. "What are you thinking?" he asked her.

Caught in her reverie she looked at him and said, "You need to scrape the whiskers from your face, Rhys FitzHugh. You look like a bear just come from its winter cave. You will find what you need on the shelf there. I must go to the chamber I share with my sisters and dress now. I will send my mother to bring you clean clothing." And Averil hurried from the bathing room.

Outside she met her mother. "He will need clean clothes," she said.

"Where are you going, daughter?" Gorawen asked.

"I must dress myself, Mother," Averil replied.

"Your possessions are no longer with your sisters. While you are here you will sleep with your husband in the small room at the top of the west tower. It is already made up. Go and put on fresh garb. When you are presentable you may both return to the hall where a feast will be set to celebrate your marriage."

Averil nodded, for she suddenly found she could not speak. She was to no longer be with Maia and Junia. She was to sleep with this husband she had gained in so reckless a manner. She almost ran up the narrow staircase to the tower chamber. Inside she found her clothing and brushes and her dower trunk. She pulled a clean chemisette from it, and removing the drying cloth from about her form she pulled it on. Her gown was of olive green silk with long tight-fitting sleeves. Over it she drew a sleeveless tunic of the same shade embroidered with gold threads. She had never before seen these garments, but she knew they were gifts from her mother on her marriage. Gorawen had exquisite taste, and was known for her generosity.

Sitting down on the bed Averil undid her hair, and taking up her brush began to brush out the long damp mass until it was reasonably dry. Then plaiting it she wrapped the braids about her head, afixing them with polished bone hairpins. She had never before dressed her hair this way but now she was a married woman, and might. She found slippers to match her gown, and slipped them on. Then she looked about for Rhys FitzHugh's clothing, but she could find nothing for him. Hurrying from the tower room she sought her mother.

"There are no fresh garments for my husband in our chamber," she told Gorawen.

"He has no clean garments," Gorawen said. "Have you not noticed that he has been wearing the same clothing since you left for Aberffraw? You are his wife. It is up to you to see what garments he has are made presentable before he dresses again, Averil."

"He must have a clean chemise and leg coverings, Mother, or washing him will have been a waste of time," Averil replied.

Gorawen nodded. "I agree," she said. "I have some clean chemises and leg coverings that belonged to your father when he was younger. I had saved them for Brynn for when he is older, but we may spare some for Rhys FitzHugh. Come along and we will fetch them."

"Let me tell him lest he put on his dirty clothing," Averil replied, and running to the bathing room she opened the door and stepped through. "Do not dress yourself yet, my lord," she said to her husband who was still scrapping the whiskers from his chin. "I will bring you some clean garments." She picked up his boots and cotte. "I will have the servants clean these." Then she was gone before he might even speak.

She gave Rhys's boots to a serving man, instructing him to clean and polish the worn footwear and then return them to her lord in the bathing room. She handed the cotte to another servant, telling her to brush the garment clean and return it to its owner in the bathing room. Then Averil hurried on, a small smile on her face as she thought of her new husband's reaction when her father's servants entered the room unannounced.

Gorawen went to the solar where all the women liked to gather. From a trunk set in an alcove she drew out a beautiful linen chemise, handing it to her daughter. "I believe this will fit Rhys," she said, and bending down again she drew out a pair of braies, giving them to Averil. "You must give his old garments to the servants to launder, but you may keep these."

"Thank you, Mother," Averil responded, and she hurried off back to the bathing room to help her husband dress.

Neither his boots nor his cotte were ready when she returned to him. He had finished taking the whiskers from his face. "You are handsome," Averil said. "My sisters have said it, and now I see it. Here is a clean chemise, my lord, and a set of braies. They are yours now. Put them on while we wait for your cotte and boots," Averil suggested to him with a small smile. She let her eyes slip quickly over him. He was a big man in every respect, well muscled and straight of limb.

Rhys FitzHugh slipped the undergarment over his now very clean frame. He sat down upon a three-legged stool to pull on the dark woolen braies. "Where did you find these?" he asked curiously.

"They were my da's when he was younger. My mother put them aside when he outgrew them for Brynn, but says she can spare them, for you are now her son," Averil told him. "My mother has taught me not to be wasteful."

"Your mother is very beautiful. But for your eyes you resemble her muchly," he replied. "She is from the house of Tewydr?"

"Aye. My bloodlines are good, my lord. You will have no cause for shame in me, though you stole the wrong maiden. Actually, my blood is better than that of my true-born sister, Maia, though I should never say it aloud to others," Averil explained.

He nodded, and then the door to the bathing room opened, and a serving maid entered carrying his cotte and his boots. She handed them to Averil, curtsied, and withdrew from the chamber.

Averil handed her husband his boots. "Put them on, Rhys FitzHugh. They are of better quality than I suspected now that I see them clean," she noted. Then she looked at his cotte. "It is blue. I could not tell before. But it is very threadbare, my lord. Have you the material at Everleigh for me to make you another? You are the bailiff of a fine estate, and cannot go about looking like a poor man."

"But I am a poor man," he reminded her. "Everleigh belongs to my sister."

"You have cattle and sheep through your marriage to me, my lord, and a purse of fifteen silver pennies, one for each year of my life," Averil reminded him. "You are no longer a poor man, and you must have a new cotte."

He laughed. "I am surprised to find that

despite your great beauty, my wife, you are a girl who will care well for me, and our children. You are not overproud, or haughty, Averil. My sister will do well to follow your instruction. Rhawn, her old nurse, cannot teach Mary how to be a lady, but you can."

"I am indeed haughty, my lord, but only where required," she responded.

He laughed again as he straightened his cotte. It was threadbare. It would be good to have a new one. "There is fabric aplenty at Everleigh, my wee Welsh wife. While you ripen with our first child this winter you will sew me a new one," he said.

"Even a well-brought up virgin knows it takes more than wishing to get a child," Averil said pithily, yet there was a small smile upon her lips.

He yanked her into his arms, and kissed her heartily. "As you will learn this very night, Averil, my wife. But for now we are expected in the hall that your family may properly celebrate our union."

Rosy with her blushes Averil nonetheless spoke up. "Then let us go, Rhys FitzHugh," she said to him. Perhaps marriage to this man would not be so bad after all. If he was not a great lord he was a charming man. That had to count for something.

Chapter 5

When Averil and her husband entered the hall of the Dragon Lord they found their entire family gathered and waiting. Normally the main meal of the day would have been served at the noon hour, but a messenger sent ahead of Merin Pendragon had warned the keep of the master's return. The lady Argel had therefore postponed the dinner, and the cook had had time to add more dishes, for the men with their lord would eat far more than the household of women and children he had been feeding. The order of their seating had been prearranged. Averil and Rhys, the feast's guests of honor, were placed to the left and the right of the Dragon Lord. The lady Argel sat to the bride's left followed by Roger Mortimer, Maia and Ysbail. To the bridegroom's right was Gorawen, Lord Mortimer, Brynn Pendragon, and Junia.

By chance there was a traveling monk from the Cistercian order who had begged a night's shelter from the Dragon Lord. He offered up a blessing for the meal and the young couple. Rhys FitzHugh was surprised when the servants set polished pewter plates and matching spoons before each diner. He had never seen such plates although he had heard of them. He noted the diners in the hall below the high board had the usual trenchers of bread. The servants then brought about the courses for the high board upon silver platters. There was trout broiled and set upon a bed of watercress. There was capon and venison, both roasted, and a rabbit pie in brown gravy. The last of the summer peas was served. Fresh bread, still warm from the ovens, and sweet butter were placed upon the table while other servants poured wine into the pewter cups at each place. When all had been consumed a final course of cheeses, pears, sugar wafers and jellies was brought forth and set upon the high board.

When the meal had been at last finished the guests at the high board washed their hands and face in bowls of scented water brought forth by the servants. Below the high board other servants were gathering up the bread trenchers, which would be distributed to the few poor gathered at the door to the kitchen garden. Lord Mortimer was impressed with Merin Pendragon's hospitality and gentility, which was every bit as fine as his many English friends. And in some instances even better.

Now the Dragon Lord's daughters got up to entertain the guests. Like most of the Welsh they were musical by inclination. Averil played upon the telyn, which was a Celtic type of harp. Maia, the pibgorn, a reed instrument peculiar to the Welsh. Junia favored the recorder, which she alternated with a small drum painted with a design, and the cymbalum, or bells, which were shaken in time with the music. She was the most skilled musician of the three sisters.

Outside the hall the day had now waned, and the twilight was followed by the night. All evidence of the meal was now gone from the high board, and the tables below it were set against the walls with their benches atop them. The large fire pit blazed, taking the damp chill off the evening. The rushes had been swept away, and the keep's dogs lay sprawled by the warmth of the hearth snoring, as the men talked among themselves.

Gorawen moved discreetly to her daughter's side. "It is time for me to escort you to your bed, Averil," she murmured low. "Keep playing," she instructed the other two girls.

Averil stood up quietly, her fingers sliding over her telyn's strings in a brief finish. Her sisters quickly took up a more spritely tune thereby distracting the others from Averil's departure. Following her mother, she left the hall. "Where are we going?" she asked her parent.

"To your chamber in the tower where you dressed earlier," Gorawen replied. "The lady Argel and I prepared it for you and your bridegroom this afternoon. You will have privacy for your wedding night, daughter."

"But what of Lord Mortimer and his son?" Averil inquired.

"They will sleep in the hall," her mother responded. "There are bed spaces that are clean and ready for visitors. They will be just as comfortable there. Besides, the guest chamber is needed that you and your husband consummate your union. Merin will not allow you to depart until he is certain it has been done, Averil. He would not allow Rhys FitzHugh any excuse to repudiate you."

"I do not think he would do such a thing, Mother. He is an honorable man," the girl said as she had earlier.

"Truly honorable men do not kidnap innocent maidens, daughter," her mother said sharply.

"But men can make mistakes, can they not?" Averil said quickly. "But if they repent of their errors are they not honorable again?"

Gorawen laughed softly. "You are defending him," she teased. "Is it just possible that you are beginning to like this husband you have?"

"Like him or not I must live with him till death parts us," Averil responded in practical tones.

Gorawen laughed again. "He is handsome, and young enough to be vigorous in bed sport. Your are right to try to find the good in him, Averil." They had reached the top of the tower. Gorawen opened the door and escorted her daughter inside. "I will help you to undress," she said, and when Averil was garbed in only her chemise her mother pointed to the basin of warm scented water that had been set in the hot ashes of the tiny fireplace. "Relieve yourself, then wash, daughter," she instructed the girl.

Averil obeyed, quickly emptying the chamber pot out the single window, and pushing it beneath the bed again. She cleaned her teeth with the cloth provided, and then bathed her private parts.

Gorawen nodded, satisfied. "Now remove the chemise," she said.

"Will he be naked too, Mother?" Averil asked nervously.

"We shall see he is delivered to you as God made him, my daughter," her mother said with a small smile. "I have always believed that lovers should be equals although such a radical thought would disturb most."

Averil removed her chemise and climbed into the big bed that seemed to take up much of the chamber. "I am ready," she said.

"Unplait your hair," her mother bade the girl, and when Averil had obeyed Gorawen said, "Now you are ready." She fluffed her daughter's pale gold hair so that it framed her face and billowed about her slender shoulders. "Yes," she said softly. Then she bent and kissed Averil upon the forehead. "Let him lead you, my daughter," she said, "and do not fear. We will speak on the morrow of this night, and I will teach you all you shall need to know. Tonight, however, your innocence will speak for you." Then turning, she left the tower room.

It was both exciting and terrifying, this unknown, Averil thought as she waited for Rhys FitzHugh to come to her. Did she need to pee again? No. She was fine. She had a vague idea of what to expect. He would lie her on her back, and mount her. Her love passage was located between her thighs. His manhood would pierce it. It was said to be painful the first time. Averil's heart hammered nervously. It sounded like a most intimate act, and she had never experienced intimacy with anyone. She drew the coverlet up higher, more aware than ever of her nakedness. And then she heard a faint sound of laughter from the stairwell that led up to the tower. The laughter grew louder. She heard Rhys protesting something, and then more laughter. She strained to hear the words, but could not quite make them out. Then there were footsteps, and the door to the chamber was flung open, and Rhys, naked as the day he had come from his mother's womb, was pushed roughly into the room.

"There he is, lady," Roger Mortimer said, leering at her wickedly. He was drunk. "We have undressed him for you, but you shall have to do the rest." He eyed her in an attempt to see her breasts.

Rhys FitzHugh turned about, pushing Roger and those who had accompanied him from the chamber. He slammed the door shut, and threw the bolt, barring it firmly. The laughter outside in the hall echoed loudly, but then they heard the sound of retreating footsteps, and the laugher slowly faded away. Rhys turned.

"Get into bed," Averil said.

"Are you anxious, then?" he asked her as he came across the room.

"I do not want you catching a chill and dying on me yet," she replied sharply.

He lifted the coverlet and slid beneath it, climbing atop her as he did, sitting back on his tight haunches to face her. Reaching out he cupped one of her small round breasts in his palm, stroking it with his other hand. "Beautiful," he said in reverent tones.

Her heart almost burst through her chest. She gasped with shock at his bold and quick actions, her eyes wide, her mouth making a small "O." For a moment she was speechless, but then she quickly recovered. "You will crush me, you great creature," she protested.

"Nay, I will not," he said. "I want to see your face when I touch you, Averil. I like the look of surprise upon it now. It tells me more than words could." He very gently pinched her nipple, smiling softly as she colored and grew rosy with blushes.

"Remember, I am a virgin," she whispered for what she knew would be the final time. It actually hurt to speak. Her throat was tight.

"I know," he replied. He leaned forward so that his lips were almost touching hers. Then he ran his tongue around those lips. He took her two small hands, saying against her mouth as he did, "Take my big boy in your hands, Averil, and caress it. Soon it will swell with its desire, and I will fill you full with my lust. Do not be afraid. Tonight I will pleasure you, and I will teach you to pleasure me." His breath was winey and hot in her face.

"My mother says that after you have satisfied yourself as to my purity she will teach me how to please you," Averil whispered back at him.

"I cannot object. Your father has the appearance of a contented man when he looks at her, which is often. He loves her above the others."

"I know," Averil said softly. She could feel his flesh on her thighs. Her hands reached out to hold him in her palm, petting him with gentle fingers, and he began to harden and swell beneath her touch.

Leaning slightly forward he fastened his mouth about a nipple of one breast, licking and suckling it.

Averil's senses spun as a sharp sensation of what she realized was desire enveloped her, and a small cry escaped her.

He lifted his dark head, looking into her green eyes. "Lovers taste and tease one another, Averil. Do you like it?"

She nodded, wordless. She was being pounded by a host of sensations, one more delicious than the other. She was afraid, and yet she was not afraid.

He rolled onto his back, lifting her so that she lay atop him. "There," he said low. "Is that not better, wife? I like the feel of you against me." Then he wrapped his arms about her, and began kissing her with slow, hot kisses that blended one into another until it seemed as if it were one long and passionate embrace.

Averil's head spun. Her mouth was burning with the touch of his lips. She could feel his manhood pressing into her soft thigh. Hot. Hard. Yet patient. Willing to wait until she was ready. She trembled more with anticipation than fear. She was very curious, yet still cautious of what was to come. Her breasts were crushed against his wide chest. Their bellies caressed as he throbbed against her.

"Open your eyes, wife," he commanded her gently. "How can I look into your soul if you hide from me?"

Averil's eyes flew open to meet his, surprise upon her visage. She hadn't realized that her eyes were closed until he had spoken. She had been totally lost in his embrace, and drugged by his sweet kisses. "I am beginning to comprehend why my mother loves my father," she told him as her light green eyes met his dark blue ones.

"This is not love, wife," he answered her. "This is lust, but it is a start." His big hands fastened about her narrow waist, and he drew her forward, raising her up so that her breasts hung over his face. "So perfect," he murmured, rubbing his cheek against her round flesh. Then his tongue slipped from between his lips, and he began to lick at her nipples.

"Ohh, I like that!" Averil told him.

He opened his mouth and sucked hard on her right nipple until she shuddered with delight. Then he transferred his attentions to her left nipple, suckling it first, and then nipped on it sharply.

Averil moaned, her pleasure undisguised. "You make me tingle in the secret place," she told him innocently.

"Let me see," he murmured, turning her onto her back once more, and leaning over her. His lips met hers again, his tongue pushing into her mouth as his fingers slipped between her nether lips to play. She was already wet with her rising desire. He found her little jewel, and began to worry it with the ball of his forefinger. She squirmed beneath his touch, making little whimpering noises. "Do you like that, Averil?" he whispered in her ear, his tongue now pushing into the shell-like whorl.

"Yesss!" she hissed. Her eyes were closed again, and the look on her face told him her fear had left her, at least for now.

The finger continued to play with her until she shivered with satisfaction, experiencing her first real knowledge of passion. He slowly pressed the foraging finger into her untried body, moving it carefully back and forth. "And do you like this?" he asked her, licking the side of her face with his broad tongue.

"Ummmm," was her reply.

It was time. He mounted her, pulling her legs wide that he might fit himself between them. Averil did not resist him. He smiled to himself. The little witch was eager even if she didn't realize it right now. Guiding his manhood he pressed against the opening to her love channel, pushing forward slowly until the head of his lover's lance was firmly engaged. She moved nervously beneath him suddenly. "Nay, wife, do not fret," he soothed her gently. "What must be, will."

"You are so big," she whispered.

"The better to satisfy your desires, Averil, and I will." He pressed himself farther, and she gasped with surprise as the truth of his words hit home.

He would surely tear her apart with his member, she thought, suddenly panicking and struggling to free herself from this great peg of flesh impaling her. But he held her fast, and before she might protest he drew himself back, and then thrust hard into her.

Averil shrieked more with surprise than pain as he filled her full. He kissed her ardently, and then began to move rhythmically upon her, starting slowly, his measured cadence increasing in tempo until she was dizzy with a pleasure flowing through her veins that threatened to overwhelm her. "Oh, God!" she half sobbed.

He was panting with his efforts, but he laughed nonetheless.

"Don't stop!" she commanded him.

"I must sooner than later," he gasped back.

"Not yet! Not yet!" she begged. She was reaching. Reaching! But for what she didn't know, or understand, but then she found it, crying out with delight as she was overcome with wave after wave of pure joy. "Ohhhh, Rhys!" she cried out.

He was lost within her, unable to contain himself any longer. His lustful tribute poured forth, drenching her hidden garden with its first taste of his love juices. He was racked with great shudders, and groaned, at last satisfied, but not unmindful of her delicate form. Rolling away from her he lay upon his back, his breath coming in great heaves of air. "Oh, Averil!" he echoed her cry. "What a passionate little virgin you were."

She began to weep. "I am no longer a virgin. I am no longer a girl," she sobbed.

"Nay," he agreed, gathering her into his arms, cuddling her against his chest, "you are not, Averil. You are my own true wife."

"It was wonderful!" she wept, her tears soaking his chest.

He wanted to laugh with his happiness, but he did not. Looking down he saw the great stain of her maidenhead on the sheet beneath them. "Your sire will be proud come morning, wife," he told her.

She drew away from his embrace slightly, and looked. "Oh!" she exclaimed, and then she blushed. "He will, indeed," she finally agreed.

"Now you must rest," he told her. "You have been very brave, wife."

"Do we only do it once a night?" she asked him. She honestly didn't know.

"We will not confine our passion only to the nights, Averil," he told her, "and in answer to your question, we can do it more than once a night. Tonight, however, we have done enough. You have proved your innocence to me, and to the world. Sleep now."

"But I liked it," she replied. "I want to do it again."

"I need my rest, too," he explained, "so that my big boy may once again be eager. Look at the poor fellow now. You have worn him out, Averil, with your lustful little nature. In the hour before the dawn we shall exercise him once again, wife. He will enjoy burying himself in your hot little nest." He kissed her, drawing the coverlet up over them. To his delight she snuggled herself against him as she fell asleep.

When Averil awoke the sky was lightening outside the tower's window. She was on her back, and there was a distinct soreness between her thighs. Rhys was also on his back, and she inspected him thoroughly for the first time. He was really a very big man. Every bit as big as her father. She considered the hours before she had slept. Her husband had proved both gentle and kind. It boded well for them, but she still did not really know him. Nor if she could trust him. Rhys FitzHugh had spoiled her dreams with no apology, and Averil knew she could not easily forgive him for it although she had to admit to having enjoyed their bed sport.

But what kind of a life was she to have at Everleigh? She would not be mistress of the house, that place belonging to a six-year-old girl. And Mary FitzHugh already had a mentor in the serving woman, Rhawn. Rhawn looked like someone who would resent any interference with her charge. Yet Rhys said his little sister needed to learn gentle ways, and Rhawn could not teach her those. The thought that she should shortly leave Dragon's Lair was not a happy one, and another unhappy truth was that she no longer belonged in her father's house. She was married, well and good, now.

Outside the tower window the sky was

growing lighter, and she heard a lark begin to sing a morning song. Averil realized she no longer felt like making love. She slipped from her bed, padding across the room to the little hearth to coax the red coals into another fire. Pouring water from a pitcher that had been set in the ashes into a copper ewer she washed herself. The water in the basin grew red as she removed the stains of her virginity from her thighs and private parts. Emptying the water out the tower window she quickly dressed herself in her chemise, a green gown and sleeveless brown tunic. She slid her feet into her slippers. Then refilling the basin she set it on the chest at the bed's foot, and woke her husband.

He opened his eyes to see her standing by the bedside fully clothed. Hiding a smile he asked no questions. "Is it morning already, wife?"

"Aye. I should like to start for Everleigh today, my lord. We have done our duty, and you have been too long away. The harvest is ready to be brought in, and the bailiff should be there to oversee the work." There! She had decided. They would go today.

He was impressed by her knowledge. He had not expected it from the Dragon Lord's proud daughter. A daughter raised to believe she would make a great marriage. He swung his legs over the bed. Then turning, pulled the sheet from the mattress, handing it to her. "Take this to your father and say we have done our duty, Averil."

"There is fresh water in the basin, my lord," she replied, taking the bloodied bed cloth from him.

He nodded, now smiling just a little, and was rewarded by a slight smile in return. She hurried from the tower bedchamber, down the narrow, twisting staircase, and into the hall. Her father was already up, spooning oat stirabout from a round bread trencher. Proudly Averil walked to the high board, and handed him the sheet. "It is done, Da," she said simply.

Merin Pendragon stood, took the fabric from her, and held it out to see the now-brown stain upon it. He nodded. "You have done your duty, daughter," he told her. "Not an easy duty given that you expected a better match than you have gotten."

"I believe I was meant for a greater man, 'tis true, Da," she agreed with him. "But fate had other plans for me. There is no use weeping over spilt milk. I suppose I could kill him and begin anew, but my value was not just in my beauty, but in my virginity. I still have my beauty," she concluded with a wry smile at her parent.

He chuckled. "And you have your mother's practical nature, too, I see now. Well, it could have been worse. At least he has a place in life, and did you not tell your mother he also has a stone cottage as well?"

"He does," Averil admitted.

"Next spring I will send the best of my builder serfs to Everleigh for you. They will rebuild your cottage into a better dwelling," the Dragon Lord said. "I will not have you living in some hovel, daughter. Remain in the manor as long as you and Mary FitzHugh can manage together though I do not worry about the little lass. It is the serving woman that dotes on her who concerns me. She is obviously used to having her own way. Her master was ill for a time and 'twas easier for him to leave his child in the care of a faithful retainer. Rhys ran the estate. But now another woman comes into the house."

"I know, Da. I cannot be mistress there, but neither will I allow a servant to rule me as she does the child," Averil replied. "My husband has asked me to teach his sister gentle ways, which the servant cannot do."

"She will be jealous of you," the Dragon Lord replied. "God's mercy, I should have killed Rhys FitzHugh for having stolen you and been done with it!"

"Once he laid his hands on me, Da, my honor was gone until he restored it," Averil responded sagely. "I would leave Dragon's Lair today, if it please you, Da. It is time for the harvest, and Rhys should be home to oversee it."

"Aye, he should. Your mother will not be happy. She says there are things she must teach you first," the Dragon Lord said.

"And I would learn from her, but my husband cannot delay, and I must go with him, Da," Averil told her parent.

"Go where?" Gorawen had entered the hall, and came to join her lord and their daughter, her eyes flicking to the stained sheet.

"We must leave today for Everleigh," Averil told her mother. "It is time for the harvest, and Rhys should be there."

"Then I shall come with you," Gorawen answered her daughter. She turned to Merin Pendragon. "It is but a few days to Lamastide, my lord. The weather is fine. You must send men to escort our daughter and her husband home. I know you can spare these men a short time. 'Twill be long enough for me to tell Averil what she must know to keep her lord content as I have kept you content all these years, my lord."

He chuckled. "You have indeed kept me

well satisfied, Gorawen. I should not deny Rhys FitzHugh the benefits of the knowledge you will impart to our daughter. Aye, you may go. If we leave today we will not arrive at Everleigh until sometime tomorrow. We will remain three full days with our child. Then we must return."

"It is barely time, but 'twill be time enough, for Rhys FitzHugh will spend his days in Everleigh's fields bringing in the harvest," Gorawen said. "I shall spend those days with Averil, teaching her, and explaining to her things only a woman knows."

"Come and eat, both of you," he said. "When you have finished go tell my lady wife of your plans; Argel will want to know, and she will miss you. My prickly Ysbail is no good company for her." He arose from the high board, for he had now finished his meal, and left the hall, the bloodied sheet in his grasp.

Mother and daughter now sat as the servants supplied them with their trenchers filled with oat stirabout. There was also a plate of hard-boiled eggs on the table, fresh bread, butter and cheese. Watered wine was poured into their pewter goblets. The two ate quietly, but when they had finished Gorawen put a hand on her daughter's hand.

"Was it all right?" she asked anxiously.

"It was wonderful," Averil replied, blushing. "But I am sore this morning."

"I have something for the soreness," Gorawen said.

"I am glad you are coming with me," Averil admitted.

"Your new home will seem less strange if I am with you at first," Gorawen answered. "Besides, this servant who has watched over the child-heiress must be dealt with, and you will need my help in that, for you are young and inexperienced."

"I would not make her my enemy," Averil said.

"Nay, you should not, but she must also understand that while her charge is the lady of Everleigh Manor, she must be guided by an equal, and not a servant. Is the woman serf, or freed?" Gorawen inquired.

"I know not, Mother," was the reply.

"It will make a difference," Gorawen said.

Rhys FitzHugh now entered the hall. He greeted Gorawen, and kissed his wife atop her golden head before sitting down at the high board. His food was immediately brought to him, and he began to eat. Averil filled his goblet herself, and cut him pieces of cheese, and peeled an egg for her husband. "I have spoken to your father, wife. We will leave for Everleigh as soon as I have eaten." He turned to Gorawen. "I understand that you will be with us, lady."

"I would see my daughter, my only child, well settled, my lord," Gorawen told him. "The lord and his son will also accompany us." She arose from the table. "I must go speak with Argel. She has spoken to me, daughter, of sending Dilys with you. She said you should not go from your father's house without your own servant."

"I must thank her. Oh, I do like Dilys!" Averil said enthusiastically.

"You will thank her before you leave," Gorawen said, and then turning she glided from the hall.

"I must send a messenger ahead to my sister so she knows we are returning, and so Rhawn may prepare for guests," Rhys told Averil.

"Is Rhawn a serf? Or is she a freedwoman?" Averil asked him. "She seems so assured of herself."

He laughed. "She is a serf, but her confidence comes from the fact that my sire trusted her completely. He always said she was a woman of good sense who was completely obedient, did well what was expected of her, and more."

"What exactly are her duties, my lord?" Averil probed gently.

"Why, she runs the household and takes

care of my sister," he replied.

"Then, what am I to do?" Averil said. "We have spoken on this before but you have never given me an answer. I am not an ornament whose sole existence is for your pleasure, Rhys. My life must have a purpose."

"What has your purpose been in your father's house?" he asked her. "The lady Argel manages here."

"My function was to learn the duties of a wife, Rhys FitzHugh, so that I might put what I have learned into effect one day. You have said your cottage is in disrepair so until it is rebuilt next year we cannot live there. And we should not live there until Mary has a husband of her own, which will be several years hence. I cannot sit in the hall at Everleigh weaving on tapestries while Rhawn manages the house. I will expect her help in learning how Everleigh's household is managed, but then it is I who should control it until Mary is old enough to take on the full responsibilities herself. Rhawn's function should be to care for your sister when I am not teaching her myself."

"She loves the child," he said slowly.

"That is to the good, then," Averil replied. "But I must be mistress of Everleigh after Mary. Would you have me answer to a serf, husband?"

"I did not think about this problem," he answered her.

"Nay, you did not. Your father, God assoil his good soul, told you to steal an heiress so you might have your own place in life. Unfortunately you stole the wrong lass. But I am your wife, Rhys FitzHugh. I am the daughter of a worthy man, a man who can trace his line of descent to a great king. My mother's family are noble, and respected. You cannot possibly expect me to give way to a serf, no matter how loyal she has been. I am not asking you to send her from the house. Just put her in her place so that I may take mine," Averil concluded. "If you cannot do that I must remain in my father's house, for I will not be shamed."

He shook his head. "Rhawn is a good woman," he said. "Mary would be lost without her, and I will not send her away."

Averil was beginning to be very annoyed. Why could he not understand that she wasn't asking him to send the serf back to the fields, she was just asking him to make certain the woman understood that Averil would manage the house once they arrived. "I repeat," she said in a tight voice. "I do not ask you to send Rhawn away."

"Let us wait until we get to Everleigh to settle this matter, wife," he told her, and before she might continue to argue her mother reentered the hall.

"Come, child," Gorawen said. "It is almost time for you to depart. You must say good-bye to your sisters, to the lady Argel and to Ysbail."

Averil arose without another word to him, and moved quickly to her mother's side, nodding. The two women departed the hall, leaving Rhys FitzHugh to contemplate his wife's words. There was much to what Averil had said, but FitzHughs valued loyalty, and Rhawn was loyal to her masters. Averil Pendragon was another matter entirely. He finished the remainder of his meal.

Averil and her mother went to the solar of the keep where the others were awaiting them. She knelt before her father's wife to receive her blessing, putting her hands into Argel's hands in a gesture of respect.

"God bless you, Averil, and may our dear Lord Jesu and his Holy Mother Mary keep you safe always. You depart your da's house with my love and my blessings on you, your husband, and the children you will bear him."

"Thank you, my Lady Mother," Averil said softly, using the name for Argel that those children not hers used. "I will miss you and our family."

"I am giving you Dilys to serve you, Averil," Argel told her. "You are the daughter of a great house, and should now have your own servant."

"Thank you."

"And I shall expect to know your children, my dear, for you shall always be welcome in the home of your youth," Argel continued. "Now get up and bid the others your farewells." She leaned forward and kissed Averil on both cheeks.

Averil stood and went to Ysbail, her father's second concubine. "Farewell, lady. May God guard you always."

"It could be worse," Ysbail said bluntly. Then she said, "Junia will miss you. I hope you will ask her to Everleigh."

"I will, lady," Averil answered, ignoring Ysbail's first words. "Will you give me your blessing too?" She bowed her head.

Ysbail was surprised, but recovering she said, "Indeed, my blessings on you and yours, Averil Pendragon." Then she, too, kissed the girl on both cheeks.

Averil now went to her two younger sisters. "I would remain longer, but Rhys must be back for the harvest."

"The sheet is flying from the tower window," Maia said excitedly. "Was it too awful? Or was it wonderful?" Her eyes were bright with her excitement, and her curiosity.

"Both," Averil said. "It does hurt, but he says only the first time, as did my mother."

"Did you do it more than once?" Maia continued.

Averil shook her head, laughing at her sister. "Nay, Maia Pendragon, I will not discuss such matters with a virgin. Besides, Junia is too young for such speech."

"No, I'm not!" Junia protested.

"Will you be happy with him?" Maia asked softly.

"I think so," Averil said.

"What if you are not?" Junia inquired.

"I must try to be, little one. It is my duty, and I am the Dragon Lord's eldest daughter. I must not shame our family," Averil responded. "This is how it is for us. We are wedded, bedded, and then we must make the best of it."

"You were meant for a great lord," Junia said, tears in her eyes.

"Aye, or so I thought," Averil agreed. "But it was not to be, Junia. Rhys FitzHugh would appear to be a good man. I will do my best to be a good wife to him as you must be to the man chosen for you one day."

"I will choose my own husband," Junia said.

"I also," Maia agreed.

"I hear the horses below," Gorawen said. "We must go, daughter."

"Travel safely," Argel said to Gorawen. She lowered her voice, "And for mercy's sake, do not linger long!"

Hearing her Averil laughed knowingly. She kissed her two sisters on their cheeks, hugging them harder than she ever had, then turned quickly away lest they see her tears. But both Maia and Junia were already beginning to weep noisily at the impending separation from their elder sister. With their sobs ringing in her ears Averil Pendragon departed the house of her father for Everleigh.

Chapter 6

Mary FitzHugh eagerly ran forward to meet her brother and his party. Rhawn, lingering behind, glared with ill-concealed anger at the sight of the beautiful golden haired girl riding by Rhys FitzHugh's side. So, he had married the Welsh wench. Well, the little savage would not lord it over her child. She would see to that. The Welsh wench would be quickly taught her place. Then Rhawn's eye touched on a second woman, very much like the first. Her mother? Well, and Rhawn laughed to herself, not even two Welsh wenches were her match. She would protect her precious little mistress from these two interlopers.

"Brother!" Mary threw herself at Rhys as he dismounted.

He lifted her up, swinging her high. "Mistress Mary!" he said, laughing, his eyes filled with love for his young sister as he held her in his arms.

Mary kissed him, smiling happily. "Have you brought home a wife, brother?" Her blue eyes went to Averil.

"I have, little one," he admitted, and slipping from her horse Averil came forward to greet her sister-in-law.

"I am grateful for your hospitality, my lady Mary," she said, and Averil curtsied.

"Oh!" Mary exclaimed. "You must not call me my lady, Averil. We are sisters now. I am just plain Mary to you as I am to my brother." Her eyes moved past the older girl to where Gorawen stood. "And this lady is surely your mother," Mary said. "She is every bit as beautiful as you are."

"And as you will be when you are grown, my child," Gorawen replied with a smile as she greeted the little girl.

"Put me down, Rhys," Mary commanded her brother. "I would greet our guests properly." And when he had complied Mary welcomed the Dragon Lord back to Everleigh, but she was looking past him even as she spoke.

Merin Pendragon drew his son forward. "This is my heir, Brynn Pendragon, Mary FitzHugh. He desired to escort his sister that he might meet you."

Brynn, a handsome lad, bowed to the little girl who curtsied in return.

"You look like your sire," Mary observed. She was more than aware why the boy was here. She was being looked over as a possible wife in several years' time.

"So it is said," Brynn answered her. His

father had told him this girl might be his wife one day. She was pretty enough, and seemed pleasant.

"Let us go into the house," Mary said, leading her guests inside to the hall where she invited them to sit before the fire while her servants hurried forth with wine to slake their thirst. Rhawn saw to the comfort of the men-at-arms, but then hurried quickly back into the hall to observe what was going on. She would not allow this Welsh wench to lord it over Everleigh folk, and push her mistress aside. No. That was not going to happen while there was breath in her body.

"Brother, you must have the master's chamber now," she heard Mary saying to Rhys. The girl turned to Averil. "It is behind the hall, and quite large and comfortable."

"But then where do you sleep?" Averil inquired. "You are Everleigh's mistress, Mary. Should not that chamber be yours?"

"It is a room for a married pair, Averil," the girl replied. "I sleep in the solar with Rhawn. When I wed one day I shall sleep there with my husband, but for now you must have it. I see you brought your servant. She will have a place in the solar with us."

"I am grateful for Dilys," Averil said politely. She didn't like the looks that the serf

175

woman, Rhawn, was casting at her. This was not going to be easy, and especially as Rhys seemed torn between her and the crone.

The supper was served. They had missed dinner, not arriving until late afternoon. There were game pies, pickled eel, half a ham, cheese, bread, and butter. And when it had been eaten a bowl of apples stewed in honey was brought forward to be served with sugar wafers and spiced wine.

"The meal was well prepared, and served. The food fresh," Gorawen noted quietly to her daughter. "This Rhawn oversees well, but I like not how she looks at you."

"I think she believes I mean to be the lady of the manor, Mother, and she is fiercely jealous of her little mistress's position. I know not what to do, for I cannot remain idle here. I have spoken to Rhys about it, but while he knows I am right, he wavers, for he says the FitzHughs prize loyalty, and Rhawn is loyal."

"The creature is a serf!" Gorawen said, outraged. "You are his wife. I will not have you insulted in this way. I shall speak to your father."

"Wait, I beg you," Averil replied. "I think I might possibly have the answer to this problem, but first I will put into effect some of the skills you taught me last night as we traveled. While I certainly have no basis for comparison, I believe my husband a lusty man. If I please him mightily he may accede to my suggestions."

"Wait another day to put your requests before him," Gorawen said. "Tomorrow while he is in the fields overseeing the harvest, I shall teach you certain things that will bind him to your side forever, my daughter." And Gorawen smiled knowingly.

"But may I practice my new skills on him this night, Mother? We have but coupled once, and having been on the road last night had no opportunity to couple again. He will be eager, I suspect," Averil concluded.

Gorawen nodded. "Of course you must offer him pleasure, daughter," she agreed.

She wondered what plan Averil was forming in order to get her way in this matter. Her child was a clever puss but she would need to be to dislodge this overproud serf.

When the evening drew to a close Mary invited Gorawen to share her bed in the solar where Rhawn, and Averil's servant, Dilys, would also sleep. Merin Pendragon and his son would each have a bed space in the hall. These were small alcoves in the stone walls of the house where bedding could be placed, making a comfortable sleeping spot for guests. Averil noted that Rhawn, in Mary's company, made certain that the fire was banked, the lamps and candles snuffed out, the doors locked and barred.

Taking his wife's hand Rhys led her into the master's chamber, which was located at the end of the hall behind the fireplace. He locked the door behind them, setting the bar in place afterwards. "This will be our wee hidey-hole," he said. "We will have a bit of privacy here." And having spoken he placed another log in the room's hearth, which shared a chimney with the hall.

Averil looked about. There were two narrow windows in the wall to the right of the large bed. There was a large wooden cupboard on another wall, a long square chest at the foot of the bed, a small settle with a cushion by the fireplace, and a single table by the bedside with a candlestick. There was no light in the room but for the fire. The candle by their bed was not lit. The floors were stone, but were covered with several woven mats. There were wooden shutters on the windows, but the chamber was high enough up that no one might peer into the room. But she would make window coverings for the winter, Averil decided. They would need them for warmth, for even narrow windows would let in the icy air. The bed curtains also needed replacement.

"I have never slept here," Rhys said quietly. "This was my sire's room."

"Well, until your sister is wedded you serve her as the master of the house," Averil said in practical tones. "But the whole place needs refurbishing, my lord husband. It is musty, and from the look of it the mattress hasn't been replaced in your father's lifetime. Still, it will serve us until we may have a new one made." She opened the cupboard doors. It was empty. "I shall store my garments here, and you will have the trunk at the bed's foot. Agreed?" She drew her tunic off, and folding it neatly, laid it on a shelf.

He came behind her and began to unlace her gown for her, his lips placing a kiss on the nape of her neck. "Agreed," he said as he pushed the gown off her, his arm going about her slender waist. His fingers reached about to untie the ribbons of her chemise, letting the silk slide sensuously though his fingers. A hand plunged into the opening to cup a firm young breast. His lips continued kissing the back of her neck.

Averil arched her body upwards, then down, and began to slowly grind her buttocks into her husband's groin. "Ummm," she murmured as he fondled her, smiling as she heard his sharp intake of breath.

He ceased his passion briefly in order to pull his cotte off. Averil turned about, shrugging the chemise from her body, reaching out to undo her husband's chemise. She pressed her naked young body against him, and he groaned as he felt every inch of her warm flesh touching him. "What a wanton you are proving to be," he said low.

"Would you have me weeping and retiring, fending you off with little cries and prayers while you took your lordly rights of me? If that would please you, Rhys, I can be that sobbing, silly creature." Her tongue snaked out to quickly run about her lips.

"So, wife," he growled in her ear, "you are hot and ready to play love games with me." He nipped hard at the fleshy pink lobe of that ear.

"Aye," Averil told him, giving a little squeal of surprise. She boldly reached down to fondle his male member in her hand. The beast did not disappoint.

"You fled me the morning after," he reminded her. "Yet the night before you were eager enough."

"If we had coupled in the early morning I should not have wanted to depart Dragon's Lair that day," Averil excused herself. "Was it not better to go then that we might be in our own bed this night?" Her little hand could barely contain him now.

He took her hand away, and kneeling before her parted her nether lips with supple fingers, and leaning forward began to lick at the delicate flesh now exposed to him.

Averil froze, surprised at first, but then she realized with shock that she liked what he was doing. The insistent tongue flicked back and forth, dodged and probed until she began to shiver with her pleasure. "Oh, yes!" she exclaimed. "Oh, yes!" She could feel her juices beginning to flow. It was at that moment he stood up, and pushing her against the rough stone wall, raised her up, his big hands cupping her buttocks, lowering her slowly onto his stiff manhood.

Averil's eyes grew wide with her surprise. This was so different from the first time. She could actually feel every inch of him as he pushed into her, and he was very, very big. "Ohh, sweet Jesu!" she gasped. And still he filled her. Her mouth opened as she struggled for air. Their eyes met. He could see the pleasure in hers. She could see the dark lust in his. She clung to him, her legs wrapped tightly now about his waist.

"Now, my wild Welsh wife, did you think one only could couple in a bed?"

"Yes," she whispered. She was burning up, and she could feel him throbbing within her love passage.

He began the incredible rhythm that had driven her so wild with excitement two nights ago. His blue eyes held her light green eyes prisoner. She could not look away. It was the most intimate and powerful moment she had ever shared with anyone. Her heart was thundering in her ears, and she was damp with their exertions.

"I will have you whenever and wherever I choose," he told her in a rough voice. "In our bed. In the stables on a pile of hay. On a hillside. Bent over the high board wondering if the servants will catch us." He laughed softly. "On the floor before the hearth, Averil." He thrust slowly and deliberately into her. "And you will yield yourself to me without question because I am your husband, and it is my right. And because you want it every bit as much as I do. Is that not right, Averil, my wild Welsh wife? You are as lustful a wench as any I have ever known."

"Yes!" she answered him. "Yes, I am, my lord husband." Her fingers stroked lightly against the back of his neck. "And each time I do this," she pulled playfully at his ear, "you will think of this moment, and you will desire me. And then, my lord, you will have to wait, for I shall only tease you when it is impossible for you to take me off to have your way with me." She leaned forward and kissed his mouth, her tongue brushing across his lips teasingly.

"What delights has your mother taught you?" he growled in her ear. Then he thrust harder and faster into her willing body.

"To drive you wild with pleasure, my lord husband," Averil murmured, and her eyes closed slowly. "Oh, yes! Oh, that is so nice! Don't stop! Don't ever stop!"

His buttocks contracting and releasing, he pushed her over the edge even as his love juices exploded into her. He was gasping with his efforts. His throat was tight, and it hurt. His fingers tightened about the cheeks of her bottom, and he groaned with the feelings of satisfaction that swept over him.

If her head had exploded Averil wouldn't have been surprised. It was as if she were being bathed in a shower of stars and honied heat. Her body craved his juices, and she could feel her love passage sucking every last drop from him. Weakness suddenly engulfed her. Her legs fell away from his body. Desperately she clung to him, her head lolling against his shoulder as he picked her up and deposited her in their bed. She was surrounded by the fragrance of lavender. She felt the mattress give way next to her, and sighed gustily as he joined her. He took her hand in his, and they lay quietly side by side recovering their strength.

Finally he spoke. "When I am inside you I don't want to leave."

"I don't want you to leave me," she admitted.

"Well," he said, his tone amused, "we know that we shall get on well in the bed, wife. As for the rest of it we shall have to see."

"I have learned it is a good thing if a man and his wife respect one another," Averil responded. "Men care for the women in their lives in different ways. My father is fond of his wife. He loves my mother with a great passion, yet Ysbail he treats with amused toleration. But he respects all of his women for who they are, and what they can do for him, his children and the family. And they respect him. I hope, Rhys FitzHugh, that when we come to know one another better, we will respect each other."

He nodded, his fingers trailing across the swell of her bosom. "Will you love me, Averil Pendragon?" he asked her.

"Will you love me?" she countered. He was so very handsome with his dark wavy hair, and his blue eyes. Could she love him? The man who had stolen all her dreams of glory? She didn't know.

He laughed. "So for now we must be satisfied that we pleasure each other well, eh, wife?"

"For now," Averil told him. She was not yet ready to broach the subject of the serf, Rhawn, with him. They needed to know one another better, and so she told her mother the next day as the two women sat together in the hall.

"What do you plan?" Gorawen asked softly, looking about to be certain that they were alone, and there was no servant to hear.

"I will ask my husband to give Rhawn her freedom," Averil said. "For her years of devotion to the FitzHughs. And a lovely little cottage for her very own. Only then do I believe will Rhys be comfortable asking her to step aside for me. But when he does this I will be with him, and I will beg her aid that I may help Everleigh's rightful mistress, my sister-in-law Mary. I will explain I am not used to being idle, having learned all manner of housewifery from my own mother, and the lady Argel."

"It is a well-considered plan," Gorawen said thoughtfully, "and it is just possible you may succeed. I have always thought you a clever girl, Averil."

"And she will no longer sleep in the house, Mother. I will appoint a younger girl to serve Mary. Rhawn is too dour, too possessive and dark. Mary needs someone young, someone filled with laughter looking after her." Averil sipped from her cup.

"Rhawn will not be entirely happy with what you suggest," Gorawen said, "but if Rhys can be brought around you will have no trouble. The woman has been so well treated that she has forgotten she is a serf. Rewarding her with her freedom is a stroke of brilliance, my daughter! But beware it does not backfire on you. Make certain Rhys understands she is to live in her own cottage, not just go there now and again."

"I will, Mother," Averil replied. Then she said, "I think little Mary likes my brother Brynn. Perhaps I should invite him for a visit soon."

"Your father considers the possibility of a match between the two, if he can keep Lord Mortimer at bay," Gorawen answered. "You will let us know if your husband's inclinations lay in that direction."

"Mary is too little for marriage although I know there are some who would set the match now, and then leave her to grow up. Rhys will not," Averil told her mother.

"Good! Having estates on both sides of the Marches is your father's hope," Gorawen confided.

Mother and daughter spent their days together as Gorawen instructed Averil in the sensual arts. But after three full days at Everleigh the Dragon Lord announced that their time was done. They would depart for home in the morning. Averil had learned well from her mother. She knew ways now of arousing Rhys that she would not have imagined before. Gorawen had taught her daughter to make potions, and lotions to encourage and aid a lagging lover. To arouse an eager one, and keep him well satisfied.

"There are other methods," Gorawen said, "but I will come again, and instruct you. For now, I believe you have enough knowledge to keep Rhys FitzHugh contented."

Averil felt overwhelmed with sadness as she watched her parents and her brother ride out and away from Everleigh. She had never before faced a permanent separation from her family. She suddenly realized how much she missed her sisters. Her servant, Dilys, put a comforting hand on hers.

"I will miss Dragon's Lair too, lady," she said. "I have never before been away from home."

"This is our home now, Dilys," Averil said.

"The way that old Rhawn talks, you're naught but an interloper," Dilys said indignantly. "She has a fine opinion of herself, does old Rhawn."

"Pay no attention to her," Averil said calmly. "She is a serf as are you, but because her responsibilities are great she does, indeed, think highly of herself. Still, I think my husband should reward her for her loyalty. I must consider it. And Dilys, you must not gossip with the other servants. I need you to be my eyes and ears."

Dilys nodded. "I know that," she said. "Lady Argel explained it to me before we left our home. Old home," she corrected herself.

Each day that followed Averil would ask Rhawn if she might have young Mary's company that she teach her the things the serf could not, but Rhawn always had an excuse to deny Averil Mary's companionship. Averil would then sit serenely at her loom in the hall weaving. She would pick flowers from the manor gardens and arrange them. She would pluck herbs to make her potions. One day she decided to make scented soaps, something that Rhawn could not do. She had taught her little mistress the art of making ordinary household soap, but scented soaps were an entirely different thing.

"Mary must learn this art," she said before her husband, and he agreed.

Rhawn was therefore unable to prevent the two from being together.

They boiled and rendered fat. The process took an entire day. They sifted ash, which they mixed with lye. This they combined with the rendered fat, olive oil, and finally the different scents. These compounds were then poured carefully into pans to harden. Some was put into stone containers. The mixes in the pans would take several months to cure, and become hard. The soaps in the stone containers would be left a month, and then used as a soft soap.

Mary loved the fragrance of roses and violets. Averil preferred honeysuckle and woodbine. After three days' work the soaps were ready to be stored. Averil suggested to the little girl that they go riding, for she had learned from Rhys that Mary loved to ride, but Rhawn would rarely allow it. And sure enough, Rhawn protested.

"Now, Rhawn," Averil said, smiling her sweetest smile, "a lady must know how to ride properly, and poor wee Mary hardly has had any chance at all to learn properly. Please do not begrudge her. We can both use the fresh air, and we will certainly be back in time for your good supper." Then taking Mary by her little hand, Averil walked her from the hall.

"That was very brave of you," Mary said as they crossed the yard to the stables. "No one ever tells Rhawn what should be done."

"Rhawn is a good woman, Mary, but she is still a serf. You are mistress here. If it is your desire to have cheese crowdie every night, then Rhawn must obey your wishes.

189

Still, I think it a shame that Rhys does not give the good woman her freedom. I know she is a bit vinegary at times, but she is faithful to the FitzHughs, and deserving of reward."

"Oh, Averil, how wise you are!" her little sister-in-law said. "Rhawn can be crotchety but she does love me, although sometimes I wish she did not love me quite so much."

"She has cared for you since your birth, little one, but I will admit I find her a bit possessive of your person," Averil murmured.

They reached the stables, and their mounts were brought forth. Mary had a small white pony with a black mane and tail. Averil had a fine bay mare. The two girls rode peaceably away from the house, and down the lane. They passed by the fields, now harvested. The gleaners were already bent among the rows. In the orchards the apples and pears were being harvested. They saw Rhys, and waved to him. He smiled broadly to see his wife and small sister riding side by side.

He told her so that night as they lay abed, but added, "I'm surprised that Rhawn allowed Mary out of the house."

Now, Averil realized, was her chance. "You have not been as good to Rhawn as you might have, Rhys. You yourself have said that her loyalty is unparalleled." She pressed herself against him, leaning over to kiss his cheek.

"What would you have me do?" he asked her, surprised.

"Make her a freedwoman, and give her her own cottage," Averil said to him. "I will need her help, of course, but it is past time I took up the duties of the hall until Mary is old enough for them. It is not right that you put a serf over your wife, Rhys, but I do understand how much you appreciate her faithful service."

He nodded slowly. "I know that you are right, Averil, but I would not seem ungrateful of Rhawn."

"You forget that she is a serf, husband, and not your equal," Averil reminded him. "Give her her freedom as a reward for her service. Let her have a cottage to call her own. I will choose a younger girl to serve your sister. Mary will never be fit for her station in life, or for a husband, as long as Rhawn remains her keeper. If you reward her so well you cannot be said to be ungrateful. I know it is difficult for you, Rhys, but I must have my place in this household. Especially now," she concluded meaningfully.

"Why now?" he asked.

"I believe I may be expecting your child," Averil told him.

"Already? Praise God, my beautiful wife,

you are a fertile field," he said excitedly.

"And you have been a diligent plowman," Averil murmured, kissing him again. She licked at his ear. "I like it when you plow a fine furrow, Rhys, my husband."

He felt his desire for her rising. "Can we?" he asked. "I know nothing of these things, Averil." Unable to help himself he stroked the insides of her thigh with his fingers.

"For now, we can," she assured him with a small smile as he drew her into his embrace.

"I cannot get enough of you, Averil," he whispered to her, nuzzling her soft golden hair. "What sorcery have you engaged to so bind me to you?"

"I am content that you still lust after me, husband," Averil told him. "Especially as we have been wed over three months." She raised her head up from his shoulder, and kissed his lips. "I am growing used to you, Rhys. I might even come to love you in time."

"Then I must certainly give you your way in this matter," he said.

"Because I said I might love you?" she questioned him, curious.

"Nay, because I have come to love you, Averil, and because you are right," he answered, surprising her. Then he kissed her with slow, deep kisses until she was hot and eager to couple their bodies, to soar with pleasure.

"I want you to love me," she told him softly. "I want you to need me, to trust me, to respect the little wisdom I can offer you. No matter how we began, Rhys, we are husband and wife now. I do not want us to be unhappy in that state." She opened herself to him, sighing as he entered her eagerly, filling her with his newly admitted passion for her. And Averil did soar with his love, and as they reached the heavens together as they so often did, she could have sworn she felt the ice about her heart crack, and she cried his name in her sudden happiness. And then she wept as she had on that first night; and he held her in his embrace as he had then. "I am so happy," she admitted to him, sniffling.

"Why?" he said. "Because you know now that I love you?" He stroked her soft hair, marveling as he always did at its color and texture.

"Aye, but also because I know now that I love you," she sobbed.

Huddled in his arms she did not see his small smile, or that he shook his head wonderingly. No one had ever spoken to him of these feelings between a man and a woman. Yet he did love her, and her admission that she loved him made him happier than he had ever been in all his life.

He wondered if his father had ever known these feelings of sweetness and completion. "I'm glad you love me," he whispered to her.

The next day they rode out together taking Mary with them to choose a cottage for Rhawn. An elderly freedman had recently died, and as he had no heirs his cottage had reverted to the manor. The little building was of stone with a hard-packed dirt floor, and a well thatched roof. It had one large room. The hearth was clean, and drew well when Rhys lit a brand and held it in the mouth of the fireplace. There was a large dresser with racks for plates and cups atop, and a cabinet with shelving below. There was a good-size bed that would need a mattress, and coverlet. There was a table, two chairs, a stool, and a wood settle by the fireplace.

"It is a very fine cottage!" Mary said excitedly.

"And near the village well," Averil noted. "And it has a small back garden."

"There is a bench in front. Rhawn would enjoy sitting and gossiping with her neighbors," Mary replied. "What do you think, Rhys? I think it is perfect!"

"So you want to get rid of your old nursie," her brother teased the child.

"Yes!" Mary said, unashamed. "I love Rhawn, and I know she loves me, but she never lets me out of her sight if she can help it. I am not allowed to ride, or to learn the things I must know from Averil, for she is jealous of your wife. But I am the lady of this manor, and I must know how to conduct myself properly. I think you very clever, brother, to give Rhawn her freedom, and this cottage."

"I will need Rhawn to help me some days," Averil quickly told the child. "I hope you will not send her away entirely."

"If you want her aid you should have it, Averil," Mary replied. "Yet while I may be a child, even I can see that she has gotten above her station. She is not the lady of this manor. I am. But I hope, Averil, you will take the burden of my duties from me until I am ready to accept them. I know I am too little now."

"And yet, Mary, you do know your duties, and you do them well," Averil said. "Still, if you wish to be a little girl for a while longer I shall be happy to aid you."

"Then we are agreed," Rhys said to them. "Rhawn is to have her freedom from her serfdom, and this cottage for her loyalty to the FitzHughs."

"Aye!" Mary and Averil told him.

They returned to the manor house, and asking Rhawn to join them in the hall they told her of their decision. Instead of the arguments they had expected, Rhawn burst into fulsome tears.

"But I must protect my child from the Welsh wench," she cried to Rhys.

"From what are you protecting me?" Mary said.

"She wants Everleigh!" Rhawn said.

"No, I don't," Averil spoke up. "Everleigh belongs to Mary FitzHugh. I am but her brother the bailiff's wife."

"You Welsh are known to steal everything that you can," Rhawn accused.

"Everleigh is Mary's, Rhawn," Rhys said quietly. "Surely you know I love my sister. I would never harm her. If I wanted to steal the manor from her I should put her in a convent not murder her."

"You are bewitched by that Welsh witch!" Rhawn accused.

"I am," he agreed, and her mouth fell open with surprise. "But my sister is no longer a babe. She needs to ride out each day and get to know her people. She needs to learn the things only Averil can teach her about being a lady. You love her, and keep her too close, but in doing so you do Mary a great disservice, Rhawn. Your loyalty and your hard work have earned you your freedom. It pleases us to give you a cottage for your own wee home. Averil will need your help. Mary has asked her to take over the duties of the lady of the manor until she is old enough for them herself. And it is right that Averil take on these duties, Rhawn, but my wife will need your help. You have lived all your life at Everleigh, and know its ways. Averil does not."

"This is what I want, Rhawn, my old dearie," Mary said, encouraging her servant.

"I but sought to keep you safe from harm," Rhawn responded, tears running down her lined face.

"I know," Mary told her, "and you have."

"Where is this cottage?" Rhawn finally said.

"I chose it myself," Mary said with a small smile. "The chimney draws well, the roof, the doors, and the windows are tight, and the thatch is new. It's in the village. Would you like to go to see it now?" Mary held out her hand to the old nurse. "We can walk. It isn't far."

"Very well," Rhawn replied, sounding less irritable. She turned to look at Averil and Rhys. "You swear on the Holy Mother's name that you will do no harm to my child?"

"Aye, I swear," Averil said quietly, her gaze meeting the old woman's directly.

"And I, also," Rhys echoed.

Rhawn nodded her grizzled head. "Very

well then, my lord. I accept the gift of my freedom, and the cot you have given me." Her lips twisted in the first smile Averil had ever seen the old woman give. She took Mary's small hand in hers. "Show me now, child, before I change my mind," she said.

When they were sure she had departed the hall both Rhys and Averil laughed.

"With a stance like hers," Averil said, "she had to be freed, husband."

"See a mattress is made for her bed quickly, wife," he told her. "And give her bowls and cups and spoons for her dresser. Whatever she may need that we may be free of her all the sooner." And he kissed his wife, lifting her up and swinging her about.

"Put me down, you great fool!" Averil scolded him. "She will come into the house by day. I need her to teach me how to run this household of yours properly so I may teach Mary."

"When is our child to be born?" he asked her softly.

"If all goes well, in May," Averil said. "But do not speak on it yet lest you bring bad luck upon us."

He nodded, understanding. "You are certain?"

"Aye, but perhaps you might send for my mother who is wise in such things,"

Averil suggested to him.

He agreed, and Gorawen was sent to come from Dragon's Lair. Arriving, she examined her daughter and concurred that Averil was with child.

"The babe is well rooted," she told Rhys. "Your seed is strong, but my daughter's womb is also a strong safe place. The child will be born in May."

"Tell me of my sisters," Averil begged.

A small shadow passed over Gorawen's brow. "Maia had several suitors this summer, but she is not yet interested. Next year when she is fifteen is a better time."

"What is it?" Averil asked, sensitive to her mother's mood.

"Your father is not pleased that she is so finicky," Gorawen said.

"She is simply not ready to give up being a girl yet," Averil said wisely.

"It is time for her to wed," Gorawen said sharply.

"Maia will do the right thing for Maia," Averil replied. "Do not fret over her, Mother. Think on the grandchild I am to give you and Da."

"Am I not still too young and beautiful to be a grandmother?" Gorawen teased them, and Rhys agreed diplomatically that it was indeed so.

Gorawen departed, having stayed but a few hours. Merin, she explained, did not like her gone from him for too long.

Rhawn was pleased with her new state, and to their surprise, with her cottage. She came to the manor house almost every day, but then, as the winter set in, she came less and less. She did not like walking in the wind, the rain, and the snows that fell now and again. Mary rode to visit her one cold winter's day, and found her old nurse sitting contentedly by her fire sewing.

"For your brother's coming infant," she said. "I can yet serve while in my own cottage, Mary child. Why have you come out in such weather? The rain is icy today. I can see it through the cottage window."

"You have not been to the manor in four days, Rhawn. I missed you, and I feared for your safety," Mary said. Then she sneezed.

"Ah, you have caught an ague!" the old woman said.

"Nay, 'tis nothing." Mary laughed.

"You cloak is wet," Rhawn said, spreading it before the fire to dry.

Mary visited with Rhawn for an hour or more, and then she rode home in the rain. When she arrived she was sneezing again, and her forehead felt hot to Averil's hand.

"Foolish child," Averil scolded her. "You should not have gone out. You did not come to ask me because you knew I should have said nay to you." She and Dilys stripped Mary of her wet clothing, putting her in a dry chemise, and tucked her into her bed. "Keep the fire going, Dilys," Averil instructed her servant. "I will brew a healing draught for Mary."

But Mary FitzHugh grew sicker as the night wore on. She developed a deep cough in her little chest, which Averil rubbed with a mixture of sheep's fat and camphor, and then covered with a flannel cloth. Her temperature rose with each passing hour. Averil made barley water, which she strained and, after adding sugar to sweeten it, fed it to Mary. She made a cough syrup of vinegar, honey and finely ground licorice, which she fed to her little sister-in-law to ease her cough. In an effort to bring down the child's fever she boiled a second batch of barley in spring water, strained the water off into a stone jar, and reboiled the barley once again with more spring water. Then, straining the water into the stone jar with the first batch, she added honey. The mixture was fed to Mary, but still her fever would not cease. Averil wept with her frustration.

Rhys rode out and fetched Rhawn from her cottage. The old woman came, and seeing the child lying on her bed so flushed with fever, she shook her head.

"What have you done for her?" she asked Averil.

Averil told her.

"All the right things," Rhawn said, nodding. " 'Tis my fault. I should not have left her. If she had not ridden out in that icy rain yesterday. Ahh, woe is me!" And she wept.

Averil found herself putting a comforting arm about the old woman's shoulders. "Fetch the priest," she said to her husband.

Rhys rode to the priest's house and banged on the door. The priest's pretty hearth mate opened the portal, and curtsied to the bailiff. "Father Kevyn, come quickly. My sister lies ill and we believe she is dying."

The two men rode back from the priest's house to the manor. Seeing him, Rhawn wept even more. Looking at Mary the priest knew her brother was correct. The child was dying.

"Mary FitzHugh," he called gently. "Open your eyes, and tell me you confess all of your sins."

Mary opened her blue eyes, focusing on the priest. She smiled weakly and nodded. "I do," she whispered.

The priest made the sign of the cross over the child, startled when Mary's little hand reached out to grasp his sleeve. "What is it my child?" he asked her. "You are indeed forgiven if that is what troubles you. Today you will be in paradise with your own good mother, your father, and our Holy Lord and sweet Mary for whom you were named."

"My brother," Mary whispered.

"Your brother?" The priest was confused.

"Everleigh. My brother's now. Swear!" She then fell into a fit of coughing.

Father Kevyn digested Mary's words for a long moment, and then he understood. "You give Everleigh, and all its goods and chattels to your brother, Rhys FitzHugh. Is that it, my child?"

"Yes!" Mary said, relieved, and then with a great sigh she breathed her last.

"I will swear to it," the priest said, and then he once again made the sign of the cross over Mary FitzHugh.

It had happened so quickly. One day Mary had been fit and hearty, and now suddenly she was dead. Outside the manor house the wind rose, keening as if it were itself mourning. The cold rain beat against the windows, now turning to sleet. Rhawn wept bitterly, huddled by the fireplace.

"I should not have left her," she repeated over and over again.

Both Averil and Rhys were stunned by Mary's swift death. They sat together at the high board staring out into the hall. Finally old Rhawn arose, and coming to

Averil she took her hand.

"We must prepare her, lady," Rhawn said bleakly.

Averil arose slowly, nodding. "I know," she said in a wan voice.

"I will help you, lady, for you must not put a strain on yourself now that you carry the next heir to Everleigh," Rhawn remarked.

"She should not be distressed at all," Rhys said, standing. His handsome face was wet with his tears, and drawn now in his sorrow.

"Mary was the lady of Everleigh," Averil said to Rhys. "She welcomed me to my new home, and loved me for your sake. But I loved her too. The child I carry is a strong child. He would want me to do my duty and prepare his aunt for her grave."

Rhys nodded, and Rhawn looked at Averil with new eyes. Perhaps the Welsh weren't all bad, she considered.

"You will help me with the child when it comes?" Averil asked Rhawn.

"I will, my lady," Rhawn said, "but I must still be free, and have my cot, for Mistress Mary chose it for me."

"I should have it no other way," Averil replied, and together the two women walked up the stairs to the solar where the body of Mary FitzHugh awaited them. Shaking his head Rhys watched them go.

His father had died exactly a year ago this day. He wondered if anyone remembered it. And when his father had told him to steal the Dragon Lord's daughter he had certainly never imagined what would happen in one short year. He would have served his sister forever, but it had not been meant to be. He was now the lord of the manor. He would have a child in the spring. But he had lost a beloved little sister in this turn of the wheel of fate. He put his head in his hands and he wept. He wept as he knelt the night before his sister's bier now set up in the hall of the manor. He wept by her graveside as she was buried into the cold winter earth. Each day he visited Mary's grave, and he thanked her for Everleigh. His sorrow eased as the spring came, but he knew it would never abate.

But then came the day that Averil Pendragon delivered his son, and old Rhawn, her weathered face wreathed in smiles, put the boy in his arms. Rhys looked down at the infant and for the first time since his sister had died, he smiled. And his eyes met those of Averil's, and she smiled, too. With the birth of this child the past was behind them.

"He's a brawny little lad," Rhys said, his big finger touching his son's cheek. "What will we call him?"

"Rhys the younger," she answered quickly. "And in a year or two as God wills it we will give him a sister who we shall call Mary."

"You are certain of that?" he teased her with another smile.

"I am certain of it," Averil said, and she wondered if he recalled that it was this very day a year ago that he had stolen her away. "Very, very certain," she concluded, and Averil Pendragon smiled up at him. He was not a great lord, this Rhys FitzHugh, but he was her husband, her lover and her friend. If there was more to life than this, she knew not what it was. Nor did she care.

Part Two

Maia

Chapter 7

The Dragon Lord looked about his hall at the worthy young men who had come to seek his daughter Maia's hand in marriage. There was one of the Great Llywelyn's bastards. The lad's mother, a Corbet, was the legitimate daughter of an English Marcher lord, and had been taken years ago in a raid. One of Gorawen's Tewydr cousins had sent a younger son for their inspection. To the Dragon Lord's surprise there were three young men from English Marcher families. Roger Mortimer, Robert Fitz-Warren, and John Ashley. Any one of them would have been more than suitable. Even the English. But Maia had no interest in any of them, and Merin Pendragon would not force his daughter into marriage. It had frustrated him that his eldest, Averil, had been boxed into a match not of her choosing no matter how well it had worked out. He would see that Maia and Junia made their own choices no matter what others might think of his decision.

"The lass is a fool," his concubine Ysbail

muttered. "What does she want, in the name of Blessed Mary? All without blemish, and strong of limb. Choosing might be difficult, but certainly she can do it."

"My daughter wants to love the man she weds," Argel said quietly.

"Bah!" Ysbail snorted. "What does love have to do with anything? And what is love? 'Tis a lot of foolishness you speak, and do not glare at me, Gorawen. I can have my opinion as you indeed have yours."

"Do you not love our lord Merin?" Gorawen said sharply.

"Does he love me?" Ysbail countered. "No, he does not! He took me for a concubine because he hoped to get a son off of me, and nothing more. I like him well enough. And I respect him, but love? Bah!"

Finally, as the summer waned, Maia's suitors departed, disappointed. Roger Mortimer was the last to go.

"You are certain," he said with a visible air of regret, "that you could not love me, Maia? I vow I should make you a very good husband, my pretty maid."

"I am sorry, Roger," Maia told him. "I do like you. I like you best of all who have come, but it is not enough for me. I must love the man I marry with all my heart and soul. That is how it must be for me. I should die otherwise."

"Then I don't suppose it would be wise to bride-nap you," he teased her with an engaging grin, his blue eyes dancing.

Maia laughed. "Nay. Be warned, Roger, that I am always armed, and I should have to kill you if you attempted to steal me. That should sadden me as you are my brother-in-law's best friend."

"If your aim is as good as your sister's, I should not be afraid," he replied.

"My aim is quite sure," she warned him. "Averil was never any good with a dagger. She is in too much of a hurry."

Roger Mortimer took the girl's hand in his, and kissed it lingeringly. "Then I must bid you a reluctant farewell, my lady Maia. I hope you will soon find your heart's desire, and live surrounded by love forever."

"What a lovely thing to say to me!" Maia exclaimed, genuinely touched, and she watched as he rode off, thinking it a pity that she couldn't love Roger Mortimer. But she couldn't, and she knew it. She could only love the faceless man who had haunted her dreams these past months since she had turned fifteen. Who was he? And why would he not come to her?

She had first dreamed of him on her birthday. Initially she had been afraid, but his low and musical voice had assured her he meant her no harm. He took her by her hand, and together they had soared over the landscape until they had come to a beautiful castle on an island in the midst of a lake. This was where they would live when she was his, he had said. The castle was like no other she had ever seen. Its towers were round, and soared into the star-filled night sky. The gardens where they strolled were filled with roses, and all manner of flowers in rich, sweet bloom. That was the first night.

He came to her every night after that, taking her hand in his, and together they would rise into the skies, traveling to his castle where soon Maia was lying in her mystery lover's arms, her head spinning with his kisses and his caresses. Her innocent heart had been engaged from the first moment he had come into her life.

"Why will you not go to my father and ask for my hand?" she inquired of him one night.

"I will come, my love, when you are certain that your heart cannot be captured by another," he told her quietly. "If you love me, Maia, you can love no other man. I would have you be certain."

"I am not even certain this is real!" she had cried to him.

She could not see the smile, for he remained faceless even when he kissed her, but she could hear the smile in his voice when he answered her.

"When you awaken in the morning, my love, you will find the proof of this night, and all the others that have gone before it, on your pillow," he promised her.

And when Maia awoke the following morning she found a tiny, delicate silver and gold replica of his castle set within a blue sapphire on a twisted silver and gold chain lying by her head. With a surprised cry she picked it up, examining it, amazed by the exquisite workmanship. Like his castle, the pendant was something the like of which she had never before seen. She slipped it about her neck, hiding it beneath her chemise. If she attempted to explain the pendant and chain her parents would become upset, for even Maia understood there was magic involved in what had been happening to her.

And now suddenly she was very curious to know just who this man who came to her every night was. She had sent her suitors away, and set about to wait. He would come. Of that she was very certain. He was as real as the pendant and chain. No figment of her imagination, or a fantasy. He would come. And then one day Maia felt compelled to wear her pendant and chain in full view of her family.

Ysbail's sharp eye was the first to see it. "Ask your daughter, Argel, where she has obtained that beautiful chain and ornament she is wearing today."

Argel reached out to finger the chain. Her look was puzzled. "Indeed, my daughter, where have you found this jewel?"

"It is a gift," Maia answered her mother.

"From whom?" Argel asked.

"From the man I will marry," Maia said. "He will come soon, Mother, and I will wed none but him."

"Who is he, my daughter? And how have you met him, and we have not?" Argel said quietly.

"I do not know," Maia said honestly. "He comes to me each night in my dreams, and we go to his castle in the middle of a beautiful lake. When I questioned the reality of these dreams he said he would leave me proof they were real. When I awoke the following morning the chain and pendant were by my head."

Argel looked stunned by her daughter's revelation, and Gorawen reached out to take her friend's hand in hers. "This is magic," she said. "And it is great magic."

"I love him," Maia spoke softly.

"She is bewitched!" Ysbail screeched, turning pale and crossing herself. "I can but hope this sorcerer has not harmed my Junia who sleeps by her sister's side!"

The other two women turned to look at Junia, and Argel spoke.

"Has any of this obvious magic disturbed you, child?" she queried the young girl. "Have you had any part in your sister's dreams?

"I do not awaken from the time my head touches my pillow until the morning, nor do I dream," Junia replied. "This is the first I have heard of Maia's dream lover. I think it very exciting. I should like to have a dream lover, too."

Ysbail jumped up and slapped her daughter's pretty face. "Foolish one! Do not tempt the devil as this proud girl has done!"

Junia cried out, and her hand went to her cheek as tears slipped down her face.

"Sit down, Ysbail," Argel ordered the woman in a quiet, but firm voice. "You should not have struck Junia. She did nothing to merit such punishment. She is yet a child. Maia, take your sister, and go into the garden. I must speak with your father. We will call you when we desire your presence once again." She smiled at the two girls as they arose, and curtseying went out of the hall. Argel signaled to a house serf. "Fetch your master. Tell him I would see him as quickly as possible."

The servant ran from the hall. "I wonder who this magician is," Ysbail said.

"I wonder when he will come for her," Gorawen replied, "for he surely will."

"Should we resist him?" Argel directed her question to Gorawen.

"I doubt that we can," Gorawen answered. "This is strong magic indeed that this man practices. Still, Maia has no fear despite the fact he remains faceless to her."

"He is probably horribly deformed," Ysbail said grimly.

"Or wonderfully beautiful," Gorwen responded.

"Then why hide his visage?" Ysbail demanded.

"Perhaps he wishes to be loved for his character, and not his face," Argel said wisely. "I wonder how long before we have the answers we seek."

"Soon, I suspect," Gorawen replied. "The year wanes. He will want her as his wife before the winter sets in, I think."

Merin Pendragon entered his hall. His wife and his women arose and curtsied to him as he settled himself before the fireplace. He had been breaking a young horse. His graying hair and his shirt were damp with his exertions. "Rafe said it was important, wife," he said. "I am not unhappy, however, to be called in. The beast is very stubborn." He motioned his three women to sit down, and they obeyed.

Argel quietly explained the tale that Maia had told them. "I expect that is why she turned down so many eligible suitors, husband," she explained.

"You are certain that she and Junia are not playing some clever jest upon you?" he asked them.

"Where would she get the pendant and chain?" Argel said.

"You are sure that it is real?" he responded.

Argel nodded.

The Dragon Lord looked to Gorawen. "You concur?" he said to her.

Gorawen nodded. "The chain is of particularly fine workmanship. As for the pendant, I know of no way but magic that that dainty replica of a castle could be enclosed within a jewel. If this man did not give it to her, how else could Maia have come by such a precious possession?"

Pendragon nodded slowly. "Is this good, or evil?" he wondered aloud.

"We cannot know until we know the man, my lord," Gorawen said.

"And she says she will marry none but this man?" He looked to his wife now.

"She will have none but him," Argel replied.

"We shall see," he said. "I wonder if he will want her without her dower of land? Perhaps it is that he seeks."

"He has a castle," Gorawen reminded the Dragon Lord.

"Or so he has led the foolish girl to believe," Ysbail spoke up sharply. "If he can do the things he does, mayhap this castle is but an illusion."

Both Argel and Gorawen snorted derisively.

"Nay, my loves," the Dragon Lord said, "she has a point. I will need to be certain there is a castle in good repair for Maia in which she may make her home."

Maia and Junia reentered their father's hall.

"It is growing dark," the older girl said.

"And the wind is beginning to rise," the younger added.

"Come by the fire," their father invited. He drew Junia into his lap, smiling as her head came to lay against his broad shoulder. "Now, my fair Maia," he said, looking at her, "is what your mother tells me the truth? This is not some jest you would play upon us?"

" 'Tis no jest, Father," Maia answered her sire.

"You have never seen his face?" Merin Pendragon was very curious. "How can you love a man whose face you do not know?" he asked his second daughter.

She shrugged. "I understand not, Da, but I can tell you that I love him for his voice, and his kind ways. Those who serve him seem to love him, too. His dogs run to him at the sound of his voice. He is gentle

218

and tender with me. I believe that he loves me, Father, and have I not said I would wed no man who did not love me?"

"Ahh," Merin Pendragon said, "there is the rub, my daughter. Is he indeed a man, or some wicked spirit come to lure you away for nefarious purposes?"

"I care not," Maia replied. "I love him, and that is all that matters."

"Then I would meet him," the Dragon Lord said quietly.

"He says he will come soon," Maia responded in sure tones.

"Good!" her father answered her, but he was troubled. What kind of man snuck into a man's house and seduced his daughter in her dreams? He was uneasy, but Argel and Gorawen seemed at ease with this situation they all faced.

That night as Maia walked with her lover in his castle garden she said softly, "Show me your face, my lord. It matters not to me if you are disfigured or scarred."

"I am not," he assured her.

"But if you do not show me your face, my lord, how am I to know you when you come to my father to ask for my hand in marriage?" Maia wanted to know.

"You will know me, my love," he promised her. "Your innocent heart has come to trust me even if you cannot see my features, and that is why I am assured that you will know me when I come to Dragon's Lair."

"Soon?" she pressed him. "Ohh, my lord, I would be with you all the time, and not just in a dream at night!"

"I promise you that I will come very soon, my love," he swore to her. "You sense it, which is why you wore your pendant today for all to see."

"I did!" she exclaimed.

He laughed, and then his thumb and his forefinger took her chin between them, and she felt his lips on hers.

Maia did not dream of her lover the next night. She awoke weeping and agitated. None could calm her until a servant ran into the hall to announce that a rider approached Dragon's Lair. Leaping to her feet the distraught girl dried her eyes as best she could. "He has come!" she cried. "He has come!" She ran from her father's hall, her long red hair flying behind her, and followed by her family.

"How does she know? How can she be certain?" Ysbail demanded. "Junia! Remain by my side."

He rode up the hill on a large black stallion. When he dismounted they could see he was tall, and lean. He wore his wavy black hair short. His eyes were a dark gray. His features were perfect. He was, Gorawen thought, the handsomest man she had ever seen. To their surprise Maia gave a sharp little cry, and threw herself into his arms.

"You have come for me, my lord!" she said, looking up adoringly at him.

His arms enclosed her in an embrace, and his eyes lit with pleasure. "I have indeed come for you, Maia, but only with your parents' permission." He kissed the top of her head. Then he set her aside, and bowed to Merin Pendragon. "I seek your daughter's hand in marriage, my lord."

"A matter to be discussed in private, my lord," Merin Pendragon said. "First, your name. We do not know it." The Dragon Lord's eyes took in the man before him.

"My name is Emrys Llyn," the deep musical voice answered him.

"The Lord of the Lake!" Gorawen exclaimed.

"I am, lady," Emrys Llyn replied with a small smile.

"How perfectly fitting," Gorawen said softly.

He laughed. "I suppose it is. I had not considered it before now."

"What is it?" Argel asked Gorawen as they entered the hall.

"This lord descends from King Arthur's knight, Lancelot de Lac, and the Lady of the Lake. Is that not so, my lord?" Gorawen said.

"Their blood flows in my veins, 'tis true, lady," Emrys Llyn said.

"But did not Lancelot betray King Arthur with the king's own queen?" Ysbail now found her voice.

"He did," Emrys Llyn replied, "and in doing so he broke the heart of the Lady of the Lake who was his wife, and who loved him too well, I fear. They say that one of Arthur's half sisters, and all were skilled mightily in the dark arts, cast a spell upon the queen and Lancelot so that they would deceive the king. Then Mordred, Arthur's other son, took advantage of the situation. Thus began the downfall of Camelot that led to King Arthur's death. 'Twas a terrible tragedy for all involved." He set his dark gaze upon the Dragon Lord. "Your ancestor took no part in any of it, did he?"

"No," Merin Pendragon acknowledged. "It was Merlin the Enchanter's decision that my ancestor would remain hidden in order for Arthur's line to continue. Arthur had not yet met his three half sisters before he was crowned. He was warned by Merlin to say naught about his son by the lady Lynior. So they never knew, and my ancestor was safe. Yet you know of my descent, Emrys Llyn. How is this possible?"

"The Lady of the Lake was one of the few in Merlin's confidence. 'Twas she who guarded the king's sword, Excalibur, before

Arthur knew his true identity. Lancelot returned Excalibur to her on Arthur's death. It is said she still keeps it safe within her watery bower. It has been believed within my family that a union between our families would wipe away Lancelot's sin against Arthur. But until now it was never possible."

The Dragon Lord nodded. "I must know you better, Emrys Llyn, before I allow you to marry my daughter Maia. While I recognize your family name and your lineage, I do not know you. Maia is dear to me, and she is my one legitimate daughter. Her dowry includes land."

"I have no need of your land, Merin Pendragon," the Lord of the Lake answered. "I will gladly accept whatever other dowry Maia possesses, but I should take her even without a dower portion. I love her."

"My lords," Argel said. "Let us sit within the hall, take refreshment while you discuss the future of my daughter." She motioned them into the chairs of honor by the fireplace, and served them sweet wine in her best silver goblets. Then she directed the other women to the benches to sit with her as they had not been forbidden to listen to the two men in their discussions.

"How came you to know of Maia?" the

Dragon Lord asked Emrys Llyn.

The Lord of the Lake smiled. "I have inherited my family's magic," he said, "and I keep myself informed. I was aware you had three daughters, two of marriageable age. I cast their star charts, which told me your golden haired daughter traveled a different path, but more important, her stars and mine were not compatible. Then I cast Maia's stars, and discovered that should I choose to make her my wife, our stars were sympathetic to one another. But first I had to know her. Sometimes when the stars are consistent with one another, the union is still not advisable for other reasons. But I loved her from the moment I knew her."

"Why did you keep your face from her, then?" Merin demanded of the younger man.

"Because more times than not an innocent maiden will fall in love with a handsome face. I do not believe I am being immodest when I say I know my visage is a beautiful one. I wished to be loved for who I am, and not for what I look like. And as you see, your daughter knew me instantly even though she had never before laid her eyes on my face." His eyes found Maia's and he smiled at her.

Her heart leapt in her chest. "Father, let us be wed today!" she begged her sire.

"No," the Dragon Lord said. "I must

know more of this man before I will entrust you to his care."

"I will die if I cannot be his!" Maia declared, distraught.

"Obey your father, my love," Emrys Llyn said. "He does what he believes is best for you. He has not forbidden us. He simply wants more time. That is his right."

"You will abide with us, my lord, will you not?" Argel said, attempting to calm both her husband and her daughter who were both known for their tempers. "Maia, you and Junia will prepare the chamber in the tower for our guest. Go, now."

The two girls arose, and casting a longing look at her lover, Maia and her sister left the hall to do as they were bid.

"There, now," Argel said quietly. She turned to look upon Emrys Llyn. "Tell me, my lord, where is your castle, for Maia has declared it beautiful and peaceful. She says it is in the middle of a lake. Is it the lake?" She smiled at him.

"Aye, 'tis that lake in which the guardian of Excalibur is said to dwell. She raised up the castle in which your daughter and I will live, for her husband, Lancelot. She planted and tended the gardens that surround it. Sometimes she is said to be seen walking in those gardens in the moonlight, for it was believed, like all magical persons, she was immortal," he told his fascinated audience.

"Humph!" grunted Merin Pendragon. "A romantic tale to be certain, but you have still not said where this castle is located."

"Not far, my lord," Emrys Llyn told them. "To the north, and to the west, just before you come to the sea is a valley, well hidden among the mountains. My lake, and my home, is there. I would like to take you to see it, Merin Pendragon, so you will know I do not lie. It is but two days' journey. If I took you there by means of magic you would not believe the evidence of your own eyes, would you?" His long mouth twitched with amusement at the look on his host's face.

But then to everyone's surprise the Dragon Lord laughed. "Nay," he said, shaking his head. "I probably would not."

"Let me have a few days with Maia in this world, and then I shall take you to see for yourself," the Lord of the Lake promised.

Gorawen spoke up. "I think that a fine idea, my lords, but I believe, Emrys Llyn, that we would all be more content if you would promise not to visit Maia's dreams while you are here at Dragon's Lair with us. What think you, Argel? Maia is your daughter, after all." It was cleverly done. Both Merin and his wife were quite taken aback by the Lord of the Lake. Gorawen realized that she would have to act for them in the area of common sense if this was to work out well for Maia.

"Yes, yes!" the Dragon Lord agreed, and Argel nodded. "You must swear to me you will not come into my daughter's dreams by night while you are with us."

"I swear," the Lord of the Lake said, and his eyes briefly met those of Gorawen's. He could see that she had some small magic about her, and was well respected by both her lord and his wife. Despite its unique nature he found Merin Pendragon's domicile both interesting and comforting.

The house serfs moved quietly about the hall preparing the household for the meal. As the wine in the two men's cups grew scant, Argel was there to fill them up. She took the opportunity to study the Lord of the Lake with a mother's eye. He was the most handsome man she had ever seen in all her life. He was fair-spoken, yet there was an air of mystery about him that lent presence to his person. And there was something that she could not quite put her finger on, Argel thought.

"Aye," Gorawen said, as if reading Argel's musings. "We know really nothing about him, do we? What of his parents? Why have many heard of him, but few seen or even treated with him before this? And from where does his great magic come?"

"From the devil, if you ask me!" Ysbail

murmured low. "No man is that beautiful naturally. Fair skin, dark hair, changeable eyes. Is he even human?"

"He is human," Gorawen said, and she firmly believed her words. "But he does have great magic. Is it inherited? Will Maia's children have it as well? I cannot help but wonder such things." Then she laughed at herself. "While Averil loves her Rhys, I think when she learns her sister is to wed a great lord she will have a moment of pure envy."

"If our lord Merin will allow such a marriage," Ysbail remarked. "I can but hope when Junia is grown she will have more sense, and choose a lordling with a good house, good lands, and a fat purse. The dramatics involved in Averil's matching, and now Maia's, is most annoying. But our lord will let his daughters have their way in such things. 'Twould be better if he found the husband and they wed according to their father's wishes. We would all be a lot better off without this love nonsense."

Junia and Maia now came back into the hall, and curtsied to the lady Argel.

"We have prepared the guest chamber, Mother," Maia said.

"Then you should have some time with Emrys Llyn, my daughter," Argel said. "But you may not leave the hall. You will be courted in full view of your family." She

228

turned to her husband. "Merin, let Emrys go now that he and Maia may be together."

The Lord of the Lake stood up quickly, and taking Maia's two small hands in his looked down into her face. "My love," he said softly.

The look on Maia's face was luminous. A blush suffused her pale cheeks. "My lord," she answered him, and then she smiled radiantly.

He tucked one of her hands in his arm, and they moved away from the others.

Gorawen shook her head. "Maia is in love, and she will never love another. Look at her face, my lord. You will not be able to forbid this."

"There is something about him," Merin Pendragon said slowly.

"I know," Gorawen responded. "I feel it too, and so do the others, but whatever it may be, good or bad, she will have him, my lord. And it is a passion that will not die, I believe."

"The silly child is bewitched!" Ysbail said. "Oh, I can but hope Junia is wiser when her turn comes to choose a mate."

"Junia will go where her heart leads her," Gorawen responded.

"The Lord Jesu and his Blessed Mother forbid!" Ysbail exclaimed. "I want a man of substance and good reputation for my daughter. She will not have to be a concubine like me. She will be a respectable man's wife, or I will know the reason why!"

The other two women said nothing in reply. Ysbail might attempt to have her way in the matter of her daughter, but both Argel and Gorawen knew that Junia's soft heart would take her wherever it would, a path that would not necessarily lead to a respectable man of substance and good repute. And they would support her as they were supporting Maia.

Finally the meal was ready to be served, and Argel invited them all to the high board, saying as she did to the Lord of the Lake, "Our meals are simple, my lord." Then she seated Emrys Llyn at her husband's right hand before taking her own place at his left hand. The remainder of the family took their places, but for Brynn, who was late. The blessing was said before the boy rushed into the hall, apologizing.

"This is your sister's suitor, Emrys Llyn, the Lord of the Lake," Merin Pendragon said to his son as the lad took his seat.

Brynn tore a chunk of bread from the loaf, and asked, "Is that your stallion in the stables, my lord? The big black one?"

"Aye, lad, that is my beast," was the reply.

"Why are his hooves so shiny?" Brynn wanted to know.

"Because I polish them with olive oil," Emrys Llyn told Brynn.

"Why?"

"Because he likes it, and because it makes him look even more beautiful," the Lord of the Lake told the boy.

"Oh." Brynn had never heard of a horse, especially a large warhorse, who liked having shiny hooves.

"And it is good for his hooves," Emrys Llyn continued. "It keeps them from becoming too brittle."

"Ahh," Brynn answered. Now that made sense.

The Lord of the Lake chuckled. "Your son will be a practical man," he said to his host. "I admire and appreciate that."

"He gets it from both his mother and from me," Merin Pendragon replied.

The servants brought in the food, and as Argel had said, the meal was simple, consisting of only three courses. There was fresh trout, pickled eel, and a salted cod in a cream sauce for the first offering. The second was made up of roasted capon, roasted lamb, a large ham, a rabbit pie, and a pottage of stewed vegetables. Lastly came a large hard yellow cheese, and a bowl of pears. There was bread upon the table as well as a large crock of sweet butter. The food had no need of spice, for it was fresh. New cider, beer, and wine were offered as well.

Emrys Llyn ate with a good appetite and complimented the Dragon Lord on the quality of his wine. Then he told Argel, "Lady, the meal may be simple, but it is well cooked, and most tasty. I cannot complain of your wifely skills in managing your servants. I can but hope your daughter is as proficient when she is running my household." And he smiled at his hostess.

Argel smiled, pleased by the compliment, and the sincerity in his tone. "I thank you, my lord, and you may rest assured that Maia is an excellent housewife."

The rest of the family waited for the Dragon Lord to say something, but he remained silent on the matter. There was much he needed to know about Emrys Llyn yet, and despite his daughter's obvious love for the man, their union was not yet fact in his mind. But he had to admit that he was already inclined to like the fellow. His lineage dovetailed nicely with Maia's. A descendant of Lancelot du Lac marrying a descendant of the great King Arthur appealed to Merin Pendragon. And yet there was something he could not quite put his finger upon that disturbed him about the man.

After the meal had been consumed, and Brynn and Junia sent to their beds, the others sat about the hearth.

Gorawen said quietly, "Tell me, my lord Emrys, why it is a fine young man such as yourself has not yet been married? And I know we are all curious as to your age."

"I am five and twenty, lady, and I have been wed twice," came the startlingly frank answer. "Both of my wives died."

"You have children?" Gorawen persisted.

"Alas, none," he answered her.

"What caused the deaths of your wives, my lord?" Argel asked.

"I cannot tell you, lady, for I do not know. Each went to sleep one evening, only to never awaken again. It was disturbing, and very strange." His handsome face was a bland mask that revealed nothing.

"Were these women ill?" Gorawen inquired.

"Not to my knowledge, lady," he responded.

"Were they perhaps cursed by an enemy?" she pressed him.

"Lady, I have no enemies that I am aware of, for I keep much to myself as did my antecedents. We are, as you know, magic folk. Ordinary people are usually afraid of us, are they not? You have some magic in you. I see it," Emrys Llyn said to Gorawen.

"I do," she admitted, "but you must admit it is strange that two seemingly healthy young women died suddenly in their beds."

He nodded.

"You will understand we are concerned that something such as that happen to Maia," Argel spoke up. "She is my only daughter, and I love her with all my heart."

"Lady, if I could, I should promise you that nothing will happen to her in my care, and I do swear it, but I cannot guarantee it," Emrys Llyn said. "But the deaths of my first two wives served no purpose that I know of, I tell you honestly. Neither came with a great dowry, nor had powerful family connections. There was no reason for them to be killed. And there were no marks of violence upon their bodies that would have indicated murder."

"Magic leaves no marks," Gorawen murmured.

He grew pale at her words, and in that moment Gorawen knew that while he might not be responsible for the deaths of his two previous wives, he did know more than he was admitting. And for whatever reason, he was not willing to speak on it yet. Or perhaps never. She considered telling Merin and Argel of her concerns, but decided she needed to get to know this man better before she spoke. Maia's heart was firmly in his keeping, and Gorawen did not believe anything they said would convince her to refuse this suitor who was as obviously in love with her as she with him.

"Lady, I know not who would practice such magic against me," Emrys Llyn said quietly. "If indeed magic is involved then I have a hidden enemy."

"Which brings us back to the matter of my daughter's safety as your wife, my lord," Merin Pendragon said. "How long ago did these deaths occur?"

"Rosyn was my first wife. I married her five years ago, and she died four months afterwards. I kept a mourning period of one year for her. Then I sought a second wife. Gwynth became my wife two years ago. Her demise came a month afterwards."

"Were these girls related in any way?" Merin Pendragon asked. There was always the possibility that they were the targets, and not the Lord of the Lake.

"They were neither related by blood nor similar in any way. Rosyn was the child of a northern lord. Her eyes were blue, and her hair light brown. Gwynth had black eyes, and dark hair. Her father was a prosperous merchant in the south," Emrys Llyn responded to his questioner.

"This is indeed strange," Argel noted.

"Why do you go on like this?" Maia demanded, and her voice had an almost hysterical edge to it. "I would wed him no matter what you say, or what has happened before. We are meant to be together, and I will allow no one to prevent this union!"

Emrys Llyn reached out and took Maia's hand in his, stroking it as if to soothe her. "Do not be distressed, beloved. Do you not see that your family is but concerned for your welfare? I am too, though I will not leave Dragon's Lair without you. We are indeed meant to be together, and I will do whatever I must to make this happen."

"Yet if we do not learn why your two previous wives died so suddenly after wedding with you, how can I give my consent to this match?" the Dragon Lord said to them.

Maia looked directly at her father, and he saw the fierce determination in her green eyes. "If you do not allow me to wed with the Lord of the Lake, Father, I will lock myself in my chamber. I will take neither food nor drink, and I will remain there until I die or until you allow us to marry. If you should attempt to break down the door, I will leap from the tower window." Then she jumped up from her seat by the fire and ran from the hall.

Astounded, they heard her quick footsteps climbing the stairs to the chamber she shared with Junia.

"She does not mean it," Merin Pendragon said. "Like all young girls she is being controlled by her emotions. In the morning she will awaken refreshed, and this foolishness will be forgotten. She will see the wisdom in our caution. Maia has never been a hysterical girl." But he himself wondered if he believed his brave words.

His three women looked at one another, knowing better, but deciding silently as one to approach the problem on the morrow when their heads were clear.

Argel stood up. "I will show you to your chamber, my lord," she said to Emrys Llyn. "Come."

The Lord of the Lake arose. "I do not know what to say," he said.

"In the morning we will solve the problem," Gorawen told him with an encouraging smile.

Emrys Llyn nodded. "Aye, in the morning," he agreed.

"Ysbail, find your own chamber," Argel commanded. "Gorawen, take our lord to your bed, and soothe his anxiety. I need to be alone this night to consider all of this so that the right decision is made for my daughter." She then moved from the hall, their guest walking in her wake.

Ysbail stood up, looking somewhat aggrieved. "Why does she always ask you to soothe our lord's anxieties?" she demanded. "I am skilled in the arts of passion, too."

Merin Pendragon laughed. "Indeed you are, my lass," he said, "but you will harp at me afterwards, and then I shall want to strangle you. Gorawen knows how to please me with both her passion and her speech." He got to his feet, and gave Ysbail a hearty kiss on the lips. "Another time, my lass, when I am in the mood to do battle with you." Then with a chuckle he pulled Gorawen to her feet and left the hall with the woman he loved above all others in his company.

Ysbail shrugged. He was honest, was Merin Pendragon. And he was good to her. She had no cause for complaint. Pouring herself another goblet of wine she sought her own bed.

Chapter 8

When Argel came down into the hall in the morning after a restless night she found Junia sleeping on the floor by the fire. She was wrapped in a coverlet, and her little face was streaked with the evidence of dried tears. By her was a willow basket piled with her clothing. Argel shook her head despairingly. Maia was not going to be easy in this matter, and had made up her mind. Her daughter could rarely be reasoned with when she came to a decision in which she strongly believed. Argel reached down and gently shook Junia by her thin little shoulder.

"Wake up, child," she said softly. " 'Tis morning, and the hall will soon bustle."

Junia's eyes opened slowly, and seeing Argel she began to weep as she sat up, clutching the coverlet to her. "Maia put me from our chamber and said she is going to kill herself. Oh, Lady Mother, what is happening? I am so afraid!"

Argel felt her anger rise. How could her daughter frighten her little sister in so cruel a manner? Maia deserved a beating for this unkindness! "It is all right, Junia," she comforted the girl, drawing her up and into an embrace. "Your sister is driven by her desire to have what she will have at all costs. She is in love and so has locked herself in the tower, and says she will take neither food nor drink until we allow her to marry the Lord of the Lake," Argel explained. "She says if we do not she will throw herself from the tower, but she will not, I promise you. She is being silly and foolish because she is very much in love with Emrys Llyn. But your father and I worry that the Lord of the Lake has had two wives who died under mysterious circumstances. We must satisfy ourselves that Maia will be safe as his wife, and in his care. He has much magic about him, yet he cannot explain the demise of his previous wives."

"Maybe he does not know why they died," Junia said innocently.

"So he says," Argel responded.

"I like the Lord of the Lake," Junia told the older woman.

"Do you?" Argel found the young girl's response interesting.

"I do not think he would lie to you and father," Junia continued. "He loves Maia greatly."

"I know," Argel replied.

"But he has such sad eyes," Junia noted.

"Why, child, what an observant little puss you are," Argel said with a small smile. Sometimes innocents like Junia saw more clearly than did adults. She hugged the girl. "Take your possessions and run along to your mother's chamber. Tell her I have said you are to sleep with her until this matter with Maia is straightened out."

"Yes, Lady Mother," Junia said, and picking up the willow basket she left the hall.

"I heard," Gorawen told Argel as she came from the shadows of the hall. "I had not realized before this what a thoughtful child Junia is. She is nothing at all like her mother."

"Nay, she is not. Thank God it will be several years before we must go through this matching game again," Argel said with a gusty sigh. "First all the drama about Averil last year, and now my Maia." She sat down in her place at the high board, and waved Gorawen to her place there.

Gorawen nodded in agreement. "Merin is soothed, and sleeping now. He is very concerned by all of this, and of a mind to refuse the Lord of the Lake."

"What do you think?" Argel asked her friend.

"Common sense would dictate he is right," Gorawen answered, "but I nonetheless think he is wrong. Maia loves Emrys

241

Llyn, and he her. I can sense no evil, no malice at all in him. His bloodline is impeccable. A match between Arthur's descendant, and Lancelot's is perfect. What children they may have!"

"But what of her safety?" Argel said.

"I will weave a spell about her that should protect her and keep her safe from any black magic. And being now warned Emrys Llyn will keep her safe from any physical threats," Gorawen replied. "You know your daughter, Argel. She is as stubborn as her father. More so. She will do exactly as she says. She will throw herself from that tower if Merin does not permit this marriage. Our good lord stands between two large rocks, and the only way out for him, if he does not wish his daughter's death on his conscience, is to acquiesce as gracefully as he can. It will be our task to see that he does." She smiled. "It will not harm Maia to go a few days without food, and I know for a fact that there is a pitcher of water in her chamber. It is there for washing, but I believe she will use it to assuage her thirst."

"Thank God and his Blessed Mother for your sensible nature," Argel said. "I remember how calm and accepting you were of Averil's marriage."

"Averil had no choice. Her fate was planned at her birth whatever she might think." Gorawen smiled again. "And while Rhys FitzHugh is no great lord, he is the lord and master of Everleigh now. And Averil has done her duty and produced a son for him. No, all is as it should be for my daughter, and will be for yours, Argel."

Ysbail now bustled into the hall, her color high. "What is this? Your proud daughter has forced my child from their chamber! I will not have it!"

"Calm yourself," Argel advised Ysbail. "It will be for but a short while. Maia will sulk, but you know it will all end well."

"If matters not to me if she marries that sorcerer, or throws herself out the window," Ysbail said meanly as she seated herself. "Junia will have the tower chamber to herself at long last. It is past time my child came into her own." She reached for the hot cottage loaf, and tore off a chunk.

"What a hard heart you have," Gorawen said, sipping at her cup. "Have you no care for Maia?"

"Maia is the heiress," Ysbail said. "She has a fine suitor, and her dowry will consist of land as well as livestock. Her suitor is a man of good lineage. Why should I feel sorry for her? My poor Junia, the youngest of our lord's daughters, will have little to recommend her, I fear. Neither of your daughters has helped her cause at all! Averil is wed to a bastard who would have lived his life as a bailiff if it had not been for his sister's convenient death," she sneered, "and as for Maia, she is determined to wed a man of dubious reputation despite his bloodline. This does not bode well for matching my daughter, does it?" Buttering her bread with her thumb, she shoved it into her mouth.

"You may rest assured that our lord Merin will do every bit as well by Junia as he has done with Averil and Maia," Argel said stiffly.

"Humph!" Ysbail replied. "That hardly reassures me given their circumstances." She reached for a hard-boiled egg from a wooden bowl on the table and began to peel it.

"Averil's dowry was a fine one," Gorawen said. "Both cattle and sheep, and fifteen silver pennies."

"Silver pennies? There was silver in her portion?" Ysbail had not known this.

"Merin puts aside a silver penny on each girl's natal day," Gorawen murmured. "You didn't know? Junia now has eleven silver pennies in her dower portion. If she weds at fifteen as did Averil, there will be fifteen silver pennies along with her share of livestock." She smiled sweetly at Ysbail.

"But Maia will have more silver, I am certain," Ysbail said, not satisfied.

"Maia will have fifteen silver pennies,

too," Argel responded. "Merin made no distinction there between his daughters. Maia, of course, will have land, which neither Averil or Junia could expect."

"Well," said Ysbail, somewhat mollified, "as long as Junia gets as much livestock as her elder sister, I suppose I have no cause for complaint. But I will not have her stinted because she is the youngest!"

"Since we have several years before Junia can be matched there would seem to be no argument," Argel remarked.

"I suppose not," Ysbail agreed grudgingly. Then dipping the peeled egg in the salt dish she popped it whole into her mouth, and ate it.

"Good morning, my women." The Dragon Lord entered the hall and joined them at the high board. He was followed by their guest. "Where is Maia?"

"She has put Junia from their chamber!" Ysbail said quickly before Argel might answer her husband. "And she has bolted the door behind her."

"What is this?" The master of the house looked irritated. "Is she not over this pettish behavior?" He reached for his goblet, which Argel quickly filled from the wine pitcher on the table. "You must go to your daughter, wife, and tell the lass that I wish to see her immediately."

"Do not send Argel on an impossible errand, my lord," Gorawen said quietly. "Maia will not obey her mother in this matter. She will obey none of us until she has her way. When you allow her to marry Emrys Llyn she will unbar her door, but not, I think until then."

"Then I must take an ax to the door myself," the Dragon Lord answered.

"My lord!" Argel cried. "Maia will throw herself from the tower if you do. She has said it."

"Nonsense!" he replied. "Maia is a sensible girl. She will do no such thing."

"Our daughter is in love, my lord, and she is much like you. She rarely threatens, but when she does you may be certain that she will follow through with her threat. If you do not think she will, then you know her not," Argel declared.

"Damn the wench!" the Dragon Lord said.

"Break your fast, my lord," Gorawen coaxed him, and she drizzled honey into his oat stirabout, and then added a generous dollop of thick golden cream. As he took up his spoon she buttered a piece of the cottage loaf lavishly, and topped it with a slice of tasty yellow cheese, setting it by his hand. Then she peeled one of the hard-boiled eggs, and lay it next to the bread, offering him the salt dish when he reached for the egg.

The Dragon Lord ate in silence now as did Emrys Llyn who had been served as nicely by his hostess. Ysbail, silent for a change, saw that the two men's wine cups were never empty. When they had finally satisfied themselves the Dragon Lord spoke.

"I suppose the first thing is to go with you, Emrys Llyn, to see whether this castle Maia speaks of is real, or but a fantasy."

"It is very real, my lord, I swear it. And I agree that we should leave this morning. It is a two-day journey, and if Maia really does refuse to eat until you give your consent it will be four to five days before we may return," the Lord of the Lake said.

"Foolish girl! She needs a good beating," Merin Pendragon grumbled.

"Fetch the horses," he called out to no one in particular, but his command would be obeyed, he knew. He put an arm about his wife, and kissed her gently. Then he gave each of his two concubines a kiss in farewell. "I am off to the north and the west, somewhere between the mountains before the sea," he told them. "At least that is the direction that Emrys Llyn has revealed to me."

"We will return in five days' time, my lady," the Lord of the Lake told Argel, and he kissed her hand. He turned to Gorawen. "Watch over Maia, my sister," he told her, and then turning, he followed his host from the hall.

"Why did he call you his sister?" Ysbail immediately wanted to know.

"Because we both practice magic, and are to a certain degree of magic," Gorawen answered the woman. "Magical folk have a special bond."

"What will we do about Maia?" Argel wondered.

"Wait until the noon hour when we will eat our main meal. By then she will be very hungry, for Maia is not used to missing her food. I think if she knows her father has gone with her lover to inspect her future home she can be coaxed into coming out and joining us until they return," Gorawen said.

"And she can take up her defensive position when her father returns in order to save her dignity." Argel chuckled.

"You both indulge the lass too much," Ysbail said. "But at least Junia can return to her rightful place if you can convince Maia to stop being so silly."

And as Gorawen had predicted Maia was cajoled from her tower chamber by her mother. She came to table at the noon hour, and ate two helpings of lamb stew and almost demolished a cottage loaf by herself. Then she offered to help her sister bring her possessions back to their chamber.

"I thought you no longer loved me because you now love Emrys Llyn," Junia said tearily, hugging her elder sister.

"What a silly goose you are, Junia! You do not stop loving everyone else because you love a man," Maia said.

"How am I to know such things?" Junia demanded in a tone so like her mother's that they all laughed, even Ysbail.

"How long did you say it would take father to reach Emrys's castle?" Maia asked.

"The Lord of the Lake said it was a two-day ride," Argel told her daughter.

"I wish I were with them," Maia said softly.

"It is a long ride," Gorawen noted, wondering how Merin was getting on, for the Dragon Lord did not travel far from his lands as a rule.

And Merin Pendragon was wondering as he rode why his daughters could not have wed men who lived closer to his home. Averil was a day and a half's journey, and now possibly Maia would be two days' riding. Still, the land was beautiful, and the weather was not too bad. With the autumn, there was a chill in the air, and he was very relieved when they camped the night in a small dry cave, and could have a fire, for the night was cold. At least they ate well, for his cook had wrapped a roasted chicken in a cloth, along with some oat cakes, cheese, apples, and the remainder of the morning's hard-boiled eggs. Each man carried a flask filled with wine. They ate half the chicken, saving the other half for the next day, and roasted apples in the fire before sleeping.

In the morning they ate the remainder of their food, but for two oat cakes and two apples. The horses were well rested, and watered. They had spent their night in the shelter of the cave away from any marauding animals, and were fed a measure of oats carried by their masters. They were ready for the day's journey that lay ahead of them.

"We should reach my castle by sunset," Emrys Llyn told his companion.

"Does it have a name?" demanded the Dragon Lord.

"Ile du Lac," the Lord of the Lake answered. "Lancelot named it."

Merin Pendragon grunted in acknowledgement.

When the sun had reached its zenith at midday they stopped and ate their scant rations while resting the horses. The countryside was very wild and very desolate and grew more so as the afternoon progressed. They had passed no cottages since midday yesterday.

"Who claims this land?" the Dragon Lord asked.

Emrys Llyn shrugged. "The great families argue back and forth over it, but no one ever comes here, my lord. I have no idea who now owns, or believes he owns, this land. It is good for little but perhaps hunting."

"How near are we to Ile du Lac?" Merin asked.

"Soon," came the answer. "Another hill or two. See, the sun is already preparing to make its descent."

"Good!" Merin Pendragon said. "I am loath to admit it, but I am not as young as I once was. I am ready for a hot meal and a comfortable bed."

"You shall have them soon, my lord," Emrys Llyn promised.

Another hour passed, and as the sun slipped towards the horizon they made their descent into a small valley taken up entirely by a beautiful deep blue lake. The hills were forested about them. The horses slowly picked their way downward until they had reached the shoreline. They stopped, and Emrys Llyn put a horn that had been hanging from his waist to his lips, and blew. The sound echoed in the clear air, and almost at once a flat-bottomed ferry came towards them from the shore of the island that sat in the midst of the waters. There was no ferryman, however.

The Lord of the Lake saw his companion's astonishment. He smiled, and then said, "I hope you will forgive me a bit of magic, Merin Pendragon. I cannot resist showing off now and again."

"Is it safe to travel in such a conveyance?" the Dragon Lord asked.

"Quite safe for us, and for the horses," he was assured as the small vessel neatly bumped the sandy beach before them.

"This is a most convenient magic you possess," the Dragon Lord remarked dryly.

Emrys Llyn laughed as he gently urged his horse aboard the ferry. "Come," he said. "The sun is near to setting, and I would show you my hospitality. Maia will be most happy here, my lord."

"Well, I will agree that the setting is a beautiful one," Merin Pendragon answered. "And you will swear to me that this is all real, and not some illusion you have wrought?"

"It is as real as your own Dragon's Lair. I swear it on the Blessed Mother and her son Jesu, Merin Pendragon. I have not the magic of the Lady of the Lake, but what magic I do possess, I use only for the good."

The Dragon Lord urged his horse onto the little ferry next to Emrys Llyn and his mount. At once the ferry began to move, and it skimmed swiftly across to the island where the castle stood, twinkling lights glittering from its narrow windows.

When they had reached the far shore there were servants awaiting them to lead them down a path from the lake's edge through a field of flowers to the castle itself. Within the courtyard of the edifice they dismounted, and their horses were taken away.

"Welcome home, my lord!" a smiling majordomo said as he hurried forward. "We did not expect you so soon."

"This is Merin Pendragon, the Dragon Lord himself, Sion," Emrys Llyn said.

The majordomo bowed low. "I welcome the descendant of the great Arthur, my lord," he said.

"You have served your master long?" Merin asked, curious.

"My family has always served in the house of the Lord of the Lake, my lord," Sion answered.

"Are the servants here real, or fairy?" Merin persisted.

Sion smiled again. "Some are real, as you put it. Some are fairy. And some of the servants are both, my lord. Is that not the way in all the world? Now, if you will follow me, my lords, the supper will be ready to be served." Turning, he led them from the entrance of the castle and into a great hall.

Merin Pendragon gaped noticeably about

the chamber. It was large. There were great beams that were carved, painted and gilded, holding up the roof. High arched windows lined two sides of the room. On a sunny day it would be bright and cheerful. There were three enormous stone fireplaces, each flanked on either side with tall carved stone knights in full armor who held their swords before them, pointed down. Enormous tapestries hung on either side of the fireplace behind the high board. They depicted King Arthur and his court going about their various pursuits. The high board itself was made of hard oak, and the table was blackened with its many years, but well polished.

Merin Pendragon sat himself at his host's right hand without being asked to do so. "Your hall is magnificent," he said quietly.

"There was a day when it would have been filled with knights, and visitors from all lands come to pay homage to the Lady of the Lake, and her mate, Lancelot. Those times are long gone," Emrys Llyn said. "Still, the hall remains a reminder of those times." There was a sadness in his voice when he spoke.

"I am weary from our journey," Merin Pendragon said. "I would eat, and find a bed, but tomorrow will you show me about this great castle of yours?"

"Gladly!" Emrys Llyn said. "You will see that Maia will be content here."

"Perhaps, but what of companions for her? Your home is beautiful, but lonely, Emrys Llyn," the Dragon Lord noted. "My daughter has grown up in a household of women, and is used to their company. What will happen when you get her with child? Who will be here to nurture and aid her? To calm her natural fears?"

"Maia is not afraid of my magic, my lord. When she desires companions they will be supplied for her. The Fair Folk are good souls, and she will easily find friends among them. She will have ladies aplenty, I promise you."

The Dragon Lord nodded. It would take some getting used to, this magical world into which his daughter would come. He thought of the majordomo's remark that some here were fairy, and some were not, and some were both. How did one tell? But then he turned his attentions to the fine meal being served.

The salmon was served with dill. There were oysters and fat prawns. And where had they come from so far from the sea? He decided he didn't care. There was roasted venison and wild forest boar. Capon in a sauce of dried berries; a duck in a sauce made from plums. The rabbit pie had a flaky golden crust. Merin Pendragon ate until he could eat no more, or so he believed. And then a bowl of roasted apples covered in heavy golden cream was brought to table, along with a platter of pears that had been sliced in half lengthwise, and sat in a sauce of rich wine and spices. Delicate little sugar wafers were set before him, and his wine cup was never allowed to be empty. Unable to help himself, he ate both apples and pears. When he belched afterwards it was a mixture of wine and cinnamon, and he smiled, well satisfied.

"I apologize for the simplicity of the meal," his host said, "but as Sion said, we were not expected."

The Dragon Lord laughed aloud. "Your jest is noted, Emrys Llyn. The meal was the finest I have ever eaten. Your cook is obviously fairy."

"Nay, he is but real folk, but he does have a talent for his work," the Lord of the Lake said.

Merin Pendragon stood up. "Now, I should like to find my bed," he said.

The majordomo was immediately at his side. "Allow me to show you, my lord," he said, bowing.

"Lead on, my good Sion," was the jovial reply, and the Dragon Lord followed Sion from the great hall of Ile du Lac. If his bed was as good as his meal, he would have no complaint. He was already beginning to think more kindly of Emrys Llyn. Everything he had seen so far would indicate that his daughter would be happy and comfortable. If only he might solve the mystery of the unfortunate deaths of the Lord of the Lake's first two wives.

The chamber to which he was shown was spacious. The windows overlooked the lake. The fireplace was ablaze, and there was water for washing. There was wine on a sideboard table.

"Is there anything I can get you, my lord?" Sion asked him.

The Dragon Lord saw his saddle pack set neatly on a stool. "No," he replied. "Thank you, Sion."

"Then I wish you a good night, my lord," the majordomo said, bowing himself from the chamber and closing the door behind him.

Merin Pendragon sat down on the edge of the curtained bed, and slowly pulled off his boots. He set them by the stool, and drawing off his cotte he lay it atop his pack. He disrobed no further, for this was a strange house, and while he felt he was safe from harm, one never knew. Climbing into the great bed he left the bed curtains open, and lay back. From what he had seen so far it was all perfect. But was it too perfect? he considered. *Tomorrow,* he thought. *Tomorrow I will be able to better judge. I am weary with our traveling. My head will be clearer in the morning. Tomorrow I shall make my decision.* He slept peacefully, and without dreams.

In the morning he arose at first light, and bathed himself, for he had not done it the previous evening before sleeping. He opened his pack, and was surprised to find not only a clean chemise, but a simple clean cotte folded up tightly. Smiling, he shook it out, thinking he must remember to thank Argel when he returned to Dragon's Lair. A man always felt more confident in clean garments. He took his worn chemise and used it to polish his boots free of dust and dirt before he pulled them on again. When he had completed his toilette he departed the chamber, and easily found his way back down to the great hall where his host was already at table. The morning meal was as tasty as the previous meal had been.

Finally Emrys Llyn said, "You will want to see all of my home now, I expect, my lord." He arose from his seat. "Come, and I will show you."

Merin Pendragon stood up, and followed the younger man. The Dragon Lord quickly discovered that while the castle was small, Ile du Lac was well thought out. There was a chamber where the lord kept scrolls and bound books, many of them obviously quite old. The kitchens were below the great hall, and there was a stone shaft with a platform within it that was raised and lowered by means of a rope and pulley. This, Emrys Llyn explained, was how food arrived in the hall hot, and how the dishes and platters were quickly cleared away. In the kitchens below the Dragon Lord saw the usual activity of a kitchen. The servants there smiled and nodded at their master and his guest as they passed by. There was a buttery and a pantry, and a cold room where game and game birds were hung.

Above the great hall there was a large master chamber, and several small but spacious chambers, including his own. In each of the four corners of the second story there were stairs leading to each of the castle's four towers. His old nursemaid, Drysi, lived in the south tower, Emrys Llyn explained.

"She is very ancient, having looked after others of my family," he explained. "She rarely leaves her rooms, and all her meals are brought to her. Would you like to meet her? I know she would consider it an honor to meet a descendant of King Arthur."

"I would, indeed," Merin Pendragon replied. This spoke well of Emrys Llyn that he housed and respected an elderly retainer. *I was right to insist on coming to Ile du Lac,* he thought. *I can learn much about this man just being here.* He followed his host up the steep and winding staircase to a door.

Emrys Llyn knocked upon the dark, worn oak portal, which was opened by a smiling young girl who curtsied.

"My lord! Drysi will be pleased that you have come." She ushered them into the chamber where an old woman sat in a high backed chair.

The eyes that looked out at them were a sharp, faded blue and the skin on her face wrinkled with age. She was a tiny woman and it was obvious that her back was crooked and hunched. She beckoned them forward with a rather imperious wave of her bony hand. "Come! Come! Let me see this seed of the great king," she said.

Merin Pendragon stepped forward and gave the old woman a courtly bow. "You know me," he said.

"Have I not ears to hear?" she asked him.

"Drysi knows everything that goes on at Ile du Lac," Emrys Llyn said in an affectionate amused tone of voice. "Sometimes she knows before even I know," he teased his old nursemaid.

Drysi cackled. " 'Tis a truth," she admitted. Then she looked again at the

Dragon Lord. "So, my lord, your daughter would wed with my master."

"And he would wed with her," Merin Pendragon responded quietly.

"Does she love him?"

"So she says," he answered.

"She must love him with all her heart and her soul," Drysi replied. "She must love him so completely that whatever happens her love will not waver. Tell me, seed of Arthur, can your daughter love that hard, that desperately? And think carefully before you answer me."

"I can only tell you, Drysi, that never before has Maia given her heart to a man, but for me, her father," the Dragon Lord said. "I can tell you that before we departed Dragon's Lair three days ago my daughter had locked herself in the tower room she shares with her sister, and swore she would not emerge from it until I gave my permission for her marriage to Emrys Llyn. She threatened to leap from the tower window if I tried to force her out before then. Aye, I believe Maia loves your master with everything of which her innocent heart is capable."

The old woman nodded. "It is promising," she said.

"Now you tell me, Drysi, who knows all. What happened to your master's first two wives? He says he does not know, but I am not certain I can believe him."

"He tells you the truth," Drysi responded. "But they were foolish girls, both of them, and the second had a greedy nature. I suppose it was their fate to die young." She shrugged. "They just went to sleep, and did not awaken. That is all I can tell you, my lord. There are some things that even I am not privileged to know, but Emrys is innocent of any deception, or complicity in their deaths. That I swear to you."

The Dragon Lord felt that perhaps the old woman knew more than she was willing to admit. She would protect her master at any cost, he thought, yet the more he was in Emrys Llyn's company, the more he liked the young man. There was nothing evil in this castle, nor among its inhabitants. The Dragon Lord had no excuse to forbid his daughter her heart's desire.

"Your daughter will be content here, seed of Arthur," Drysi said. "But remember, she must love Emrys Llyn no matter the circumstance."

"I believe she will," the Dragon Lord replied. He turned to his host. "Show me these gardens Maia raves about. My wife and my women will want to know all about them."

They took their leave of Drysi, moving down the staircases and finally out into the

Lord of the Lake's gardens. Maia had been right. The gardens moved from an inner courtyard out into a large walled area that spilled down to the lakeside. The day was bright and sunny. A day such as Merin Pendragon had rarely seen. The air was soft around him, and the smell of roses, rosemary and lavender tickled his nose. There were several apple trees in the large section of the garden, now heavy with fruit. He looked about him, and knew in his heart that his daughter could be happy nowhere else.

"There is one final place I would show you," Emrys Llyn said. "Come with me, my lord." And he led his guest back into the castle, up a staircase that the Dragon Lord didn't remember having seen before, into a long chamber with windows along one entire side that overlooked the lake. The chamber was bright with sunshine and the sparkle of the water that reflected through the tall windows. Opposite the windows the other wall appeared bare until Emrys Llyn waved his hand slowly, and to the Dragon Lord's amazement lifelike figures appeared upon the wall. "I thought you would enjoy seeing your ancestor," the Lord of the Lake said. "You much resemble him." He pointed to the figure of a tall distinguished man in full armor, the red Pendragon emblazoned across his breastplate. In one arm the man held a helmet. In the other a great sword. On his dark head was a narrow gold crown.

Merin Pendragon stared. "That is Arthur?" This was an amazing magic.

"Aye, 'tis the once and future king himself, my lord. Now look to his right, and see Lancelot, and on the king's left is his queen."

Gwynefr was exquisite, the Dragon Lord thought to himself. No wonder Arthur had fallen hopelessly in love with her. And as Merin resembled his ancestor, so did Emrys Llyn resemble Lancelot. "Show me more," he begged the Lord of the Lake.

Emrys Llyn smiled, and led his guest down the chamber. Farther down the wall a trio of incredibly beautiful women could be seen. "Arthur's half sisters. Morgause, who was married to King Lot of Orkney, Morgan le Fey, who seduced Arthur before he knew who she was, and bore his son, Mordred, who was responsible for the downfall of Camelot; and lastly the youngest of them, Elaine, the lady of Shallot who died of her unrequited love for my ancestor, Lancelot, who betrayed her first with my mother, and then with Gwynefr."

"I have never seen such beautiful women," Merin Pendragon said softly.

"Aye, they were famed for it, but their hearts were evil. They never forgot that

264

Uther Pendragon was responsible for the death of the duke of Cornwall, who was their father; and all because of Uther's desperate passion for Igraine, who was the duke's wife before she was Uther Pendragon's wife. They hated their stepfather though he treated them as if they were his own blood. They hated their mother after Cornwall's death, for they held her equally culpable. One night Uther Pendragon, with the help of Merlin the Enchanter, took Cornwall's form, entered his castle, and seduced Igraine. The sisters believed that she was aware of the deception, yet allowed herself to be swept away. That is why your ancestor, Arthur, was hidden away until it was time for him to become the king," Emrys explained. He moved on down the wall, waving his hand as he went. "Here is Merlin himself, and with him the beauteous Vivian the Enchantress who was his mate, and finally betrayed him."

"And the Lady of the Lake, your ancestress?" Merin Pendragon asked, curious.

"The final image, my lord," Emrys Llyn said softly.

The Dragon Lord stared hard. If Arthur's half sisters had been divinely fair, this otherworldly creature was incredible in her exquisite beauty. Her face was shaped like a heart. Her skin was pure and creamy with just the faintest hint of rose in her cheeks. Her golden hair curled and swirled about her as if being blown in a breeze. Her eyes were the same blue as the sky above her, and the lake below her gown, the hem of which seemed to be made of the lake's very waves. She brandished Arthur's sword, the fabled Excalibur, above her, her fingers wrapped about its gem-encrusted hilt.

"Usually," Emrys Llyn said quietly, "the only glimpse people have of the Lady is her arm holding the sword. For my father's sake she agreed to be displayed here, but only on the condition that all the portraitures be rendered invisible to the everyday eye. Only the master of the castle would be able to reveal them."

"I am honored to have seen them," the Dragon Lord said.

"There is one final view," the Lord of the Lake replied. He waved his hand, and there before them was the famed Round Table with Arthur and his knights in the great hall at Camelot.

"It is magnificent," the Dragon Lord said. His eyes were filled with tears. "Thank you, Emrys Llyn, for showing me this. Thank you!" He wiped his eyes with his sleeve.

"Have you seen all you need to see, my lord?" the younger man asked him.

Merin Pendragon nodded. "Aye, I have."

"And have you made your decision?" Emrys Llyn asked.

"Aye, I have." The Dragon Lord sighed. "While I still cannot help but wonder what happened to your two previous wives, I am content that you will do whatever you must to protect and cherish my daughter Maia. She is yours."

"I would give my life for Maia," Emrys Llyn said.

"I hope that it will not come to that," Merin Pendragon said. "Now, let us go back to your hall, my lord, and drink to the union of our two families."

Chapter 9

Brynn Pendragon could see the two riders from the top of the north tower where he stood watching. They came from the north-west. Even from this distance he recognized his father's horse. The day was gray, damp and misty, but the boy remained at his post. There was plenty of time, and the moment he delivered his news to the hall his mother and the other women would set up a great to-do. And his silly sister would dash up to her chamber in the south tower, and lock herself in her room until she was certain she was getting her own way. And she was. The very fact that Emrys Llyn rode with his father told the boy that. The Lord of the Lake would have hardly returned with Merin Pendragon so that he might be publicly refused and humiliated. But Maia would play at her game of histrionics. His sister, Brynn decided, had the wit of a goose.

The watchman on the south tower looked to him for instruction. He pointed to the hills, but Brynn shook his head. "Not yet," he called to the man. The man-at-arms nodded his understanding, and turned away. So Maia would be wed, Brynn thought. And that would leave only Junia for him to tease. He grinned to himself. Junia was a lot of fun for a girl. She could race him on both horseback and foot. He could beat her ahorse, but Junia ran faster than anyone he had ever known. It would seem odd with just the two of them now. He still missed his eldest sibling, Averil, and now Maia was to go.

The two riders were halfway across the field before the keep now. Brynn called down to the men-at-arms below. "My father comes with a guest. Make ready!" Then he opened the trapdoor in the roof, and climbed down a ladder into a small room below, pulling the door shut behind him and barring it. He lay the ladder against the far wall as he had been taught. Then he exited the chamber and ran down the stairs into the hallway below. Dashing down the steps from the upper hallway he entered the hall. "Father is coming," he said.

Maia jumped up with a little shriek and made for the stairs.

"Your lover is with him, you muttonhead," Brynn called after her. "He isn't coming back because father has refused him. You're going to get your way."

Maia stopped for a moment, and turned.

" 'Tis a matter of principal," she told her little brother in lofty tones. "And don't you dare tell them that I've been out of my chamber while they've been gone, or I will make you very sorry, Brynn Pendragon."

"Yah! Yah! Yah!" he mocked her with a grin. "Maybe I will, and maybe I won't. I'm not afraid of you, Maia. Oh? Is that our father I hear at the portal?" And he laughed uproariously as his elder sister turned again, and picking up her skirts dashed up the stairs.

"Brynn," Argel gently chided her son, but she was smiling, and the others were as well, but for Junia who began to giggle openly.

Brynn winked at her. "Soon it will be just you and me, Juni," he said to her.

Junia stopped giggling, and her lower lip began to quiver. Two large fat tears rolled down her face. "I don't want Maia to go," she sobbed.

"Now you have done it, you little roughneck," Ysbail snapped. She turned on her daughter. "Stop howling, Junia! Soon you will be old enough to be married."

"I don't want to marry!" Junia wailed. "I want everything to be as it was. I want my sisters baaaaack!"

"Life moves on, my child," Argel said quietly. "Averil is content with her husband, and son. And Maia loves Emrys

Llyn, and is glad to be his wife. I know you love your sisters so you must be happy that they are happy. Someday, sooner than even I would wish, you will find that same happiness in the arms of a man." Argel embraced the young girl, and stroked her dark hair. "Do not let your father see such a sad face upon his return, my child." She wiped Junia's tears with the heel of her hand.

"Yes, Lady Mother," Junia said obediently, and she gave Argel a tremulous smile.

Merin Pendragon came into his hall in the company of Emrys Llyn. He looked tired, his women noted. Argel and Gorawen hurried forward to greet the two men while Ysbail poured out two goblets of wine for the travelers. The Dragon Lord embraced his wife, and then Gorawen. Seeing Ysbail standing with the wine he nodded his approval, and greeted her as he took one of the goblets from her hand. She handed the other to the Lord of the Lake. The two men sat by the late afternoon fire while the others clustered about them on the settle, and the two youngsters sat upon the floor next to their father.

"My lord," Argel began formally, "as you have returned in the company of Emrys Llyn, I must assume that you have decided to allow a match between him and our daughter Maia."

"I have," the Dragon Lord answered.

"And his home is fit for our daughter's arrival?" Argel continued.

"His castle, which is called Ile du Lac, is beautifully situated and in excellent repair. The servants are well trained, and pleasant. They are anxious for a new mistress," Merin Pendragon told his audience.

"And you have found the cause of his previous wives deaths?" Argel persisted.

"It would seem there is no mystery, my lady wife. It was but a coincidence that both of these young women died suddenly, and seemingly without cause," Merin Pendragon told his audience. "I am satisfied there is no evil involved."

"Then we may plan a wedding?" Argel asked.

"You may plan a wedding," the Dragon Lord told his wife.

"Then you must send Emrys Llyn to Maia's chamber to tell her all is well, my lord," Argel said with a smile.

"I will show you!" Junia jumped up and held out her hand to Emrys Llyn.

He looked to the Dragon Lord, who nodded with a grin. "Fetch the wench," he said. "Junia, you may show him, but then you are to come right back to the hall, lass."

"Yes, Da," she answered him, and then

she hurried off with Emrys Llyn.

When they had left the hall Gorawen said, "Tell us all, my lord." She knew there was far more than Merin had revealed so far. "Is there magic at Ile du Lac?"

He nodded. "Aye, but of a gentle sort. The castle sits on an island in the midst of the lake. A ferry, without a ferryman to steer it, came at the sound of Emrys Llyn's horn. It took us over to the island, which is very beautiful, filled with all manner of green and growing things. The castle is lovely with four tall towers with peaked witch's caps for roofs. The towers each face a different compass point. The servants, his majordomo told me, are human, fairy, and a mixture of both. He is loved by all. I met his old nursemaid, Drysi. She lives in isolated splendor in the south tower. I asked her about the two previous wives, but she assured me, and I did believe her, that it was but a tragic coincidence. She says if Maia loves Emrys there can be no difficulty, and predicts the marriage will be happy."

Drysi, Gorawen thought. The word meant "thorn." Merin was not repeating exactly what the old woman had said. He was abbreviating it for them. She would speak to him later, and coax him to remember everything. Maia's very life could depend upon it, Gorawen considered.

"But the most amazing thing I saw at Ile du Lac was in a long gallery that faced the lake. Emrys showed me with his magic a wall of portraiture so lifelike that I expected the figures to step from the wall and converse with us. I saw my ancestor, King Arthur, his queen, Lancelot, and all those who lived at Arthur's court in that time. And when Emrys waved his hand again they were all gone, and the wall was a blank. I shall never forget it as long as I live."

"That is, indeed, wonderful magic," Gorawen said softly.

"I am convinced that the Lord of the Lake loves Maia truly. I am convinced that there was no evil in the demise of his previous wives. That is why I have given him my consent to marry our daughter. It is a good match, Arthur's descendant and Lancelot's descendant," Merin concluded.

"They will want to be wed soon," Argel remarked.

"Emrys and I have chosen the first day of the Celtic New Year, November first," the Dragon Lord said.

"That is less than a month, my lord!" Argel exclaimed.

"Do you think Maia will wait longer?" Gorawen chuckled dryly.

"It does not have to be a grand affair. Invite the Mortimers, Averil and her family. 'Twill be enough, and Maia will not care as long as the family is together," the Dragon Lord told his wife.

"And we are all here to help," Ysbail chimed in, to their surprise.

Junia returned to the hall. "Maia and Emrys won't stop kissing," she announced, plopping herself down next to her brother again.

"They are in love," Gorawen murmured.

"Do all people in love kiss without ceasing? I do not see how they can even breathe," Junia responded. "You and father don't spend all your time kissing."

The adults laughed, and then Argel said, "When you are young, and love is new, you do a lot of kissing, Junia."

"You mean that I will have to do all that kissing someday?" the young girl asked incredulously. She wrinkled her little nose with distaste.

"Only if you want to," Gorawen replied, "but if it is the right man, you will want to, my child."

Maia and her lover now came into the hall, and Maia ran to her father. "Thank you, Da!" she told him, and she hugged him.

"I should have beat you more," he growled, hugging her back.

"You never beat me at all!" Maia exclaimed.

"And you see what a willful wench you turned out to be," he teased her.

"My lord Emrys says we will wed on November first, and I am content to know it," Maia said meekly.

"Love," Argel murmured, and she rolled her eyes.

Gorawen and Ysbail laughed.

It had grown dark outside, and the lamps were lit in the hall. The evening meal was served, and those at the table were merry. Afterwards, Junia and Brynn, tired with all the excitement, found their beds. Ysbail arose, yawning, and saying that if she was to do the embroidery on Maia's wedding gown she must get her rest. As her embroidery was the finest of Merin Pendragon's women, she was not detained. Argel then stood, and kissed her daughter good night before departing the hall. Merin Pendragon was quickly on his feet, taking Gorawen's hand in his.

"I will see that the door is barred, and tell the servants to douse the lamps," he said to no one in particular. Then he left the hall in Gorawen's company.

"They are not very subtle," Maia said softly, looking at her lover.

"Did you really keep to your chamber and starve yourself while we were gone?" he asked her.

Maia laughed, and then she flushed.

"Nay, my lord. I was coaxed from my room as soon as my father had gone. I missed no meals at all I blush to tell you."

"If you father had refused my suit, and not gone to Ile du Lac, would you have carried out your threat?" he wondered aloud.

She nodded. "I am yours, Emrys. I can belong to no other," Maia told him.

He held out his hand to her. "Come and sit in my lap, Maia.

She came at once to his invitation, for she had cuddled in his arms in her dreams. She had no fear of him at all.

When she was comfortably settled he reached around her, and began to unlace her gown. Then he drew the upper half of the gown from her arms and shoulders. The fabric settled itself about her waist. "I want to caress you," he told her. "I want to feel your skin against my hands." His fingers undid the ribbons holding her chemise closed.

"We have not done this before," Maia whispered, her pulses beginning to race.

"Nay," he said. "We have not." He let his hand push past the opening of her chemise.

"Why?" she asked him.

"Because you were not really mine until your father agreed," Emrys Llyn said, his long fingers brushing her skin lightly.

"I was yours from the moment you first came to me, my lord," Maia told him. She looked up at him adoringly.

His dark head dipped, and he brushed his lips lightly against hers over and over. Then his tongue traced the shape of her mouth lingeringly, and when she murmured with her pleasure his mouth took hers in a fierce hard kiss that seemed as if it would never end. His hand plunged deep, finding a full and generous round breast. He cupped it. Then he squeezed it while his lips relaxed against hers, and he said against her mouth, "You have no idea, Maia, the white-hot desire I have for you!"

Her head was spinning, and she was having difficulty breathing for a long moment. Then she whispered daringly against his mouth, "Remove your cotte, my lord."

"What if someone comes?" he asked her.

"They will go away," she assured him.

He released his hold on her, and pulled the cotte off even as he watched with surprised eyes as Maia shrugged her chemise down to join the top of her gown. Then reaching out she undid his chemise, and drew it off.

"I am a virgin," she said, "but I have desires and instincts which I feel need to be sated, my lord. Will you satisfy them?" Her bare arms slipped about his neck, and she looked up at him with open longing. The tips of her nipples were temptingly close to his smooth chest. Her little pointed tongue imitated his actions of a few moments earlier.

He was astounded by her daring impudence.

"Do you not want me, Emrys?" she asked him. She pulled him against her breasts.

He groaned with longing. The soft flesh of her bosom was the most intoxicating thing he had ever experienced. All the other women he had known in his life faded in his lust for this beautiful girl. "Your nature is, I can see, as fiery as your hair," he murmured low in her ear. His tongue encircled the curved whorl of delicate flesh, licking at it slowly. He blew gently into it, smiling to himself as she shivered openly. Her instincts might be leading her, but her experience was nil.

"Your flesh on mine," she whispered at him. "It feels so good, Emrys. I could stay this way forever!"

He loosened her hold on his neck, and tipped her into the curve of his arm. "I want to look at your breasts, Maia. And when I have had my fill of them, I want to suckle on you. Jesu! You have the most beautiful and perfect round breasts." He stroked her flesh gently, and she trembled with a rising hunger she could not understand. Then his dark head lowered itself again, and his seeking mouth fastened itself about a nipple.

Maia gasped softly. Feeling his wet and hungry mouth feeding on her was the most exciting thing that had ever happened to her. His mouth sucked harder, and she felt a corresponding tug in her secret place. Unable to help herself she arched her body against him. "Ohh, Emrys." She sighed. "Don't stop, I beg you." The mouth tugged harder and harder at her until she actually felt a humid moistness that stuck against her thighs. "Oh!" she exclaimed, surprised.

His hand slipped beneath her skirts, slithering up until he, too, felt the first rush of her virginal juices. He wanted to take her then and there, but he did not. By their wedding night Maia would fear nothing, but he had to be patient with her, and with himself. He removed his hand and lifted his head from her breasts, kissing her mouth as he did. "It is enough, my love, for now."

"It will never be enough," she told him.

He laughed. "Do you crave my passion so, then, my love?"

Maia nodded. "You and no other, Emrys Llyn. I should die before I would allow another to have me."

"Be patient, my love. In just a few short

weeks we will be wed. And in the mean-time we will make love when and where we can that you may be ready to accept me on our wedding night," he told her.

Maia nodded. "I am not afraid of passion," she told him.

"I know," he answered her, and then pulling her chemise up, he threaded the ribbons used to close it shut. He drew up the top of her gown, and she slipped her arms back into the sleeves even as he laced the garment shut.

"I don't know why we bother." Maia laughed. "We will go to our chambers, and disrobe now."

"The little Junia will be waiting for you, I am certain," he said, laughter in his deep voice. "She will want to know all that has transpired between us, my love."

"She is much too young!" Maia said, scandalized.

"Nonetheless, she will ask. Did you not ask Averil after she had mated with her husband?" he teased, and laughed when she blushed. "Therefore we must at least give the appearance of propriety," he concluded.

Maia sighed. "Aye," she agreed, "but I should far rather go to your bed tonight, my lord, than share a bed with my little sister."

He laughed again, tipping her from his

lap. "You will behave yourself, Maia. Remember that you are soon to be a respectable married woman. Go now."

"You don't know where the guest chamber is, my lord," she told him mischievously, grinning.

"A servant will show me, my love," he said.

She pouted a moment, but then she gave him a quick kiss, and hurried off. Emrys Llyn sat staring into the flames of the fire. He loved this girl as he had never before loved. His previous unions had been of necessity. He had not wanted to wed, for he knew that somewhere out in the world beyond Ile du Lac there was a girl who would love him, and him alone. Who would not be afraid of the truth when he told her, or look at him as if he were a monster as his first wife had done.

Rosyn had been an innocent daughter of a northern family. She had been meant for the church, but he had seen her and thought that perhaps she would suit him. She was a meek and gentle girl. Her uncles had been more than willing, and so they had wed. But Rosyn had been devout. His magic had frightened her. And when the Lady had come forth from the lake to inspect her, she had fled to the top of one of the castle towers, and flung herself over the edge. He felt great guilt at her death, and it had been put about that the poor lass died suddenly in her bed.

In choosing a second wife he looked for a stronger, bolder girl. He found her in Gwynth, a merchant's beautiful daughter. Gwynth had skin as white as the snow, and hair like a raven's wing. Her eyes were as black as the cherries that came from Brittany in June. Emrys Llyn was willing to accept Gwynth's small dower portion. Her father was content to overlook the strange rumors about the Lord of the Lake, and the marriage was celebrated. But no sooner had it been than Gwynth began to change from a cheerful girl into a shrew. She mistreated the servants. There was nothing that caught her eye that she did not desire, and she would whine and complain until she got it. Emrys Llyn did everything he could think of to please this second wife, but she was never content. Enough was never enough for Gwynth.

To amuse her one day he showed her the portraiture in the gallery overlooking the lake. Gwynth was immediately transfixed by King Arthur's sword, Excalibur. She demanded to know what had happened to it, and he told her that Lancelot had brought the sword back to the lake, and hurled it into the water. He explained that the Lady's hand had come from the water to reclaim the sword, which she would hold until Arthur returned to recover the throne of Britain.

"Then the sword is in the lake," Gwynth said.

"The sword is with the Lady," Emrys replied.

"It should be here in the castle, hanging over the main fireplace in the great hall," Gwynth replied. "You must tell the Lady we want it."

"Nay," he responded quietly. "The sword belongs with the Lady. 'Tis she who gave it to Merlin the Enchanter for Arthur."

"Have you no idea of the prestige the sword would bring you, my lord," Gwynth railed at her husband. "If you will not ask the Lady for it, then I will!"

Several days later Gwynth was found on the edge of the shore. She was dead. And once again the story was put about that Emrys Llyn's wife had suddenly died in her bed.

He had not loved Rosyn, but she had been a sweet girl. He had not loved the beauteous but greedy Gwynth, but he had hoped she would love him. Now he was to take a third wife, and he wondered if he was doing Maia Pendragon a disservice in wedding her. Yet she knew of his magic, and was not afraid of it. And she had shown no unpleasant traits so far. But did she love him enough? He didn't want the death of another wife on his conscience. Yet he could not resist her, and he loved her as he had never loved another. And the plain truth was that he had no choice if he was to move on with his life.

"My lord?"

He started, and turned to face a servant. "Yes?"

"If I may show you to your chamber, my lord. The doors are barred, and the lamps doused. I should like to seek my own bed, but if you are not ready, I will wait."

Emrys Llyn arose, and stretched. "Nay, 'tis past time for me to find my bed, but it is so comfortable here before the fire. Forgive me that I have kept you from your own rest. Lead on." And he followed the servant from the hall.

Though Maia protested it was decided the following day that the Lord of the Lake would return home until just before the marriage was to be celebrated. And in his daughter's presence Merin Pendragon obtained Emrys Llyn's promise not to visit Maia in her dreams. They would be separated until a day before the wedding. Reluctantly Maia bade her lover farewell, and watched sadly as he rode away from Dragon's Lair.

But in the days that followed she had little time to weep over his leaving, for the preparations for her wedding began in earnest. Messengers carrying invitations were sent out to Everleigh and Lord Mortimer. Her father, her brother, and the castle huntsmen went into the forest to find a fine boar for the wedding feast. Ysbail worked tirelessly on the embroidery that would be added to Maia's wedding gown. And in the kitchens the cook began preparing for the feast he would have to create on the wedding day.

Argel wanted her daughter's wedding dress to bespeak her status as the legitimate daughter of the house. She chose a rich violet silk brocade for the undergown. The garment had long, tight sleeves, and a simple round neckline. The sleeveless overgown was the same shade of violet, but embroidered in rich gold thread with a matching fabric girdle. The color but highlighted Maia's pale skin, and rich red-gold hair. The effect would be one of graceful simplicity. Beneath her fine clothes Maia would wear a simple white chemise designed as her undergown with a round neckline and long fitted sleeves. The chemise, however, was fashioned of a very thin silk that would not bunch beneath the brocade. The three older women of the house worked hard on Maia's wedding garments, and Ysbail even embroidered the pointed toes of the bride's shoes, as well as her white silk hose, with small flowers and leaves.

"I shall not have a gown that fine," Junia said enviously, "and Averil was wed in just what she had brought with her to Aberffraw. Yours is surely the most beautiful gown in the whole wide world, Maia."

"I should have chosen a lighter color," Maia answered her younger sister.

"The violet is stunning with your hair and skin," Junia replied. "I think your mother chose well, Sister."

"As do I," said the eldest of the sisters, entering the solar.

"Averil!" Both Maia and Junia turned, squealing with delight.

"Put the baby down, Dilys," Averil said to her maid. "That is what the cradle by the fireplace is for, lass. And try not to wake him, or he'll be howling to suckle again." She turned to her sisters. "I am naught but a milk cow to the little devil." She hugged each of her siblings in turn. "So, Maia Pendragon, you are to be married at last. You are closer to sixteen than fifteen now, I fear. Had you wasted any more time you should have found yourself considered too old, but then there is gossip that this Lord of the Lake has outlived two wives to date, and no children to show for it. Tell me what you know, for I am overcome with curiosity."

"He is handsomer than your husband!" Junia burst out. "And he practices magic! And I like him so very much. I hope my husband is as nice."

Averil laughed. "Well," she said, "that tells me a great deal."

"I cannot live without him," Maia said softly. "It is as if he is the other half of both my heart and my soul."

"So, Sister, you are very much in love, I see," Averil replied. "I do not know if that is good, or if it is bad. I suppose only time will tell."

The harvest gathered in at Everleigh, Averil and Rhys had a day before the wedding day. The Dragon Lord and Gorawen were happy to see that Averil's marriage was a good one despite the manner in which it had been begun. Emrys Llyn arrived at Dragon's Lair in time to celebrate Samhain, the last day of the Celtic calendar year, which was still kept in parts of Wales, Ireland, and Brittany. Maia flew into his arms, and they embraced eagerly.

"They kiss all the time," Junia said, a disapproving tone in her young voice.

Averil looked at her husband, and they smiled knowingly, for they understood what Junia was not yet old enough to understand.

The meal was simple that night. Roast venison, broiled fish, a pottage of lamb and vegetables, bread, cheese, and pears stewed in red wine. And afterwards they all went outdoors to light their fire as the last of the sun sank behind the western hills. And on the hillsides all around them other fires sprang to life as they began to dance about the flames welcoming in the New Year according to the ancient calendar of their ancestors.

Finally, as the night deepened and the air grew very chill, they returned to the hall, leaving the servants to tend to the Samhain fire, which would be allowed to burn itself out eventually. The Dragon Lord looked about his hall, and smiled, well pleased. Two daughters matched, and matched well, to his eye. "Find your beds," he commanded. "The marriage will be celebrated early." He turned to his son-in-law, the lord of Everleigh. "I thank you, Rhys FitzHugh, for bringing the priest with you. And he has not complained that we keep some of the old ways."

"Being a good Christian, my lord, does not mean one must cease revering the customs of our people," Father Kevyn said quietly. "It does our Lord Christ no disservice to do so."

Maia slipped her hand into that of Emrys Llyn. "Come," she said low, and led him from the hall back out into the night.

"Would you seduce me, then?" he teased

her, but his eyes were eagerly devouring her beauty.

"We have had little time alone since your return from Ile du Lac. I would know if you still are certain that you love me, Emrys, my lord," Maia said softly.

"I have loved you since time began, Maia, and I shall love you forever," he told her, and his arms wrapped about her as he bent to kiss her.

But Maia stopped his lips with her fingers. "Did you say those words to Rosyn and Gwynth?" she asked him.

"Never!" he declared vehemently.

"You loved neither as you love me?" Maia persisted.

"I loved neither at all," he told her honestly.

"Then why did you wed? One I can understand, but two wives, and neither loved? I cannot believe your heart that hard, my lord Emrys." Maia told him. "The man who would do that is not the man I love. I want to understand."

"I am ten years your senior, Maia," he began. "It is expected that a man wed for the good of his family. I am alone in the world as both my parents are gone. I thought I must wed that my family continue. It was wrong."

"Why was it wrong?" she asked him.

"Because the voice within me said that

you were out there waiting for me," he told her. "I ignored my true voice, and did what I thought I must do. I allowed my foolish impatience to guide my actions, Maia. Because of that I hold myself responsible for the deaths of Rosyn and Gwynth. If I had listened to my own voice I should not have wed either of them. Rosyn was delicate and frail, poor lass. She was fearful of her own shadow. Gwynth turned greedy and discontent from the moment our vows were spoken. I misjudged them both, and they suffered for it."

Maia looked into his eyes, and she saw genuine regret on the part of Emrys Llyn. "But you are certain that I am the wife for you, my lord Emrys?" Her own look was searching as she scanned his handsome face.

"I swear to you on the sacred memory of our ancestors, Maia, that I have never before loved a woman, but I do love you. I shall never love another. Are you considering withdrawing your consent to my proposal?"

Maia smiled up at him. "Nay, my lord Emrys, I am not. But I needed to hear the words you have just spoken. I have never before loved a man until I loved you. I shall never love another, but it was necessary to my peace of mind that you love me, and I be certain of it."

"God, what a fool I have been!" he cried.

"Aye," Maia agreed quietly, "you have been a fool, but do not fear, Emrys Llyn. I shall not let you make a fool of yourself ever again."

He laughed aloud, and then he kissed her cherry red lips until Maia's head was spinning. "Ohh, Maia, my darling, I have so much love I have stored up over the years to give to you, and I will!"

"But not tonight, my lord," and they heard Argel's voice.

Guiltily they broke apart.

"The marriage ceremony will be early in the morning," the lady of Dragon's Lair said. "Since I doubt you will get much sleep tomorrow night, I should suggest you both find your separate beds now." She took her daughter's hand. "Come, child. Averil will be sharing your bed again tonight while Rhys and the other men sleep in the hall. You will find your place there, Emrys Llyn," Argel told him. Then she led Maia away.

He followed sheepishly behind, but he felt no anger towards Argel for intruding upon them. She was right, and they both knew it. As he entered the hall again he watched as she took her daughter up the staircase, and then he joined the other male guests. Lord Mortimer and his son had arrived just as the Samhain fires were being lit. Roger Mortimer teased Emrys Llyn good-naturedly.

"You have had the advantage of me with Maia, my lord," he said.

"What advantage?" the Lord of the Lake asked, puzzled.

"Well," Roger said thoughtfully, "you are well over six feet in height, while I am under six feet by at least two inches. You are not pockmarked whereas I must keep a beard to hide the few scars of my youth. Your features are chisled, whereas mine resemble that of every Mortimer ever born. We both have blue eyes, black hair, small mouths, and big noses. Your figure is fit. Mine shows the results of a healthy appetite."

Emrys Llyn was laughing now. "Surely my lady is not so shallow as to choose a handsome face over a Mortimer," he teased back.

"I fear the wench did," Roger replied with a grin.

"There is always Junia," the Lord of the Lake said.

"God's mercy, I must take a wife before that little hoyden is old enough!" Roger said. "Besides, her mother is a dragon. I should not have her in the house, but then neither, I suspect, will Junia."

The men all laughed uproariously at his

remark. They congregated companionably about the hearth, drinking the Dragon Lord's good October ale for some time, but then slowly, one by one, each found a bed space, and fell asleep. The hall was soon filled with the sounds of men snoring, and breaking wind.

Emrys Llyn was awakened on his wedding day by his soon-to-be mother-in-law. She beckoned him silently, and he followed her down a flight of stairs into the kitchen, which was beginning to bustle with preparations for the wedding feast.

"I thought you might want to bathe," Argel said to him, pointing to an oaken tub that had been set before the fire. "Let me help you with your garments. I have had your wedding clothes brought." She aided him to disrobe, and got him into the tub where she washed first his dark wavy hair, and then his lean hard body. Maia would not be unhappy with the husband she had chosen, Argel thought as she bathed Emrys Llyn. When she finished she wrapped him in a towel, and sitting him before the fire dried his hair.

"I thank you, lady," he said.

"You bathe regularly I am happy to see," Argel answered him.

"How can you tell?" He was curious.

"You did not stink of yourself, your hair was dusty, but not really dirty," Argel said.

"And your clothing is clean. I am glad, for Maia has a delicate nose, and bathes regularly. We have a bathing chamber, but this will be quicker this morning."

"Then we have much in common, lady," he agreed.

"You no longer need my help," she said with a smile. "Dress yourself. I have put your wedding garments on the rack here. I will go help my daughter. She will be a beautiful bride, Emrys Llyn."

He smiled back at her. "I will care for her as if she were a queen," he promised.

"I know that," Argel responded. "If I did not believe it you should not have her." And leaving him openmouthed with surprise, Argel ran quickly up the stairs.

Chapter 10

Argel found her daughter awake, and sitting up in bed chattering with her two sisters. The conversation ceased as she entered the chamber, and a small smile touched her lips. She suspected they had been speaking of men, and while she did not think Junia old enough yet for such knowledge she supposed the child must learn sooner than later. At least a married older sister would have correct information.

"Good morrow, lasses," she greeted them.

"Good morrow, Lady Mother," they chorused back.

"You must come to the bathing chamber, Maia," her mother said. "I have already seen to Emrys's ablutions, and he will be back in the hall now putting the finishing touches on his garb for today. Hurry, now!"

Maia climbed from the bed. "Yes, Mother," she replied dutifully.

"Averil, make certain that Junia's gown is neat," Argel instructed her husband's eldest child.

"Yes, Lady Mother," Averil answered.

"And see she washes behind her neck and her ears," Argel said as she hurried from the little tower chamber.

"I wash behind my neck," Junia said, sounding just slightly aggrieved.

"When you remember to do so," Averil teased her, climbing from the bed. "Come on, little one, and let us get ready. What have you chosen to wear?"

"I have a new gown!" Junia said excitedly. "It is scarlet, and my mother embroidered the neckline and a girdle for me in gold threads." She jumped from their bed. "I shall look very grown up in it, Averil."

"First we wash," Averil said sternly, and pointed to the pitcher and basin warming in the ashes of the chamber's little hearth.

"You sound more like a grown-up than you ever did," Junia complained.

"I *am* a grown-up, little one. Remember, I have a child, and he will soon need to be fed." She looked into the cradle by their bed where her son, Rhys the younger, lay awake, and playing with his toes. "Let me nurse him first while you wash," she suggested. She picked up the baby, and opening her chemise put him to her breast.

"What does it feel like to nurse a child?" Junia asked, curious.

"Wonderful," Averil said. "And just right. You know when you place your child

297

at your breast that this is how it is meant to be."

"Is it different than when a man sucks on your breasts?" Junia inquired.

Averil blushed, astounded. "Who told you that men do such things?"

"Maia said it happens when a man loves you. Is it different than having your child at your breast?" she asked again.

"Yes," Averil replied, "and that is all I intend saying on the matter. You are too young for such information. I cannot imagine what has possessed Maia to share it with you."

"Maia said I should know, and that as both of you were gone, there would be no one to tell me," Junia responded innocently.

"Maia is wrong," Averil said. "You can always send for me, and I will come, sister. When you meet the right man, and you are certain you are in love, I will tell you whatever you need or want to know. My mother, and our lady mother Argel will also enlighten you, little one. Now put Maia's foolishness from your head, and wash your face and neck. I am almost finished nursing my son, and will want to bathe, too."

Her words were barely spoken when Dilys, her serving woman, arrived to take the baby from Averil so she might dress.

The two sisters washed themselves in the basin, emptying the dirty water out the tower window. Then they dressed themselves. Junia in her scarlet gown with its gold embroidery at the neck and down the narrow girdle. She had a matching ribbon with which she tied back her dark hair. Averil's gown was a sky blue silk brocade with laced-in contrast fabric sleeves. The side of the gown was laced, and she wore no girdle about her still supple waist, the skirt falling gracefully. Her golden hair was parted in the center, and plaited, the braids set around her head. She wore a sheer veil with a silver filigreed chaplet holding it firmly.

Maia dashed back into the chamber, a large drying cloth wrapped about her. "I barely had time to get back upstairs, for the men are all awake now," she said. "Good! You are both dressed. You must help me now. Mother is behind me with my wedding garments."

Argel entered the chamber with the gown and its accessories. She lay her burden carefully upon the bed. "You will not need me to help," she said, knowing full well the sisters wanted these few moments together. "I will go down to see the hall is in readiness." With a smile at the trio, she left them.

They stared at the rich violet gown on the bed.

Finally Averil said, "If you are dry, Sister, you had best put on the chemise."

"Aye," Maia said, and dropping the damp cloth she had been clutching about her she donned the delicate silk chemise.

Averil and Junia lifted the violet silk brocade undergown, and helped their sister into it, lacing the gown up the back. Maia made certain that the sleeves of her chemise did not bunch, or wrinkle the long tight sleeves of her garment. When she was satisfied that all was well she let her sisters slip the sleeveless overgown with its gold thread embroidery over the undergown. Averil affixed the embroidered gold girdle about Maia.

"Ohh, Maia," Junia said worshipfully, "you are the most beautiful girl in the world in that gown!"

"You must brush my hair," Maia said to Averil, but she gave Junia a quick smile of gratitude. She was beginning to be very nervous. Was she doing the right thing in marrying Emrys Llyn? Did she really want a husband who knew magic? What had really happened to his first two wives? How could two such coincidences occur?

Averil brushed her sister's long red-gold hair with several quick swipes of the brush. Then she set a delicate chaplet of golden flowers with tiny jeweled centers atop Maia's head. "From Da. His mother wore it when she wed our grandfather. You will get to wear it one day, Junia. It remains with the house of Pendragon."

"Oh!" Junia said, and her face was wreathed in smiles. Then her little face grew sad. "But you never got to wear it, Averil."

"Yes I did, little one. I carried it with me to Aberffraw. But I've a good man, and 'tis more important than fine jewels as Maia now knows, and you will, too, one day."

There was a knock upon the door, and Dilys stuck her head into the chamber. "The lord says the eldest and the youngest are to come into the hall. He will come for the bride in a minute or two."

Averil and Junia each took the time to hug their sister, kissing her on both cheeks. Then they departed the tower chamber, and went down into the hall as they had been bidden. Seeing them, Merin Pendragon went to fetch the bride. He found Maia weeping in her chamber.

"What is the matter, daughter?" he demanded. "Will you go to your husband with a sad face? The priest will think we are forcing the union."

"I don't know if I am doing the right thing," Maia sobbed, and she flung herself into her father's arms.

Grasping the girl by her upper arms he set her back from him. "You will stain my

301

very best cotte with your tears, lass," he told her. "Have you stopped loving the man?"

"Naaay." Maia wept noisily. "I can see myself wed to no other."

"Why is it that women never make any sense?" the Dragon Lord muttered to himself. "Daughter, the Lord of the Lake, your family and our guests wait below. Either you are marrying the man or you are not, but make your decision now!" he roared at her.

Startled out of her hysteria Maia looked up at her father questioningly. Then she drew a deep breath, and said as she wiped her face, "Of course I am marrying Emrys, my lord father. Who else would I have?"

Merin Pendragon swore beneath his breath a word Maia had never before heard. In fact, she wasn't even certain she recognized such a word. A vein throbbed visibly in Merin's left temple, and then he said, "Well, then, lass, come along." And he escorted her from the little tower room down into the hall of his keep.

The hall had been decorated in branches of green pine, and late flowers from the keep's sheltered garden. It was a rainy morning, but candles burned everywhere lighting the space with a warm glow. Father Kevyn from Everleigh awaited the bridal, and with reluctance the Dragon

Lord handed his daughter off to the Lord of the Lake. Together the couple stood before the priest, and pledged themselves to each other in marriage. Argel stood between her husband and their son, weeping softly. Behind them Gorawen and Ysbail, their daughters by their sides, stood quietly watching with the remainder of the guests. When Father Kevyn finally pronounced that Maia and Emrys Llyn were husband and wife a great cheer arose from those assembled in the hall.

The servants who had been watching from the shadows now began to bring the food into the hall that the wedding feast might begin. There were eggs poached in a herbed cream sauce; fresh trout served on a bed of watercress; there was bacon fried crisp; trenchers of oat stirabout mixed with dried apple, honey and heavy cream; there were newly baked loaves of bread; crocks of sweet butter, plum jam, and a fine hard cheese. A great dish of apples baked in sugar and cinnamon and swimming in golden cream was the last dish offered. There was wine, October ale, a carafe of honied mead, and a jug of sweet cider to drink.

Many toasts were raised to the bridal couple. The three sisters entertained the gathering with their musical talents, and Brynn Pendragon sang for them in his high sweet voice. In late afternoon another meal was served consisting of roasted boar, venison, lamb, ducks cooked crisp with plum sauce, lettuces steamed in white wine, a pottage of rabbit, onion, and carrots, bread, butter and cheese. There was more wine, ale, mead, and cider to drink. More toasts were offered. It was already dark outside when the servants brought in a dish of pears stewed in wine, and crisp sugar wafers. The guests were overfull of good food and drink. Lord Mortimer had fallen asleep by the warm fire. Merin Pendragon was playing chess with Rhys FitzHugh, and the other men were dicing. No one noticed when Argel and the other women quietly escorted the bride from the hall.

They led her upstairs to the guest chamber in the opposite tower from where she had slept her entire life. They took her beautiful wedding gown from her, and folded it neatly in her trunk, which was at the foot of the bed. They divested Maia of her delicate silk chemise. Naked, she washed her face and hands, and scrubbed her teeth with a cloth.

"Come and get into bed, daughter," Argel said. "If you have no questions to ask of us we will leave you to await your husband."

"My sister has explained all, Mother," Maia said politely.

Argel nodded, and then each of the women and Junia kissed Maia upon her cheek, and wishing her well, departed the bedchamber.

Maia sat straight up in the bed. She hoped that the bedsheet she gave her father in the morning was as bloody as the one Averil had offered him the previous year. Her maidenhood must be attested to very clearly. She remembered how all the men had brought a naked Rhys to Averil. Would they do the same again? Then to her surprise the door to the bedchamber opened, and her husband stepped quietly inside. He threw the bolt, locking them in, and then coming to her, took her hands in his, and kissed them.

"I am glad the men did not strip you naked," she said softly.

"They are either asleep, or gambling," he told her. "They did not even see me go. I waited to see your mother return to the hall." He sat down on the bed next to her. "Now, my love, it is rare that I use serious magic, but tonight I would make an exception with your permission."

"What would you do, my lord Emrys?" she asked him.

"This chamber is small, and its little fire gives scant warmth on a late autumn's night, Maia. The chamber you and I will share at Ile du Lac is spacious and warm. I would not offend your family, but I should far prefer to spend our wedding night there than here, my love. With your permission, of course." His dark eyes met hers.

"Shall we be more private?" she asked softly.

He nodded. "There will be none to hear our cries of pleasure," he told her.

"You are certain we will have pleasure, then?" She teased him gently with a small smile, her emerald eyes dancing.

He nodded again, and a slow smile lit his features. "Aye, I am sure, Maia."

"We will not be missed?" she asked him.

"No one will disturb us on our wedding night, my love, and we will awaken, I promise you, in this bed on the morrow," he told her.

"Take us home, then, my lord Emrys, that you may begin to teach me what it is to be a woman," Maia told him. She closed her eyes.

The Lord of the Lake wrapped his arms about his wife, whispering, "Do not be afraid, Maia," and his right hand moved from the top of their heads downward.

Her head spun for just a quick moment, and then she heard his voice.

"We are home, my love," he said.

Maia opened her eyes to find herself in a beautiful room with a large fireplace in which a bright fire was even now burning.

The bed in which she now sat was oak, and it was carved all about with beasts, flowers, vines and leaves. The bed curtains were a dark forest green velvet. Though it had been raining at Dragon's Lair, she could see the moon shining on the waters of the lake through her windows here. The pillows behind her were encased in silk, and very soft. The silk coverlet she clutched to her breasts was filled with down, and light as a feather. The linens on the bed smelled of lavender.

"Aye, this is much nicer," she said softly.

"And there is no one to hear us," he murmured, kissing her ear.

She shivered. "If you are going to do things like that, Emrys, my love," she told him, "then you had best get out of your clothes."

He grinned, arose from her side, and began to undress. "My magic does not frighten you, does it, Maia?" he said.

"Nay," she answered. "Is not our land of Wales steeped in magic? We have both grown up with magic all about us."

"But I use my magic," he said, "and I know far more than most folk."

"You love me, and I love you. 'Tis all I care about," Maia answered him. "Tomorrow when we leave Dragon's Lair, can we come home using magic instead of traveling two days? I should like it if we could."

He nodded. "It shall be as you desire, Maia."

"And you will show me the wall of portraiture of our ancestors that you revealed to my father?" she asked him.

"I will," he promised as he pulled off his chemise.

"Oh," Maia said as she saw him completely naked for the first time. "You are very beautiful, my lord husband. Your limbs are perfectly shaped."

He laughed. "Another might have admired my other attributes," he teased her.

"They are in goodly proportion, too," she replied with a small smile, "but I should hope they would be bigger eventually. Averil says the manroot grows in relation to the excitement my body generates in you."

He climbed into bed next to her. "She is correct," he said. Then he embraced her with one arm while he tipped her face up to him with his other hand. His lips descended gently upon Maia's, and they kissed a long, slow kiss.

"That is a nice beginning," she told him when his mouth freed hers at last. One of her hands caressed the nape of his neck. The other pressed flat against his broad smooth chest. She could feel the prickles of excitement on the back of his neck.

He smiled down into her eyes, and for a

moment found himself lost within her gaze. It surprised him, for no woman had ever had such an effect upon him. Was she the one? He did not dare even entertain the thought. The hand that had been upon his chest now reached up, and her fingers brushed across his lips. He knew that she was an innocent, and yet her actions were born of an instinct deep within the female soul. He took the little hand in his, and kissed each fingertip. "Do you love me, Maia?" he asked her.

"Oh, yes, Emrys!" she answered him. "From that first moment, my dear lord, when you entered my dreams." Then a blush suffused her cheeks as she boldly asked, "Do you love me, my Lord of the Lake? Really love me? Not just because you needed to take another wife, but do you love me above all others? Would my loss break your heart?" Her young face was anxious for his answer.

"Yes!" he answered her without hesitation, and then he kissed her again.

His mouth was hot upon hers. The kiss was deep, and very passionate. More so than any he had offered her before. It was as if he sought to prove his words to her so that there would never be any doubt in her heart as to how he felt about her. Her arms slid about his neck, and she arched her lush young body, pressing against him. Her head spun with the excitement his kiss was generating within her. She felt his tongue pushing past her lips suddenly. Instinctively those lips parted for him. She shivered hard at the first contact his tongue made with hers, but she easily caught the sense of what he wanted from her, and she gave it to him willingly.

Then his kisses were blazing a burning trail down her throat. He kissed the hollow in her throat where her pulse beat wildly with her own accelerating excitement. Lingering there he felt the throb beneath his lips. Unable to help himself he licked at the graceful column of her neck, reveling in the taste of her before moving on to worship at her wonderfully round breasts. They were deliciously full breasts for a girl. His kissed them first, then licked at them. Then his mouth closed over a pert nipple, and he suckled upon her eagerly.

She gave a little cry, but the sound held no distress in it. His lips tugging at her nipple was the most exciting thing that had ever happened to her. Oh, he had fondled her, and suckled before, but she had always been clothed. This was different, and it was but the beginning of the passion they would share tonight. She caressed the dark head at her breast, and murmured, "Yes!" She could lie here with him like this forever, Maia thought, and she was not afraid of what was to come.

He lifted his head from her nipple. His dark eyes were glazed with his own desire. "You have the most perfect breasts, my love," he told her. "I shall be jealous of our children." Then he lowered his head, and moved to enjoy her other breast.

"I feel so strange," she told him.

"How?" he asked, and licked the nipple he had been suckling upon.

"The hidden spot tingles, Emrys," she said.

"Does it?" He smiled. "That is good."

"I want something," she spoke softly.

"What?" he asked her, and he took the nipple in his mouth, and sucked hard upon it again.

"I do not know," she admitted, "but my need is growing greater with each passing minute, Emrys."

"I am being selfish," he replied. He kissed her breasts, and his head moved to kiss the lush young body she offered him now. "I want to salute every part of you," he told her. "You are so delicious, Maia, I cannot resist you."

"Will it soothe my need?" she inquired.

"Nay, not right away," he told her. "It will, in fact, but increase your desire, for that is what it is. Your desire is rising as I love your luscious body. But if you will trust me, my adorable wife, I will quench your passion shortly."

"I will trust you," she said.

He turned her over, laying her flat on her belly, and pushing her flowing hair from her neck he kissed the soft nape of it. He planted kisses across her shoulders, and then his warm tongue traced the outline of her spine down to her buttocks, which he kissed, each in its turn.

"You are making me blush," she cried, giggling as he licked her thighs, and nibbled his way down her shapely calves. "Ohh!" she felt his hot kiss on the arch of each foot, and then he surprised her as he turned her onto her back once again, nibbling at her toes. "Emrys!"

"What?" he replied.

"Would you eat me up?" she demanded.

"If I could and yet still have you, aye! I know you are a virgin, and yet you have no fear of me, or my actions," he told her.

"I love you," she answered him, "and you love me. Why would I be afraid?"

"Maia! Maia!" he murmured her name, and then he was kissing her mouth again, hungrily, his long lean body covering hers, feeling the heat between them.

She felt it then. The hard length that was his manhood. It was no longer small and soft. It was big and it was very hard. Her heart hammered in her ears. This, then, would be the moment as Averil had explained. It was exciting and terrifying all at once, and yet as she had told him, she was not afraid. She knew he but waited for her assent. "It is time, Emrys," she whispered in his ear, "isn't it?"

"Aye," he said as softly.

"This is what the longing is about." He was spreading her thighs.

"Aye," he told her.

She felt the wet tip of him pressing against her own moisture. Her breath was coming in short pants of anticipation.

He pressed forward, the head of his lover's lance pushing slowly, ever so gently into her. She was so wonderfully tight. He moved slowly, slowly, opening her to his pleasure. And then suddenly he could go no farther, for he had reached the barrier of her maidenhead. She winced slightly, and he knew it was kinder to penetrate her quickly than wait any longer. He pulled back just enough, and then thrust hard, shattering her innocence in a single swift movement.

Maia cried out. The pain was cruel and sharp. She struggled to dislodge him, and her nails raked down his back in an effort at her defense. He held her tightly, and whispered hotly against her mouth, but she didn't know if she believed him when he told her the pain would be quickly gone. She sobbed into his shoulder. But then the pain faded as quickly as it had come, and Maia was very aware of his manhood within her. "Oh!" she cried softly, and without further explanation he began to move within her. The rhythm was intoxicating, and the heat he generated within her was amazing. She was astounded that she did not burst into flame. "Oh! Oh, Emrys!" she cried out again. He ground himself into her, and suddenly her head was spinning. Stars appeared, and burst behind her closed eyelids, and she was, without warning, racked with such pleasure that Maia thought surely she was dying. And then he was kissing her again. Her mouth, her closed eyelids, her face.

"You are amazing," he told her. "For a virgin to have obtained such heights her first time! It is surely because I love you, my darling." He lifted himself from atop her.

"It is because I love you, too," she agreed, curling herself against him. "Averil did not explain this all to me. She said I must experience it to understand, and she was right."

He arose from their bed, and going to a carved oak sideboard poured them each a goblet of rich, sweet wine. Maia sat up against the pillows, and accepted one of the goblets as he returned to their bed. "It will strengthen you," he told her.

"Do I need to be strengthened?" she asked him, smiling.

He nodded. "I will never get enough of you, Maia, but I will try!"

She sipped her wine, looking at him seductively over her goblet. "Nor I you!" she told him. "Why did you wait so long to come to me, my husband?"

"I was a fool, my darling. I did not listen to my own heart, and voice within. I will never again do that no matter how desperate I believe the situation to be," he swore to her.

"I cannot believe that I am so happy," Maia told him softly. "I cannot believe that it is right to be so happy. Tell me I am not being greedy?"

"You are not being greedy," he replied.

When they had finished their wine Maia arose from their bed. She found a basin and warmed water on a shelf built into the hearth. There was a soft cloth next to the basin. Gathering it all up she returned to her husband, and bathed his male member. Then she bathed herself. "Gorawen says it is necessary after passion for passion may reignite once again, and there should be no barriers between lovers." She stared at the brown water in the ewer, realizing it was her own blood. Her eye went quickly to the sheet beneath them, and saw the great evidence of her lost maidenhood. A little smile touched her lips. The stain was even greater than Averil's. Her father would be proud.

"Do you understand what Gorawen meant by no barriers?" he asked her.

Maia shook her head. "Nay, but I know you will teach me, Emrys, my lord."

He nodded. "Aye, I will, my love, but perhaps not quite yet. Put your basin aside now, and come back into bed with me. I am going to need to make love to you again before we sleep this night."

She looked and saw his manhood once again beginning to stir with his longings for her. Maia set the basin and cloth down back on the hearth ledge. Then she returned into her husband's welcoming arms. "Do not linger this time, my lord," she told him. "I am already hot for you, and need you within my lover's sheath."

His fingers began to play almost at once with her. He found the tiny nub of her womanly jewel, and he teased it with a single finger. Maia moaned with her rising excitement. Soon she was wet with juices, and he pushed two fingers into her sheath even as he pushed his tongue into her ear, whispering, "You are a shameless wench, my fair wife. Totally and utterly shameless!"

"Would you have me any other way, Emrys, my husband?" she taunted him low. "Come! You long to fill me with your own hunger. Do it! Do it now! Ahhhhh, yes!" He was inside her again, and instinctively Maia wrapped her legs about him that he might push himself even farther within her.

"Ah, Maia!" he cried low. "How I want you, my love! How I want you!"

Their entwined bodies heaved and thrust creating a heat that almost caused steam to arise from them, so great was their lust for one another. Their mouths were bruised with their kisses. They ached with their mutual pleasure. He filled her with his hot juices, and she craved more. He cried out with his desire as she did. Finally exhausted the lovers fell into a deep sleep, and when they awoke in the light of the dawn, they were back in the tower room at Dragon's Lair as he had promised her.

Maia stretched her limbs with a contented sigh, noting that the little chamber was cold. She arose, and moving quickly across the stone floor added a bit of wood to the glowing coals. The fire sprang up once again. She quickly snatched the basin from the ashes with it's water lukewarm from the coals. Then she washed herself again, her face first, then the rest of her. Opening the shutters she dumped the basin of water and refilled it from the pitcher in the coals. Then she gently shook Emrys's shoulder. "Wake up, my lord. The sun is already arising."

"If you do not put on some clothing, lady, I may never come forth from our bed, and neither will you!" He reached for her, but laughing, Maia dodged his grasp.

"I have water for you to bathe in," she said. Then she drew on her silk chemise, noting that there was a simple nut brown gown on the same chair with it. She drew the garment on over her head. "You must lace me," she told her husband. "I cannot reach."

"I should rather unlace you," he said mischievously.

"Emrys! My father will want to see I have survived a night with you, and he will want to see the sheet, for you know he will fly it from the window above this room." Then Maia paled. "Emrys! We were not here, but at Ile du Lac. What are we to do?"

He climbed from the bed, and she could see the sheet beneath as pristine as it had been the night before, but with a wave of his hand the stain of her innocence appeared. "I have just shifted it from there to here," he said calmly. "Now, come, wife, and let me fasten your gown for you."

She felt his fingers threading the laces, and the gown was made fast. "It is very convenient to have a husband with such

318

talents as yours, my lord," Maia told him with a smile, and he grinned back at her.

"Help me dress, woman," he said.

"First you wash," she returned.

"That I will do myself, for I recall when you did it for me last night it but led to further delights. I want to go home today. Do you?"

"Aye," Maia told him, "I do. Can we ride until sunset, and then travel the rest of the way by means of your magic, my lord?"

He nodded. "The day is fair, and while I can think of a nicer way to spend our day, I will acquiesce, my love." Then he took up the damp cloth and began to wash.

"What will it be like to live at Ile du Lac?" she asked him. "Is it like other households, Emrys? Will I manage our servants, and see to the other chores a good wife does for her husband and family? You do not use magic all the time, do you?"

"Nay," he replied. "The household is yours to manage as you wish, my love. The servants will all obey you. I but request you use Sion to guide your path until you are certain of how to manage the castle."

"Of course," she agreed. Then she asked him, "Do you have many visitors?"

"Nay," he said. "Ile du Lac is far off the more traveled tracks, Maia, but your family may come to visit us whenever you so desire it. I do not want you unhappy or lonely, my love. But you will make friends among the castle's inhabitants. Not all who inhabit Ile du Lac are servants. I have distant relations who live in the castle. Most are from among the Fair Folk."

"Averil has Fair Folk in her heritage. That is why she is so golden," Maia said. "I am just an ordinary lass."

"There is nothing ordinary about you, my love," the Lord of the Lake told his wife. Then having completed his toilette he dressed himself in a clean chemise, braies, and cotte from the trunk at the foot of the bed.

Maia took her pear wood hairbrush, and brushed his wavy black hair into a semblance of order. "Your hair is as thick as mine," she noted.

He took the brush from her hand, and seating her upon the room's single stool began to brush out her red-gold locks. "Today, my lady, you will bind your hair up as is fitting for a married woman. I love the color of your hair, Maia. It is like the sunset." He set the brush down.

Maia affixed her hair in a soft knot at the nape of her neck, and turning, smiled up at him. "Does this please you, my lord?" she asked.

"It suits you well," he replied.

"I did not want to wear plaits wrapped about my head as Averil does," Maia told him. "I wanted my own fashion."

"The plaits suit Averil, for she is tall, but this love knot suits you, for you are more elegant," he flattered her.

"Do not ever say that in front of Averil." Maia laughed as she gathered the sheet from their bed.

They left their tower, and descended into the great hall below where their family awaited them. With quiet ceremony Maia handed the bedsheet to her father, and while Argel winced at the great stain upon it, Merin Pendragon congratulated his daughter on her entry into womanhood. Then he left the hall to hang the sheet himself from the roof of the tower above the bridal chamber. When he returned the Dragon Lord invited all to table that they might break their fast.

After the meal had been eaten the guests began to depart. First Lord Mortimer, and his son, Roger, who had been betrothed in early autumn to a cousin. Then Averil, Rhys and their party. Maia cradled her nephew for a long moment.

"Mayhap by this time next year," she said, "I shall have a son."

"You look so happy," Averil said softly. "I am glad that you have found love, dearest sister."

"Are you happy?" Maia replied. "Rhys certainly looks content."

"Aye, I am," Averil admitted, "though I did not think I would be. I believe little Mary's death brought us closer, and she would be glad, God assoil her sweet soul."

"Emrys and I wish to keep the Yuletide at Ile du Lac," Maia said. "Will you try to come? Please!"

"We will try, but you know the weather can be difficult in December, Sister."

"If it is, you will come for midsummer," Maia responded. Then the two sisters hugged one another.

"Do not forget me!" Junia cried, pushing between them. "Oh, we shall never be together again! I do not think I can bear it!" She hugged both of her elder sisters.

"We cannot forget you, little one," Averil said, and Maia nodded her agreement.

"Will you invite me to Ile du Lac soon, sister?" Junia pleaded.

"You shall come at Christmas if the weather allows, and if not then, in the spring I shall send for you," Maia promised, brushing the tears from Junia's rosy cheeks. "Now, do not weep, little one. It is not the end of the world, and soon you will find love and marriage yourself."

"I hate being twelve!" Junia declared passionately.

Her older sisters laughed at their sibling's remark.

"You will be fifteen before you know it,"

Averil said. "Now before Rhys begins to roar, I bid you both farewell." And turning she left them to join her party.

Now just the remainder of the immediate family lingered in the hall of Dragon's Lair. Emrys Llyn looked at his bride, and she nodded.

"Now it is our turn to depart," Maia said quietly.

Argel began to weep. "I cannot bear to see you go, my daughter," she said.

"My place is with my husband now, Mother. Is that not what you have taught me? I am not so far away that you cannot visit me, but I will be honest with you. I am eager to go to my new home." She put a comforting arm about Argel, and kissed her soft cheek.

"I will send a troop of men with you," Merin Pendragon said.

"There is no need," the Lord of the Lake told his father-in-law with a meaningful look. "We shall be safe. Our path has been cleared by my own people. We shall reach Ile du Lac by nightfall."

The Dragon Lord nodded. He needed no further explanation. "Maia's possessions have been sent to your castle previously so there is naught for you to do but go now before my wife floods the keep with her tears." He turned to his daughter. "Make your farewells now, Maia, and be quickly gone."

323

"Yes, Da," she said with a little smile. Then she embraced Gorawen, and Ysbail, and Junia a final time.

"Remember your promises to Junia," Ysbail said sharply.

Not in the least offended, Maia nodded. "I will, lady. I think her no less my sister because you are her mother." Maia embraced her mother a final time, and then her father. "Farewell to you all," she said, and taking Emrys Llyn's hand she walked from the hall and out into the courtyard where their horses awaited them in the cold sunny air of the morning. She did not look back as she rode away from Dragon's Lair. It was her past. It was her future that far more interested Maia.

Chapter 11

"He should be mine, old woman! Why is it that Emrys cannot see that I love him?" demanded the beautiful girl with the sable hair.

"Be silent, Morgant!" Drysi said sharply. "It has never been your fate to wed with the Lord of the Lake. Why do you persist in this quest?"

"My blood is every bit as good as hers is," Morgant replied angrily.

"Your blood is curst, girl, and you know it!" Drysi replied. "You descend from Mordred, who betrayed Arthur."

"Did not Lancelot betray Arthur as well?" Morgant said slyly.

"Aye, he did, and he lived to bitterly regret his actions. He tried to attone for them. Mordred neither regretted what he did, nor did he repent of his wickedness," Drysi answered her companion.

"Mordred was Arthur's son, and so I descend from Arthur too," Morgant said.

"The Lord of the Lake loves his wife. But more important, she loves him. She will be tested soon, and when her love is proven, the curse will finally be broken on Lancelot's descendants," Drysi said.

"But then everything will change for us," Morgant replied. "I do not want things to change, old woman!"

"Change is the natural order, child," Drysi responded.

"Perhaps she will fail the test," Morgant said slyly. "Or perhaps she will die like the other two."

"You think I do not know what you did?" Drysi said.

"But you kept silent, old woman," Morgant murmured low.

"The other two were not worthy of him, and they did not love him completely. The lady Maia does. Let it be, Morgant, or I will tell the lord what you have done."

"I wish I were all fairy, and not half-human," Morgant whined.

"You are what you are," Drysi said. "But remember I hold a certain amount of power in this house. Behave yourself or I will see you punished."

"I hate you!" Morgant said fiercely.

"I know," Drysi replied with a wicked smile. "Now go, for your puling complaints are beginning to bore me."

Morgant slammed from the old woman's tower apartment.

"She is dangerous, mistress," Drysi's servant, Efa, said. "Why do you not have the lord send her from Ile du Lac?"·

"I should have to tell him why I was asking such a favor," Drysi responded. "I made a great mistake when I did not tell Emrys that Morgant killed his first two wives. Now I am afraid to say it lest I lose his love. I have never before betrayed him. I pray that the Lady tests this new bride, and she proves worthy, before Morgant can cause any more difficulty. If the curse is lifted, then the lord will send Morgant into one of the two worlds where she must remain. She longs to be all fairy, and he knows it."

"You should tell him, mistress. He would forgive you. You are old, and made an error in judgement. The lord loves you as he would his mother."

"I cannot," Drysi said. "I am truly afraid that he would not forgive me."

Efa sighed. "Then at least warn our master that Morgant longs for him, and is jealous of the young mistress," she suggested. "You know that she has made herself the lady Maia's confidant, and that poor lady, eager for a friend, has embraced her totally."

"I will attempt to warn him that the young mistress should beware," Drysi agreed.

But Emrys Llyn, while listening to his

old nurse's admonition, said, "I know that Morgant fancies herself in love with me, but she has eyes, Drysi. She can see that I love my wife. Maia misses the company of her sisters, and Morgant is her only friend. If I take away that friend, she will pine away. Morgant keeps Maia's mind from a child, for my wife longs to have one. She is distressed she has not yet conceived."

"Nor will she, as you well know, until the curse is lifted, my lad," Drysi said dourly. "Surely you cannot doubt your wife's love for you, Emrys. You must call the Lady, and let her test Maia Pendragon. The sooner it is done, the better off we will all be, and you know that I speak truth."

"I am not ready for Maia to know the truth, Drysi," Emrys Llyn said. "It is too soon. Let her remain innocent for a while longer."

"The longer you wait, the longer Morgant has to cause trouble, Emrys," the old lady told him firmly. "And she will. Of that, you may be certain."

The Winter Solstice was celebrated, but Maia's family could not get to Ile du Lac, for the early snows had been heavy. Strangely she did not mind. She had her new friend, Morgant, a half-human, half-fairy girl, keeping her company by day. And she had her husband making love to her in the nights. Life at Ile du Lac was almost too perfect, Maia thought, as she watched the snow falling onto the frozen lake. If she lacked one thing, it was the hope of a child. Was she to be like her mother? Slow to conceive? She voiced her fears to Morgant as they sat together in the Great Hall one afternoon.

Morgant's half-fairy blood gave her a piquant look. Her eyes were almond-shaped, and a silvery-gold in color. Her skin was so pale it was almost translucent. And her long, sable locks fell in rippling waves to below her buttocks. Morgant made no secret of the fact she was beautiful.

"You are a year older than I am," Maia said to her. "I do not know why you have not been wed. You are even more beautiful than my sister Averil."

"It takes a brave man to wed a half-fairy girl," Morgant replied. "And to give her a child. The lord, your husband, is a magical man, though I have never heard it said he has fairy blood. Perhaps he does, and that is why he will not give you a child. You should ask him why you do not conceive. I think it very sad that you want a child and the lord will not give you one."

"Perhaps I am like my mother," Maia responded. "I have told you how difficult it was for her to conceive."

"It is said such weaknesses usually skip several generations," Morgant murmured.

"I still believe you must speak with the lord himself. You do love him, and he says he loves you. But then, men always say they love you. It doesn't mean they really do. I mean — didn't the boys who courted you cry love?"

"Nay," Maia said. "They didn't. The only man who has ever claimed to love me is my husband. And I do believe him when he says it, for Emrys is not a man to lie."

"No, no, of course not!" Morgant said, realizing that Maia was not as cow-eyed over her husband as to be led astray. "The Lord of the Lake is a most honorable man."

But some of Morgant's words had disturbed Maia. She knew little about these things, but was it possible that Emrys was withholding a child from her? She would ask him, for she wanted to give her husband an heir. After they had made love that night, and Maia lay contented in her husband's arms, she spoke up.

"Why is it I cannot conceive of your seed, my lord? Do you withhold our child from me? And if you do, why would you? I love you with all my heart, and I have no doubt in your love for me."

Emrys Llyn sighed. He would have to tell her the truth, and while he had told Drysi earlier that he did not believe Maia was ready for the truth, he supposed he had no choice now. He had hated keeping the secret from her, but he feared when she learned the truth she might be sickened by the knowledge of it. "Come," he said to her. "Get up, and I will tell you all you need to know, Maia, but I would look into your face when I speak on it, my love." Helping her up, he wrapped her in a velvet robe lined in softest rabbit fur. He donned a matching robe, and then pouring them each a goblet of wine he led her to the cushioned window seat overlooking the lake.

"Do you know what my name means, Maia?" he asked her.

"It means immortal," she answered him.

"Aye, it does." He sipped deeply from the goblet. "You know me as a descendant of Lancelot and the Lady of the Lake, but I am not their descendant. I am their son."

Now it was Maia who drank deeply, almost draining her goblet empty. "How can this be? Lancelot lived centuries ago, my lord."

"My father was a man who enjoyed women greatly," the Lord of the Lake began. "That is why it was so easy for Arthur's witch-sisters to enchant him to seduce the king's wife even though he was wed to my mother at the time. But there was another woman in his life as well. She was the youngest of the king's half-sisters.

Her name was Elaine, and she was the Lady of Shallot. He knew her before he knew my mother, and I believe at one time he held her in some small affection."

"How old are you?" Maia asked him, staring hard.

Emrys Llyn had to laugh, but the sound was a rueful one, not one filled with humor. "I am twenty-five, my love, as you know. Let me continue on, and I will explain further."

Maia nodded. "Please do," she said, but then she reached out and took his hand in hers. "This is indeed a tale of magic, my lord."

"Aye, magic has much to do with it," he agreed, and he lifted the hand that had taken his to his lips to kiss it tenderly. "The Lady of the Lake rarely left her own castle beneath the lake. Her duty had been to guard the sword, Excalibur, until Arthur could claim it. But she was curious at all she heard about the court at Camelot, and she finally went to see it. She arrived as befitted her station, in a great train of fairy folk. The moment she saw my father she fell in love with him, and he with her — at least briefly, for Lancelot's heart could never belong to just one woman, as many learned to their great sadness.

"Yet he loved the Lady enough to ask her to be his wife, and in doing so set in motion much of the tragedy that was to follow. The Lady of Shallot was at first furious at my father's betrayal of her. There had been talk of his marrying this youngest of the king's half-sisters, although nothing formal had been agreed upon. So my father married my mother at Camelot in the presence of King Arthur, Queen Gwynefr, and all their court. And they returned here, where my mother raised up this castle for my father. She was already with child by the time they returned from Camelot.

"They spent a few months together, and then the king called my father back to his side, for Lancelot was the greatest of his warriors. While he had been gone, however, the king's half-sisters decided to revenge themselves upon Lancelot for his betrayal of Elaine, the youngest of the trio. They worked a spell that easily caused my father to fall in love with Arthur's queen. You know that story so I need not recall it to you."

Maia nodded. She was actually quite fascinated by her husband's tale, and she wanted to know more. She sipped at the wine left in her cup.

"One evening, my mother appeared at the court with her newborn son wrapped and swaddled. The Lady of Shallot made certain that her rival knew that once again Lancelot was betraying the woman he claimed to have loved enough to wed. Then Elaine laid a curse upon me to revenge herself upon my father. I would reach the age of twenty-five, but I would grow no older. I would be a man who if he knew love would suffer, for should I love, the woman would age as the years passed, yet I would not. I would see all I cared for grow old, and die, yet I would not. I would be young, handsome, immortal. Yet I would forever lose those I loved, and never know the peace that comes with true love. He shall be known as Emrys Llyn, Elaine of Shallot told my mother. The Immortal of the Lake, though in time people will forget how he came by the name."

The Lord of the Lake refilled his goblet, and his wife's, before continuing on with his dark tale. "The next day Elaine, the Lady of Shallot, drank poison, and laying herself in a richly caparisoned barge in the river by her tower home, floated down past the battlements of Camelot beneath which she breathed her last, and finally out to sea where she disappeared beyond the horizon. My mother was furious. My father was devastated by the havoc his behavior was wreaking. He returned with her to Ile du Lac to do penance. But he was still troubled by the enchantment surrounding him.

"My mother, of course, despite her great magic, could not entirely undo the curse placed upon me by the king's half-sister, but she was able to amend it slightly," the Lord of the Lake explained to his wife.

"How?" Maia asked her husband.

"While I am a half-human, half-magical man, my humanity is stronger. Sons born of human fathers to fairy women are. Daughters, however, who are half-fairy, are more of the fairy kingdom. My mother knew that I would fall in love over the centuries to come and so she ameliorated the curse upon me. When I reached the age of twenty-five, Ile du Lac and all in it were put into a deep sleep by my mother. She then rendered the castle invisible, and so we all remained until five years ago. In this way, we were protected from outsiders and others who might discover that I never aged.

"Then she said that when the day came that a woman could love me no matter my history; and would be willing to sacrifice herself for me; and if I were willing to renounce my fairy side in favor of the mortal one, the curse placed upon me by the Lady of Shallot should be lifted, and dissolved. I would then begin to live a totally mortal life as a mortal man. I should age as other men. I should beget heirs."

"And your magic?" Maia asked.

"If I am mortal, my dearest, my magic will be gone," he told her.

"I don't care!" Maia said. "As long as we may be together for ever and always, Emrys, I shall be content. I never sought anything other than a husband who would love me as I loved him, and children of our union. Let your magic be gone, that we may live as ordinary mortals."

"Then," he said, "you will have to meet the Lady of the Lake herself, my love. It is she who must be convinced of your sincerity before I may be released from this ancient curse." He drew her into his arms. "I knew you would be the one to free me, Maia! I knew it. Drysi said I must seek a female descendant of Arthur who would love me for myself. I did not know of any but for Morgant, and I could never love her."

"Morgant descends from Arthur? I did not know that," Maia said softly.

"She comes through Mordred's line," Emrys explained. "She was very surprised to learn of your family's existence."

"What will happen to the fairy folk when we live as mortals?" Maia asked.

"They will return to their own world," he answered her.

"Even those with only half-fairy blood?" she persisted.

"They will be given the choice, but most will prefer to return to fairyland."

"And you, my lord husband," Maia said

softly. "Are you truly willing to give up your mother's heritage to live as a full mortal? To grow old? To know pain and sorrow?" She reached up and touched his smooth cheek. "I love you, Emrys, and I know in my heart that I shall never love another. But this is a very serious decision that you must now make. You cannot go back once you have, can you?"

"Nay, I cannot, Maia," he told her.

"Be certain what you want, my husband," she warned him. "If you would remain as you are, never growing old, I will understand."

"But you would grow old," he reminded her.

"Aye, I would," she agreed.

"And if we had children they would grow old as well. You would all leave me behind, Maia. I should rather grow old myself than lose you," he told her.

"How will your mother test me?" Maia asked him.

"I do not know," he admitted. "It did not come to that with my other wives. They never knew the full story. I tried to tell Rosyn, but she fled me."

"I am afraid," Maia said, "but on the morrow you must call your mother to us. We dare not wait if this is to be done, Emrys. There will be those among your people who will not be happy to see this magical world of yours come to an end."

He nodded. "You are right, my love."

They remained seated in the window looking out over the lake for some minutes. The snow had stopped falling, and the skies had cleared. The moon silvered the landscape, and the stars twinkled brightly in the black night sky. The lake was frozen. Maia wondered how the Lady of the Lake would emerge from her underwater home under the circumstances. Well, she would know on the morrow. She began to feel sleepy again, and her head drooped upon her husband's shoulder. He smiled down at her, and picking her up, carried her to their bed.

"Do not call the Lady without me," she murmured to him as he laid her down.

"I won't," he said, and he gently kissed her lips before joining her.

It was almost dawn, but yet still dark when Emrys arose and dressed himself. He slipped from their bedchamber, and climbed to the south tower of Ile du Lac to speak with Drysi. She was awake, and obviously expecting him. "I have told her," he said as he entered the old woman's chamber.

Drysi nodded. "And what said she?"

"That she loved me, no matter. That if I chose to remain as I am she would be willing to grow old by my side," he replied to his old nurse.

"She is the one," Drysi said. "I knew it from the beginning."

"How did you know of the Pendragon family, Drysi?" he asked her.

"There were rumors now and again at Camelot, my lord. And I was younger and fairer then. Once I lay with Sir Cai, the king's foster brother. He was in his cups, and he told me of the king's first love, and the child born of that union. He said Merlin the Enchanter had hidden the boy and his mother in the hills of Wales, that Arthur's true blood might survive. Merlin saw far into the future when he chose to do so. I think he knew that Arthur's half-sister, Morgan le Fey, would seduce him, but he knew he could not prevent it. I kept that information to myself."

"But Arthur's blood by his young lover might not have survived," Emrys pointed out to his old nurse.

She cackled knowingly. "If Merlin took the trouble to hide the child and its mother, he knew by doing so that the line would survive," she said. "I wonder in what cave the old sorcerer sleeps today, just waiting to be recalled."

"Have Efa bring me the crystal in the Great Hall," Emrys Llyn said quietly. "I will go and awaken my wife."

Drysi nodded. "I know not what your mother will do, my lord," she said. "Her

339

opinion of humanity is not very high, given her experience at Camelot and with your father. She protected you as best she could, but even you must beware of her, for I do not think she ever meant for you to choose your full mortality. Do you understand me?"

"I know my mother," he said, "and I will indeed be mindful, for she can be overproud and overprotective of me. But I will do what I must for Maia."

"It is your lady wife who must face whatever challenge your mother gives her," Drysi said. "Go to her now, my lord. Assure Maia of your great love before she must face the Lady of the Lake herself."

He left his old nurse, and returned to the chamber where Maia lay still sleeping in her innocence of what was to come. Bending, Emrys kissed his wife's lips and gently shook her by her shoulder. "Awaken, my love," he said to her softly.

Maia's emerald green eyes flew open. "Did I dream last night?" she asked him.

"Nay," he said. "You did not dream our conversation. I have not yet called my mother from her castle beneath the lake. Do you still want me to do so, my love?"

Maia sighed. "You must, Emrys, if we are to have a normal life together. It is what I want, but I will accept whatever you want. You know that."

"I want what you want," he said quietly. "Dress yourself in your finest gown, my love, for my mother will consider it a sign of respect, and be pleased. I would not frighten you, but be warned that she is not an easy woman."

"I will wear my wedding gown," Maia said. "It is my best." She called her servant to her, and while he awaited her in the hall, Maia prepared to meet the Lady of the Lake. Her serving woman dressed her hair in the graceful knot at the nape of her neck, and Maia wore her silver and gold chaplet, but no veil. About her neck she slipped a filigreed chain of gold at the end of which dangled a pendant with the red dragon of her father's house. Her woman held up a polished silver mirror. Maia nodded, and thanked the woman for her help. Then she hurried down to the hall to meet her husband.

Emrys Llyn smiled as his wife came before him. She was pale, but her look was a resolute one. "Come," he said holding out his hand to her, leading her to the high board in the center of which had been placed a tall diamond crystal next to which was a small and slender wand of purest gold. They stood before the crystal, and taking it in his hand Emrys Llyn asked his wife a final time, "Are you ready, my love? Once I summon my mother, there can be no going back for either of us."

Maia nodded. "I am ready," she replied. Her throat was tight with the words.

He took up the delicate wand, but at that moment Morgant entered the hall. Seeing him she cried out, "What are you doing, my lord? Are you mad?" She ran across the chamber to stand before them.

"I am calling the Lady, as you can see," he said. "It is time."

"No!" Morgant said. Her tone was desperate. "No!"

"This is not your decision, cousin," he told her quietly. "It is ours, and we have made it. My wife would be tested. We would live as mortals do."

"You cannot!" Morgant began to sob. "You would give up your magic to live as a mere man? Like your father? You would die one day, and allow your bones to rot away within the bosom of the Mother? No, Emrys! No!"

He struck the crystal with the golden wand in reply. Once. Twice. A third time.

Morgant gasped, shocked. Her hand flew to her mouth to still her cry of despair.

Maia was stunned by the girl's desperation, and not just a little angry. Emrys was her husband! This half-fairy girl behaved as if Maia were merely incidental to her plans. *I would scratch her eyes out if I could,* Maia thought jealously.

The wand striking the crystal made the most exquisite sound that echoed throughout the entire castle of Ile du Lac. And then a pale smoke appeared in the center of the hall, writhing and twisting upward, slowly taking shape, its color a thousand shades of blue, until finally the Lady of the Lake herself was visible to them. She stepped forward, smiling, her eyes only for her son.

"Emrys!" she said, and he stepped down from the dais to greet her, taking both of her elegant slender hands in his, and kissing them.

"Mother," he greeted her. "It is good to see you once again."

"Why have you called me?" the Lady of the Lake asked him, but her eyes were sweeping over Maia, and her expression as she looked at the girl was unreadable.

"I have called you to meet my wife, Maia Pendragon," he said, and he drew Maia forward.

She curtsied deeply to her husband's mother. "Lady, I am honored," she said.

The Lady of the Lake reached out, and inspected the pendant that Maia wore. "Is this not the symbol of Arthur, once king of Britain?" she asked.

"It is," Maia replied quietly.

"By what right do you wear this symbol?" the Lady demanded.

"I am the descendant of Arthur through his first son, Gwydre, who was born to Lynior, daughter of ap Evan," Maia responded proudly.

"The child the old enchanter, Merlin, hid away?" the Lady said.

"Aye, the very same," Maia told her.

"A union between Arthur and Lancelot's blood," the Lady considered. "Interesting." She looked at her son. "For how long have you had this wife, my son?"

"We wed November first," he answered his mother.

"Just three months ago," the Lady mused. "And Morgant has not taken her life yet? I am surprised."

"What?" Emrys looked astounded. "What did you say?"

The Lady of the Lake laughed. "Be careful, my son. Your humanity is showing far more than I would have it show. Did you not know that Morgant is responsible for the demise of both Rosyn and Gwynth?" She laughed coldly. "She frightened them with hints and innuendo, did you not, Morgant? And so Rosyn flung herself from a height, and Gwynth drowned, did they not, Morgant?"

"Lady, they did not love him!" Morgant cried. "But I do, and I descend from Arthur too! My blood is equal to hers."

Maia was shocked. Emrys had told her

his previous wives had died in their beds. What else was he possibly keeping from her? And then it occurred to her that the explanation given her family was a more palatable one than the truth. Her parents would not have let her wed with a man whose first two wives were apparent suicides. She kept silent.

The Lady of the Lake laughed scornfully. "Seed of Arthur, and his evil spawn Mordred, you do not know what love is. It is Emrys's power and prestige you seek." Her look turned to Maia. "But you are different, girl. You love my son, I can see it in your eyes — but more important, I can see it in your heart. The question is, just how *much* do you love him?"

"What do you want of me, my lady?" Maia said bravely. "I will do what I must to prove my love for Emrys, and to lift the curse that binds him."

"Will you, indeed?" The Lady's voice was tinged with amusement. "We shall see, Maia Pendragon. We must consider well the trial you will face to prove your worth to me. I will not let my son go easily, you understand. I have protected him his entire life, and I will continue to do so if you cannot."

"I will make you no promises other than to do my best for my husband," Maia said. "I do not dissemble, and am known as a woman of my word, my lady."

The Lady of the Lake nodded. "We will set you an ordeal, Maia Pendragon, and you are free to refuse it if you think it too difficult. But if you refuse it, or if you fail, my son will retain his immortality, and you will be driven from Ile du Lac to grow old alone."

"I will do whatever it is you ask of me," Maia said, "yet I wonder why you would ask further proof of my love for Emrys when you say you see that love, both in my eyes and in my heart." She looked directly at the Lady when she spoke.

"It is my right to ask because I am his mother. I want what is best for my son, Maia Pendragon." The Lady's blue eyes narrowed with her burgeoning annoyance.

"I can understand that," Maia responded, "but Emrys is no longer a boy. He is a man. Do you not think him capable of making his own decisions?"

"You are a bold creature!" the Lady said. "I could destroy you with a wave of my hand, Maia Pendragon."

"I have no doubt of that," Maia answered, "but you will not destroy me if you truly love your son as you claim."

"Hear my conditions!" the Lady began.

"No!" the Lord of the Lake suddenly spoke up. "Say not another word, my mother. I have always revered you, and I have respected you, but I have at last found true love. I will not let you take it from me in an effort to destroy it."

"Emrys!" the beautiful fairy cried, "you are so human, and humans are weak! Your father was weak. And Arthur of Britain was weak. You must not be weak!"

"Oh, Mother," he responded softly, "I far prefer my human side, I fear. You have protected me for over seven hundred years, but this is a different age from the one into which I was born. Britain is no more, and while Wales is yet wild, the land beyond it, England, is a civilized country. The Northmen are long gone. I love my wife, and she me. Will we have bad times as well as good? Aye, we probably will, but it is our love for one another that will help us to survive. I have no doubt in Maia's love for me, and I know she has no doubt in my love for her. Accept my decision in this matter, for it is my life, our lives, that are important here."

"Humankind is unstable and vacillating, my son. You can trust no one, least of all a human," the Lady said.

"Then you do not trust me," Emrys Llyn replied.

"No! No!" the Lady cried. "It was your father I could not trust. He betrayed every woman he ever involved himself with, my son."

"You are wiser than most," the Lord of the Lake said to her. "You must have known the kind of man he was, and yet you wanted him, Mother."

"I thought my love for him would change him," she said brokenly, and then catching herself up, she continued, "but Lancelot was weak as all his kind are weak."

"He ensorcelled you with his beauty, and his charm," Emrys Llyn said. "So much so that you deliberately set out to steal him from the king's half-sister. You knew, mother, that he would be flattered by your interest. I suspect that my father did not seduce you, but rather you seduced him. He was a weak man, but not all men are like that. I know I look like my father, but I am not my father. You can no longer revenge yourself on Lancelot through me for the heartbreak he caused you. I have found the one woman I shall love through eternity. I have married her. You amended Elaine of Shallot's curse so that my immortality would vanish when I found true love. I have found it, mother. You must release me!"

The Lady of the Lake looked at her son, and she saw the truth in his eyes. With a cry that was half despair, half anger, she vanished before their eyes. And in the lake beyond the castle's Great Hall, they heard the ice cracking with the sound of terrible fury.

"What have you done?" Maia asked her husband.

"I am not yet certain," Emrys answered her.

Old Drysi hobbled forward, for she had come down from her tower. "You have bearded her, my lad. 'Twas time. She has never forgiven your father, and she has been deluding herself that she protected you for love of her son. But in her heart she meant to keep you caught between worlds forever as a means of revenge against Lancelot."

"She could destroy us all, you fool!" Morgant cried.

"I would rather be destroyed than live without Maia," the Lord of the Lake snapped back.

"We must make our peace with her," Maia said.

"Not if it means exposing you to one of her mad schemes, my love," Emrys told his wife. "I have found you, and I shall not lose you!"

"If she lets you have your full humanity," Morgant said bitterly, "you will grow old, and die one day."

"Aye," he said, "I will."

"You have lost your wits!" Morgant said angrily. "It is her fault!" She glared at

Maia. "I should have killed you immediately!"

Maia laughed aloud. "I am not the meek Rosyn, afraid of her own shadow, Morgant. Nor am I the greedy and jealous Gwynth. I knew you coveted Emrys, but he did not want you, else he should not have come and wed me," Maia mocked Morgant.

"I have magic, and you do not," Morgant threatened.

Again Maia laughed. "You cannot harm me, Morgant. Do your worst! I am protected from creatures like you."

Morgant's odd-colored eyes narrowed, and she flung her hand out toward Maia. Almost immediately she was thrown back herself. A look of fear crossed her beautiful face, but she pointed a finger at Maia nonetheless, only to cry out with pain. "What is this magic?" she gasped. "Emrys, let me destroy her! We can be happy together, I swear it!"

"It is not my magic that surrounds my wife, Morgant," he told the half-fairy girl, "but by threatening Maia in my very presence, and by the knowledge I have gained this day about your cruelty, I must send you from Ile du Lac now. You have a choice to make, Morgant. Will you choose to be all human, or all fairy?" He knew the answer even as he asked her.

"I shall be happy to be relieved of my

humanity!" Morgant cried. "But once I have my full powers, I shall be revenged upon you, Emrys Llyn. You and your wife!"

"Go!" his deep voice thundered. "By the power I still retain as Lord of the Lake, I release you from your humanity. Go, Morgant, and do not return to trouble us! You will be welcomed in my mother's realm, but never again in mine!"

And before their eyes Morgant faded from their sight, and was gone.

"Twice today you have been my knight," Maia said softly to Emrys.

He took her into his arms, and looked down into her face. "I love you," he said simply. "And now, tell me how you are protected from fairy magic."

"Gorawen, my father's concubine. You know she practices magic. My mother feared for my safety here at Ile du Lac, and it would appear that her fears were indeed justified," Maia said with a small smile. "Gorawen wove a small spell of protection about me before I left Dragon's Lair. I doubt it would protect me from your mother, but Morgant had not such strong powers that I could be harmed."

"My mother is wrong," he replied. "Humans are not weak, but rather most resourceful, I think." Then he bent and kissed her. "Now, my love, we must consider well how to convince my mother to release me from the curse so you and I can get on with our lives."

"And you must give the other fairy folk here the option of remaining with us, or going into the fairy kingdom," Maia told him. "Some may now be afraid, as you have refused to allow your mother to test my love."

"I need no further proof, Maia," he responded.

"I know," she said. "I will always love you, Emrys. From the moment you entered my life I knew there was no other man for me. And if I must grow old while you remain youthful, then so be it, for I shall be happy that you remain at my side."

"Yet if you grew old, and I did not, I do not think I could bear it," he replied softly. "We must convince my mother to release me."

"She will be softened by a grandchild," old Drysi spoke up. "And convinced by your determination to stand by each other. Do not allow her to bully you, my children."

"We will not," Emrys Llyn told his old nurse.

"Never!" Maia echoed her husband's sentiments.

Chapter 12

Maia awoke with the awareness that she was very cold. Emrys was not by her side, and she half rose to see that the fire was out in the hearth. *How odd,* she thought, realizing at the same time that the castle was deathly quiet. Reluctantly she climbed from her bed, picking up and quickly donning the fur-lined robe, slipping her feet into a pair of fur-lined house boots. "Emrys," she called, but he did not answer. Maia moved through their apartment, noting as she did that the fire in the dayroom hearth was also dead. She departed their private apartments, making her way to the great hall of the castle, finding it empty, dead coals in all of the fireplaces. There was no one to be found. She descended the stairs into the kitchens. Empty. The cook fires out.

Maia was beginning to become very frightened. What had happened? Where was Emrys? Where were all the other inhabitants of Ile du Lac? Why were all the fires out? With great difficulty she pulled open the great front door to the castle. The storm had blown itself out and away, but it was bitter cold. The courtyard was high with snow, none of which had been shoveled away to make a path to any of the outbuildings. Maia pushed the door shut, and then she climbed the staircase to Drysi's tower rooms. To her relief the old woman was still there.

"Drysi! Praise God and his Blessed Mother. The castle is deserted. The fires are all out. I cannot find Emrys."

" 'Tis the Lady's doing," Drysi said, shaking her head. "She means to test you despite her son's wishes. He has not the power to overcome her, I fear."

"Can you walk, Drysi?" Maia asked the old lady. "I cannot keep all the fireplaces in the castle burning, but I will keep the two in our apartment alight, and we will be comfortable and safe there."

"I can get down," Drysi answered Maia. "It is the getting up that is difficult, child. But I must have my things with me."

"Tell me what you want, and I will bring them," Maia told her.

The old lady instructed Maia to pack a basket with her hairbrush, and several warm gowns. She nodded her thanks as Maia helped her from her bed, wrapping her in a robe, and slipping house slippers on her wrinkled feet. "You are a good child," she said.

Maia helped Drysi down the winding staircase from her tower room, and into the apartments she shared with her husband. Settling Drysi in a chair she tucked a fur robe about the old lady, then hurried to relight the fires, working the flint and stone until the pile of straw in the thick kindling finally blazed up. When the fire was well established Maia took a torch, and lit the hearth in the bedchamber as well.

"We will have to cook here, too," she said. "I will go to the kitchens to find what food I can. At least it is winter, and the food will not spoil if it doesn't freeze. Ile du Lac is constructed of stone. I noted earlier that the hoarfrost is already beginning to touch the interior walls. Without heat the castle will become frigid." She turned to her companion. "Why has she done this, Drysi, and what can she hope to accomplish by it?"

"She seeks to drive you away, child," Drysi responded. "Yesterday her son did something that he had never before done. He stood against her. And he stood with another woman by his side. The Lady both loves and hates her son. She cannot forgive him his mortality, nor can she forget that he is Lancelot's son as well as hers."

"But she loved Lancelot, and she protected their son from Elaine of Shallot's curse. She has kept him safe for centuries, and he has had two other wives before me," Maia said.

"Aye, but she knew that her son did not love those poor girls, and she knew that the jealous Morgan 'twould see to their demise," Drysi replied. "Emrys would remain hers, and that is what she wants. He is all she has left of Lancelot, and if he embraces his mortality he will grow old and die like all humans. Then who will she have to love? The Lady is like all of us, human or fairy. She needs love, Maia, my child."

"Are you human or fairy, Drysi?" Maia asked.

"Lord, child, I am as human as you are. I was just preserved along with all the other inhabitants of Ile du Lac those many centuries ago. I will die sooner than later, but I will not die until I have seen my laddie safe," Drysi told the girl.

"What am I to do?" Maia asked the old woman. "How am I to get my husband back from the Lady? I will not be driven away! I love Emrys!"

Drysi shook her head. "I do not know," she said. "The Lady will come to you, you may be certain of it. She will tell you what she wants."

"But if she loves Emrys as you say she does, what can I possibly give her in exchange for him?" Maia wondered aloud. Then she straightened her shoulders, and said, "I will go to the kitchens and find us some breakfast. You will be here when I return, won't you, Drysi?"

"If the Lady had wanted me, child, she would have taken me with all the others," Drysi said. "I will be here."

Maia ran from the chamber and hurried to the kitchens. She found a tray and put a pitcher of frosty milk on it. She found a loaf of yesterday's bread on a shelf, a slab of bacon, and a wedge of cheese. She piled them with a knife, a toasting fork, two plates, and two mugs onto the tray, and made her way back upstairs to her apartment. To her vast relief Drysi was still there, dozing in her chair. Setting the tray down Maia sliced the bread, cheese and bacon. She toasted the bread on the end of the fork. Then using the same utensil she fried each of the bacon slices, laying each across the toasted bread as it was done with a slice of cheese. And while she cooked she took the chill off the pitcher, placing it carefully in the ashes of the fireplace. Finally she took a pear from the bowl on the sideboard, and peeling it, she sliced it into several juicy pieces, dividing the fruit equally between herself and the old woman. Then she woke Drysi.

"I have prepared us a meal," she told her.

"You are resourceful, my child," Drysi said.

"All of my father's daughters know how to cook, and keep house," Maia replied as she poured them each a mug of the slightly warmed milk. "My mother said a woman could not know if her servants were doing their duty if she did not know that duty herself."

Drysi nodded as she eagerly ate. She seemed to have more teeth than most old women, or else her gums were very hard. She particularly appreciated the slices of fruit, and the juice from it drizzled down her pointed chin. She nodded her thanks when Maia leaned over and wiped the sticky sweetness from her face. When she had finished all the young woman had set before her she said, "Now, my child, what will you do?"

Maia sighed deeply, but then she said, "If the Lady hopes to wait us out we will freeze to death, Drysi. There is wood by all of the fireplaces in the hall, and I will haul it up here so these two rooms at least will remain warmer than the rest of the castle. But when the wood is gone we are, I fear, lost. The courtyard is filled with snow, and no paths cleared to the woodsheds, stables, or barns. The creatures will die without food or water. I cannot even escape this place and attempt to return to my father's house for help. We cannot wait upon the Lady's pleasure, Drysi. This matter between us must be settled quickly!"

"But how?" the old woman wanted to know.

"I am not certain," Maia admitted. She wanted to cry with her fear and her frustration, but she bravely swallowed back her tears. They would gain her nothing, and she could not let Drysi see her distress. Her companion needed to believe that there was hope, and that shortly all would be restored to its natural state. "I need to speak with the Lady," she decided aloud, "but will she speak with me?"

"Call her," Drysi said.

"What?"

"Call her," the old lady repeated. "Go up to the battlements and call her. You must be able to see the lake itself or she will not answer you. She will pretend she doesn't hear you, but with the lake in your view she has to answer you, child."

"Will you be all right here alone?" Maia wondered.

"Put some more wood on the fire and I will be fine," Drysi assured her.

Maia set two more good pieces of wood into the blaze, and then she took up her outdoor cape from her trunk and wrapped herself in it. "Wish me luck, Drysi," she said to her elderly companion.

"I do," Drysi responded, "but you will need more than luck, child. The Lady is clever and she will seek to outwit you. She does not want her son choosing his mortality over his magical heritage. But Emrys is in love with you, and that is just what he wants. He has always wanted to be just a man. The Lady does not understand that, but unless you can convince her that losing her son to humanity will not cost her her son, she will fight you with every magical skill at her command," Drysi warned.

"If she truly loves him she will sacrifice her own needs for his," Maia replied.

Drysi laughed. "Child, child, it is clear you know little of fairy folk. They can be the most selfish of creatures ever created, and the Lady is. You will need to outwit her, or you are lost, and Emrys too. My laddie is not a man to give his heart lightly. He loves you, Maia Pendragon. Whatever happens he will never love another. If you lose this battle with the Lady, both of you are condemned to a loveless existence."

Maia bent down and kissed the old woman's withered cheek. "Then wish me good fortune, Drysi," she said, "for all our sakes." Then she hurried from the chamber. Climbing the narrow winding stairs to the top of the castle Maia shivered with the bitter cold that had invaded Ile du Lac. At last she reached the door that opened out onto the battlements. It was barred. She struggled to lift up the heavy wooden beam, and after some minutes was successful. It dropped noisily to the cold stone floor with a thunk, but the door was also locked. Undefeated Maia drew forth her chatelaine's keys, and finding the right key inserted it and unlocked the door. The door swung open. She was grateful it did not open out, for the battlements were deep in snow.

Maia stepped gingerly out. She had gauged carefully the number of steps she would have to take to reach the edge of the battlements and see the lake. They were thankfully few, and while her feet were cold, the snow did not soak through her fur house boots. Although the snow had ceased, the skies above her were lowering and both gray and white in color. Only the dark color of the forest beyond the lake broke the monotony of white. The lake appeared frozen, but Maia knew that the lady could rise above it should she choose to do so. The cold air was beginning to burn her lungs, but Maia nonetheless took a deep breath, and called loudly, "I ask the Lady of the Lake to come forth and treat with me!"

Silence greeted her. Even the birds were quiet this morning.

"Lady, I know you are there," Maia called. "You have used your great magic in your attempt to overcome the love your son and I have for each other. Are you so afraid of me that you cannot face me, Lady?"

The silence was now broken by a faint rumble, but nothing more.

"I know fairy folk do not play by the same rules as we mortals," Maia continued, "but you cannot change Emrys's heart by separating us, Lady. And knowing that you fear me gives me power over you, does it not?"

The rumble from beneath the lake now was quite discernable. Fog swirled over the ice, which suddenly cracked loudly, and Maia saw her rival standing just above the water in the center of the lake. She thought again as she had the first time she had seen the Lady that this fairy woman was incredibly beautiful with her swirling silver-gold hair and her deep blue eyes. Her gown, all in shades of blue, blew in the faint breeze her arrival had caused to spring up.

"What makes you think that I would be afraid of you, bold girl?" she demanded of Maia in an icy voice.

"If you are not afraid of me then why take Emrys from me? And all the others who dwell at Ile du Lac but for old Drysi?" Maia demanded. "Why isolate me? You have even made it impossible for me to flee you. Will you have me dead then, Lady?"

"I care not if you live or die," the Lady said coldly.

"You care," Maia murmured softly.

"You play a dangerous game, Pendragon's daughter," the Lady responded.

"I play no game with you, Lady. I simply want my husband returned to me," Maia told the Lady. "You had no right to steal him unwillingly away."

"What makes you think it was unwilling?" the Lady replied. "Perhaps my son has grown bored with you, and needed my help to rid himself of you."

Maia laughed aloud. "Nay, Lady, Emrys is not bored with me, nor will he ever be, I promise you." Then she grew serious. "Oh, Lady, you are his mother, and I cannot take that away from him, nor would I. But I am his wife. Emrys loves me. You cannot replace that love in his heart for me any more than I could replace the love in his heart for you. A mother and a wife share the man. Each has her place in his life. Surely you understand that."

"He would be mortal," the Lady said. "This is your doing, and I will not have it!"

"He is already half mortal. It is his right to choose the world in which he prefers to reside, Lady. He had, I believe, made that choice even before we met."

"I can wipe the memory of you from his

very thoughts!" the Lady threatened.

"Aye," Maia agreed, "you can, Lady. But you will never wipe the memory of me from his heart any more than you were able to extinguish the memory of Lancelot from your heart."

"Do not dare to speak to me of that . . . that man!" the Lady cried. Her hair and her skirts swirled about her in her agitation.

"Are fairy folk perfect?" Maia asked.

"Nay, of course not!" the Lady said impatiently. "Why do you ask such a foolish question, girl?"

"You can make mistakes like mortals," Maia said.

"Aye, but not as many," the Lady said.

"Then accept the fact that while you love your son, Lady, you erred in your judgment of his father," Maia responded. "The Lancelot of legend was brave and noble. The Lancelot you knew was brave, yet frail. A man easily bewitched into misbehavior with other women. Had you not stolen him away from Elaine of Shallot you might not have suffered this tragedy of your heart. You are every bit as responsible for what followed as he was, yet you set the blame entirely upon my race." She shivered now as the rising wind began to cut through her cloak, and her feet grew numb in their boots.

"Bold girl, you know nothing!" the Lady cried, and then in a clap of thunder she disappeared.

Maia sighed. Then turning from the battlements she reentered the castle, locking and barring the door behind her, and returned to her apartments. Drysi sat dozing by the fire. Maia added more wood to the hearth, and sat down heavily. The old woman was immediately alert.

"You have returned, child," she said.

Maia nodded.

"Did the Lady answer your summons?" Drysi wanted to know.

"She did," Maia acknowledged, and proceeded to tell the old lady what had transpired between her and the Lady of the Lake. When she had completed her recitation she stood up again. "I must bring wood up from the hall if we are to get through the night, Drysi. The Lady is not yet ready to admit her defeat. I will be back." Then Maia left the nursemaid again, going down the stairs into the hall. For the next several hours she brought armload after armload of wood upstairs into her apartments so that she might keep the fires going through the night and into the next day. She foraged in the kitchens a second time, bringing back a cold meat pie, a ham, more bread, and a half wheel of cheese. She chopped up winter vegetables,

365

and a dressed duck she found in the cold pantry, putting them into a pot with water and wine. All of this she carried upstairs and then returned downstairs for several skins of water and a carafe of wine. When she had finally finished the winter day was ending. She set the pot over the fire to boil itself into a stew. As long as she could find food and fuel they would survive.

Drysi spent her day dozing and watching the girl as she went about the task of making their confinement comfortable. She spooned up the dish of duck stew that Maia had prepared, mopping every bit of gravy from her bowl with a chunk of bread. She shared a bit of cheese and an apple with her young companion thinking that if anyone could save Emrys Llyn it was his wife.

"Come, Drysi," Maia finally said when she had cleaned up the remnants of their supper, "and I will help you into bed. I can sleep on the trundle."

"Nay, child," Drysi told her. "I am more comfortable in my chair here before the fire than I would be in bed. Wrap that fur lap robe about me, and build up the fire."

Maia did as she was bid, putting a foot-stool beneath the old woman's feet. Then she kissed Drysi good night, and found her own bed, waking twice in the night to be certain that the fires were still going in both her hearth and Drysi's. She did not sleep well, for there were too many thoughts swirling about in her brain. Where was Emrys?

And would she actually be able to overcome the Lady of the Lake, and regain her husband again? What would happen to her if she couldn't? Her father's keep was two days away, and she wasn't even certain she knew how to get there. And right now it was impossible, for she could not reach the stables to get a horse. And what was happening to the animals? They must be very hungry and thirsty by now. Tomorrow she would attempt to get across the castle courtyard. There was so much to do, and she was but one girl. Maia felt the tears come, and she wept silently into her pillow. She had to prevail. She simply had to prevail over the Lady! Her happiness depended upon it.

The next morning Maia awoke before the dawn, and dressed herself in the warmest clothing she could find. Bringing Drysi a cup of hot milk with a slice of bread and cheese, she left the old woman. The hall outside the apartment was bitterly cold. The castle walls were covered in a layer of silvery white frost, and she could see her breath.

"Damn the creature!" Maia muttered beneath her breath as she hurried along.

Reaching the main door to the castle she unbarred it and pulled it open. The sun was beginning to rise, coloring the skies above with red, orange, lavender and a deep pink. Maia drew a deep breath, and the icy air burned her lungs. Undeterred she set forth from the castle, slowly making her way across the courtyard to the stables. Finally reaching them she pulled the doors open. The stables were as empty of inhabitants as the castle was. She closed the doors to the building and struggled on to the barn. It, too, was empty. Not even a cat remained. Maia followed her footprints in the snow back to the castle, yanking the door shut behind her.

Now she began the climb back upstairs to the battlements of Ile du Lac. Unbarring the door and unlocking it she went out again to the precipice overlooking the lake. The winter sun was skimming across the horizon and turning the surface of the lake golden with its light. Maia snuggled into her hood and drew her cloak about her.

"Lady, come forth, damn it! It is time we settled this matter between us. I want my husband back! I need him, and he needs me." Her voice echoed in the silence. Not even a bird called back.

"I am with child!" Maia said.

The rumble came in a fierce rush, and then the Lady appeared in the middle of the lake as was her custom.

"Bold girl, you lie!" she said, but the very tone of her voice indicated that she was not certain if Maia lied or not.

"I do not," Maia responded calmly, standing straight and looking directly at this beautiful fairy who was her mother-in-law. "I am with child," she repeated.

"How can you be certain?" the Lady demanded.

"Lady, I am the second of four children, and my eldest sister has two," Maia answered. "You amended the curse on him yourself. You said he would regain his full mortality and sire children when he found true love. Is this not the real proof you seek, Lady? Emrys is now a mortal as he has wanted to be, and I carry his child!"

"Does my son know?" the Lady asked.

"I wanted to make certain I was not mistaken," Maia said. "I planned to tell him the morning I awoke only to find you had stolen him away. I had been so concerned that I was not with child as quickly as my sister that I missed the first signs of my condition."

For a long moment the Lady of the Lake was silent. Then she said, "I will send you in safety to your father's keep, Maia Pendragon."

"No," Maia told her. "This is your grandchild, Lady. This is how we members

369

of humankind gain our immortality. It is through our offspring, and those that follow from their blood. Give me back my husband that he may know his child."

"No! I above all others know the pain of seeing those you love grow old and die. I will not do that to my son."

"Were you there when Lancelot died, Lady?" Maia asked the fairy.

The Lady nodded. "He came back here. Here to Ile du Lac. Here to me. But I had already wrapped the castle and its inhabitants in my spell. His home was gone, and so I raised up a small dwelling on the lakeshore where he might take his ease. He had been fighting in France, and anywhere his sword could be hired. Now he was old and could no longer fight, so he came back to me. Came back, and I saw my handsome and unfaithful husband, his limbs thin, his face drawn and gray, his once beautiful dark hair faded and streaked with white."

"Yet you loved him still," Maia said softly.

The Lady nodded. "I loved him still," she agreed, "but alas, my magic could not protect him forever, for you mortals are so very frail. I told him what I had done to protect our child, and he smiled, pleased. But as each day passed he grew weaker, and finally, as I sat by his bedside, and held his hand, he died, another woman's name upon his lips. Gwynefr. Your ancestor's cursed queen, Maia Pendragon."

"She was no blood of mine, Lady," Maia responded. Then she said, "Emrys would choose his mortal side, Lady. He would live as a man lives. Let him!"

"I cannot see my son grow old and die," the Lady said.

"Why?" Maia demanded. "Because you would be alone, Lady?"

The Lady of the Lake grew agitated with the girl's words. "You dare . . ." she began.

"I would dare anything to regain my husband!" Maia cried. "Give him back to me, Lady! You cannot keep his love by keeping him from me, and from his child."

"You are the most stubborn girl!" the Lady said, and then she disappeared in a rumble of thunder as she had the day before.

Sighing, Maia reentered the castle. Every time she backed the fairy woman into a corner with her logic, the Lady disappeared. It was impossible to reason with someone who wasn't there. She spent the rest of the day as she had the previous. Hauling wood from the great hall to her apartments. Going out into the kitchen courtyard she lowered the bucket into the well, banging it several times against the glaze of ice covering the surface until the bucket dipped into the water. Maia filled the water skins from the bucket, and returned to her chambers.

"What had the Lady to say this day?" Drysi asked her.

"How do you know I spoke with the Lady?" Maia returned.

"Of course you spoke with her," Drysi said. "You have not given up hope of finding your husband."

"I told her I am with child," Maia replied.

"And are you?" Drysi asked.

Maia nodded, and then a few tears slid down her face. "I was going to tell Emrys that day," she explained to Drysi.

"What did the Lady say?" Drysi demanded to know.

"She offered to return me to my father's house," Maia responded. "I refused."

"Of course you refused," Drysi said. "You were wise to do so. She knows that if her son learns he is to be a father she will lose him as she lost his father."

Maia brushed the tears from her face. "I will not give up my husband," she said. "In the spring I will go to my father, and he will give me the loan of servants. I will remain at Ile du Lac until my husband returns to me, and I will raise our child alone if I must, Drysi."

Maia toasted bread and cheese that evening, setting a slice of ham upon it. She and Drysi drank wine from the carafe on her sideboard. And then they slept. When Maia awoke the following morning she sensed that something was different than the two previous days. Arising she went out into the dayroom where Drysi still slept. Gingerly she opened the door to her apartment, and stepped out into the hallway. The air within the passage was warm, and the frost had gone from the walls. She moved back into her own apartments. The pile of firewood she had so laboriously hauled upstairs from the great hall was gone. So was her cache of food, but on the sideboard was a covered tray.

Maia lifted the cover off the tray. Beneath she discovered two trenchers of bread filled with hot oat stirabout flavored with honey and heavy cream. There was a bowl of hard-boiled eggs, a cottage loaf, a dish of plum jam, and a little crock of sweet butter. She heard Drysi awakening behind her, and turned to her saying, "Look, old woman, we are to be magically fed this morning."

Drysi cackled a dry laugh. "So your husband's mother has a conscience," she remarked. "I do not know if I am surprised or not."

"But how?" Maia wondered aloud.

"Ask not, child. Let us just eat, and be glad," Drysi replied.

They split the contents of the tray between them. Maia had to admit that she felt better for the hot cereal. When they had finished she set the tray back upon the sideboard, and when she looked again it was gone.

"The castle is warm again," Maia said. "The frost is gone from the walls."

"Go down and see if anyone is here but us," Drysi suggested.

Maia took up her cloak, and leaving the old lady, inspected the entire castle; but though the fireplaces were all burning, and the frost was indeed gone, there was no one about that she could see. She opened the door to the courtyard, and saw that a path had been shoveled to the various outbuildings nestled beneath the castle walls. The castle gates were wide open. Wrapping her cloak tightly about her Maia walked through them and down the shoveled path to the lakeside.

"Thank you, Lady," she called, but all was silent. Not even the wind made a sound, and the icy surface of the lake remained smooth. Maia turned, and walked back to the castle. For the next few days she and Drysi ate from the trays that magically appeared in Maia's dayroom twice daily. Their fires burned without wood being added. The Lady was caring for them for whatever reason, but the Lord of the Lake remained missing. Finally, when ten days had passed, Maia had had enough. She climbed to the battlements one bright morning, and called forth the Lady of the Lake once again.

The air had the faintest hint of warmth in it this day. It would be March shortly.

Maia stood straight. Her voice was stronger than it had ever been. She had to do this. For herself, for the child now growing in her belly, for Emrys. "Lady, come forth! It is not enough! You must return my husband to me."

"Must? Must?" The Lady appeared without her usual trumpet of thunder. "You are in no position to make demands of me, bold girl," she told Maia.

"You fear being alone in this world where magic is fast disappearing," Maia said quietly. "But it need not be that way, Lady."

"What do you mean?" the Lady asked. "If my son grows old and dies I will be alone. If he embraces his mortality that is what must happen. If I convince him to let only fairy blood run in his veins, he will be forced to watch you grow old and die. I know he loves you, and such a happening would break his heart."

"He is a mortal, Lady. And, aye, he will

grow old one day and die. But his blood will live on in his sons, and his sons' sons," Maia explained. "You need never be alone. Ever! And as long as there are those who believe in you, your magic will never die."

"It is the way of the world to forget, Pendragon's daughter. To see, and yet to not believe. Emrys knows of the olden times for he was born into them. He will never forget, and he will always believe," the Lady said.

"And for this you would condemn him to a loveless life?" Maia replied softly. "Your very actions make true Elaine of Shallot's curse upon the son of Lancelot. You have not protected him at all, Lady."

"You do not understand!" the Lady cried.

"Nay!" Maia cried back, "I do not! Listen to me, Lady. I did not seek out your son. He sought me out, coming to me first in my dreams, until I sent away all of my suitors and waited for him to come to me. He did, and when he did he asked my father for my hand. My father was reluctant to give his permission, for he sensed that something was not right with your son. But I swore I should have no other, and so we were married. I conceived this child in my belly, Lady. It was meant to be. Emrys and I were meant to be. Give him back to me! Give him back!"

And Maia stamped her foot in frustration.

For a long moment the Lady looked as if she could not make up her mind. Maia's words but gave proof of what she had been refusing to see or understand. Her son wanted to embrace his mortality. He loved this mortal woman. She was ripening with his child. And this morning the Lady of the Lake had seen a single silver strand in her son's ebony hair. The locks of fairy men never changed. Though she sought to prevent it, Emrys had embraced his mortality even without her permission. The reality of it all pained her greatly, and with a great cry of sorrow the Lady disappeared beneath the lake.

Maia began to weep with her desperation, and then she felt his hands upon her shoulders. "Emrys?" she whispered, half frightened.

He turned her so that she was facing him. "It is I," he said, his deep blue eyes hungrily scanning her beautiful face.

Maia burst into a great flood of tears. "Is it really you?" she sobbed. "This is not some magical trick of your mother's?" Her hands ran over his face and shoulders.

"It is I," he promised her, and then his mouth descended upon hers in a burning kiss. And when he had satisfied himself with her lips he kissed her eyelids, her cheeks, the very tip of her nose.

"But how?" Maia sobbed. "She was so obdurate."

"I am not certain, my darling," he said, "but I suspect the strength of your love for me was too great even for her magic, and that was what finally overcame her." His big hand caressed her face.

"Are you really mortal now?" Maia demanded to know, sniffling.

"I am mortal," he said. "When she spirited me away I told her it was what I wanted. Under fairy law she had no choice but to accept my wishes though she tried hard to convince me otherwise, my love."

"I am with child," Maia told him, a small smile touching her lips now. He was safe! Emrys was back with her, and he was safe.

His whole face lit up with the evidence of his joy at her words. "We are to have a child, Maia?"

She nodded.

"Does my mother know?" he asked her.

"Aye. I told her when I demanded your return," Maia replied.

He laughed aloud. "You demanded of my mother? You are a brave woman, wife. I do not think anyone has ever demanded anything of the Lady." He chuckled, imagining how his mother had reacted to this girl's behavior. "Let us go in and see if my mother has returned everyone back to the castle. Were you all alone, my darling?" He helped her through the door into the hallway, locking and barring the door behind them.

"Nay, Drysi was with me. The Lady forgot her, and I found her in her tower, Emrys. I helped her to our apartments, and took care of her. I brought wood for the fires, and found food in the kitchens with which I fed us until the last few days when your mother began to relent. The frost fell from the castle walls. The fires never went out although there was no one tending them. And food appeared beneath a covered tray on our sideboard. I had so little to do then that Drysi and I played chess, and hare and hounds. She is good company, Emrys."

"Drysi was with the rest of us, Maia," he told her. "I think it was my mother who must have taken her form in order to see what kind of a human you really were, my love."

"Your mother?" Maia gasped. "No, no! It was Drysi. You should have heard the things she told me, Emrys. It had to be Drysi."

"And I tell you that Drysi was with me," he told her. "She was very irritated to be removed from her cozy tower, and complained bitterly to my mother. And she does not play chess, or hare and hounds,

Maia. Her sight is not good enough. Nay, it was my mother, and you surely impressed her else nothing you said could have saved us."

"Then I owe her more than I can ever repay her," Maia said. "Still, she might have trusted you to have chosen the right woman to marry."

"After the first two debacles?" He chuckled as they entered their apartments to find them empty. "I think not, knowing my mother. She never had a high regard for humanity to begin with, and my father's behavior but compounded her opinions."

"Her greatest fear is being alone, Emrys," Maia said. "I have told her with our progeny, and their descendants, she will never be alone, for we will teach them to know and respect her. I am not certain she believed me."

"Then you and I must prove her wrong," the Lord of the Lake said to his wife.

The winter loosened its grip upon the land about Ile du Lac. The Dragon Lord, his women, his son and remaining daughter came at Beltaine on May first. They celebrated beneath the full moon, honoring the old ways. Three months later Maia was delivered of her first child, a daughter. Several days after the child's birth Emrys and his wife took the infant down to the lakeshore, and called on the Lady to come to them.

Rising from the blue waters the Lady reached out to take her grandchild into her arms. Her beautiful imperious face softened as the infant looked up at her with eyes as blue as her own, and a tuft of silver-blond hair. "What is her name?" the Lady asked.

"We would have you name her. It shall become custom that as long as it pleases you, you will name your descendants, Lady," Maia said.

"Call her Seren, for her eyes are like stars," the Lady said. Then she placed a kiss upon the infant's forehead, and handed her back to her parents.

"And I have passed your challenge, Lady?" Maia asked, her eyes twinkling.

The Lady of the Lake laughed. "Aye, Daughter," she told Maia, "you have, indeed. If I had chosen for my son, I could not have done better."

"And we will be friends?" Maia persisted.

The Lady nodded, and then with a loving smile at them she sank once more beneath the lake, which was her home.

"I never thought to know such happiness," Emrys Llyn told his wife.

"Nor I, my lord," Maia responded. She lifted her head up to him for a kiss, and the infant in her arms protested as she was squeezed between her two parents.

They laughed, breaking away.

"She is already exhibiting my mother's disposition," Emrys said with a grin.

And Maia laughed again. She was indeed happy. Averil was happy. Now it but remained for Junia to find the same happiness, she thought. And together the Lord of the Lake and his wife walked back into their castle, their child in Maia's arms now sleeping.

Part Three

Junia

Chapter 13

Gorawen watched as Junia slipped silently from the hall. The last of the Dragon Lord's daughters was now fourteen. She was a tall, slender girl with wonderfully thick hair the color of ebony with faint gold and red highlights in it; and like her two elder sisters, Junia had green eyes. But unlike Averil whose eyes were a pale green, and Maia who had eyes the color of an emerald, Junia's eyes were a deep leaf green. She had already outgrown her coltishness, and was now a bit taller than her eldest sister, Averil. Her face was a perfect oval, her eyes more round than almond in shape. Her elegant little nose turned up just slightly, and her mouth was long. She had become in a few short years a very beautiful young woman.

They saw little of her, however, for Junia was always out of doors on her horse. She had missed her elder siblings greatly, and when they had first gone she had spent much time with their brother, Brynn; but Brynn was still a boy, and Junia had outgrown him and his games. So she chose to study with the keep's best sword master, and its finest archer. She rode daily, and for hours, often returning home with plants for Gorawen, asking what they were and whether they were of use in making medicines. Gorawen gladly explained the origin and nature of the plants, and taught Junia how to use them, making salves, ointments, pills, and teas.

Junia absorbed all this knowledge but when it came to the lessons of housewifery she was not in the least interested. Cooking bored her. Embroidery was a chore to be avoided. She had not her mother's talent with the needle, and could barely darn her stockings. She learned to make candles, soap and preserves grudgingly. She was happy to hunt for her family, but the dressing of her kill needed to be done by others, for Junia would not do it. With her sisters' departures Junia Pendragon had developed an entirely new personality. She was not longer the littlest sister. She became a very independent girl, and was beginning to exhibit a strong will.

Ysbail came into the hall, looking about. "Have you seen Junia?" she asked Gorawen. "She is to have another embroidery lesson with me though frankly I despair. I have never known anyone so clumsy with a needle."

"I suspect she has gone out," Gorawen

answered. "The day is fair."

"If she were older I would swear she was meeting someone," Ysbail said irritably. "I think it is time for Merin to start seeking a husband for her. She is too wild a girl by far, and before she gets out of control she should have a husband."

Gorawen nodded. "I agree," she said, surprising Ysbail. "Junia has grown into a beautiful young woman. I believe our lord will be able to make a good match for her."

"But I would still wish she was more skilled in the womanly arts," Ysbail said.

"She need only be skilled in one," Gorawen said with a small smile. "Have you taught her the things she needs to know to please a husband?"

"Nay," Ysbail replied. "Each time I try to broach the subject Junia tells me she does not want to hear such things. That she is not ready." Then Ysbail looked at Gorwen, and said, "Would you try with her? You are far more skilled in the arts of love than either Argel or me. And Junia likes you."

"If you are certain you want me to speak with her, I will," Gorawen replied. And the sooner the better. She had believed for some time that Junia was indeed meeting someone even if her mother did not. She did not think these meetings had led to anything yet, but Junia was growing up very quickly. She had also, like her sisters, become very willful in her character, and determined to have her own way when she wanted it. Argel entered the hall to join them, and Gorawen after a few minutes departed to find Brynn. Brynn would know something about where his sister went, and if she was meeting anyone.

Brynn was in the courtyard of the keep practicing hand-to-hand sword combat with the keep's captain-at-arms, Walter. Gorawen watched with interest. The boy was only eleven, but he had a natural skill that promised to turn him into a great warrior one day. Gorawen hoped he should never have to go to war. Merin had gone off now and again in the service of his prince, Llywelyn ap Iowerth. The prince of the Welsh was forever having to protect his rights against the young English king, Henry III, and his nobles. Gorawen was glad for the isolation which kept Dragon's Lair safe.

The lesson done, Brynn walked over to his father's concubine, a woman he loved every bit as much as his mother. "What think you, lady? Am I improving?"

"Greatly," she told him. "Now come walk with me to cool off, for I would not have you get a chill, son of Merin."

The boy grinned. He liked Gorawen. She

was clever, and she never treated him like a child as did his own mother, and Ysbail. "I have my father's good health, I am happy to say," he told her as they walked from the courtyard into the small walled garden. It was late summer.

"Tell me where Junia goes each day when she rides out," Gorawen said without any preamble.

The boy did not flinch. "She rides all over the district, but her favorite spot is the old ruins near Mryddin Water," he said.

"Who does she meet there?" Gorawen asked.

"Sometimes a Marcher lad. I don't know his family name."

"You have spied on them?" Gorawen said.

"Nay, I used to go with Junia. The ruins are a grand place to play, Gorawen," he explained. "Then one day this older boy came riding up. We became friends, the three of us. He has helped me with my swordplay and I have learned a great deal from him."

"But you do not go with Junia anymore to Mryddin Water?" Gorawen asked.

"Nay, a couple of months ago Junia asked me not to come with her all the time. I think she likes Simon. For a while she giggled at everything he said," Brynn finished disgustedly.

Gorawen laughed. "Girls do that when they like a boy," she explained to him.

Brynn rolled his eyes. "I never saw Juni behave in so silly a fashion," he said.

"Just what do you know of this boy?" she queried him.

"Simon," he said. "He is Simon."

"But Simon who?"

Brynn shook his dark head. "I don't know," he answered her. "He's just Simon to us as we are Brynn and Junia to him."

Gorawen nodded. It would be that way with young people. The boy rode. That would mean he was from a good family. Peasants did not have horses to ride, nor could they ride. But who was he? And how old was he? And what were he and Junia doing alone in the ruins by Myrddin Water? Yes, it was time for Junia to be matched and wed before she could not be. *And I must learn more about this boy,* Gorawen thought. She would not tell Ysbail, however. Ysbail would immediately jump to all the wrong conclusions and forbid Junia to ride out. And then Junia would disobey her mother, and the war would be on between them. *No,* Gorawen considered silently. *I will learn what this is all about first before I say anything to either Merin or Ysbail.*

Unfortunately at the evening meal Ysbail began to complain to the Dragon Lord.

"Junia is past fourteen now, my lord, yet you make no effort of which I am aware to find her a husband. Why is that? Do you not hold her in as great esteem as your two other daughters? I know I disappointed you when I did not bear you a son, my lord, but Junia is of your blood as are Averil and Maia."

The Dragon Lord looked startled at Ysbail's accusation, but it was Argel who quickly spoke up.

"Junia is as highly treasured as any of our good lord's children, Ysbail. Why do you say such things to him? You know your words are not true. When the time is right for a marriage to be made for Junia it will be." Argel had the strongest urge to slap Ysbail for her outburst.

"I am not ready to marry," Junia said, surprising them all.

"Your sisters were fifteen when they wed," Ysbail snapped at her daughter. "Do you think good matches are easily come by, and especially for the daughter of a concubine?"

"I could be content at Dragon's Lair for the rest of my life," Junia replied calmly. "Perhaps I never want to marry, Mother."

Ysbail gave a screech, and her hand flew to her heart. "Never want to wed? What foolishness is this, girl? Of course you will marry! What else is there for a girl?" Then a terrified look came into her eye. "You do not have a passion for the church, do you?" *What a catastrophe that would be,* Ysbail thought. She had anticipated spending the rest of her life in comfort with her daughter's family. If Junia preferred a convent she would be forced to remain at Dragon's Lair.

"I have no tendre for the cloistered life, Mother," Junia said. "I am simply not ready to marry yet. Why do you wish to hurry me along that path?"

"If you wait much longer you will be considered too old," Ysbail said, trying to calm herself. "You are just nervous, but once your father presents several suitors to you, Junia, you will no longer be afraid."

"I am neither nervous or afraid," Junia responded. "I am just not ready."

"The discussion is ended," Merin Pendragon said firmly. "In the spring I will seek among the young men for a husband for this youngest of my daughters, but not now, Ysbail. And do not nag me about it again."

Ysbail clamped her lips shut, but they could all tell she was not satisfied with her lord's answer. Yet she would get no aid from either Argel or Gorawen she knew, for they were in agreement with the Dragon Lord. Still, if she did not stand up for her child, who would? Gorawen could be content with her son-in-law, the lord of Everleigh. Argel was happy that her Maia was married to the Lord of the Lake. But what of poor Junia? She was not the first child born to Merin Pendragon. Nor was she the heiress of Merin Pendragon. Nay, she was the baby born who was not the son they had wanted. Brynn Pendragon held that honor. No, poor Junia was just the youngest daughter. But she had her mother, and Ysbail knew she would stand up for the best match they could obtain for Junia. She had to, else her own old age would not be the contented one she had always envisioned.

Junia grit her teeth and tried not to let her mother annoy her. Why was Ysbail so intent on marrying her off? She was tempted to go up to her room, but she was not yet ready for solitude.

"Come play chess with me, Junia," Gorawen invited.

"I'll get the board," Junia replied enthusiastically.

Gorawen brought a small flat table from its place next to the wall, setting it before the hearth between two chairs. Junia brought the board and the chess pieces. Sitting down she set it all up. The board was made of ebony and holly wood. The matching pieces had been carved from ebony and holly, as well. Gorawen took the dark colored pieces as she always did, and they began to play. The early moves were swift and easy, but then they became more difficult.

"Brynn tells me you and he have made a friend of a boy named Simon," Gorawen said as she moved her knight. "Who is he? From where does he come?"

"You haven't told my mother, have you?" Junia answered the question with a question. "Is that why she has begun nattering at Da to find me a husband?"

"Why would I tell anyone? Yet," Gorawen responded low.

"He is from the Englishry," Junia said. "Brynn and I met him several years ago when we began to explore the ruins by Mryddin Water." She blocked Gorawen's knight.

Gorawen pondered her next move. "How old is he?" she asked.

"When we first met he was sixteen," Junia said. "Now he is eighteen."

"I think it not wise you meet him alone now," Gorawen gently suggested. "Take Brynn with you the next time you go to Mryddin Water."

"Why? Because I am of an age to wed?" Junia said. "I do not need a nursemaid when Simon and I meet, Gorawen. We do nothing wrong."

"I did not say you did, my child, and

394

keep your voice down lest you alert your mother who I know would have you confined to the keep should she learn you are riding out to meet with a young man, Junia," Gorawen warned the girl. "If you like this young man, your father can approach his father about a match. Provided, of course, that he is not already betrothed." Unable to decide what to do, Gorawen moved another of her pawns. Junia was really a very good player, and always offered her a challenge.

"He is not yet betrothed," Junia said. "Do you really think Da would try to arrange a match for me with Simon?"

"Do you think Simon would like such a match?" Gorawen said.

"I don't know," the girl replied, her smooth brow furrowing as she considered the possibility.

"I think the first thing we must know is who Simon's family are," Gorawen replied. "I assume that since he has a horse he is of good breeding."

"He is well-spoken, and educated," Junia volunteered. "We talk on all manner of things. His father knows King Henry." Her green eyes were sparkling as she offered this bit of information. "And Simon is so handsome, Gorawen!"

"Is he?" Gorawen smiled. "Tell me, Junia."

"He has dark hair like mine, and his eyes are the purest gray I have ever seen. I think he is every bit as handsome as my sister Maia's husband; and he is certainly handsomer than Rhys FitzHugh," Junia said.

"Indeed," Gorawen noted. Her son-in-law was a fine-looking man, but he was nowhere near as handsome as Emrys Llyn. But Gorawen was concerned, for Junia already sounded as if she were falling in love with this Simon. "Learn his surname, my child, and then come tell me so I may speak to your father for you."

"Oh, thank you, Gorawen!" Junia said, and then a look of regret passed over her face. She bit her lower lip. "Check and mate," she said ruefully.

But Gorawen just laughed aloud and said, "You are really becoming a fine player, Junia. I am proud of you. Neither of your sisters play as well."

Junia smiled happily. Suddenly life was just wonderful. She had Simon, and Gorawen had just complimented her. She asked Brynn to come with her the following day when she rode out to Mryddin Water to meet Simon.

"Gorawen says I should not meet Simon alone now that I am of a marriageable age," she confided to her younger sibling.

"And you actually listened?" Brynn said unbelievingly. "There is more to this than you are telling me, Sister."

Junia's pale skin grew pink. "Gorawen says if his family is a respectable one Da might be willing to make a match beween Simon and me!"

"And what if his family is not suitable?" Brynn demanded to know. "What will you do then, Sister?"

"Do not even think such a thing!" Junia cried. "Of course Simon's family will be suitable, Brynn. They must be!"

"But if they are not?" he persisted.

"I will not think about it," Junia replied.

"You must think about it, Sister," the boy pressed her. "Would you run away with him, that is, if he would do it? Would you refuse to marry at all?"

"I don't know," Junia admitted. "But Simon's family will be acceptable to Da. I just know it will, Brynn! Why are you always so dour?"

"Always have a plan, Sister," Brynn replied. "And another plan if the first one fails. 'Tis only prudent."

Reaching Mryddin Water they dismounted and secured their horses. Brynn began to climb the stairs of the ruined castle to their very top, which offered him a fine view of the surrounding countryside. Junia picked a bunch of daisies, and began to weave crowns from the flowers. She was very nervous. She had met Simon when she was twelve. Knowing his surname had never been necessary until today. How was she to go about learning that surname? Could she ask him outright?

"He's coming," Brynn Pendragon called out from his aerie atop the stairs.

Junia's heart began to beat rapidly. She pinched her cheeks to bring some color into them. Why was she so damned pale? She sat on her perch over the little river, watching as his big horse picked its way across the shallows to the other side. Seeing him entering the clearing she came forth to greet him along with Brynn, who dashed down from his watch post atop the stairs.

"Brynn! It is good to see you again," Simon said as he saw the boy. "What brings you here today?"

"Juni shouldn't be meeting you alone," Brynn said. "You are both of an age to make a match. I can't have my sister's reputation tarnished, now, can I, Simon?"

"Brynn!" Junia was blushing. "Oh, Simon, I do apologize for my little brother's quick tongue," she said.

"He's right, Junia, but the de Bohuns are honorable folk. I swear it," Simon de Bohun said with a smile. She was so fair, his Junia.

"As are Pendragons," Brynn replied. There! That answered the question they needed to know, and told him as well.

Brynn was pleased with himself. "I'm going rabbitting," he said. "I'll be back." And he trudged off, his traps in his hand, ready to set.

"Two years," Junia said, "and this is the first time I have known your surname."

"And I yours," he agreed.

"Simon?" She looked just a little bit anxious.

"Yes, Junia?" he answered her.

"Simon, I know of no other way of asking this than to come right out and say the words. Please do not think me forward."

He put his arm about her shoulders, and drew her against him. "What is it, sweeting? Why, I can see your little heart beating in the hollow of your throat. Tell me."

Junia drew a deep breath. Somehow his arm about her made her feel braver. "In a few months' time my father will seek a husband for me. If he approached your father, would you be amenable to such a match? Ohh, please tell me the truth! If you are not then I shall never speak on it again, and you must promise we will remain friends."

Simon de Bohun turned the girl about. His hands rested lightly on her shoulders. He looked directly into her eyes. "Junia, do you not know that I love you?" he said softly. "My innocent maid, you are the only girl I could ever wed. My father is not an easy man. Some say he is a cruel man, and I will admit that I have seen that side of him. But I am his only son. Certainly he will want me happy in my marriage, for the one good thing they say about Hugo de Bohun is that he loved my mother. I will speak with my father, and have him approach yours about a match now that I know it would please us both." Then he brushed her lips gently with his, and Junia almost swooned, for she had never before been kissed; but his arms wrapped about her, holding her close.

"Simon," was all she could say. Junia couldn't ever remember a time when she had been so happy. His cotte chafed her cheek, but she didn't care.

"I will approach my father tonight," Simon promised her, smiling into her green eyes, his hand caressing her face.

"They will not let me wed until I have past my fifteenth birthday next June," she finally said. "We must wait until then, I fear."

"It will give my family time to know you, and your family time to know me," he said. "I can wait, for you, sweeting, are a prize worth having."

"I have set my traps," Brynn said, returning.

"Unset them!" Junia said. "I want no blood spilled here, Brother, for this is a joyous place."

"Jesu!" Brynn swore, and stamped off to fulfill her unreasonable request. What the hell was wrong with Junia? When he returned she was alone again. "Where's Simon?" he asked her.

"He has gone home. We will meet again in three days' time. Come on! I don't want to be riding in the twilight, Brother. Who knows who is lurking about." She mounted her horse and looked impatiently to him.

Brynn climbed up into his saddle, gathering the reins into his hand. "What happened to put you in such a mood, Sister?"

"We are going to be married!" Junia exclaimed excitedly.

"What?" Brynn looked surprised.

"He loves me, brother! He loves me! He is going to have his father ask Da for my hand in marriage."

"Jesu!" the boy exclaimed again.

"You can tell no one, brother! Do you swear it?" she demanded of him.

"Why not?" Brynn laughed. "I cannot wait to see the look on your mother's face when the offer comes. She does not like the English. Even the Marcher English. Just knowing what I know will be worth the wait."

"I will have none but Simon," Junia said firmly.

"Now you sound like Maia, but at least we knew the Lord of the Lake was a man of means. What does Simon de Bohun have that will make him an acceptable husband for you in Da's eyes?" Brynn asked his sister. "Is he the eldest son, or a younger son? Will his family accept the circumstances of your birth? Will they accept your mother?"

"He is an only son," Junia said, "and what does the rest of it have to do with a marriage between us if we love one another?"

"Sister, sister," Brynn lamented. "Love has nothing to do with a good match. Matches are made for gold and for land. A match must give an advantage to both parties. Even I, young as I am, understand that. And so should you. Do you not recall that Da was considering matching me with Mary FitzHugh before she died? Had she been my wife it would have gained us the manor of Everleigh, and a toehold in the Englishry. Marcher lords always seek lands on both sides of the border. It is practical."

"I am the Dragon Lord's daughter," Junia responded.

"His youngest daughter. Born to a second concubine, and not a wife. You have little to offer the heir to an estate,"

Brynn reminded her. "Unless he's poorer than you."

"My sisters —" Junia began, but her brother cut her short.

"Averil's marriage was good fortune for her based on Rhys's stupidity. Maia was born a legitimate child, and had land to offer along with her dower of silver and cattle. Do not pin your hopes upon Simon's father agreeing to even consider a match between you two. He will be looking higher, seeking an heiress with lands to add to his as well as livestock and gold."

"You are wrong," Junia said firmly. "Simon will convince his father otherwise despite what you believe are my shortcomings."

"Your mother bore but one child, and a daughter at that," Brynn said.

Junia countered gamely, "Gorawen bore but one child, and yet her daughter now has two children."

Brynn laughed again. "Well," he said, "I can see you will fight to the death for what you want, Juni. I wish you naught but good luck, Sister."

"I wonder how far it is to Simon's home from Mryddin Water," Junia said.

It was not far, and Simon had ridden quickly, for he was anxious to tell his father that he had fallen in love and wanted to marry. At eighteen he was more than ready to take on the responsibility of a wife, and children of his own. His only qualm was bringing Junia into the de Bohun household where his father ruled with an iron hand. Junia was such an innocent girl, and from the stories she had told him of her family her house was a kinder place than his had ever been.

Simon had not lied when he said his father was not an easy man. That he was considered cruel by some. A few said the death of his beloved wife had been what changed him, but the old nurse who had raised Simon said otherwise. He was always cruel, she told Simon. But he had loved the lady Anne, and she had softened him while she lived. She had never really recovered from Simon's birth. Yet his father loved and treasured her. When Simon was twelve his mother found herself with child again. She had died shortly thereafter, unable to sustain either herself or her unborn babe. Hugo de Bohun had bitterly mourned her passing for a year before he reverted to his old and wicked ways. He had left the raising of his son to his beloved wife, and her elderly nurse. After Lady Anne's death no women would serve willingly in Hugo de Bohun's household, for most who did were prey to the lord and his men. His serfs either hid their daughters or disfigured them to keep them safe from rapine. Simon could but hope that Junia would have as civilizing an effect on his father's house as his mother once had.

That evening the hall was unusually quiet, and Simon took the opportunity to approach his father who was not yet in his cups, and without his latest whore in his lap.

"I want to marry," he said.

"Aye, I have been thinking it was time for you to take a wife," Hugo agreed. "There's this little heiress whose lands match ours to the east. Her father would be amenable to a match, I suspect. The de Bohun name means something in this land though we are but a minor branch of it." He picked up his goblet and drank deeply.

"I have chosen my own wife," Simon said boldly. "I would marry for love as you once did, Father."

"I married for love, aye, and what did it get me? One son, and a broken heart. 'Twas foolish, and you will wed where I say you'll wed, boy."

"I will not marry some bucktoothed wench for her lands, damn it!" Simon said angrily. "I want Junia Pendragon, and by God, Father, I shall have her!"

"Who did you say?" Hugo de Bohun asked, his look suddenly dark.

"Her name is Junia Pendragon. She is Welsh, and while I know you profess to dislike the Welsh, many of your fellow Marcher lords mix their blood with the Welsh. It gives them lands on both sides of the border, and a stronger position."

"No de Bohun will ever marry a Pendragon, Simon! Are you a fool that you do not know the story? Do not tell me there is something old Elga has not told you?" he sneered, draining his cup and slamming it on the board to indicated his need for more.

A servant quickly filled the cup to the brim.

"What story?" Simon demanded. Until today he never remembered even hearing the name of Pendragon.

"Several generations back, I think it was in the time of my great-grandfather, a de Bohun son was to wed a Pendragon daughter. The bethrothal papers were signed, the dower delivered, when the bridegroom died unexpectedly before the wedding could be celebrated. The greedy Welsh Pendragons then demanded the return of the dower from us. Of course, we refused them. It was not our fault that the de Bohun lad died after the papers were signed. The girl's property was rightfully ours. Then the damned wench went and killed herself by jumping from the top of her father's keep because without her dower lands she could not wed another, and no convent would have her. The Pendragons blamed us, but it was not our fault. The dower was ours.

"It might have ended there had the Welsh been willing to let it go, but they were not. They kidnapped the de Bohun heir, and castrated him in retaliation for their daughter's death. Of course, he did not live long after it, but at least his wife bore him twin sons several months afterwards. She raised them to hate the Welsh, and particularly the Pendragons. It has been that way ever since. Pendragons do not wed de Bohuns, Simon, and there is an end to it."

"How long ago did this happen, Father? A hundred or more years ago? Is it not time for this feud, or whatever it is, to be ended? And what better way than by a marriage between a Pendragon and a de Bohun? A marriage that this time will be celebrated and consummated, and lead to de Bohun heirs," Simon said to his father. "A betrothal began this feud. Let a marriage end it."

"Jesu!" Hugo de Bohun swore violently. "It is as I have always feared. You are a damned weakling with a soft heart. Fuck the girl if you must, but you will wed the girl I choose for you to wed. You will not disobey me in this."

"I will marry no one but Junia Pendragon," Simon said angrily.

"You will wed Aceline de Bellaud," Hugo roared. "She is an only child, and her father is as anxious for the match as I am."

"First you speak of this girl as if you are merely considering it. Now suddenly it appears that you have already set the negotiations in motion, yet you have not consulted me in the matter. I am eighteen, Father, not a stripling of twelve."

"Under the law, however, you are bound to obey my wishes, Simon."

"I could leave Agramant," Simon threatened his father.

"Leave your home?" Hugo shouted, and he slammed his cup onto the high board, sloshing wine across it. "Where the hell do you think you would go? And what would you do, you damned weakling?"

"I could go to my mother's family," Simon said.

"Do not think your grandfather would take you in under the circumstances. He would send you packing as soon as he learned why you had come! Your mother's father is a man who understands the necessity of an advantageous marriage. Aceline de Bellaud will make you an excellent wife. Her lands are fertile. She has livestock aplenty. And she has a dower of both silver and gold."

"If she is so well-propertied, Father, then why would her father consider us?" Simon queried his father. "We are a minor branch of the de Bohuns."

"But we are still de Bohuns," Hugo replied. "And while the de Bellauds have wealth, they have not a great name. We do. Aceline is an only child. Her father's line dies with her, but can live on in her de Bohun sons. I have seen the wench myself. She is ripe for fucking, and you'll get a houseful of sons off such a toothsome little bitch."

"It sounds as if you would like to have at her yourself, Father. Why don't you wed her? Why must I be the sacrificial lamb to your greed? And while I am thinking about it, what the hell was the matter with the de Bohuns that they would not return the dower belonging to the Pendragon girl? The marriage had not been celebrated, and the death of the bridegroom was not their fault. The dower should have been returned. It was not the Pendragons who were greedy, Father. It was the de Bohuns."

"They killed the de Bohun heir," Hugo growled.

"After their daughter was cheated, shamed, and killed herself," Simon countered. "I expect they considered it as much justice as they would ever receive from us."

"It matters not just what I say or think, Simon," his father replied. "The Dragon Lord will never allow you to wed his child. The Pendragons hate us every bit as much as we hate them. Put the girl from your thoughts and concentrate on a marriage with Aceline de Bellaud, for it is she who will be your wife, and not this Junia Pendragon."

"I will not marry this girl of your choosing," Simon said firmly. "I will wed with Junia, or I will not wed at all."

"You will obey me, Simon, for I am your father," Hugo said. "Whatever made you think you could choose your own wife?"

"You did," was the answer.

"Aye, I did, but I was lord of Agramant when I did. My father was long dead, but I followed in the path I knew would please him when I chose your mother. I could not have known how frail she would become after your birth," Hugo de Bohun replied. "You have not the authority to pick your own wife, and so you will obey your father who does."

"Must I kill you and become lord of Agramant to gain Junia as my wife?" Simon shouted angrily.

"You have not the balls for it, lad," Hugo mocked his son. "You are far too civilized and good-hearted. The bride I have chosen for you is a strong young woman. She will make up for your lack, and make certain you do what you should when I am gone one day." He laughed at the look on Simon's handsome face. "Sulk for a bit if you must, boy," he told his son. "Satisfy your longing for the girl if you are man enough. When you are ready to see reason we shall visit the de Bellaud family, and you can meet your bride, Simon. As I have said, a most toothsome little bitch."

"Go to hell, Father!"

"I undoubtedly will one day," Hugo responded, "but I shall have a fine time getting there, I promise you, boy!" And he laughed as his son stormed from his hall.

Simon found the sanctuary of his own chamber, and flung himself across his bed. What a disaster this was! But he loved Junia, and he was not yet ready to give up his quest for her hand in marriage. He would go to her father himself! He would do whatever he had to do to gain the Dragon Lord's permission to wed Junia. He heard the door to his chamber open and close, and looking up he saw old Elga.

"My poor laddie," she began.

"Were you in the hall?" he asked her, "Or did someone else report the conversation my father and I had? More a shouting match, I fear, Elga."

She sat down next to him on the bed. "You must give up this girl, my lad. If you do not, your father will do whatever he must to see that you do. Hugo de Bohun is a bad man. You have not yet seen the length and breath of his wickedness. Only your mother, God assoil her good soul, could keep his demons under control. If you truly love this lass you must part with her, for if you do not you put her in the gravest danger."

"I would go to her father and plead my case with him," Simon said. "Certainly if he sees how much I love Junia he will allow us to wed."

Elga was pained by her nursling's naivete. "Laddie, even if the Dragon Lord would take into account the love you and his daughter have for one another, what have you to offer if your father disinherits you? And he will if you disobey him."

"But I do not care if he casts me out, Elga! Junia has become my very life! Today when she said she loved me I thought my heart would crack within my chest from the sheer happiness I experienced. How can I give her up?"

Elga sighed. "You must, Simon. If you do not, then whatever vile revenge your father takes on this innocent maiden will be your fault. Can you live with that? And in the end you will still be forced to do his bidding and marry the bride of Hugo de Bohun's choosing. And the Pendragon girl will be forced to marry the man of her father's choosing despite her love for you. Better you break off this unfortunate liaison now so that both of your hearts may have time to heal," Elga advised. She patted his shoulder. "I am so sorry, laddie. More often in this life we do not get to do the things we want, or have the things our hearts desire. It is the way of the world."

He sighed. It was a deep and desperate sound. "I am to meet her again in three days at Mryddin Water," Simon said.

"And you will tell her then that this union between you is not possible?" Elga probed.

"I do not know," Simon replied.

"You have not breached her, laddie, have you?" Elga's worn face had a worried look upon it.

"Jesu, no!" he said with such fervor that she knew he spoke the truth. "I love her, Elga. I would not shame her."

"Of course, laddie, but I thought it wise to ask," she answered him. Then she arose. "I will leave you now to consider what you must say. You have three days in which to decide." And she departed his chamber.

"I will not give her up," Simon said softly to himself. "There has to be a way. There has to be!"

Chapter 14

She couldn't keep it to herself. She just couldn't! Seeking out Gorawen in the hall she caught up the older woman's hands in hers saying, "Simon is going to ask his father to ask for me in marriage!" Junia's eyes were sparkling. Her whole demeanor mirrored her happiness. She sat next to Gorawen.

"And Simon's family is?" the Dragon Lord's favorite probed gently.

"He is Simon de Bohun! It is an honorable name, Gorawen, is it not?"

Gorawen grew deathly pale. "Oh, my dearest child," she said, "you cannot wed with a de Bohun. Your father will never allow it. I am so, so sorry!" She reached out to embrace Junia, but the girl drew back as if she had been scalded.

"What are you saying?" she gasped.

"We must speak with your father now," Gorawen said, her eyes filled with tears.

Junia sat as if she had been carved out of stone. "You must say nothing until his father comes to ask for me," she responded woodenly.

"His father will not come, Junia. Merin! Please hear this," Gorawen called to the Dragon Lord. "Junia, tell your father of your meetings at Mryddin Water with Simon."

"What is this?" Ysbail was immediately on her feet. She ran to stand before Gorawen and Junia. "Have you been meeting with a man, you slut?" She slapped her daughter's face. "Will you ruin yourself, you little fool? Who will have you if it is known you are a road already well traveled?"

Gorawen jumped to her feet. "Do not dare to hit Junia," she said angrily. "You know naught, but you have already assumed the worst. Are the daughters of this house raised to behave like common whores?"

"Do not tell me how to discipline my daughter," Ysbail screeched. "I did not raise her to behave like some trull!"

"And she has not!" Gorawen said sharply. "If you will shut your mouth and keep your evil thoughts to yourself you will learn the tragedy that is befalling your child. Her sweet and innocent heart is about to be broken."

Ysbail sat down heavily. "What has happened, Junia?" she queried her daughter in calmer tones. "Tell me."

"No," Merin Pendragon said. "Tell me, daughter," and he came and sat on the other side of her from Gorawen, pushing Ysbail away as he did so, curious that Brynn came and sat down on the floor before his sister.

"His name is Simon de Bohun," Junia began, hearing both her mother and Argel gasp. "Brynn and I met him two years ago in the ruins at Mryddin Water." Two large tears slipped down her pale face. "We are in love, Father. He wants to marry me. Why is that so wrong?"

"It is not wrong to be in love, Juni," her father began. "And it is not wrong to want to wed. But there is bad blood between the Pendragons and the de Bohuns, my daughter. No marriage between you and this Simon can ever be celebrated. I am sorry."

"Why is there bad blood between our families, Da?" Junia asked, her voice shaking with her shock.

"One hundred and twenty-two years ago Bronwyn Pendragon was to marry Robert de Bohun. The betrothal papers had been signed, and then in a quirk of fate Robert de Bohun died before the marriage could be celebrated. His family refused to return Bronwyn's dower portion. They claimed the very agreement signed by both families led them to it. That it was not their fa— —ir son had died. It was a dastardly and —ly act. You know that the Pendragons— never been a wealthy family, Juni. Wit— the return of her dower Bronwyn c— —t be rematched. Not even the riches— —gious house would take her without a portion of some kind, and there was simply nothing left. Because of the de Bohun name we had scraped together everything we could. But Bronwyn had loved Robert de Bohun. Heartbroken by his death, and by the fact his family's refusal to return her dower had caused a breach between the Pendragons and the de Bohun's, Bronwyn threw herself from the top of the north tower."

"Oh, Da!" Junia said softly.

"That was not the end of it, daughter," the Dragon Lord continued. "Bronwyn's father sought out the de Bohun heir, the family's other son. He castrated him, causing his eventual death. He had hoped by this brutal act to wipe out the family thus restoring his daughter's honor. However, the de Bohun heir's wife was enceinte. She gave birth to twin sons seven months later, and raised her children to hate the Pendragons as has every generation of de Bohuns since. And that, Juni, is why you cannot wed with a de Bohun."

Junia was silent for a long moment, and

then she said, "That is ridiculous, Da! Are you telling me that because of a feud that was begun one hundred and twenty-two years ago, Simon and I cannot wed? Have neither the Pendragons or the de Bohuns ever considered healing this terrible breach? Is not now a good time to do it? Until this day neither Simon or I was aware of the other's surname, and certainly we did not know of this feud. We have fallen in love. We want to marry. Can the love we have for each other not cure the ancient bitterness between our families? Is not love stronger than hate? I think it is, and I would have Simon de Bohun to wed. No other."

"Junia," her father said, "I would give you this if I could, but I cannot. Your Simon's father is a man with a particularly cruel reputation. For a time he ceased his wickedness, for his wife was known to be a very good woman. But after her death he once again took up his old ways. He will not consider a match between our families. I am sorry."

"If no one will try to make peace then there will never be peace," Junia replied.

Merin Pendragon nodded. "That is true, daughter, but it is the way of the world."

"I will have no other to husband me," Junia said stubbornly.

"Aye, you will, one day, Juni," the

Dragon Lord told his youngest daughter, "but for now your heart needs time to heal itself. I will not force you into marriage with any man until you tell me you are ready to consider it," he promised her.

Junia stood up. The look she gave them was so tragic that Argel, Ysbail and Gorawen all began to weep. Then the young girl ran from the hall sobbing bitterly.

"Is there no hope?" Gorawen finally said.

The Dragon Lord shook his head. "If Hugo de Bohun did not have so foul a reputation I might attempt to end the bad blood between us for Juni's sake, but I want no daughter of mine in that man's house. And who is to say this Simon did not know Junia was my child? Who is to say he is not like his father, and was attempting to seduce her?"

"Simon is a good man, Da!" Brynn spoke up. "He has always treated my sister with the utmost respect."

"But you have not been with them always," Gorawen reminded the boy. Like his sister he was yet trusting of the world.

"You left them alone?" The Dragon Lord sounded displeased.

"My sister asked me not to trail after her," Brynn said, the very memory of it offending him. "It was only a few times, but I spied on them twice. All they were doing

419

was sitting and talking. And they weren't even close to each other."

"We raised her to have pride in her honor," Argel said quietly.

Gorawen concurred, saying, "I trust Junia, and she has told me nothing happened between them. I believe her, Merin."

"I will beat her senseless if I learn she has been loose in her behavior," Ysbail muttered. "What a pity there is bad blood between the de Bohuns and us. What a fine match that would have been for my daughter! A de Bohun for a husband would certainly have been a better catch than a FitzHugh, and perhaps even Emrys Llyn."

"Put it from your mind, woman," Merin Pendragon said harshly. "Hugo de Bohun's serfs are said to scar their own daughters to keep them from his roving eye and that of his men. I should not like our daughter in such a house."

"To think that Junia could attract such a fine name," Ysbail said, half ignoring him. "You will have to go some, my lord, to find an equally good husband for Junia now. I shall not be satisfied with just anyone."

Argel and Gorawen looked at each other, both tempted to laugh. They managed to restrain themselves. As always, Ysbail was being selfish. They knew she hoped to leave Dragon's Lair to live in her daughter's house when Junia was finally wed one day. Both knew she would be doomed to disappointment in that matter. Still, both women wished that Ysbail understood the heartbreak that Junia would suffer from this incident. They could but hope to console the young girl's disappointment in her stead.

Junia did not appear in the hall the following day. She kept to her tower chamber.

Argel sent a servant up twice with a tray for the girl. Both trays were returned untouched. Junia would allow no one into her chamber. Listening at the door Gorawen heard her weeping piteously, and hurried away lest she weep herself. They left her to herself, for they knew that Junia needed time to come to terms with the unfortunate situation. And then on the evening of the second day the young girl appeared in the hall, and took her place at the high board. She was pale, and very quiet, and she did not speak a great deal but to answer when spoken to, but this was in keeping with her past behavior.

The following morning Junia came into the hall, and broke her fast. She seemed a bit more cheerful, and Brynn noted it aloud. They were alone.

"Today is the day I am to meet Simon,"

Junia said softly, her eyes shining. "I know he will have overcome his father's objections to a match, for he loves me. Together we will surmount my father's objections. It is past time this feud was ended, Brynn."

"Don't tell me you are going to Mryddin Water, Juni," the boy said.

"Simon said he would meet me in three days' time. Today is the third day, Brother," Junia replied calmly.

"If his da is as bad as our da says, he'll not be there. It might even be dangerous for you to go, sister," Brynn warned her.

"Simon will let nothing happen to me, Brynn," Junia assured her brother.

"Then I will go with you," he answered her.

"Nay, you must not," Junia responded. "Given that both Simon and I now know the story of our families estrangement, it would appear that I did not trust him if you came. There is naught for me to fear."

"Let me go," Brynn pleaded with her. "If he is not there, you have your answer. If he is, then I will ascertain the lay of the land for you."

"Nay," Junia replied. "I trust Simon, and if you tell Da, I will follow the example of Bronwyn Pendragon, and jump from the north tower, Brynn."

Brynn grew silent. There was no reasoning with Junia when she got this way.

In that sense she and Maia were much alike. He would simply follow his sister to be certain she came to no harm. It was not likely that Simon de Bohun would show up anyhow. Like Junia he was bound to obey his father's wishes, too. Junia would make the trip, see the truth of the matter, and cry, but that would be the end of it. And he already felt badly for his sister. A feud such as the one his father had described in the hall three nights ago seemed so foolish. Brynn arose from the high board, and bidding his sister be careful, left the hall.

Junia went back up to her tower chamber. She washed her face, and brushing out her long black hair replaited it in a single braid, which she tied with a small bit of ivory ribbon. Her gown was a deep green. It was her second best gown, but she wanted Simon to be proud when they met today. Going to the stables Junia called for her horse, and it was brought. She mounted the beast, and rode from her father's keep, watching carefully to be certain that no one of note saw her go. The stable yard was quite empty, and the sentries posted at the entry to the keep merely nodded as she moved by them. They were used to Junia's wanderings.

Brynn Pendragon watched his sister leave their father's keep. As he knew where she was going, he also knew he need not hurry after her, and risk being seen. Simon never arrived at the ruins by Mryddin until after they did. Brynn suspected he waited to see them come before coming himself. There was more than enough time to reach the place of assignation. Brynn did not pray often, but he now prayed that Simon de Bohun would not come to meet his sister. No matter what he said, Junia would believe she could overcome the great odds of the ancient feud between their families. And knowing Simon de Bohun, another dreamer, Brynn thought, he would think so, too. It was a pity. They were very well matched. Perhaps one day when this Hugo de Bohun was gone to hell, Brynn considered, he could approach Simon, and together they would put a stop to this foolishness. Of course, by then it would be too late for Simon and Junia. Both would be wed to others.

Brynn now went to the stables to fetch his horse. As an afterthought he strapped on the sword his father had given him on his last birthday when he had turned eleven. His bow and quiver he affixed to his saddle before mounting the beast. Then he rode out of his father's keep, following the barely visible track that would bring him to Mryddin Water. He was far enough behind his sister that she would not hear him to her rear. By the time he reached the water the sound of the little weir would muffle the sound of his animal's hooves. Brynn was rather pleased with himself, and he thought his father would be, too. He was thinking like a warrior.

Ahead of him Junia's heart was hammering with her excitement. Simon would come! Of course he would come. He loved her. She could barely wait to see him again. She heard the sound of the little weir tumbling over the rocks before she even reached Mryddin Water. She loved that little waterfall. There was something magical about it that had always called to her. And then her path ended as she entered the small clearing by the water. Dismounting, she tied her horse to a tree so it would not wander, and waited for her lover to arrive.

"Junia!" His voice called to her.

"Simon!"

He was here. She watched as his mount picked its way across the stream just above the weir. He dismounted, and they flew into each other's arms.

"I love you!" she cried. "I don't care that you are a de Bohun!"

"I love you too, sweeting," he answered her, his arms enclosing her in an embrace. "I did not know of the feud until my father told me the other night."

"Nor did I," Junia answered. "Oh,

Simon, what are we to do?"

"What can we do?" he responded. "Without my father's approval, without your father's approval, how can we marry, how will we live, Junia?"

"I do not care as long as we are together," Junia declared passionately.

"Sweeting, you must have a home to lay your head. Food. And so much more," he told her. "How can I provide this for you if I am disinherited?"

"You could sell your sword, Simon. There is talk of another Crusade. I would go with you. We would survive the better for being together," Junia said.

"You have said your father would not permit your marriage until you are fifteen. Let me have until then to try to persuade my father to end this feud, Junia. And you will speak with your sire," he responded.

"What if your father decides to match you with another?" she cried.

"He has already made the suggestion, but I have told him I will have no other, and I will not, Junia. You know as well as I do that the church will not sanction any union that is coerced. There is no way on this earth that my father could force me to marry another, sweeting. I am yours. I swear it!"

"And my father has said he will not force me to any marriage unless I am content to be a bride," Junia responded, smiling up into his handsome face.

"This whole thing is so foolish," Simon said. "It goes back several generations, and until a few days ago I had not heard of it. How important can it now be to our families if we did not know?" He took her hands in his, and they sat facing one another on the stones about the clearing by the stream. "Junia, you must know that my father is not a good man. He was different while my mother lived, but after she died they say he reverted to his old ways. He is a cruel man. Frankly, I have done my best to stay out of his way these past few years. He does not care as long as I do his bidding. His lands and his passions are all that interest him."

"I am told your serfs disfigure their daughters to keep them from him," Junia said quietly. "Is it so, Simon?"

He nodded. "It is true, I am ashamed to admit."

"I think if his reputation were not quite so bad," Junia murmured, "I might cajole my father into making peace. Da is a good man, and loved by all who know him."

"If only I had my own wealth," Simon said desperately, "but I am beholden to my father for everything. The clothes I wear, every bite I eat, even my horse."

"But surely if your father loves you he

would want you happy in your marriage," Junia said innocently. "He did love your mother I have been told."

"My father does not love me," Simon replied. "I am little more to him than a possession, sweet Junia. Something to be made use of, nothing more."

"Who is the girl your father would have you wed?" she asked, unable to help herself, or stifle her curiosity.

"Her lands border ours in one direction. She is an only child, and while richer than we are, her name is not as noble. So in exchange for our name we gain her riches. Or so my father hopes; but I will not marry this girl, Junia. I will not!"

"I am Da's youngest daughter, Simon. My mother is nothing more than a concubine. My dower portion is very modest. Some sheep and cattle. Fifteen silver pennies when I reach the age of fifteen. Nothing more. I have no lands. Only my sister, Maia, who is the legitimate daughter, had a small portion of land in her dower."

"But you have said your two elder sisters married well," he said.

"They did," Junia admitted.

"Then you have useful relations," Simon told her with a smile. "That is something." He raised her hands to his lips, and kissed them. "Fifteen silver pennies is a goodly sum, Junia." His pure gray eyes smiled into her green ones.

She laughed softly. "You are making fun of me," she said. Oh, how she loved this man!

"It is a respectable dower, sweeting, and let none tell you otherwise. Your da has been very wise in setting aside such a sum, for it makes you a desirable bride despite your lack of lands. The silver can buy available lands," Simon told her.

"Well." Junia chuckled. "I am not the poorest prospect, I suppose." Then she grew serious. "We must play a waiting game, my love. As long as I know you love me I can do it, Simon. When will I see you again?"

"We need be careful, Junia," he said. "I want no harm coming to you."

And at that same moment they heard the thunder of hoofbeats, and a party of armed men galloped across Mryddin Water into the clearing. Junia and Simon jumped to their feet, but before he might get her on her horse they found themselves surrounded.

Hugo de Bohun smiled down cruelly on the pair. "So, my son, this is your little Welsh whore. Did I not tell you this affair was ended? You have disobeyed me, Simon. You know how angry I become when I am disobeyed, don't you?"

"We but met to say farewell, Father," Simon quickly said. "You were correct that Junia's father would not have a de Bohun as a son-in-law any more than you would have a Pendragon for a daughter-in-law." His arms held Junia close to his side in a vain attempt to protect her from the danger he sensed surrounding them.

Hugo de Bohun laughed aloud. "How noble you are, my son. You make me want to puke, you reek so of goodness." The men accompanying him laughed with their master, and their horses shifted nervously at the rough sound.

Junia moved from Simon's side, and looking up at Hugo de Bohun said in a firm voice, "I will go now, my lord." She made to push past his stallion, but Hugo de Bohun moved the beast to block her.

"And just where do you think you will go, mistress?" he growled. He was a stocky man with a black beard and shaggy black hair.

"Home," Junia answered bravely. "Get out of my way!" She shoved at the large horse, attempting to get by it.

"The wench has more backbone than you do, Simon." His father laughed. "If she were not a Pendragon I might reconsider my decision." Then he looked down at Junia. "You will come with us, my pretty wench. My men could use some new amusement to entertain them, and I suspect you will put up a good fight."

Simon jumped forward. "You will not touch her, Father! I will not let you! I will kill you if you do! As God is my witness, I will kill you!"

"You want her, then?" Hugo de Bohun said, laughing heartily.

"Yes, damn you, I want her!" Simon shouted.

"Then take her," his father answered, a cruel smile upon his face.

"What?" What mischief was his sire plotting, Simon wondered.

"Take her! Here! Now!" Hugo de Bohun replied. "You say you want her."

"Have you lost your mind?" Simon responded, the look of shock upon his face palpable. "You have finally gone mad, my lord. Junia is a virgin of good family. You cannot mean what you are saying."

"If you do not take her here and now, my son, I shall have her first, and then I will give her to my men; and they will use her very well, I assure you. But make her your leman now. Here, before us all, and I will spare her that. The choice is yours, Simon, but make your decision quickly."

Simon de Bohun could not move for a moment he was so shocked by his father's words. He had always known his father was a cruel man, but this went beyond the very bounds of decency.

"I will count to three, Simon," his father spoke again, "and then the girl is prey for me first and then my men."

Junia had listened to all of this with growing horror, but then she realized that to show fear was exactly what would give this horrible man pleasure. "I am not afraid, Simon," she said bravely.

Hugo de Bohun laughed. "One," he said.

"Junia! Do you realize what he is suggesting that I do to you?"

"Yes," Junia answered calmly. "He wants us to make love before him."

"Two," Hugo de Bohun growled.

"Nay! He wants me to rape you before them all," Simon gasped.

"Do it!" she begged him. "The alternative is worse, Simon! Do it!"

"Three!" Hugo de Bohun cried, and he looked to his son.

"Very well," Simon said, turning to look at his sire, "but I will damn you to hell with my dying breath, Father. May you roast in eternal damnation for this!"

"Strip her!" Hugo said coldly, nodding to his captain, "and hold my son back until she is as naked as the day she was born. At least we will get a good look at what we are missing." He turned to his son, grinning. "If you cannot get it up, my lad, I shall do the deed for you. It has been some time since I had a juicy young virgin such as this wench."

Simon was quickly restrained, but Junia snapped at the men who had surrounded her, "Do not touch me! I have not clothing to spare. I will remove them myself."

"No!" Brynn Pendragon jumped from behind the rocks surrounding the clearing by Mryddin Water, his sword in hand. Surprising them, he engaged the nearest man, blooding him. "Run, sister!" he shouted at Junia.

Hugo de Bohun leapt forward, knocking the sword from the boy's hand, and hitting him a blow that sent him unconscious to the ground. "By God! By God! It gets better! This is the Dragon Lord's son! Bind him up and throw him over my saddle," he directed his men. Then turning back to Junia, he said, "Now, wench, disrobe, and do it prettily for I would be amused by your performance."

"Go to hell!" Junia snapped angrily. "If you hurt my brother my father will kill you for certain. If I do not stick a knife in you first, de Bohun!" She pulled her gown off and lay it over a rock.

"Give me your boots, wench," he snarled at her. "You'll not go running off easily without them."

Junia sat down on the rock with her

gown, and yanking her boots from her feet threw them at Hugo de Bohun. Standing up again she undid her hair, hoping it would offer her some shield for modesty. Then, taking a deep breath, she pulled her chemise over her head, and lay it atop her gown. She was quite naked. She had to struggle to keep her fear down, and to maintain her composure.

Hugo de Bohun and his men stared lustfully at the young girl. Finally Hugo said, "I am a man of my word, but by God and his Blessed Mother, Simon, we have given up much, I think." He reached out and pulled Junia back against him, his hands reaching around to grab at her breasts. Unable to restrain herself Junia struggled against him even as Simon struggled in his captor's grasp. "Come, my son," Hugo taunted the younger man, "does not the sight of this naked beauty arouse your passions?" He grinned, and then said, "Take my son's tunic off, and let's see whether his manly cock can be brought to salute his virgin love."

"You are vile!" Junia cried out at her captor.

"If he doesn't take you, wench, I surely will, but having seen you I may relent a bit and not give you to my men. At least not for a few months," Hugo told her, and he kissed Junia's bare shoulder as his big hands crushed the tender flesh of her breasts.

His men had in the meantime stripped off Simon's tunic, and fumbling with his chausses bared his manhood, which had begun to react to the sight of Junia's nude, struggling form. They dragged him over to where their master held the girl, and pushed the young man against the naked girl, rubbing the two bodies together while laughing wildly. Hugo de Bohun forced Junia to the ground on her back as two of his men knelt and yanked her legs wide. Two others knelt by the girl's head, grinning as they pinioned her slender arms down. Then they shoved Simon between the girl's spread limbs.

"We've done all we can, boy," Hugo said crudely. "Now fuck her! And fuck her hard! Unless, of course, you want me to do it for you, and I could. I want to hear her scream when you pluck her cherry, boy. You can teach her the niceties later, but for now you will deflower the little Welsh bitch, and make her howl for more!"

Junia bit her lip, but then she whispered to Simon, "We have no choice, my love. I want no other but you. I care not the circumstances."

"This is barbaric," he whispered back, touching her face tenderly. "Junia, I am so sorry, for I do love you." He was ashamed, for his manhood was now as hard as the rocks that stood about this clearing, and he lusted for Junia as he had never lusted for another. Encircled by his father and his men, he was being forced to rape the girl he loved. And what was worse, he wanted to take her. He couldn't help himself.

"Think of another time and place," Junia murmured in his ear. "We are there. Not here. We are alone, Simon. Alone to indulge our passions for each other. Make love to me, my darling. Make love to me here and now!" Her words were braver than she was feeling, and what of her little brother, now trussed like a slaughtered deer on Hugo de Bohun's saddle.

"Do you know the first time hurts?" he whispered, and when she nodded he said, "You must scream loudly else my father will not be satisfied, sweeting. I don't want him hurting you again." He found the soft entry into her body, relieved that she was moist.

"Get on with it!" his father shouted. "Will you just lay atop her like a wet coverlet, boy? Ride her hard, Simon! Ride her hard!"

"I am not afraid," Junia told him. "I love you, Simon de Bohun!" She felt him pushing carefully into her inexperienced body, and she was grateful for his care of her in this terrible circumstance.

"Have you got it in her yet?" Hugo shouted.

Junia moaned convincingly, and her tormentor grinned, pleased.

"Am I hurting you?" Simon gasped.

Junia almost laughed, but she swallowed back her giggle. "Nay, it is for effect, my love." Then her green eyes widened as he pushed farther within her innocent body, and she felt herself opening to take him. "Oh! Ohh! Ohhh!" she cried out, and her eyes closed, for she could not bear to look at the cruel and lustful faces of the men staring down on them another moment. The two men holding her legs apart now stood, pulling her legs up and wider as Simon's manhood slid deeper.

Hugo de Bohun was not yet satisfied with his son's performance. The lad was coddling the girl. Walking over to his stallion he pulled a leather strap from the saddle. The boy thrown across his mount glared with angry eyes at him, but could say naught for they had gagged him. Hugo walked back into the circle where his son was carefully moving on the girl now. Raising the leather in his hand he brought it down across Simon's bare buttocks, laughing as his son jerked in surprise.

"Enough of this shilly-shallying, lad!" he cried. "Impale her fully. I'll not stop whipping you until you do!" He brought the leather strap down again and again on Simon's bared bottom until his son began to move swiftly upon the girl beneath him.

"I am sorry, my love," Simon groaned, and then he thrust hard, shattering Junia's maidenhead, almost weeping at her genuine scream of pain.

"Keep it going, lad!" his father shouted, beating Simon all the harder with the leather strap. "I want her furrow well plowed, and watered with your juices."

Junia thought for a moment that she was going to die, but she quickly realized better. She kept her eyes tightly shut, but she could not drown out the sound of Hugo de Bohun's vile words, nor the sounds the men surrounding them were making as they watched the spectacle before them. Her head thrashed back and forth with the pain. The worst of it was quickly gone, but the continued friction of Simon's manhood was irritating her. Then she felt him stiffen atop her. He shuddered, and there was the sensation of something filling her body. He slumped for a moment atop her, but then regaining his composure arose, pulling Junia up with him.

"You've had your entertainment, you devil!" he snarled at his father. "Now let Junia go. And her little brother."

"Nay, lad," his father told him. "They

are coming with us. The boy will spend the rest of his days in my dungeons. And your Welsh whore will spend her time in your bed awaiting your pleasure. You love her. I can see it in your eyes, Simon. You won't be able to resist using her despite your vaunted nobility. I have done you a great kindness, my son. You will have your cake, and eat it too. Your Welsh leman, and Aceline de Bellaud as your wife with her lands matching ours, and all her other wealth." Hugo de Bohun smiled at his son, but it was more a sneer than a smile.

"No! I won't have it!" Simon shouted at the older man.

Hugo laughed. "You won't have it? Oh, have you tired already of your Welsh whore, my son? Will you give her to me, or perhaps to my men? For if you do not protect her that is what will happen to her. The wench's only chance at survival is if she belongs to you, Simon. Do you understand me? If she does not belong to you, then she is fair game for my soldiers. Now pull up your chausses and get dressed. There is rain coming, and I do not wish to be caught out in a late summer's downpour." He turned away from his son, his lustful look going to Junia. "Did you enjoy your first cock, girl? You'll take mine, and many others, before you finally die. But for now my son will keep you safe. His wife, however, may not be as open-minded."

Junia glared at him, and pulled on her chemise. "Give me my boots, old man," she snarled. She was bleeding, and she hurt, but she would say nothing.

"You'll ride barefoot, bitch," he growled back. "Slave whores don't wear shoes. And if you ever throw anything at me again I'll take this strap I used on your lover and beat you myself. Do you understand me, girl?"

Junia nodded, pulling her green gown over her head. As she quickly rebraided her hair her eyes went to her brother. His face was wet with his tears. Dear God, had he seen it all? *I will kill Hugo de Bohun one day*, Junia thought to herself. *I swear by the blessed St. David that I will kill him!* She walked over to Brynn and brushed the tears off his cheeks. "It's all right, Brynn," she told him. "Simon loves me. We will get through this."

"Get away from the prisoner, girl!" Hugo de Bohun ordered her, his thick fingers grasping hard at her arm and dragging her away from the boy.

Junia drew away from him saying, "He's just a child, my lord. Let him go."

"He is your father's only son," Hugo de Bohun said, grinning evilly, "isn't he?"

Junia stared stony-faced at her tormentor.

"And so ends the proud line of Arthur," Hugo de Bohun sneered. "Get on your horse, wench. One of my men will lead it, and your hands are to be bound."

"Do what pleases you, my lord," Junia replied.

He laughed again. "You're a hard wench. You'll give my son a goodly number of strong little bastards. I shall look forward to dandling them on my knee."

"I will strangle them at birth," Junia answered him, smiling wickedly.

"By God, wench, I have, I think, made a mistake giving you to my son instead of keeping you for myself. I thought you to be a weak as water little bitch, for my son is a weak as water man. But you are all fire and fight. Still, I could tame you."

"Not even at the height of your powers, my lord," Junia told him, "but you are long past those days, are you not?"

Hugo de Bohun laughed again. He had always enjoyed a challenge. He would leave the Pendragon girl to his son as he had promised, but come Simon's wedding night to Aceline de Bellaud, his fiery Welsh leman would be fair game, Hugo decided. He would have the wench beneath him then. And when he had finished with her she would never again be satisfied with his son Simon. But there was plenty of time

441

for that, and the wait for Junia Pendragon would make having her all the better. Licking his lips in anticipation he led the girl to her horse and lifted her up, sliding his hand beneath her bottom and squeezing her buttocks as he did so. He laughed when she swore at him.

Chapter 15

The de Bohun home of Agramant was fashioned of dark stone. It was a small castle with four square towers, and black slate roofs. They rode across a drawbridge which lay over a water moat, and beneath an iron portcullis into the courtyard. This would not, Junia, realized, be an easy place from which to escape. She watched helplessly as her brother was pulled from Hugo de Bohun's horse. Brynn fell heavily to his knees, unable at first to stand, for he had been left across de Bohun's horse head down for several hours now. The men-at-arms who had been accompanying them laughed, and prodded him up cruelly, but Brynn was yet dizzy and could not remain upright. When he could not, the master of Agramant kicked the boy, shouting at him to arise.

Simon stepped between Brynn and his father. "Let the boy alone, Father. He will stand in a moment or two when he is able. His head is surely spinning from being across your horse all that time."

"Pah! What a weakling you are," Hugo said irritably. "A real man would not show compassion for an enemy."

"Brynn is eleven, Father, and hardly dangerous," Simon replied.

"The brat injured one of my men and tried to skewer me," Hugo growled. "He showed considerable skill with that little weapon of his. He had no right to attack us."

"You were threatening his sister, Father," Simon reminded Hugo. Turning away from the older man Simon bent and put an arm about Brynn. "Can you rise now, lad?" he asked the boy gently.

Brynn nodded, eyes wary.

"I didn't know they followed me, Brynn, I swear it," Simon murmured low as he undid the binding about the boy's mouth and helped him up.

Brynn licked his dry lips several times, and swallowed once or twice before saying, "Thank you, Simon. I'm all right now."

"Take the brat to my dungeons," Hugo de Bohun said. "Look about you, boy. 'Tis the last glimpse of the world you are likely to see except for the scrap of sky from your cell." And he laughed.

"If I had been but a moment quicker, de Bohun, I could have killed you," Brynn said boldly. "Next time, and there will be a next time, I will succeed."

"Brave words, boy, but after a few weeks in my dungeons you will see the futility of those words. Take him away!" Hugo de Bohun now turned to Junia who was still sitting, hands bound, upon her horse. Licking his lips he leered at her, jumping back quickly as she spat at him. "Take your bitch to your chamber, Simon, and keep her there until I say she may come into the hall," Hugo said irritably. "You did well today, my son. Her screams were most gratifying." Then turning away he entered his castle followed by the men who had accompanied him.

Simon walked over to Junia and gently undid the rough strip of leather that had bound her slender wrists to the saddle's pommel. Junia slid immediately from her mount, but her legs buckled as her feet touched the ground. Simon caught her, preventing her fall, but was disturbed by the great shudder that racked her body when he touched her.

"Junia, my love, what is the matter?" he queried her.

Junia closed her green eyes briefly. "I want a place to hide," she whispered to him in an odd little voice. She drew away from him, and he saw her face was very pale.

He nodded, immediately understanding that the shock of the past few hours was finally beginning to affect her. "Can you walk unaided?" he asked her.

"I th-think so," she said low.

He held out his hand, but she drew back. "Come with me, then," he said with a sigh, his hand dropping.

"Don't let him see me," Junia pleaded softly as Simon brought her into the castle. "I cannot be brave any longer."

"You'll be brave again after a meal, and a good night's sleep," Simon said as he led her up a flight of stone stairs and down a dim hallway.

"I hurt," Junia replied, following him through a door into a small chamber.

"So do I," he responded. "I know my father took great pleasure in laying that strap across my buttocks. They still burn. I'll see you have water to bathe yourself, Junia, and the ache will be gone come the morrow, I am certain."

Junia looked about the chamber. The walls and the floor were stone. There was a bed, a chest, a stool, and little else. There was no hearth for a fire. The single window was shuttered with two sturdy wooden shutters. The bed, however, was curtained, and would provide some shelter against the winds that would creep through the cracks in the walls and the window.

"What does he mean to do with my brother?" Junia asked Simon.

"I am not certain yet, but I do not think he will kill him," came the reply.

"Will he torture him?" Junia pressed.

"I don't know, but I will do my best to dissuade him from harming Brynn," Simon answered. He couldn't lie to her, but perhaps he could convince Hugo to leave the boy alone. Merin Pendragon would eventually come for his children, and Simon determined to do all in his power to help the Dragon Lord regain their custody even if it meant going against his father. Hugo's cruelty this afternoon had surpassed his previous worst efforts. Simon remembered his mother, and how she had struggled to see that her only child did not grow up to be the man his father was. Anne de Bohun had been a compassionate and kind woman of great faith. So much so that his father had gone against his very nature to please her while she lived. He had been unable to maintain his reformation once she had died. Anne had held his demons at bay. Without her he was helpless to do so, and not even the son they had created together could help him.

Simon considered how horrified his mother would have been at the rape of Junia Pendragon. And it had been rape despite the fact Junia had cooperated. It had not been at all the way he had envisioned their first coming together. It had been lewd, and violent. And now he saw Junia's brave façade beginning to crumble as fear began to overcome her. He had to prevent those fears from overwhelming her. And he had to keep his father from seeing her afraid.

"I want to see my brother," Junia said in a quavering voice.

"My father will not let you, sweeting," Simon replied, "but later I will go below to the dungeons and reassure Brynn. His main concern is for you right now."

"The Dragon Lord will come, Simon. Oh, God! By our actions we have only revived the feud between our families!" She began to weep.

He reached out to gather her into his arms, but she drew back, the fear in her eyes now very visible. "Junia?"

"Please, Simon, do not touch me," she whispered. "I do not think I can bear it if you touch me now! Please, I beg of you!" The tears ran down her pale cheeks.

He nodded helplessly. "Junia, I am so sorry. So very, very sorry! You know I would have never touched you but for my father. Say that you can forgive me," he pleaded. "How can I live knowing what I have done and how it has hurt you?"

Reaching out with a tentative hand Junia patted his hand. "Like the pain between my thighs, Simon, these fears I now harbor will also recede eventually."

"I will not touch you again in that way until we are wed," he swore.

Junia shook her dark head. "Oh, Simon, we will never be wed," she said. "Your father will have his way, and you will marry this girl he has chosen for you. But my father will come, and he will not rest until Brynn and I are free. As for me, no man will have me now. I have been despoiled. But perhaps some convent will accept me despite my modest dower. I have no real calling for the church, but what other road is there for me?"

"I will not marry this Aceline de Bellaud," Simon responded stubbornly, "and one day I will teach you how sweet passion is between two people who love one another, Junia. I will kill my father before I let him harm you again!"

"Nay, Simon, I will kill him myself one day," Junia whispered.

There came a scratching upon the door to the chamber, and Simon called, "Enter!"

The door opened to reveal a tiny wizened woman followed by a young girl with a scar across her face that ran from her right temple over the bridge of her nose, and to the left corner of her mouth. The girl carried a basin of water in her hands, and across her arms were several clean cloths.

"Elga!" Simon was relieved to see his nurse.

"Your father boasts of his foul deeds today in the hall," Elga said, shutting the door behind them. "Put the basin on the stool, Cadi." Her attention then turned to Junia. "My poor child," she said. "I am Elga, she who nurtured this laddie, and before him his mother, the Lady Anne of blessed memory. I have come to take care of you now, my chick. Simon, leave us, and do not come back until I tell you." She shooed him from the chamber, turning back to Junia. "Tell me your name, child."

"I am Junia Pendragon," the girl responded.

"And you have been cruelly treated this day, Junia Pendragon," Elga said. "Let Cadi help you off with your gown, and I will make you feel better if you will allow it."

"I am so ashamed," Junia said low, realizing that she was embarrassed. What had she done that had caused Hugo de Bohun to order her rape?

" 'Tis not you who should be ashamed," Elga said fiercely, "but rather that fiend who is master here. Do you see Cadi's face? Lord Hugo took her eldest sister for his amusement, and so Cadi's father disfigured his own younger child to protect her. I then took her to help me with my chores,

450

for I am an old woman now. But at least no man will hurt her as you were this day, Junia Pendragon."

Junia began to cry again, the tears running down her face in dirty runnels.

Elga gathered the girl to her bosom. "There, child, there. My laddie loves you, and he will make it all right. He is a good soul as was his mother, God assoil her. If my lady had been alive this foolish feud between your families might have been settled once and for all. Now I fear for what will happen."

"My da will come." Junia sniffled as Cadi helped her from her gown.

"Of course he will," Elga agreed.

"My brother is in your dungeons," Junia said. "Elga, he is just a boy!"

"And a brave lad, too. I heard Lord Hugo said the boy might have killed him had he been a bit quicker. Well, better luck next time to him, and then my laddie will rule here at Agramant." Elga chortled. Then she grew serious once more. "Lie down upon the bed now, my child, and draw your chemise up so I may treat you. Cadi, put a cloth beneath the lady."

Junia lay down as she had been bidden. She closed her eyes but felt the heat of her embarrassment in her cheeks. Elga *tched* and clucked as she bathed Junia, wiping the blood from her thighs and private parts with a soft cloth and warm water.

"There is an herbal potion in the water that will help to ease the soreness, my child," Elga told Junia. "You are, of course, no longer a virgin, but there is no real damage done you otherwise. There," she finished, waving away Cadi and the basin. She drew Junia's chemise back down. "I am going to give you something that will help you to sleep, my child. You will feel better on the morrow, I promise you."

"But if I sleep I am helpless should he come into this chamber," Junia whispered fearfully.

"Who, child? Surely not Simon." Elga's face wore a puzzled look.

"Nay, his father!" Junia cried.

"Lord Hugo will not bother you. He has said aloud in the hall that you are his son's leman. He possesses a strange honor, that monster. He will not touch you as long as Simon protects you by his possession of you. Nay." She shook her grizzled head. "You need have no fear of Lord Hugo."

"I must be certain Brynn, my brother, is safe," Junia said desperately.

"Cadi, slip down to the dungeons and ask after the boy," Elga said. "I will stay with you, Junia Pendragon, until she returns."

"Thank you!" Junia replied, and then she

accepted the mint-flavored liquid that Elga offered her, asking before she drank it down, "Will you stay with me until I sleep, Elga? I feel safe with you."

Elga nodded, and then said, "Hurry, Cadi!"

Cadi sped down the stairs, and slipped like a shadow through the hall, taking the flight of steps that led down into the de Bohun dungeon. There was but one guard on duty. Cadi smiled her crooked smile. "Let me see the prisoner," she cajoled him.

"No one is to see him," the guard said surlily.

"I'll let you feel my titties if you do," Cadi tempted the guard. "I just want to have a look. I ain't never seen a Welshman before."

The guard considered her offer. Her face might be scarred, but he could see by the bulges in her gown that she had big breasts. "Come here!" he told her with a grin.

"Nay. First I get my look, and then you get your feel," she replied.

He thought a moment, and then he nodded. Even if she didn't mean to keep her promise she still had to get by him to get out of the dungeons so he'd get his feel, all right. "He's over here," the guard said, leading her to a small wooden door with an iron grill in it. "Hey, laddie, this wench would have a look at you."

"Your sister wants to know if you're all right," Cadi said.

Brynn nodded. "Is she?"

"Aye," Cadi responded.

"That's enough now," the guard said, pulling Cadi away. "I didn't say you could talk to him." He pulled her against him, and began to fumble her breasts.

"I'll make it up to you, then," Cadi told him, and she fondled his cock with skilled fingers. "Do you like this?"

The guard groaned. "Jesu, wench!"

Cadi laughed, and pulled away from him. "That's enough, now. Thank you!" and she sped off up the stairs again, leaving the guard rubbing himself.

She might have an ugly face, the guard thought, but by God and his Blessed Mother, the wench had a lust for life a man could appreciate. He wouldn't tell any of his friends of this little adventure. He intended keeping that hot little piece for himself. Eventually he'd get her against the wall with her skirts up. He grinned and wondered what her name was.

Cadi hurried back to the chamber where Junia was imprisoned. "I saw your brother myself, lady. He says he is all right and worries for your safety," she reported.

Junia was already half asleep, but she heard Cadi's words, and smiled weakly.

"Thank you," she murmured before slipping into a deep sleep.

There was a faint scratching at the door, and Elga nodded to Cadi to see who it was. It was Simon.

"How is she?" he asked. His eyes went to the sleeping girl.

"Frightened. Ashamed," Elga said. "Why on earth did you let your father force you to rape, laddie? Your mother would be furious."

"I didn't know he had followed me when I left here today to meet with Junia at Mryddin Water. He came upon us so quickly that I couldn't get her to her horse. He said if I didn't take her then and there that he and his men would. He meant it, Elga. The devil was hoping I would refuse so he could have my sweet love. I had no choice in the matter. I tried to be gentle with her, but my father took a strap and beat my buttocks in order to make me perform more vigorously. I begged him to let her go afterwards, but he said if I do not keep her as my leman, he will give her to his men. And, Elga, he means to wed me to Aceline de Bellaud."

The old woman nodded. Then she said, "You are fortunate he holds both of the Dragon Lord's children captive else that outraged father come down on Agramant with a cruel vengeance and more innocent folk be harmed. Now, laddie, did I not tell you I should call for you when I wanted you?"

"I just came back to tell Junia that her brother is all right. I visited the dungeons myself a short while ago," he replied.

"We know. Cadi went herself for your lady," Elga said. "Now go into the hall and eat, Simon. Your Junia will sleep the night through, and she needs that healing sleep far more than food right now. I will remain with her until you return."

"Have you eaten?" he asked her.

"Cadi will bring me a bowl of pottage, laddie. Go now else your sire come looking for you," Elga advised.

"He won't come here," Simon said with a small smile. "He is too busy in the hall boasting of his escape from the dangerous knife attack of an eleven-year-old boy."

"The laddie is but eleven?" Elga cackled her laughter. "Ah, no wonder his sister is worried about him."

"I'll be back as soon as I can," Simon said as he left them.

"The dungeon guard was cooperative?" Elga asked Cadi when Simon had gone.

Cadi nodded, giving the old lady a crooked smile. "Man who spends most of his waking hours in a dungeon gets lonely," she said with a mischievous wink.

"And?" Elga said, her grizzled head

cocked to one side.

"I let him feel my titties," Cadi said. "But not until after he had let me see the boy, and talk a moment with him. Master shouldn't imprison a boy like that, and for what? The lad was trying to save his sister. Seems it don't make no difference if you're rich or poor if you're a woman. Men will have their way."

Elga nodded. "You've a sharp eye, lass," she said, nodding. "But be careful when you play such games."

"I know what to do," she told the old lady. "Don't you worry none about me, Elga."

Junia slept through the night as her young body recovered from the shock it had sustained. She awoke, unsure for a moment just where she was, but then remembering, rolled over to find Simon next to her in the bed. Her sharp gasp woke him.

"How do you feel, sweeting?" he asked her, his gray eyes scanning her face.

"What are you doing here?" she demanded to know.

"My father has ordered that you be my leman, Junia. Do you not remember? You are in my chamber. If I do not sleep here he will think I am not coupling with you, and then he will take you for himself and afterwards give you to his men. This is the only way I can protect you, sweeting."

Her hand flew to her mouth. "Oh, God, Simon!" And the terrible memory of the previous day welled up. "Brynn!" she said.

"He is safe in my father's dungeons. He had not been harmed, and I will do my best to see that he is not, Junia."

"I want to go home," Junia whispered, low.

Simon de Bohun sighed. "I know," he said. "And I want to take you and Brynn home, but for now my father is adamant. You are safe here in my chamber where he has ordered that you remain until he gives you permission to come into the hall. Elga and Cadi will look after you when I am not here. How do you feel?"

She blushed. "The soreness is gone," she told him.

"Good," he replied. "Junia, I told you last night, and I say it again, I am sorry. I beg your forgiveness, sweeting. Tell me you do not hate me for what happened."

"I do not hate you, Simon," she answered him. "How could I when I love you, but I know now that love cannot be. Your father is a strong-willed man. He will have this girl he has chosen for your wife, and you cannot escape it. But you must aid Brynn and me. We must escape Agramant before this ancient feud escalates into something far worse, Simon. You are aware that Brynn is my father's only son. He will be wild with anger over his kidnapping."

"And what of you?" Simon asked her.

"I am his youngest daughter, my love. Daughter of his second concubine. He loves me as much as the others, but I am a daughter. Brynn is the son. My father's heir. If I cannot get away, at least help my brother, I beg you!"

"I will do what I can, Junia," he promised her, and he leaned over to kiss her lips, but Junia pulled back from him. He looked at her, puzzled.

"I am sorry, Simon, but I told you last night that I cannot bear to be touched right now," Junia reminded him.

He closed his eyes a moment feeling physical pain throughout his whole body as her words reached him. Then opening his eyes he looked into hers, which were filled with disgust and loathing as she stared back at him. "It will not get better, Junia, until I have held you in my arms again, and comforted you," he said quietly. "Each time you reject me your fears will grow larger. I swear to you that I will not touch you with disrespect. We will pretend for my father's sake that we are lovers now, but I will not make love to you, my darling girl, until you are ready again. But how can I believe that you have forgiven me unless I can hold you, and kiss your lips?"

"Oh, Simon, I am afraid," she admitted. "I can still hear the shouts of your father and his men as you took my virginity. I close my eyes, and I see their faces leering down at us. I see some of them rubbing themselves while you labored atop me. It was horrible!" Her eyes were now filled with tears.

"Aye, it was," he agreed with her. "I was so afraid for you that it was difficult for me to maintain my arousal. My father knew it, and that is why he beat me — that I would remain hard and plunder your virtue."

"I never knew people did things like that," she cried. "I thought love was good and fine. The love my father has for his women and his family is that way. My sisters are so happy in their marriages. I thought it would be that way for me, Simon. I did not know this darkness existed." The tears were now running down her face.

"Oh, Junia," he replied, "it should not have been the way it was for us. I am as much a victim as you. I am so ashamed that I was forced to violate the girl I love, and wish to make my wife. But I swear to you that I did not know what else to do. He threatened you, and he would have carried out that threat had we not obeyed him. He is the most wicked of men, and there is no stopping him." There were tears running down his face now, too.

Seeing them Junia reached up and caressed his cheek. Then she lay her head against his shoulder, sighing as his arms gently enfolded her. "What are we to do, my love?" she asked him.

He kissed the top of her head, rubbing his chin against her hair. "I do not know," he told her. "For now, all I can do is keep you safe in this chamber, and see that no harm comes to your brother."

"I think my fear is receding," she told him. "I told you last night and I meant it, Simon, that should the opportunity arise I will kill your father myself. He has made a mockery of our love, forcing us to couple before him and his men."

"Be careful, my love, for he is clever as most madmen are. Remember that as long as he holds Brynn his captive he has your cooperation whether you will or not." Simon kissed the top of her head again. "I will send Elga to you, sweeting," he said, and arising from the bed he quickly dressed, leaving her.

Junia got up when he had gone, and picking up her gown from the stool where Cadi had laid it the previous evening, she drew it on. She felt better dressed. She had no hairbrush so she ran her fingers through her long hair until it was untangled. Then she plaited it into a single, thick black braid. Bored, she made the bed, fluffing up the feather bed, and tucking the coverlet neatly. She had no sooner finished when there was a scratching upon the door.

"Come in," Junia called and both Elga and Cadi entered the room. The younger girl carried a tray.

"You should be hungry now, lass," Elga said. "I've brought you a nice trencher of hot porridge, along with some bread and honey."

Junia thanked the two women, and sitting on the stool quickly devoured the meal that they had delivered. When she had finished she looked about her, and said, "If I must remain here in this chamber then I must have something to do. Is there a loom upon which I may weave?"

"Aye! My lady Anne had a fine loom," Elga said. "Cadi, you must remain with the lass while I go to arrange for the loom to be brought here." She hurried from the chamber.

"Thank you for going into the dungeons last night, and seeing that my little brother was all right," Junia said.

" 'Tweren't no trouble," Cadi said. "He's a brave laddie. I wouldn't want to be in a cell with the rats, and no water."

"He has no water?" Junia was shocked.

"Master gave orders," Cadi replied. "No

food and no water for the boy. He's going to starve him to death, he says, and then send his body back to your father."

"Merciful Mother!" Junia cried, realizing with certainty now that Simon's father was indeed an evil man. Then she swallowed back her fear and asked Cadi, "How did you get to see Brynn last night?"

"Gave the guard what he wanted, what they all wants," Cadi responded.

"I do not understand," Junia said.

"I let him feel me up," Cadi answered matter-of-factly. "He's lonely down in that dungeon, lady. He does me a favor. I do him one. There is nothing unusual in it."

"You bargain with your body?" Junia was both astounded and shocked.

"Women ain't got nothing else of value to bargain with," Cadi replied sanguinely.

"I have to see my brother," Junia said. "And I have to get a skin of water to him that he may keep hidden. He can live without food, Cadi, but he cannot live long without water. When my father comes to get us I will tell him how good you were to me, and he will reward you. But his reward will be greater if his only son is still alive."

Cadi nodded. "I'd do it for nothing just to get back at the master for what he did to my sister," she said. "But I got to be practical, too."

Junia nodded. "I understand," she told the girl.

"Master will soon go out hunting with his son and his men. That would be the best time for us to sneak down to the dungeons. There will be no one in the hall then, for they will all be in the kitchens preparing the meal for when master returns. When he gets back from hunting he wants his dinner hot, and ready, else the kitchen staff suffers. I can get a skin of water. You will hide it beneath your gown. I'll do all the talking, and keep my friend busy."

"Thank you," Junia said.

"Will your da really come for you?" Cadi asked, curious.

"Aye," Junia said. "He will come, and woe to Hugo de Bohun when he does."

Elga returned accompanied by two men carrying a fine loom, and a basket of multicolored wools. The loom was set up by the chamber's single window, and with it a lovely padded bench.

"This is what my mistress sat upon when she was at her loom," Elga explained.

"Is the master gone hunting yet?" Cadi asked innocently as the two serving men departed the chamber.

"Aye, he's just off else I should never have gotten this loom from the corner of the hall he consigned it to when Lady

Anne died," Elga explained.

"The young mistress has got to see her brother," Cadi began, "and I got a plan."

"If he finds out you've taken her into the dungeons," Elga said, "he'll beat you senseless, girl. What if you're seen?"

"They'll all be below in the kitchens, Elga. You know how he is when he gets back from hunting. No one will see us so no one can tell," Cadi reasoned.

Elga thought for a long moment. "I'll go down to the hall and keep watch," she said. "Will your friend cooperate with you again? He'll want more than you offered last time, girl. Are you prepared to give it?"

"I knows just what I'll give him," Cadi said with a grin, "and he'll be a very happy man, Elga, I promise you. First, however, I need a water skin for the young mistress to take to her brother."

"There's one here," Elga said. "When I ask for another later I'll say someone must have taken it to fill it and forgot to return it." She took down the water skin from a peg on the far wall and shook it. "It's full."

Junia took the water skin from the old woman. She removed her gown and put the water skin about her neck, then replaced the gown. The skin was well hidden, and only someone looking closely at Junia would have wondered what the long lump beneath her clothing was.

The three women left the bedchamber, and slipped quietly down the stairs. As Cadi had predicted there was no one about, and the castle was extremely quiet. They left Elga to keep watch, and descended the staircase into the dungeons where the single guard remained on duty.

"Stay here a moment," Cadi instructed Junia, and then she called out to the guard, "I've come back to see you, handsome laddie."

The guard turned. "You want to see the boy again?" he asked, grinning.

"It ain't me who wants to see him, but his sister. Let her, and I promise to make it worth your while," Cadi tempted.

"The master would kill me if he found out," the guard said nervously.

"The master is out hunting with all his men," Cadi murmured, and she moved closer to the guard. "Don't you want to know what I'll give you, handsome?" she purred.

"Tell me, and I tell you if it's worth the chance," the guard said, pulling her close.

Cadi leaned into the man, and whispered softly in his ear. Then she licked the ear.

The guard's eyes widened. "You swear you'll do that?" he asked her. One hand plunged into her chemise top, and squeezed a breast. "What about the boy's sister?"

"She'll be locked in the cell with her brother having a nice little visit, while I give you the pleasuring that you deserve for being so kind to a girl like me," Cadi said, giving him a wink and a smile.

"All right," the guard said, his voice filled with his excited anticipation. He took his keys up and opened the cell in which Brynn was imprisoned. "Come on, lady," he called to Junia, and when she had slipped quickly by him into the cell he locked the door behind her, turning to Cadi with a grin. "Now, my girl, you must keep your promise to me. And do it slowly, lass. No kiss me quick, for as soon as you are done the girl must leave the cell. So if you wants her to have a good visit, you'll take your time."

"I'll give you the best time you have ever had, my handsome laddie," Cadi said, slipping to her knees and reaching beneath his garment for his manhood. Finding it she looked up at him coyly, and licked her lips slowly. "You're going to like this," she said, and took the flaccid manhood into her hand, and began to lick on it with leisurely strokes of her tongue. The guard moaned softly almost at once. Damn, she thought, he would not be able to hold himself back once she got him in her mouth. She'd really have to take her time if Junia was to have time with her brother.

Within the cell the brother and sister hugged each other silently. Finally Junia put Brynn back from her, and looked at him. "Your face? What happened to your face?" she asked him.

"It was when Hugo de Bohun hit me," Brynn said. "It hurts like the devil. I suppose it looks bad."

"Aye," Junia told him, and then pulling her gown over her head she lifted the water skin from around her neck, and handed it to him. "Don't drink too much," she cautioned him. "Lord Hugo means to starve you, and give you no water. Hide the skin beneath the straw. Only drink it when you must. I don't know if I can get another to you. He's out hunting, or I couldn't have snuck down from my chamber. I am confined there." She drew her gown back on as she spoke.

"What of Simon?"

"Filled with remorse. He does love me, Brynn, but alas, he is helpless before his father for he has naught but what Lord Hugo will give him."

"Da will kill the de Bohuns, father and son, when he gets here," Brynn said.

"Let him kill the father," Junia said. "I still want the son for my husband."

"The castle is well fortified," Brynn noted. "You'd be surprised what you can see hanging upside down on a horse." He gave her a small grin.

"Oh, Brynn, this is all my fault! I am so sorry!" Junia cried.

"Shut up," he muttered. "You couldn't help falling in love, and you didn't know he was the wrong man. Da will come for us, you may be certain, sister. And then Hugo de Bohun will regret his perfidy."

"Simon and I have in our ignorance but escalated the feud," Junia said sadly.

"There will be no more feud after Da comes," Brynn replied grimly. "He will wipe the de Bohuns out root and branch, and I will help him."

"Brynn!" Junia was shocked by the venom in his voice.

"I'll never forget what was done to you, sister," he told her grimly. "Never!"

"It wasn't Simon's fault, Brynn. By doing what he did he saved me from his father and his rough soldiers," Junia tried to explain.

"He should have fought his father to preserve your honor before he allowed himself to be put to you like a stallion to a mare," Brynn replied. "Do you not understand, Juni? You have been cruelly dishonored. No man will have you now."

"Simon —" she began, but he cut her short with a wave of his hand.

"Our da will kill Simon, sister. Pray God his foul seed did not take root in your womb," Brynn responded angrily.

Junia pressed her lips together to keep from screaming. Her brother was right. Their father would take his revenge on all the de Bohuns for what they had done. She put her hand into the pocket of her gown, and pulled out a chunk of bread. "Here," she said, handing it to her brother. "I don't know when or even if I can get any more food to you. Don't let the rats get it, Brynn."

He took it from her, and began cramming the bread into his mouth. He was hungry, and he was a growing boy. He had had no food since the previous morning, and his sister was correct when she said he was unlikely to see food again soon. Outside the wooden cell door they heard the guard begin to moan and sob. Brynn looked to his sister questioningly. "What the hell is she doing to him?" he asked.

"Look if you will," Junia said. "I don't want to know."

Brynn walked over to the door and looked through the grate. The serving wench was on her knees before the guard, and she was sucking on his cock for all she was worth. The look on the guard's face was one of pure bliss. Brynn grinned. He had been recently entertained in such a manner by one of his father's serving girls. It was a most pleasurable experience. He would remember to see the girl was spared when his father brought fire and sword to lay waste to Agramant. "Give the wench my thanks for what she has done," he told Junia, carefully blocking her view of the grate. "Tell her she need have no fear of the Pendragons even when they bring war to this castle."

Junia nodded. "Take a sip of your water, and then hide the skin well," she advised him. " 'Tis all I'm likely to be able to get you."

Outside of the cell they heard the guard give a muffled shout, and after a moment or two Cadi's voice said, "Now wasn't that worth the risk, handsome?", and the guard's assent. Another moment passed, and they heard the key in the lock of the cell door. Brother and sister embraced quickly.

"You must go now, lady," the guard said.

"Take care of yourself, Brother," Junia told him.

"And you also," he replied as she left him. The door was firmly closed and locked. Brynn Pendragon found himself alone again. He listened as his sister's footsteps faded away.

The two young women hurried up the winding stone steps and back into the hall again where Elga was awaiting them.

Without a word the trio quickly made their way upstairs to the chamber where Junia was supposed to be imprisoned. Once there they heaved a collective sigh of relief.

"I don't know what you did to that guard, Cadi, but thank you!" Junia said. "He certainly seemed happy enough when we departed the dungeons, and you gave me time for a good visit with Brynn."

Elga raised an eyebrow, while giving Cadi a swift look. Then she said to Junia, "How is the laddie?"

"His face is bruised terribly from where your master hit him yesterday," Junia said, "but he will live, and his spirit is not broken." She did not mention that Brynn spoke of nothing but revenge upon the de Bohuns. Elga and Cadi had been kind to her, but they still belonged to the de Bohuns and would have a certain loyalty to them.

"The loom is set up for you, child," Elga said.

"Then I shall sit down and weave," Junia replied. "It is as good a way to pass the day as any."

"Will you be all right if we leave you for a short while?" Elga asked. "We do have other duties about the household, for there are few women to serve. We shall replace the water skin when we return."

"I will be fine," Junia assured the two

472

women, and bowing, they left her, but Junia heard the key in the door's lock turn with a click. She was truly imprisoned now.

Chapter 16

Merin Pendragon looked about the hall. "Where are Junia and Brynn?" he asked of no one in particular.

Ysbail shrugged. "I never know where my daughter goes these days," she said, and looked to Argel and Gorawen.

"I have not seen either of them today," Gorawen said, and that knowledge gave her a sudden uneasy feeling. She turned to Argel questioningly.

"Brynn came to give me a morning greeting, but I have not seen him since," Argel answered.

"This is most strange," Gorawen replied slowly, looking past them to the windows in the hall where the sun could now be seen setting.

"I have never known my son to miss a meal," Argel noted. "Where could they be, if indeed they are together?"

"Search the castle!" the Dragon Lord said.

"Nay, they are not here," Gorawen replied. "I am certain of it! They are past games, and if they were here would now be in the hall for the meal." She looked to the Dragon Lord. "My lord, you must go to the men at the keep's entrance and ask if they have seen Brynn and Junia."

He nodded, and swiftly departed the hall. At his gate Merin Pendragon questioned the men now on guard duty. "Were you here this morning?" he asked them.

"Aye, my lord, both of us were. We will be off duty shortly," one of the men-at-arms responded.

"Did you see my daughter or my son leave the keep today?"

"Aye, my lord," the man answered. "The lady left first, and the young lord went perhaps fifteen minutes afterwards. Both traveled in the same direction."

"And they have not returned?" the Dragon Lord questioned.

"Nay, my lord, they have not returned," came the reply.

"And you did not think it odd that my son and my daughter departed here this morning and have not yet come home? Nor have you thought to inform me of this fact. You have already locked the gate!" He was shouting now.

"But the young lord and his sister always ride out," the guard protested.

"And they also ride back," Merin Pendragon said angrily. "When have you ever known my children to remain outside the gates after sunset, you witless boob!" He shouted for the captain of his guard, and when the man had come running he told him what had happened. Then the Dragon Lord said, "Send these two witless dullards back to the fields where they obviously belong, and gather together a troop of men with torches. I think I know where my children have gone. But whether they are still there is another matter entirely." Then turning, he hurried back into his hall where his women awaited him anxiously.

"They both rode out this morning, Brynn a short while after his sister. I suspect he was following her, and I suspect she was going to Mryddin Water to meet with that cursed de Bohun boy," the Dragon Lord told the trio.

"Aii! She will ruin herself, the foolish slut!" Ysbail cried.

Gorawen sent the woman an angry look, then said to her lord, "They would have come back by now. I think Junia may have just been going to tell this boy good-bye. She has always been obedient. But of course, she is in love, and young girls in love are apt to behave foolishly."

"Brynn must have either known of her plan to go, or seen her go, and followed her," Argel reasoned.

"Then why is he not back?" Ysbail wanted to know.

"Because he tried to protect his sister," Gorawen responded.

"From what?" Ysbail said.

"From whatever threatened her, and it must have been a terrible threat else he would have come home and told us," Gorawen said softly.

"The de Bohuns?" Argel paled. "Oh, God! Have they killed my son?" She began to weep wildly and tear at her hair.

"Nay, nay!" Gorawen quickly answered her. "Brynn is far more valuable as a hostage. The de Bohuns have always preferred money to anything else, Argel. Brynn will be safe. I am certain of it. It is Junia for whom we must fear. If this boy pursued his relationship with her in order to entrap her she is in far greater danger than Brynn."

"Aii!" Ysbail wailed again. "Now who will have the bitch to wife? She has ruined herself in spite of all our warnings!"

"Be silent!" Argel snapped, recovering herself. "Do you think our revenge on the de Bohuns will be any less because Junia is a girl?"

"But if she has been despoiled, what bounty will restore her honor?" Ysbail cried. "No man of good lineage and property will have such a wife."

"Let us not get ahead of ourselves," Gorawen spoke up again. Her palm was itching to slap Ysbail whose care was more for herself than for her daughter. "The de Bohuns may not have them at all. They may have escaped any trap and are just hiding, waiting for our good lord to come to their rescue." But in her heart Gorawen was far more concerned than she showed.

"My lord, the men are ready," the captain said as he entered the hall.

"Where are you going?" Argel asked her husband.

"To Mryddin Water," he replied. "If there was an ambush and attempted kidnapping of our children, and they did escape, they will surely be glad we have come to bring them home." He did not address the possibility that his only son and his youngest daughter had actually been kidnapped and might at this very minute be in de Bohun hands. Turning, he followed his captain from the hall.

Ysbail sat down and began to cry.

"Do you weep for your daughter or for yourself, Ysbail?" Argel said cruelly.

"You are a wife. You hold a position of esteem," Ysbail said bleakly. "A good match for my daughter was the one chance I had of living a comfortable old age."

"Our lord Merin will take care of you. He loves us all," Gorawen said softly.

"He loves you," Ysbail said. "He respects Argel as his wife. He took me to get a son upon, and I failed him, birthing another daughter instead. He has no use for me, nor would he be sorry to see me go."

"You do our lord a disservice," Argel replied. "Your daughter is his daughter. Junia shares blood with both you and her father, with my children and Gorawen's daughter. For that he will always regard you with kindness. You have never suffered in this house, or been in any sort of disfavor, Ysbail. Each of us, you, Gorawen, and I have our place in Merin Pendragon's heart. If Gorawen holds a larger portion of our lord's heart, I am not dissatisfied, for Merin has been a good husband to me, and a good lord to you and Gorawen. Why should you carp and cry? For now, our main concern is the safety of our children. My son, and your daughter. Their return home is all I pray for, Ysbail. So should you instead of feeling sorry for yourself."

"But what if my daughter has been debauched?" Ysbail said unhappily.

"Then we shall see her wed to the de Bohun boy before we kill him," Gorawen answered her. "We cannot allow such an insult to go unavenged. The marriage restores Junia's honor. His death restores ours. As a widow Junia would be eminently marriageable, Ysbail. And she will have her full dower as well."

"I had not thought of that," Ysbail said. "It is not as bad as I thought."

"It seldom is," Argel murmured. "Let us to table, ladies. The supper grows cold as we stand here gossiping."

The three women sat themselves at the high board, and ate the pottage of rabbit with onions and carrots, along with the rest of the day's bread with butter and cheese. Afterwards Ysbail excused herself, and hurried off to her own chamber. Argel and Gorawen were relieved. It was not easy being with Ysbail.

"Do you think the children will be found safe?" Argel wondered aloud.

"Nay," Gorawen said frankly. "They departed this morning long before the noon hour. If they escaped a de Bohun ambush they would have been home long since. They have been taken, I fear, and we must prepare to expect the worst for poor Junia. Unharmed, Brynn will bring a goodly ransom, and the de Bohun lord knows it. He is unlikely to harm the boy, but to dishonor Junia gives de Bohun an excellent opportunity for retribution against the Pendragons. This feud should have been settled long ago. Now it must be ended, for as long as the de Bohuns go on believing that they were somehow insulted those hundred some odd years ago, neither our children nor theirs can be safe."

"The feud had been quiet until Junia met the de Bohun boy," Argel said. "What an unfortunate happenstance."

"She says she is certain he did not know as she did not know, but I cannot believe it. I think he met her, told his father, and together they planned this mischief," Gorawen answered. "Poor Junia! He is her first love. Would that he might have been her last."

"But what if he is innocent of duplicity?" Argel asked. "If we wed them then we might end this foolishness for good and all. I say slay his father but leave the boy alive. It is only simple justice that a Pendragon daughter wed a de Bohun after all these years, and then live happily ever after."

Gorawen smiled. "It is possible, I suppose. That decision must be up to our good lord. He will know what the right thing is to do."

"He will know if we tell him," Argel said with a wicked smile, and Gorawen laughed. "We could both tell him," Argel considered, and Gorawen smiled at her friend.

"I know that Merin needed to go out tonight, and find out what he could, but I wonder what he can learn on a moonless night, even with torches lighting his way," Gorawen responded thoughtfully. "It is not an easy ride to Mryddin Water."

The object of her conversation was discovering that a hard trail to follow in the daylight was near impossible to find at night. Merin Pendragon and his men moved carefully, and far too slowly to suit the Dragon Lord, but there was no other choice. The trail they followed was winding and steep. In many places it was so narrow that it was hard to traverse it, but they moved onward toward Mryddin Water. Finally, after almost two hours riding they saw the clearing ahead of them.

Merin Pendragon silently signaled his men to stop. "I would go in on foot as to not disturb any evidence of what has happened here this day. Come with me to the edge of the wood, and then let me go forth with my torch."

"I would go with you, my lord," his captain said.

"Very well, but follow in my footsteps, Ivor," the Dragon Lord said.

The two men moved into the sandy clearing, one directly behind the other. The evidence of a large party of men and horses was obvious. Torches held high, they saw the smaller footprints of a boy, and recognized Brynn's shoe, for the heel of his left boot was always worn down more on the right side. And then they saw it. A deep imprint in the sand of a girl's body, arms and legs spread, the knee-prints of her captors on either side. The knee-prints of her violator between her legs.

"Jesu!" Merin Pendragon swore. "Here? Before all?" And just how many, he wondered silently, had raped his innocent daughter? Lord de Bohun would pay dearly for this brutality. And Brynn had undoubtedly seen it all.

"My lord!" His captain's voice was shaking as he spoke the two words.

"We will return to Dragon's Lair now," the Dragon Lord said. "There is nothing further we can do tonight, Ivor. But tomorrow is another thing. Do not tell the others of what we have seen. I just mean to say that my children were taken by de Bohun and his ilk. I will destroy him and his son. I will burn Agramant to ashes for what has happened to my daughter. A hundred-year-old falling-out between our families is no excuse for what obviously took place here this day." Then Merin Pendragon turned and walked back to the woods with Ivor behind him. Mounting his horse, he signaled their return home.

After several hours more, with their torches flickering low, they reached the keep of the Pendragons. The lord of the castle dismounted, and going inside first sought out Ysbail, telling her that both children had obviously been taken hostage, and that on the morrow negotiations for their return would begin. Ysbail nodded, but she was no fool, and knew he was leaving out much. Still, she did not press him, for he was obviously both tired and angry.

The Dragon Lord found his wife and favored concubine seated together by the hearth in the hall, sewing. They looked up simultaneously at the sound of his footsteps, their single look questioning. "They've been taken," Merin Pendragon began.

Gorawen rose quickly and fetched her lord a large goblet of wine. Then she sat back down again, and waited for what he had to say.

"It's de Bohun, without a doubt. Brynn was there. That damned left heel of his was obvious in the sand of the clearing by Mryddin Water."

"And Junia?" Argel asked. She was no longer fearful for her son. He would be ransomed, and she had no doubt it would cost the Pendragons a pretty penny.

"There, too," Merin said tersely, and his jaw tightened with his memory.

"What else did you see?" Gorawen probed. "Was she ra—"

"Aye! And ask me no more, woman! And neither of you is to tell Ysbail. I have told her they were taken, but nothing else. If she begins to howl and whine at me I shall kill her, I swear it! Right there, the devil! In a circle of boots, and how many I do not know! I shall wipe the de Bohuns off the face of the earth for this cruelty. As God is my witness, I will destroy them and theirs! I shall leave not a stone of their castle unbroken or not burned to avenge my innocent daughter."

"First we wed her to the de Bohun boy," Argel said. "Her honor must be restored so we may find her a good husband afterwards. A respectable widow with her dower portion still intact."

"I cannot think on such a plan right now," the Dragon Lord admitted. "My blood lust is too great. I will follow the example of my ancestor before me, and castrate the son before his father. Then I will chop off the father's manhood and balls myself. The de Bohuns of Agramant are finished!" He drank the contents of his goblet in several deep swallows, and slammed the vessel down on the arm of his chair.

Both women jumped, startled. Neither had ever seen Merin Pendragon so angry. They looked at one another questioningly.

"My good lord, you are justifiably upset," Argel said. "Come to bed, now. I fear you will burst if you cannot calm yourself."

Reaching out he took her hand in his, and raising it to his lips kissed it, giving her a small smile as he did so. "Go to your bed, Argel," he said. "I will come eventually."

The lady of Dragon's Lair arose, and curtsied to her husband. She knew he would take Gorawen to his bed, for Gorawen was better able to defuse his anger. When he was calmed once again he would leave the woman he loved, and come to his wife to comfort her. *Why do I feel no resentment over that?* Argel asked herself. But she didn't, and she never had. Perhaps because Merin respected her position as his wife, and treated her with kindness. Perhaps because Gorawen never attempted to overstep her own position in their lives because she loved their shared lord deeply. *As do I,* Argel thought. *And that is why we are such good friends.* She moved quietly from the hall to find her own chamber.

When she had gone Gorawen arose and held out her hand to Merin Pendragon. "Come, my lord. Argel is right. You need to calm yourself. If you do not you will not think clearly." She took him by the hand and led him from the hall to her chamber. There she disrobed herself, and Merin. She brought him more wine, taking a goblet for herself as well. Then together they entered her bed. "Shall I offer you comfort, my lord?" she asked him softly, but he shook his head at her.

"I could not," he answered her. "Not after what I have seen tonight, Gorawen."

"Tell me what you would not tell the others," she coaxed him gently, a skilled hand massaging the back of his thick neck. "You cannot keep it bottled within you like an evil fairy, my lord. What did you see at Mryddin Water?"

He groaned. It was a sound of deep pain. "A ring of boots in the sand surrounding the deep imprint of my daughter's body. Men knelt by her four limbs, spreading them wide, forcing her to submit. And between her legs the mark of more knees denting the soft ground. I know not how many men knelt there violating Junia!" He swallowed down his wine, setting the cup aside, his head falling onto his chest as he sobbed with his grief.

Gorawen took him into her arms and let him weep. When the sounds of his sorrow began to ease she said to him, "I want you to think back on that scene, Merin."

"I cannot!" he cried, anguished.

"You must!" she insisted. "Do you see footprints anywhere within the circle moving into it, Merin? Think, my lord. Think!"

He was silent for a long moment, and then he answered her, "Nay. I see only the marks of the circle. Wait! One set of footprints behind the knee marks."

"Nothing else?" she pressed him.

"Nay," he said slowly, and then more forcefully, "Nay!"

"Then in all likelihood Junia's violation was by but one man," Gorawen told her lord. "Let that be of some small comfort to you."

"It is so?" he asked, grasping at her words as a drowning man grasps at a straw.

"If there were no footprints of men moving in and out of the circle then there was only one man to do the deed, my lord. Not that it is any less abhorrent, but it was probably the boy who violated her. His father has a foul reputation, as you know. I am sorry the boy takes after him."

"I will kill him!" Merin Pendragon said again.

"Of course you will, my lord, but not until after we have seen them wed. It will be far easier to find a suitable husband for Junia if she is a widow with her full dower portion than if she is the victim, however innocent, of a cruel assault," Gorawen reasoned. "But, my dear lord, you cannot punish the de Bohuns without help. You must call upon Lord Mortimer for aid."

"You would make this matter public?" he said, outraged.

"Lord Mortimer can be convinced to remain silent if he knows the truth of the matter. He is an honorable man, Merin, and he can accomplish what you cannot," Gorawen told him.

"What?" the Dragon Lord demanded of Gorawen.

"He can get into Agramant without a fight," she replied. "The most important thing in all of this is to ransom Junia and Brynn so we may gain their safe return. Lord Mortimer can negotiate for you, Merin. Once we have your son and daughter back in our custody, then, my lord, you can attack Agramant. It will be a difficult siege, Merin. You do not want the children caught in it else de Bohun kill them out of spite."

He thought for several long moments during which time she continued to massage his neck. Finally he said, "Aye, lovey, you are right! But will de Bohun believe that all I want is my son and daughter?"

"Of course he will," she replied with a small chuckle. "He will believe you the weakling for sending Lord Mortimer to parlay with him instead of coming yourself. He will consider the ransom he wants, and be greedy. We will give him what he wants, for when Agramant falls you will retrieve it. First and foremost we want Brynn and Junia safe home," Gorawen concluded.

"But it will take several days to get to Mortimer, and convince him to agree.

What if he will not help me?" the Dragon Lord said.

"He will give you aid. Lord Mortimer is a vain man, and to have you pleading for his help will be most flattering. He bears you no ill will, Merin, and he will be shocked to learn of what the de Bohuns have done," Gorawen responded.

"But to have to leave my son and my daughter, especially Junia, in their hands for any longer than necessary," the Dragon Lord answered her, "breaks my heart."

"The damage is already done, my lord," Gorawen said sensibly. "Nothing will change by it taking longer to gain their release. Besides, you cannot successfully besiege Agramant. It is too well fortified. We must get Brynn and Junia back, and then gain custody of the de Bohuns, *pere et fil,* by means of some clever ruse."

"You are the cleverest of women, Gorawen," he told her admiringly. "I am fortunate in having you."

"Aye, you are, my dear lord," she agreed with him, and she laughed.

"You have set my mind at ease in this matter," he replied. "I feel hope in my heart where I did not earlier." He drank down his wine, and then arose from her bed. "I had best go to Argel now, and tell her of your wise counsel." He pulled his tunic over his dark head.

"Do not say that it was my advice, my lord. Let her believe you have thought on the matter, and decided it yourself," Gorawen said. "Argel is your wife, and you should not make her feel any less because of your love for me. If you had spent this last hour with her she very well might have offered you the same ideas as I had," Gorawen said.

"It is not likely," he told her, "for Argel, good woman she is, has not your keen mind, my love, but if I tell her these are my thoughts she will believe me, for she is, bless her, a trusting soul."

"Do not underestimate her, my dear lord, for Argel's heart is yours, and her duty first and foremost is to the Pendragons," Gorawen replied sagely.

He bent and gave her a swift kiss. "You are a clever creature," he told her with a chuckle, and then he left her.

Gorawen shook her golden head. She loved him, but he was not the quickest man where strategy was concerned. She wondered if Lord Mortimer would be able to convince the de Bohuns to accept ransom for the Pendragon brother and sister. There had been no need for them to kidnap Brynn and Junia. Why had they reignited a feud that had lain dormant for many years? And why had they felt it necessary to violate Junia? Was it possible that

Lord de Bohun meant to wipe out the Pendragons? And why did he feel a need to do such a thing if it was indeed his purpose? Junia's plight was making the trials suffered by her two elder sisters seem like child's play in comparison. *I must sleep on this,* Gorawen thought to herself. Merin would not return to her tonight. The reality of what he had seen earlier rendered it impossible for him to make love to any woman this night, and possibly for many nights to come.

In the morning a messenger was dispatched to Lord Mortimer. The messenger returned four days later with both Lord Mortimer and his son in tow. They were accompanied by Rhys FitzHugh. They were surprised to see the lord of Everleigh, for it was harvest time.

"Averil is capable of overseeing the estate," Rhys explained. "This is obviously a family matter, my lord Merin. I would help in whatever way I can."

The Dragon Lord was pleased, but he asked, "How did you learn of my request to Lord Mortimer for help?"

"They stopped at Everleigh to water their horses and beg a meal," Rhys replied.

Merin Pendragon nodded. "Sit down then, my lords, and I will tell you why it is I have called upon you for your aid. My daughter Junia and my son Brynn have been taken by Hugo de Bohun and his son Simon. They are imprisoned at Agramant." Then the Dragon Lord went on to explain the entire situation in careful detail to the trio.

They were shocked by his story.

"Hugo de Bohun was always a bad sort," Lord Mortimer said. "Only his wife could keep him from mischief, but she, poor lady, is long dead. I had not heard evil of the son before this, Merin. I am sorry he has followed in his father's boot steps."

"What do you want us to do?" Rhys FitzHugh asked.

"I cannot take my revenge on the de Bohuns while they retain custody of my children," Merin Pendragon began. "And so, my lords, I would have you go to Hugo de Bohun, and ask him what ransom he will require to release my son and my daughter to me. I will pay it, whatever it is, for I will retrieve said ransom once I have my children returned, and seek out the de Bohuns that I may have my revenge upon them. The feud between our families burned hot for many years, but for the last five and twenty years it has lain dormant. I know not what caused Hugo de Bohun to revive it, but when he and his son are finally in my hands, I will end this quarrel between our families forever."

Lord Mortimer nodded. "Aye, that

would be best, old friend. And you will have no difficulty from his more powerful de Bohun relations. They will look the other way, and be glad his branch has been pruned from the family tree. That I can promise you, Merin. Hugo de Bohun has been causing trouble in one place or another for years."

"Then you will go to him, and ask what is required of me that my children be safely returned to Dragon's Lair?" the Dragon Lord said.

"Of course I will go," Lord Mortimer said.

"We will all three go," Rhys added. "Lord Mortimer and Roger as your own personal emissaries, and I as a member of your family."

Lord Mortimer nodded. "We will make an impressive delegation, I think. Even de Bohun should be impressed, if not a bit intimidated, and we need to intimidate him perhaps a little. If he believes that the English Marcher lords are involved in this we may be able to move him." Then Lord Mortimer said to Merin Pendragon, "I am sorry about Junia, old friend. I remember her as a child. A most charming little girl."

"The vision of what I saw that night will remain with me always," the Dragon Lord replied. "The hard knowledge that my daughter was violated so cruelly."

"Try to put it from your mind, old friend," Lord Mortimer said. "Not an easy thing, I know, but for Junia's sake you must. She will be greatly shamed by what has happened to her while she has been in de Bohun hands. I regret we must wait until the morrow to travel onward, but the sun is already setting over the western hills."

Argel entered the hall as he spoke, with Gorawen at her side. "Welcome, my lords," she greeted them as Gorawen went to her son-in-law, and kissed his cheek.

There were tears in her eyes, but he understood the unspoken words she did not utter, and put an arm about her. "*Belle Mere*, you grow more beautiful with each year," he told her, and gave her a kiss in return.

"Thank you for coming," Gorawen finally managed to say softly.

"Junia is my wife's little sister, *Belle Mere*. Your lord should have sent to me also. I am disturbed he did not."

"He knows how important the harvest is to you," Gorawen defended, "and too, he is not thinking clearly these days. The knowledge of what has happened to Junia has almost rendered him mad with grief."

"What if my wife's sister is already with child?" Rhys said, low.

Gorawen paled. "Pray God we are

spared that tragedy," she whispered back.

"You will rest the night, and go forth on the morrow," Argel was saying. "I have a good hot supper for you, my lords, and comfortable bed spaces here in the hall." She was all the dutiful chatelaine.

Ysbail came into the hall, looking about her with curiosity. "We have guests?" She was surprised.

"They have come to aid us regain the children," Argel replied.

"You will want your son back, of course," Ysbail said, "but as for Junia she is de Bohun's whore now, and not worth having in our hall."

"She is your daughter, lady!" Rhys FitzHugh said, shocked by Ysbail's words.

"She was my daughter, my lord. She is no longer my daughter. She is de Bohun's whore. By her own willful actions she brought disaster upon herself. She would not listen to anyone. She would, foolish creature, follow her heart. But do we not all know that the heart is not a reliable indicator?" Ysbail sat down by the fire. "I do not care if you retrieve her or not. I have no daughter," she finished bleakly.

"She hoped to join her daughter in the household of a well-to-do son-in-law," Gorawen said acidly. "Now her plans gone awry, she realizes she must live out her old age with the rest of us."

Ysbail jumped up from her seat. "Do not dare to judge me!" she cried angrily. "You have his love and his heart. Argel has his care and respect. My tenuous hold on him was but my child who is now shamed and would be better off dead! A place in my daughter's house would have been one of honor and respect. What have I here? I am a second concubine whose daughter has brought dishonor to the house of Pendragon, and worse, led its heir into terrible danger!" Her narrow face was wet with tears of self-pity.

"No one is blaming Junia that Brynn followed her," Merin Pendragon said. "Be silent now, Ysbail. We have guests, and I would not have them think ill of you. I know my daughter has been shamed. Did I not see the evidence of it with my own eyes? But I will never desert any child of mine for any reason. Dry your tears, woman, and come to supper with the rest of us." He reached out and awkwardly patted her shoulder.

"You do not blame Junia for Brynn's plight?" She sniffled.

"Nay, I do not, nor should you, woman," he replied. "Brynn is my son, and noble in his heart. But he lacks the experience of a seasoned warrior who would have not gone to Junia's aid when the odds were so obviously against him. A wiser warrior would have slipped away, and hurried back to Dragon's Lair to tell me what was happening. Had he, we might have rescued Junia before they took her back to Agramant. Nay, I do not blame Junia for what has happened. She is but a girl in love. I blame Brynn for reacting, instead of acting in Junia's best interests, and ours."

She took his hand and kissed it. "Thank you, my lord," she said.

The meal was served, and afterwards their guests were given bed spaces.

"We must leave before the dawn," Lord Mortimer said, and his companions agreed. "If we do we may be able to reach Agramant late tomorrow."

"If the lord does not want Junia back," Rhys murmured to Gorawen before she left the hall, "Averil and I will take her."

"In this house it is only Ysbail who carps and cries about Junia," Gorawen told her son-in-law. "Her father loves her, and so do the rest of us. We will be here for her in her sorrow, but dear Rhys, I thank you for your kindness. I will tell Merin. We did not begin well, I fear, but I can see you are a good man. My daughter, I suspect, is fortunate in her husband. She is well? I have not asked before now for obvious reasons."

"She is well, and expecting another child in the spring," he responded with a smile.

"I hope for a daughter this time. Two sons is a good start, lady. When this is over, and the matter settled, I hope you will come and spend some time at Everleigh. Your daughter misses you, and you have not seen your grandsons in months now."

Gorawen nodded. "I will come," she promised, "but first we must make everything all right for sweet Junia. And it will not be finished until my lord has slain the de Bohuns, father and son, Rhys. And if Junia still loves her Simon, she will grieve deeply, I know."

"What if the son is innocent of the father's evil?" Rhys asked.

"It will matter not to Merin, for the younger de Bohun did not protect Junia from his father's wickedness. Junia was a sheltered and well-born virgin. In all her life she never met such evil as the de Bohuns have shown her. They will not have broken her spirit, for I know Junia is strong-willed. But they have ruined her future, and insulted this family's honor. Honor must be avenged, Rhys. You know that yourself."

"But you did not have me slain. You had me marry Averil," Rhys said.

"You did not rape Averil before the vows were said," she reminded him.

"You believe he is the one?" Rhys was shocked that an honorable man professing to love an innocent girl would violate her.

"If he is not then it is worse, for that would mean he stood by while the deed was done. But it no longer matters," Gorawen said. "Junia is ruined."

"We will bring her back, *Belle Mere*," Rhys responded.

"I know that Junia will be safely returned eventually," Gorawen agreed, and then she left him to get his rest. She found Merin awaiting her in her chamber. She went to him, and kissed him softly. He was seated in the chair by her hearth. She sat down in his lap with a sigh.

"I wish I could go with them," he told her.

"I know," she replied, "but they have a better chance of regaining the children if de Bohun does not see you. He will see you soon enough, my lord. Is that not so?"

"I think about killing him," Merin Pendragon said. "I debate with myself if it should be slow and painful, or quick and sure. Should I kill his son before his very eyes, or should I wait and kill the father before the son? I think of stripping the flesh from de Bohun's bones while he yet lives. Of cutting him open and pulling his innards out, and feeding them to the dogs. Should I blind him with a red-hot poker, or slice off his nose and give it to the castle cats as a plaything. I am filled with such dark thoughts, Gorawen, and I do not like it."

"You should not," she agreed. "Such thoughts make you no better than the man who saw to your daughter's public violation. Kill de Bohun swiftly, my lord. See the son wed to Junia, and then send him to hell with his father as quickly. Do not draw it out. If Junia yet loves Simon de Bohun you must not add any more to her pain than is necessary for honor to be satisfied. She will say she will never forgive you, but she will one day."

"What if she is with child?" he asked the question she had hoped he would not.

"It can be managed, my lord," Gorawen told him.

"I have always suspected you had such means at your disposal, my love," he remarked quietly.

"Junia cannot be allowed to have a child with de Bohun blood," Gorawen said. "It is unlikely she will ever know what I have done, my lord, and so we may spare her that sorrow. It will be far easier to find a husband for a widow with a good dower and no children than a widow with another man's babe."

"I agree," he said. "So it is settled, then. And all that remains is to reclaim the children."

"It is settled," Gorawen replied to him,

and she kissed him.

In the morning Lord Mortimer, his son, and Rhys FitzHugh left before the dawn. Ahorse, and carrying torches they followed the winding narrow track to Mryddin Water, reaching it as the sun slid above the horizon. It had rained in the days since Junia and her brother had been abducted by the de Bohuns, but even so the evidence of the crime was still visible in the sandy ground.

"If I thought we could kill him ourselves at Agramant, I would," Lord Mortimer said in a tight voice.

"Nay," Rhys replied. " 'Tis the Dragon Lord's privilege, and his alone. However, it could not hurt to ascertain Agramant's weaknesses, could it?"

Roger Mortimer grinned. "God, Rhys, 'tis good to be together with you, and out on the hunt. Marriage is a bloody bore!"

"Not for me," Rhys said with an answering grin.

"Well, if I had a wife like Averil . . ." Roger began.

"You didn't deserve a wife like Averil Pendragon." His father chuckled. "I am not even certain you deserve the wife you have, my son."

The three men rode the day long, stopping to relieve themselves, eat and give their animals a rest. The countryside through which they rode was quiet, and they saw no one.

Then just as the sun was preparing to set they saw the dark stone towers of Agramant ahead of them. Lord Mortimer raised his hand to slow their advance, and they stopped as he contemplated their next move.

Finally he said, "Roger, you will remain here while Rhys and I enter the castle. If we are not back within two days' time, return to Dragon's Lair, and tell the lord."

Roger nodded. He was disappointed, but he did not argue. "I will wait two days," he said. And then he watched as his father and the lord of Everleigh continued onward towards the castle of Agramant.

Chapter 17

Lord Mortimer and his companion were granted entry into Agramant just before the drawbridge was drawn up, the doors shut, and the iron portcullis lowered for the night. Dismounting, their horses were taken to a stable, and a house servant brought them into the great hall of the castle.

Hugo de Bohun was already at table with his son, and Junia. He looked surprised to see them, but motioned them forward. "Come! Come! Eat! You look as if you have traveled a long ways this day. We have venison, and it's been well hung, my lords." He looked for a servitor as they took their seats next to Simon. "Wine for my guests, you lazy bastards!" he shouted. Then he shoved a large loaf of bread down the table at them as his servants brought pewter plates piled high with venison, and goblets of wine. "Eat!" he commanded them again. "Then you will tell me what brings you to Agramant. Who is this with you, Mortimer?"

"Lord FitzHugh of Everleigh," Lord

Mortimer replied.

Hugo de Bohun grunted, and his curiosity satisfied, went on eating.

Rhys could not look at Junia without being noticed, but from the brief glimpse he had had of her when they entered the hall she appeared unharmed. He wondered where young Brynn was. Then hungry, he took his knife from its scabbard and began spearing pieces of the meat and eating them. It would all be revealed in due time.

When the places had been cleared away Hugo de Bohun looked to Lord Mortimer, and said, "Why have you come to Agramant? We rarely have visitors." He leaned back in his chair.

"Merin Pendragon would like his son and his daughter returned, and he is willing to pay a goodly ransom for them, my lord," Lord Mortimer said.

Hugo de Bohun laughed uproariously as if Lord Mortimer had just told the most amusing jest. "I will keep to the laws of hospitality, my lords," he replied, "but come the morrow return to the Dragon Lord and tell him there is no amount of ransom that I would take in exchange for his children. My son is soon to wed Aceline de Bellaud, but he would keep his little Welsh whore as well. As for Pendragon's son, he resides in my dungeons where he will eventually die, as I have given orders he is to have no food or water."

"Jesu, de Bohun, Brynn Pendragon is but a lad!" Lord Mortimer said.

"But when he is dead," the lord of Agramant continued, "I will return his body to his father so he may see that Arthur's line is finished, and bury his only heir." Then he laughed. "As for the wench, she will remain with Simon until he is bored with her, and then I will give her to my men for the castle whore."

"Why have you done this?" Lord Mortimer asked.

"The Pendragons are our enemies," Hugo de Bohun replied.

"The feud between you has been dormant for years now," Lord Mortimer said.

"Until my weakling of a son met Pendragon's daughter by Mryddin Water, and she lured him with her wiles from the path I had chosen for him to take. He wanted to marry the little slut with her meager dower instead of the fine landed heiress I had chosen for him. He would have run away with her, but that I put a stop to it."

"Surely you did not think Pendragon would have a de Bohun for a son-in-law, my lord?" Lord Mortimer said, shocked by the venom in his host's voice, and puzzled by the silence of young Simon de Bohun.

"Willful, both of them," Hugo de Bohun responded, "but I put a stop to it. I followed my son that day he planned to meet with his wench. I thought at first to kill her and be done with it, but then I decided instead to break her father's heart. I made my son take the girl as my men and I watched. How she howled when he stole her cherry from her. Her brother, a lad I will admit with more guts than my own son, tried to save her. Now he will end his days in my dungeons. I have beaten him twice, but he will not utter a single cry, and I admire him for it. But he will, before I am through with him, beg for mercy, and when he does I will give him the gift of death to reward him."

"My lord, you are a monster!" Lord Mortimer said, genuinely disgusted.

Hugo de Bohun laughed. "Have some more wine, my lords, and then I will have my son's leman dance for us. She is quite skilled at the dance, are you not, whore?" He looked down the board at Junia, leering.

"You are truly a pig's turd, my lord," Junia replied sweetly.

"Junia, for God's sake, do not enrage him," Simon told her nervously.

But de Bohun merely laughed heartily again. "His mother was a good woman, but she gave me a weakling for a son. But this little bitch will give my son strong bastards, will you not, girl?"

"Go to hell, my lord," Junia answered him in pleasant tones.

Now Rhys took the opportunity to lean forward and look down the high board so he might see Junia, and she get a good look at him. To his host it would appear no more than Lord Mortimer's companion was interested in seeing the girl. Junia's eyes met his but a moment, and then she glanced away. It had been enough for Rhys to see that her spirit was indeed not broken as Gorawen had said. The urge to get up and strangle Hugo de Bohun with his bare hands was a strong one, which he wisely pushed away.

"Do not be foolish, de Bohun," Lord Mortimer said. "Your son has had his way with the girl, and you have accomplished your purpose to ruin her. Who will marry her now, especially with her little dower portion? Ransom her. Surely you do not want your son's bride brought into Agramant under such circumstances. The de Bellaud family will desire their daughter be happy, and it is an insult to them that your son's mistress will be in residence when the blushing bride arrives. Surely your coffers can benefit by the addition of two fat ransoms. You can beggar Pendragon, and accomplish your revenge more easily."

"Why do you tell me this? Are you not

the Dragon Lord's friend?" de Bohun asked suspiciously.

"I am his friend, but I have known all his children since their birth. It pains me to see Junia like this, and to know that young Brynn lies starved and beaten in your dungeons. If you kill them, what is left to you? But if you take all of the Dragon Lordwealth from him in exchange for his children, the daughter ruined without chance of marriage, and the son damaged, you will have destroyed the entire family in the end. Is that not a greater revenge, Hugo de Bohun?"

"I must think on it, and especially of why you, who claim to be Pendragon's friend, would even suggest it to me," Hugo de Bohun replied.

"You have the upper hand, de Bohun," Lord Mortimer replied. "How many men do you know who prefer their children to their wealth, eh?" He chuckled. "As for me, Pendragon's lands match with mine. I could use them. A man must think of himself, eh?" And he chuckled again in such a knowing manner that de Bohun laughed, too.

"For all your civility, Mortimer, it would appear you are a man after my own heart, though you hide it well. But as I said, I must think on it." Then turning away from Lord Mortimer, he looked back down the high board, and said, "Get up on the table and dance, you bold Welsh bitch! I want my guests well entertained."

"There is no music, my lord," she said. "I cannot dance without music." Then rising from the table she began to leave the hall.

But de Bohun was around the table and after her, with Simon also in pursuit. The older man caught Junia first, and raising his hand hit her a heavy blow, and then another and another. "When I give you an order, whore, you will obey me!" he shouted.

"For mercy's sake, Father, leave her alone," Simon said, and he pulled his sire away from Junia whose nose was bloodied. "She is right. She can't dance without music."

"Then," Hugo de Bohun said angrily, "find one of the servants to play for her. I would have her dance for our guests."

"Let her go up to my chamber, Father," Simon cajoled. "Her nose is bleeding, and she is already showing a bruise on her cheekbone. She is hardly a pretty sight, is she?"

"The bitch deserves a good beating," he growled.

"And I will give it to her later, I swear it," Simon promised. "You can stand outside my chamber and hear her cries."

"Nay, I will stand in your chamber, and I will watch as you punish her," he said with a cruel smile." Then he looked at Junia. "Get upstairs, you little bitch, and wait for your master to come."

Junia ran from the hall without another word. At the high board Rhys FitzHugh again pushed back his urge to slay Hugo de Bohun. Junia was being foolishly brave. She could have avoided a beating by simply saying there was no music instead of defying Hugo de Bohun. This was a man who very much enjoyed giving pain, but then Rhys realized that it was Junia's very defiance that was keeping her alive. Had she lost her courage and gone to pieces, Hugo de Bohun would have given her to his men and been done with it. She would have never survived. Poor gentle Simon found it near impossible to stand up to his father. He could not save her, and Junia realized it.

The evening had been ended with the terrible scene between de Bohun and Junia. Simon had slipped away after the girl. Lord Mortimer and Rhys watched as Hugo de Bohun rummaged among the firewood by the hall's hearth. Finally he drew forth a stick about a foot and a half in length, and the thickness of his thumb. He smiled cruelly.

"This will do nicely," he said to them.

"The servants will show you to a chamber, my lords. We will speak again on the morrow." Then he was quickly gone from the hall.

"I think young Simon made an error in judgment saying he would beat Junia," Lord Mortimer said, shaking his head. "De Bohun realized it was a ruse and called his son's bluff. Junia is in for it now, I fear."

"My wife's sister is brave, but foolish," Rhys agreed. "With de Bohun in the chamber watching, Simon will have to lay his punishment on hard. Junia will be sore come the morrow, but she will survive."

Simon had hurried to his chamber knowing his father would be close behind him. He burst into the room, and Junia turned, startled. "He wants to watch, damn him! I don't want to beat you, but if I don't he will, and it will be the worse for you, my darling. I am so sorry!" He took her into his arms, and felt her tremble.

"I do not know how much longer I can be brave, Simon," Junia told him, her young voice quavering.

"Try to bear the first few blows, and then yell your head off," he advised her. "That will please him, and then perhaps he will let me let you off. And Junia, do whatever I order you to do no matter how it angers you. He needs to feel I am as much a monster as he is. If I hear him refer to me again as a weakling, I will kill him," Simon said grimly. "Why is a gentle man considered weak, and a brutal one strong?"

The words were barely out of his mouth when the door to the chamber flew open, and Hugo de Bohun entered. "Here," he said, handing his son the stick he had chosen. "Wield that well, and the little bitch will learn her lesson fast enough." He sat down on the bed. "Well?" he demanded.

"Take your gown and chemise off, girl!" Simon ordered Junia. "I'll not have them damaged. Do you think good coin for clothing grows on bushes? Hurry up, now! It is past time you were taught the lesson of obedience."

Hugo de Bohun looked at his son, approval in his dark eyes. He watched as Junia quickly obeyed, his glance moving swiftly over her pretty little body. Again he regretted his decision to let Simon have her. She really was a toothsome piece.

"Get over here!" Simon barked at the girl, and when she came he tucked her beneath his left arm, turning her delightfully round little bottom towards his father. Then raising his arm he brought the thick stick down on Junia's rump. At the fourth blow she began to whimper. By the sixth she was howling. By the tenth she was begging for mercy. Simon looked to his father, but Hugo shook his head.

"Give her a bit more," he said. "She can take it. If you want, I'll do it." He licked his lips in anticipation.

"Nay, I will finish what I began," Simon said, and began beating Junia once again. At the thirteenth blow she began to sob piteously, continuing to beg him to stop.

"Give her twenty," Hugo order his son.

"Nay, fifteen will be enough or I'll not have my pleasure of her tonight," Simon said. "Those strips on her buttocks will burn for three days as it is." He brought his weapon down on her twice more, and then shoved her to the floor. "There, wench, I hope you have learned your lesson. In the future you will address my lord father in a proper manner, will you not?"

"Yes, my lord Simon," Junia sobbed.

"Now kiss the rod that has chastised you, wench, and thank me."

Junia did as he commanded, whispering, "Thank you, my lord Simon."

Hugo de Bohun stood up. "By the rood, my son, I didn't think you had the balls for punishing a woman, but you have proved me wrong. I will leave you. Fuck her well tonight, and you, wench," he bent and pulled Junia up by her long dark hair, "give your master the pleasure he deserves. He has done well." Then Hugo de Bohun left them.

Simon moved swiftly to the door, and slammed the bolt home. He heard his father laugh knowingly outside in the hall, and then his footsteps moved away. Turning back to Junia he enclosed her in his arms.

"Did you have to hit me so hard?" Junia said.

"Did you want him to beat you? It would have been far worse if he had, and he would have given you twenty blows, Junia. You know I am sorry," Simon told her. "Let me find some salve for your welts."

"If you hadn't suggested beating me in the first place . . ." Junia said irritably.

"I didn't think he would want to watch," Simon replied. "I thought I would beat the bed and you would howl while he listened outside the door."

"Considering how I was violated, Simon," Junia told him tartly, "you might have realized he is a man who enjoys watching pain."

"Bend over," he told her. "I'll put the salve on you."

"Ouch! Oww!" she cried as his fingers rubbed the ointment over her wounds.

"I'm sorry, Junia. Oh, damn! All I wanted to do was to love you, and to wed with you. How did it come to this nightmare we are both living?"

"No more," she told him, straightening up, and she took his face between her hands. "I feel the same way, Simon. I just wanted to be your wife. Nothing more. Now there will be war again between our families, and we cannot stop it."

"He's a greedy man, Junia, and Lord Mortimer made a strong case for ransom," Simon noted. "Who is the man with him? Lord FitzHugh."

"My sister Averil's husband," Junia said. "I would speak with Rhys if I could. Have you seen my brother today?"

"Aye. He is in remarkably good condition considering he has been denied sustenance these last few days. Father gave him a good hiding with his favorite leather strap yesterday, but your brother is still strong," Simon told her.

"He has always been a brave lad," Junia remarked.

"Junia," he said low, pulling her close.

"No," Junia said. "I cannot bear it. I am sorry, my love, but you must give me more time. And I am truly sore from the beating you have given me. I think I will not sleep in my chemise tonight. I don't want to get the ointment on it."

He sighed, and let her go. "You will have to sleep on your belly, I think," he told her. Since that terrible day at Mryddin Water they had not coupled. Junia claimed she could not bear to be touched, and he understood, although he longed desperately for her. He knew to have her again would be but to dishonor her further. Junia was not his wife, and unless a miracle occurred she would never be his wife. How his father would have laughed him to scorn, but he still remembered the look on her lovely face when he was forced between her spread thighs that day. Her cry of pain when he shattered her maidenhead would remain in his memory forever. He could not force her again. He knew she still loved him. He saw it in her eyes. But if Junia would not have him as a lover, then he must abide by her decision. He joined her in his bed, turning away from her so as not to disturb her.

In the morning Hugo de Bohun met again with Lord Mortimer. "I will make an agreement with you," he said. "You may have the lands bordering your own, but I want everything else, including Dragon's Lair. If Merin Pendragon will agree to that, I will return his children to him."

"Alive and well," Lord Mortimer said sharply. "You will not damage them."

"Alive and well," Hugo de Bohun agreed, "and I will not damage them."

"That means you feed the boy, and release him from his dungeon," Lord Mortimer pressed his companion.

"I will feed him, but he stays in the dungeons until I have his father's word," de Bohun countered.

"And his sister can see the boy," Lord Mortimer said.

"Why not?" Hugo de Bohun laughed.

"Then we are agreed?" Lord Mortimer said.

"We are agreed," Hugo de Bohun replied.

"I will return to the Dragon Lord and tell him of your wishes," Lord Mortimer said.

"He will not agree," Hugo de Bohun answered.

"I think he will," Lord Mortimer responded. "He loves his children well."

"Then he is a bigger fool than I have always believed," the lord of Agramant said. "Have some breakfast, Mortimer. Where is your companion?"

"He wanted to check the horses before we depart. I think my beast got a stone in his shoe yesterday. Rhys said he would look at the animal's foot, and remove the stone," Lord Mortimer replied without hesitation, but he wondered where Rhys FitzHugh was.

The lord of Everleigh was with Junia in Simon's chamber. He had been brought to her by Cadi, and Simon had left them alone to speak.

"My father is coming?" Junia said.

"Aye, he will come, but it will not be an easy or a simple thing to breach the walls of this castle. Why the hell did you disobey your father and meet with young de Bohun that day, Juni? Have you any idea the troubles you have caused with your willful behavior? You've been raped, and are now without honor, lass. What are we to do with you when we get you back? Not even a convent will have you now."

"I only went to say good-bye," Junia said. "And I hoped that his father would have been willing to end the feud between our families."

"Your lover is a good lad, but a weakling, Junia. He did not protect you from his father and his father's men. He allowed Brynn to be captured. He is afraid of his father, and frankly I'm not surprised. Hugo de Bohun is a monster. It would take a very strong man to stand up to such a beast, and young Simon has not the courage or the fortitude to do so."

"But he did protect me, Rhys. He is the one who had my maidenhead. No one else. And we have not joined our bodies since. He loves me, and he wants me for his wife. He was forced to take me by his odious father who threatened to have me himself, and then pass me on to his men. Simon did what he could under the circumstances, and as for Brynn, there was no way to aid him. He jumped down into the midst of de Bohun's men, wounding one, and then immediately going after the master."

"I will tell your father what you have said, but the problem still remains that we are going to have a hell of a time successfully storming Agramant to rescue you and your brother," Rhys replied.

"I know another way into the castle," Cadi, who had been sitting in the shadows, said as she arose and came forward. She curtsied to Lord FitzHugh. "But if I tell you, my lord, you must swear to me that old Elga and I will be spared the Dragon Lord's wrath. We have done our best to help the lady Junia, and keep her safe."

"Oh, Cadi!" Junia cried. "You must tell us!" She turned to her brother-in-law. "Rhys? Swear to me that Cadi and Elga will be safe from Da. They really have been very good to me. Cadi has helped me to see Brynn. We got a water skin to him, which he has kept hidden, and that is why even without food he can survive. Please! I cannot bear much more of this terror I face each day in Hugo de Bohun's custody. You must swear these two women will be safe!"

"Cadi, you have my pledge and my warrant that you and Elga will be kept safe from the Dragon Lord's revenge. I will tell him of your care of his daughter. But you must both remain by her side when the castle is taken else you be mistaken for the others," Rhys explained to the girl.

"We two are the only women servants in the castle, my lord," Cadi said.

He nodded. "Now tell me of how we may enter Agramant undetected."

"There is a passage that goes from the dungeons beneath the walls and the moat. It opens out into a cave in the forest beyond," Cadi explained.

"How do you know this?" Rhys asked her.

Cadi grinned. "My friend, who is stationed to guard the lad, my lady's brother, showed me a few days ago."

"Why would he show you such a thing?" Rhys wanted to know.

"Well, my lord, I've been giving Davy certain pleasurings so that my lady can visit her brother. He finally wanted more than I have been offering, and so I told him to meet me in the forest where I would give him whatever he desired as long as my lady could keep on seeing the lad. Being a lusty fellow, he agreed," Cadi said with a grin.

" 'Meet me in the dungeons,' he told me.

" 'I said in the woods,' I told him.

" 'Trust me, lass,' he said.

"So when the mistress and I snuck down

into the dungeons two days ago," Cadi continued, "he let her into the cell as usual, and then taking me by the hand led me around the corner and there, my lord, was a door in the stone wall. Davy selected a key from his warder's ring, and opening the door, let me through. He had taken a torch from the wall before we entered this tunnel, and so I could see more or less where we was going. It were a nasty place, but when we reached the end of it, there was another door that opened out into a cave. I was so surprised, and he laughed. After I'd given him his pleasuring I walked from the cave to discover I was in the woods just beyond the clearing. I could see the castle, and everything. We returned the same way we came."

Rhys nodded slowly. He took the girl by her arm, and looked down into her plain face. "This is the truth, lass?"

"Aye." Cadi nodded vigorously.

"You weren't told to tell me this, were you?" Rhys searched the girl's face for any sign of deceit or betrayal.

"Nay, my lord!" she told him. "I long for the day that Hugo de Bohun is slain. My sister was twelve when he saw her. She was a beauty was our Mary. He dragged her screaming from our hovel, and brought her here. And when he had finished with her he released her naked into the fields, and

522

let his men hunt her down that they might take their pleasure of her. She died. And the same day he took her off," Cadi said, "me da took his knife and cut my face so that I am scarred as you now see me. I was only nine years old, my lord. But where others then turned away from me, Elga took me and made me her helper. That, and the hope of revenge, has been my salvation, my lord."

"Yet you are not a virgin," Rhys noted.

" 'Tis said all cats are black in the dark, my lord," Cadi told him with a wink.

Rhys laughed softly. "You're a bold baggage, lass, but you have a good heart. I will keep my promise, and see that you and Elga are kept from harm. I suspect that the Dragon Lord will give you a home to reward you for your kindness."

"Breaking into the castle tunnel at the forest cave should not attract anyone's notice," Junia said, "but when you start beating on the door in the dungeons, they will surely hear you. You will lose the element of surprise."

"I'll loosen the hinges of that door," Cadi promised. "One light shove and the door will go down, my lord."

"You must do it in the next day or two, lass," he told her.

"That soon?" Cadi was awestruck.

"I'll ride today until I reach Dragon's

Lair," Rhys said quietly. "The Dragon Lord will be on his way in two days' time." He turned to Junia. "You must tell no one. Not your Simon, and not Elga."

"But Simon —" Junia began.

"Simon is weak, lass. Charming, but weak. He will give us away without meaning to do so. Swear to me, Junia! Swear you will not tell him. If you do you will have the death of your father, your brother, and many good men on your soul. As for Elga, she cannot help but be protective of the lad she helped to raise. The child of the girl she raised. Cadi?"

"I swear, my lord! Elga has not the hatred for the de Bohuns as do I," the girl replied.

"Junia?" He looked hard at her.

"I swear, Rhys, but you are wrong about Simon," Junia replied.

"You had best go now, my lord," Cadi advised.

Rhys nodded in agreement, and taking his sister-in-law into his strong arms hugged her, kissing the top of her dark head. "Be brave, Junia. Your deliverance is at hand, I promise you. And Cadi, I will not forget." Then turning, Rhys moved swiftly from the chamber where they had been. He hurried down into the hall in hopes that he might gain a meal before they departed.

Lord Mortimer arose from the high board as he entered the hall. "Was it indeed a stone in my horse's shoe, Rhys? Did you get it out?"

"Aye, the front right hoof," Rhys answered, catching on to the excuse Lord Mortimer had obviously offered to mask his absence. "Is there time for me to eat, my lord?"

"Best take what you want, and eat while we ride," Lord Mortimer said. "We would reach Dragon's Lair in two days' time with the ransom proposal."

Rhys reached for the loaf of fresh bread, and sliced himself two thick slices. He buttered the bread lavishly, and then lay the remaining strips of bacon, and slices of a hard-boiled egg between the two slices. He filled his flask with wine from the table carafe, and stood again, bowing to Hugo de Bohun. "My thanks, my lord, for your hospitality," he said. "I am ready, Mortimer."

As the two men strode from the hall Hugo de Bohun called out to them, "Safe journey, my lords. Give my regards to Merin Pendragon when you tell him I want all he has for the safe return of his children." And he laughed uproariously.

"Bastard!" Rhys muttered beneath his breath.

"Go gently, my lord," Mortimer advised. "At least until we have escaped Agramant, and met up again with my son."

Their horses were brought forth from the stables, and mounting them the two men rode slowly from the courtyard, across the heavy drawbridge, and over the field before the castle into the wood beyond. As they rode Rhys told Lord Mortimer what he had learned, and when they had again met up with Roger Mortimer they sought for the cave that Cadi had told him about. Finding it they discovered that the hinges on it were made of leather. They cut through the hinges, and lifted the door off, laying it down. Making a torch of some nearby reeds they lit it, and Roger, anxious to play some part in their mission, went through into the tunnel. When he returned he told them, "There's another door at the other end just like the girl said. I was able to see through a crack in the door. It's a dungeon all right."

They replaced the door carefully, and to a cursory glance it would appear that no damage had been done to the door's hinges. Returning, they mounted their horses and rode from the cave out onto the faint forest track. The day was gray, but dry.

"We'll go as far as Mryddin Water," Lord Mortimer said. "I will then go on to Dragon's Lair to fetch Merin and his men. You two remain hidden on the chance that de Bohun sends anyone to watch for the Dragon Lord's coming. If you see anyone, kill them. It is the element of surprise that will assure us of success in this venture."

By the time they had reached Mryddin Water it was already dark, and Lord Mortimer decided to remain until it was light enough again for him to travel on. He assured his son and Rhys that he would be back that same day with the Dragon Lord and his men. When he departed the two men remained hidden in the rocks about the water keeping watch, and when the sun was directly at mid-level they saw two men wearing the de Bohun badge on their sleeves come to the other side of the water and dismount, tying their horses in the trees. The two men walked along the bank of the broad stream.

Rhys caught Roger's eye. He nodded to the bows tied to the back of their saddles. Roger nodded back, and slipped back farther into the rocks to fetch the weapons. He returned, handing Rhys his bow and two arrows. Then he notched his own bow with an arrow while tucking a second carefully beneath his other arm. Each man picked his target, and then Roger gave the piercing cry of a hawk. The two men across the stream immediately looked up even as the two men across from them let their arrows fly. Both of de Bohun's men were killed instantly, and falling into the fast-running water, were swept downstream.

"Damn!" Roger exclaimed. "I meant to get our arrows back. Do you think de Bohun will send any more?"

"Unlikely. These two were sent to give early warning to their master. They won't be expecting our return so quickly," Rhys replied.

"How is the girl?" Roger asked.

"Unbroken, but foolish yet. The de Bohun son is a kind young man, but weak. He lives in terror of his sire, as well he should. Hugo de Bohun is a beast. Still, Junia cries love, as does her Simon. My father-in-law will kill him, of course, after he has wed him to Junia and restored her honor, and that of the Pendragons."

"Does Junia realize that?" Roger asked.

"Nay, she does not. Had I told her she would have remained at Agramant in bondage to the de Bohuns rather than let harm come to her lover. The father has negotiated a marriage for the son with Aceline de Bellaud. Do you know the family?"

Roger shook his head in the negative. "Nay, but she must be propertied if de Bohun wants her for Simon. I will tell my uncle. He is looking for an heiress for his younger son. He's a FitzWarren, and the name is every bit as good as de Bohun."

Rhys nodded. "Rest now, Rog, and I will keep watch for a bit. The Dragon Lord will be here soon enough to surprise Hugo de Bohun and end this feud."

In mid-afternoon Merin Pendragon and his men arrived in the company of Lord Mortimer. They stopped long enough to give their horses a brief rest, and then the armed party crossed Mryddin Water, and continued onward towards Agramant. Rhys moved his mount up alongside his father-in-law.

"You have brought the priest?" he asked softly.

"He rides at the rear. I sent to the Cistercian monastery the day you departed for Agramant," the Dragon Lord replied.

Rhys nodded. "What will happen to Junia afterwards?"

"I will look for a match for my widowed daughter," the older man replied. "There will be someone who will have her. Her dower is respectable enough."

Rhys nodded. Junia had brought it all upon herself with her willfulness, but he still could not help but feel sorry for his wife's youngest sister. "Let me kill Simon de Bohun," he offered. "Better she hate me than you, my lord."

Merin Pendragon turned to look at his son-in-law. His face was one of deep sorrow. "Nay, it is my duty, for she is my daughter."

"The young de Bohun tried to protect her," Rhys said. "He is still doing his best to keep her from harm's way. The two women servants, too. I promised them you will give them their lives in return for all the aid they have rendered Junia."

"So Mortimer told me. I will honor your word to the two women, but as for Simon it makes no difference. When you stole Averil away you were willing to accept your responsibility in the matter. Simon de Bohun and Junia have caused their own misery. He knew he could not wed her, and she knew the same of him. Yet they met again at Mryddin Water in defiance of parental authority, for Hugo de Bohun would have told his son what I told my daughter," the Dragon Lord said stonily.

"I do not believe that Simon ever considered his father would follow him," Rhys made a small attempt at the young man's defense.

"He should not have gone to meet Junia at all that damnable day," Merin Pendragon said angrily. "He was the man. He should have known better. Junia's foolishness I can more easily forgive, for she is a lass. Now that is an end to it, my son."

Rhys grew quiet. His father-in-law was right. Honor was all, and honor must be restored to the Pendragon name. What had happened to Junia was not simply barbaric, and the behavior of another age; it was totally unforgivable that de Bohun had caused the public deflowering of an innocent girl of good family. Both father and son had to pay for the insult to this line of the legendary King Arthur.

It grew dark, and finally when they could no longer see their way, they stopped. They dared not light the torches they carried for fear of exposure. A small fire was lit in a sheltered grove. Their mounts tied to trees, the men settled down to eat the oat cakes they carried, and drink whatever they had in their flasks.

"I believe we are fairly near to Agramant," Roger Mortimer said quietly.

"We leave at earliest light," Merin Pendragon replied.

When false dawn was lighting the skies, it was just enough to allow them to move onward again, albeit slowly, until finally the skies grew lighter with the approach of the dawn.

"There!" Rhys said, and he pointed to the rock formation in the grove they had just entered. "There is the entrance to the cave, my lord."

"You are certain?" Merin Pendragon said.

"Come this way a moment, my lord, and

you can see Agramant through the trees," Roger suggested.

"We could not choose a better time," Lord Mortimer said. "The castle will not yet be awake but for the servants, Merin."

"Aye," came the terse reply. "Is the cave big enough to hide all the horses?"

"Yes, my lord," Rhys replied.

"Then let us do so now, and begin our assault," the Dragon Lord responded.

One by one the armed men moved into the cave, dismounting. The youngest of them would be left behind to shepherd the horses, and keep them inside. To this end they had carried several bales of hay with them, and a bag of oats. The hay, mixed with the oats would be spread about to keep the animals occupied. The door to the secret tunnel was removed, and the Dragon Lord congratulated Rhys on his foresight.

"Are there torch holders along the walls of the tunnel?" he asked.

Rhys nodded. "The tunnel is about half a mile from here to the dungeons beneath the castle," he said.

Merin Pendragon turned to his men. "The first dozen of you light your torches. You will place them in the holders beginning with the first one you come upon. That man will then drop back allowing the other torchbearers to light the way forward until all the holders have been filled. Be silent now," he told them, waving the torch-bearers ahead, and ducking his head he moved after them through the door, and into the darkened tunnel beyond. As each holder was filled the Dragon Lord moved forward until as the last torch was placed, he was leading his men. Finally they reached the end of the tunnel. The doorway to the dungeons stood before them.

"The girl, Cadi, said she would weaken the hinges," Rhys said. He put his shoulder against the portal, and felt it give way, swinging open on its half-cut hinges, and hanging askew. "She should have her freedom for this," he murmured low.

"She will," he heard his father-in-law say as they stepped through into the dungeons of Agramant Castle. "Set the door aside, Rhys, so it does not fall." He moved quickly around the corner, and seeing the sleeping guard slit his throat swiftly and neatly, lowering the body to the ground. Taking the man's keys he opened the cell door, and Brynn, grinning broadly, stepped silently out. The Dragon Lord nodded, pleased, and then signaled his men to follow him up the stairs into the great hall of the castle where the servants were quickly hunted down, and were killed. "Bar the door," Merin Pendragon said softly. "We'll take care of the castle's garrison after we have killed its master."

The men-at-arms within the castle were sought and slain. Then Rhys led his father-in-law to the chamber where he knew Junia and Simon were sleeping. The girl was awake immediately as if she had been expecting her father that morning. She jumped from the bed, clad in her dirty chemise, and taking up her gown quickly drew it on as her lover was pulled from the bed.

Confused, and still half asleep Simon's handsome face was suddenly aware of what was going on. "Allow me to dress, my lords," he said.

"Where is your father's chamber?" the Dragon Lord asked.

"He sleeps in the east tower," Simon said without hesitation as he drew on his garments. His own death was very near, and he knew it. For some reason he did not understand he felt at peace with the knowledge. "You have a priest with you?" he asked of them. "I will need to make my confession, my lords."

Merin Pendragon nodded. "We do."

"You will allow me to be shrived?" the young man asked.

"I am no barbarian, Simon de Bohun," the Dragon Lord answered him. "Aye. You may make your confession before you die."

Junia grew pale. "Da . . ." she began.

"Be silent, Daughter! This is not over

yet," he told her. "Bring her and her lover to the hall, Roger. Rhys, you come with me." He strode from the chamber.

Together the two men crept up the narrow staircase to the east tower, and upon trying the door were surprised to find it unlocked. Slipping into the room they found Hugo de Bohun lying upon his back, snoring, an empty carafe and goblet on the floor. He was alone, which was to the good. Neither Merin nor Rhys enjoyed killing women.

"Hugo de Bohun, I have come to take my children home," Merin Pendragon said in a loud voice, and as his enemy's eyes flew open, a startled expression upon his visage, the Dragon Lord's sword swiftly descended, cutting the head of Hugo de Bohun from his body in a single sharp stroke. Then Merin Pendragon reached out and lifted the coverlet off his enemy. Pulling up de Bohun's chemise he took his knife and sliced the manhood and balls from the body. These he stuffed into de Bohun's open mouth. Finally he lifted the severed head from its trunk. "We will put it on a pike. Perhaps it will save me the trouble of killing the garrison, and the serfs. We will fire Agramant, however," he said. "Let this be a warning to those who would follow this man's example."

"I will take the head of the beast into the

castle courtyard, and see if the rest of the men-at-arms will surrender," Rhys said. "The sight of this may help them make the correct decision," he said with a grim smile.

"And send Roger back through the tunnel with several men. I want the horses brought around into the courtyard of the castle," the Dragon Lord ordered.

The head of Hugo de Bohun, master of Agramant, his genitals spilling forth from his mouth, was displayed openly upon a pike within the courtyard.

"I am Rhys FitzHugh, lord of Everleigh, and son-in-law to the Dragon Lord. We are within the castle, and have slain your lord. You are given the opportunity to surrender yourselves, and serve Merin Pendragon. This castle will be destroyed."

"What of Simon de Bohun?" a voice from among the small garrison called.

"He will soon be in hell with his sire," Rhys replied coldly. "Put down your weapons if you would swear a new allegiance to the Pendragons."

The sound of falling weaponry filled the courtyard, and the men there fell to their knees.

"Two of you," Rhys said, "open the gates wide, now, and watch for our horses. The rest of you come into the hall." And he led them into the castle, the head of

Hugo de Bohun leading them on. They were then put into the dungeons, and locked in the cells there, for Merin Pendragon would want each man interviewed before he would trust any allegiance they would make. The de Bohun men understood that, and made no protest. Rhys then rejoined his father-in-law and the Mortimers.

Junia and Simon were standing separately, each guarded by two of the Dragon Lord's men-at-arms.

"Where is the priest?" Merin Pendragon called loudly, and the cleric hurried forward. "You know what to do, priest," the Dragon Lord said. "Bring my daughter and the young de Bohun lord forward."

"Da!" Junia attempted to speak with her father once again.

"You are to be married to your lover, girl. Is that not what you wanted?" he asked her coldly.

"Have mercy, Da!" she begged him.

"I will show him more mercy than he showed you. Now be silent, girl, and speak your vows with this man you would marry," Merin Pendragon said in harsh tones.

"If you mean to kill him once we are wed I will not say the vows," Junia cried defiantly. "If that is the only way I can keep him alive then I will!"

"Junia, in the name of all that is holy," Simon said to her, "let me restore your honor to you before I die! Do not let me go to my death with the sin of what I did on my conscience, I beg you!"

"But if I will not wed you, he will not kill you, for my honor will still be in question," Junia reasoned innocently.

"Junia, I am already a dead man," Simon told her softly. "Marry me and let me go to my grave forgiven. Our love was doomed from the start." He took her two hands in his hands. "Please, my love, do this for me that I may rest in peace."

The tears began to slip down Junia's face. She nodded reluctantly.

The young couple were pushed forward before the priest, and were told to join hands. The priest hurriedly droned the words of the marriage ceremony, and when he had finished Junia and Simon were man and wife. They kissed a lingering kiss. Then the priest drew Simon de Bohun off, and Junia watched with growing horror as her husband knelt and began to speak in low words that she could not make out. She turned to her father now, her slender hands held out pleadingly in a gesture of silent desperation.

"Da! In the name of all that is holy, spare Simon!" The tears began to pour down her fair face. "He is all I have ever wanted. I love him!" She threw herself at her father's feet pleading, her hands raised up to him in supplication. "Let him go away! I will never see him again! Da! Da! I beseech you to have mercy!"

Merin Pendragon turned his head away from his weeping daughter. "The Pendragon honor, Junia, your honor, my honor, must be restored. There is no other way. I am sorry, my daughter."

"You are a worse monster than Hugo de Bohun!" she accused him angrily. "If you do this thing I will never forgive you!"

"Is he shrived yet, priest?" the Dragon Lord asked.

Simon de Bohun stood up and walked over to them. "But a moment, my lord," he said calmly to Merin Pendragon. Then he took Junia in his arms, and looking down into her face said, "Your father is right, my love. By stealing your virtue I stole your honor as well. Our marriage has but partly restored that honor. Only my life can atone for what has happened. I should never have come that day to meet you, but I needed to see you one more time. I am so sorry, Junia, for I would have never intentionally harmed you, my precious love."

"Simon! I love you!" she cried. The tears would not stop flowing. She would spend the rest of her life in tears and mourning for him, Junia thought to herself.

"And I love you, my dear wife," he responded. "But now I must go, and you, Junia, must continue on with your life as it was intended." His lips touched hers in a final tender kiss, and then putting the girl from him he turned to Merin Pendragon. "I am ready now, my lord," he said.

The Dragon Lord handed Simon de Bohun a cup of wine. "My beloved Gorawen sent me with a packet of poison, Simon de Bohun. She said if I felt you deserved a kind death I was to give it you, mixed within a cup of wine. There will be no pain, I promise you. Just sleep."

"No!" Junia flung herself towards the two men in a futile attempt to take the cup. She was restrained by Rhys FitzHugh.

"Shut up, damn you, Junia!" he hissed in her ear. "He is exhibiting great bravery. Would you break his spirit now?" His fingers dug into her arms.

Simon de Bohun's elegant fingers wrapped about the stem of the goblet. Then raising it to his lips he drank it down without stopping. The cup dropped from his hand almost at once, and he collapsed to his knees. "Junia!" he said, and then he crumpled over, his heart slowly coming to a stop. His last conscious thought was that Merin Pendragon hadn't lied. There was no pain. No pain at all.

Chapter 18

Junia began to scream. She wrenched herself free of Rhys's iron grip, and threw herself across Simon's now prone form. Her hand reached out to take the cup. She would drink whatever dregs were left in it, but Rhys, anticipating her, kicked the cup across the hall. Gazing up at him, the look she gave him was filled with venom. Then she turned towards her father. "You have murdered Simon, damn you!"

"I have restored our honor, you foolish child," he told her.

"What good is honor to me when I have lost the one man, the only man I shall ever love?" she screamed at him. "Will honor keep me warm on a cold winter's night, Da? Will honor give me a son? Curse you and your honor to hell!" She cradled the body of her dead husband protectively.

"Lay him out upon the high board," Merin Pendragon said. "He will burn with the castle."

"No!" Junia told her father fiercely. "You will bury him honorably, next to his mother. Let his father burn with Agramant as he is now burning in hell, but Simon will be treated with dignity, Da. It will be your bridal gift to me." Her look was one of pure determination.

"Let her have this boon, my lord," Lord Mortimer interceded for Junia. "It is little enough your daughter asks of you."

"Very well," Merin Pendragon replied. "Take some of the de Bohun men, daughter, and bury your husband." He turned to Rhys. "Fetch two from the dungeons, and go with them."

"I will go too," young Brynn Pendragon said.

The Dragon Lord looked to his son, surprised.

"He was my friend, Da," the boy said quietly. "He was kind to me."

"He took our family's honor, Brynn," Merin Pendragon responded.

"But he was my friend," Brynn repeated, and going to his sister raised her up from where she knelt, gently loosening her grip from Simon's dead body. "Come, Junia, we must bury him now, sister." Then he turned to Cadi and old Elga, both of whom were weeping softly, afraid to incur the wrath of the Dragon Lord. "Come with us."

"A shroud," Elga quavered. "He must have a shroud."

"There is no time, old woman," Lord Mortimer told her. "Be grateful the Dragon Lord allows him to be laid by his mam."

Rhys returned from the dungeons with two strong men in tow. On his command they picked up the body of Simon de Bohun, and departed the hall.

Merin Pendragon turned to the two de Bohun women servants. "If there is anything of yours that you would take with you," he said, "fetch it now while the grave is being dug. I am almost ready to fire the castle."

The two women scampered off while Brynn led his sister out of the castle onto the hillside where Anne de Bohun was buried in a family plot marked with a small stone cross. The two men-at-arms set the body they carried down, and began to dig the grave that would contain Simon de Bohun. The earth was soft with the recent rains, and the two worked quickly. Elga and Cadi joined Brynn and Junia just as Rhys declared the grave ready. The two servants carried small bundles wrapped in shawls.

Junia was sitting on the grass next to the body. She was speaking softly, but they could not make out her words. The tears that continued to pour down her face seemed endless, and her eyes were beginning to swell shut with her sorrow.

Rhys touched her shoulder gently. "Say your farewell, Junia. It is time."

The face that looked up at him was anguished and drawn, but she nodded, bending to kiss the icy lips of the young man who had been so briefly her husband. Then she let Brynn help her up, and watched, trembling, as Simon was laid in his grave. Old Elga was sobbing bitterly, and her keening grew in intensity as the dirt was shoveled over the body of the young man she had helped to raise. The air was suddenly damp with impending rain, and as the wind began to rise they suddenly smelled an odor of burning. Turning they saw Agramant fully ablaze, flames leaping from the castle roof and from every opening in the building. Even the heavy wooden drawbridge was afire.

The serfs belonging to Agramant had come forth from their hovels. They stood staring openmouthed at the destruction, and particularly at the bloodied head of Hugo de Bohun looking down at them from atop its pike. Merin Pendragon spoke to them in a loud and strong voice.

"I am the Dragon Lord, and so end those who insult my family's honor. Take what few possessions you have, and follow in my train. You now belong to me, but you will find me a far better master than the one whose head now adorns my pike."

"My lord!" A tall man among the serfs came forward. "What of the young lord?"

Merin Pendragon pointed with a long finger to the hillside. "He is now next to the lady Anne. May God and his Blessed Mother have mercy on him."

At his words many among the serfs began to weep.

"Find my daughter," the Dragon Lord said. "She will ride by my side."

It was Rhys FitzHugh and Brynn Pendragon who lifted Junia off her husband's grave. They aided her to mount her horse, and put the reins in her hands. She spoke not a word. Her eyes were now almost entirely shut from the salt of her tears, which refused to stop flowing. Seeing her deep anguish Brynn attached a leading rein to his sister's mount, which he kept himself. Merin Pendragon said nothing. It was natural for his daughter to mourn the man she had believed she loved. He would give her a full year's mourning, for if he did not it would seem odd to any considering her for a wife. She would not be allowed to ride out from Dragon's Lair unless she was accompanied by his men. There would be no more problems such as Junia had caused with the de Bohuns.

They came home two days later, their journey having been slowed by the serfs with them. Argel and Gorawen were waiting for them in the great hall of Dragon's Lair. When they saw the state the young girl was in they both hurried forward, but before they might speak to her Ysbail came into the hall, and seeing her daughter ran forward.

"So, you are returned despoiled and unfit to be a decent man's wife, my daughter!" she cried. "How could you bring dishonor upon the Pendragon name, Junia?"

"I am widowed, Mother," Junia spoke the first words they had heard her utter since departing Agramant.

"Well, that is at least something," Ysbail replied. "Our honor has been restored. I knew your father would do the right thing. Pray God there is no child in your womb."

"I curse the day the Dragon Lord ever laid eyes on you, Mother," Junia said. "I curse the day you laid with him and conceived a daughter. Get away from me! Your words offend, and the sight of you makes me want to puke!"

Ysbail fell back, openmouthed. She tried to speak, but she could not.

Junia turned away from her, and stalked from the hall proudly.

"Jesu!" Argel whispered. "I have never seen such bitterness."

"She loved him," Gorawen replied simply.

"Here is your son, safe, lady," Merin

Pendragon said to his wife.

Argel held out her arms to Brynn, and with a grin he slipped into them, and hugged her. "You are your father's son," she told him, "and I am proud of you, Brynn."

"It was Juni who saved me," he told her. "She saw I had water, for Hugo de Bohun planned to starve me to death. Juni said I could survive as long as I had water, and she was right, Mother. She was the brave one, for she bearded Hugo de Bohun daily."

Argel kissed her son's forehead, and then released him. "I will remember to thank your sister," she promised.

"I would wait a while," Brynn replied wisely. "She is very angry that father slew her husband. Simon was not a brave man until the very end, but he did his best to protect her. He really loved her." Then Brynn turned to greet both Gorawen and Ysbail. "I am happy to see you both," he told them.

"I am sorry my daughter put you in danger, Brynn," Ysbail whispered in a quavery tone. "I am glad you have survived to come home to us."

Brynn realized suddenly that he felt sorry for Ysbail. With a show of his generous nature he embraced her, saying, "Lady, I am as much to blame as is my sister. But we are both now safe, praise God and his angels." Then he kissed her cheek.

Ysbail burst into fulsome tears, and ran from the hall.

" 'Twas nicely done, my son," Argel approved, and Gorawen nodded in agreement. "When Junia ran to her Simon, all of Ysbail's dreams came crashing down around her, I fear. She is at a loss now as to what to do."

"She brought up one thing we has best consider," the Dragon Lord said. "What if Junia is with child?"

"I will take care of it," Gorawen said. "I have already prepared a draught for Junia to drink. It will settle the problem, my lord."

"God forgive us!" he responded.

"Would you prefer a de Bohun grandchild?" she asked him. "And how easy will it be to find a husband for Junia if she is burdened with another man's child?"

"Do it now," he said. "Junia grows more obdurate with each passing day."

Gorawen bowed to him, and hurried off. In her chamber she opened a small packet of fine powder that she had prepared while he had been gone. Emptying it carefully into a simple pewter goblet she poured wine from her own carafe, and painstakingly mixed the two until the powder was well dissolved. Then taking up the cup she went up the winding staircase to the tower room where Junia slept. Opening the door with one hand, she entered.

Junia turned, but there was no welcome in her look. "What do you want?" she asked. Her normally sweet voice was cold as ice.

But Gorawen did not flinch. She held out the cup. "Drink it," she said.

Junia took the cup from the older woman. For a long moment she hesitated, but then she drank it down as swiftly as Simon had imbibed his poisoned cup.

"You did not ask me what it was," Gorawen said, taking the cup back.

"I would wish the same poison that you gave my husband, but I know better. This brew of yours is to make certain I bear no child, is it not?"

"Aye," Gorawen answered, her gaze refusing to flinch beneath Junia's hard look.

"I will never forgive any of you," Junia told her.

"Perhaps you will not," Gorawen said calmly, "but I would remind you that this is not the fault of your mother, or Argel, or me. What has happened to you is not the fault of your father, or your brother, either, Junia. What has happened is your fault, and Simon de Bohun's fault. He has paid the ultimate price with his death. Now you must pay the ultimate price by living without him whether you will or no." And then turning about, Gorawen left the surprised girl. The older woman understood the girl's grief, but Junia had to come to terms with the truth sooner or later. *Let her consider my words well*, Gorawen thought to herself as she made her way back down into the hall.

The autumn came, and they celebrated on the last day of October in the old way. The fires burned on the hillsides from the moment of the sunset and through the night, sending off the old year, and welcoming in the new year. The preparations were made for the winter. The lord and his men hunted daily. New hovels were built to house the additional serfs before the cold rains and bitter snows of winter arrived.

The winter came, and it was no better or worse than many before it. Junia remained cold and sullen to her family, but for Brynn. She wove at her loom incessantly, and prayed constantly. Cadi and old Elga had been absorbed into the household. Argel had asked Elga to serve young Brynn in hopes that having another boy would ease the woman's sorrow over Simon de Bohun. Brynn did not really need a nursemaid any longer, but he understood, and found little things that Elga might do for him. Cadi was given to Gorawen. It was thought better she not serve Junia for she could be nothing more than a reminder of the girl's time at Agramant, which had ended so unhappily.

Spring finally came, and seated in the hall one night Merin Pendragon brought up the subject they had been expecting him to bring up. "It is seven months since our return from Agramant," he began, "and Junia will be sixteen in two more months. The time has come for me to seek out another husband for her."

"She will fight you over it, my lord," Ysbail said.

"Perhaps, and perhaps not," Gorawen responded.

"Aye," Argel agreed. "She is still angry at us, and may take any excuse to leave Dragon's Lair."

"Have you a man in mind?" Gorawen asked their lord.

"Possibly. Mortimer and I discussed it last autumn when we were hunting," Merin Pendragon replied. "He has a widowed cousin, William le Clare, who was wed for many years to his childhood sweetheart. It was a true love match between them," the Dragon Lord said, "but alas, they had no children. William le Clare's wife died two years ago. He might be willing to take a young wife in hopes of at last siring an heir."

"How old is he?" Argel inquired.

"Five and thirty," the Dragon Lord answered. "Almost twenty years Junia's senior, but I do not think she would willingly wed a young man after Simon de Bohun. William le Clare has lost a beloved wife. He will surely understand Junia's sorrow."

"If you think this is best, husband," Argel said, "then by all means pursue it."

The other two women nodded in agreement.

The Dragon Lord rode the next day to Lord Mortimer's fine stone keep. When Lord Mortimer learned the reason for his visit he clapped his friend upon the back, saying, "You could not have come at a better time. My cousin arrives tomorrow for a visit. He has written me that he is indeed considering another marriage, and wishes my advice as to seeking a suitable bride."

"I do not have a great name," the Dragon Lord said.

"You descend from Arthur, and your lineage is impeccable. One thing, however, old friend. My cousin must be told the entire truth of Junia's unfortunate adventures."

"It is the honorable thing," Merin Pendragon agreed. "Will my daughter's dower be enough, though?"

"William does not seek a rich wife. He

needs a young and fecund wife," Lord Mortimer said. "The more I consider it, the more I believe Junia would be perfect for him. William loved Adele right well even as Junia loved her Simon. Neither of them will expect it to be anything more than a good match. Junia is well bred, and knows how to manage a household. My cousin is not a cruel man, but he will know how to be firm with a young wife."

"Then I will remain and meet William le Clare," Merin Pendragon said.

Lord Mortimer's expected guest arrived the following morning, and the three men spent the afternoon hunting. After the evening meal as they sat before the fire in the hall, wine cups in their hands, William le Clare explained to his cousin the purpose of his visit.

"I have decided that I need another wife," he said. "I do not want one, for it seems almost a betrayal of my beloved Adele, but I need an heir, and I am still young enough to sire one, Cousin."

"And have you anyone in mind?" Edmund Mortimer asked his cousin.

William le Clare shook his head in the negative. "Nay. How would I know any suitable young girls?" He chuckled.

"Then it is possible I may have a prospect for you, Cousin," Lord Mortimer said. "The Dragon Lord is seeking a husband for his widowed daughter. The girl will be sixteen in two months. She is the child of his second concubine, and her dower portion is intact. As you do not seek love, neither does Junia Pendragon, for she loved her husband well and true, cousin. She is very fair, well-spoken and well-bred."

William le Clare turned to Merin Pendragon. "You would consider me, my lord?"

Merin nodded. "But first you must know why my daughter is widowed, sir," he said. "My family and another have been locked in a feud for over a century, but for the last few years the quarrel lay dormant. My daughter knew naught of the dispute, and neither did the young man she met several years ago while riding with her brother. A friendship grew between the three young people. My daughter and this boy fell in love."

"He was of the other family?" William le Clare immediately guessed.

"Aye." Merin Pendragon sighed deeply. "Of course, no marriage could be contracted between them, and both were told this. Unfortunately, my daughter and Simon de Bohun arranged to meet again. The boy's father followed with his men, and caught the two. Hugo de Bohun forced his son to rape my daughter while he and his men watched. My only son, Brynn, attempted to rescue his sister and was captured and imprisoned for his trouble. I will not bore you at this time with all the details, especially if your interest in my daughter has waned with my telling. I rescued my children. I slew Hugo de Bohun. I saw Junia wed to Simon de Bohun, that our honor be restored. Then he was also slain."

"You are a good father, my lord. You did exactly what needed to be done," William le Clare said.

"She loved the de Bohun boy. She loves him yet, I fear," Merin Pendragon said.

"I loved my wife, and love her yet," William le Clare responded. "If your daughter is willing, then there would be no illusory expectations between us. I seek a young wife who will give me an heir. Nothing more. I will treat her kindly as long as she is obedient and a good chatelaine."

"Her dower is not great," Merin Pendragon said.

"What is it?" the younger man asked.

"Livestock, cattle and sheep both. A dower chest of linens and clothing. Her horse. And sixteen silver pennies, sir," the Dragon Lord answered.

"I consider her very well dowered, my lord," William le Clare replied. "I would, however, for both of our sakes, see your daughter before any arrangement is made between us. While I seek a young wife, I do not want an unwilling wife. I do not, I fear, have the patience for it," he finished with a small smile.

"Agreed," the Dragon Lord responded. "I will return home tomorrow. Come to Dragon's Lair when you have concluded your visit with your cousin, and you will meet my daughter Junia. You will find her very fair." He arose. "If I am to leave early then I will to my bed, gentlemen," he said.

When Merin Pendragon had found his bed space at the end of the hall William le Clare turned to Lord Mortimer. "Do you know the girl?"

"Since she was a child. Merin has three daughters. The eldest by his first concubine, Gorawen, a most beautiful and clever woman. A second daughter, as well as his son, by his wife, the lady Argel. Junia is the daughter of his other concubine, Ysbail. Averil, the eldest sister has always been considered the most beautiful. She is the wife of the lord of Everleigh. The second daughter, Maia, is the wife of Emrys Llyn, the Lord of the Lake. Junia, the youngest, was coltish and charming as a little girl. Now I find her every bit as beautiful as her eldest sister despite their different coloring. The girl is pale, with hair like a raven's wing. Her eyes are the green of a sunlit forest pool. She is nicely made and sweetly spoken. She plays several instruments, and is skilled on them all. Beware her mother though, cousin. Ysbail is greedy and sharp-spoken. However, you could do worse than to wed Pendragon's daughter."

"You like her," William le Clare said.

"Aye, I do," Lord Mortimer admitted. "And I will admit that even I wished it had not been necessary to kill young Simon de Bohun. The boy loved her, for all that happened. Merin tells me that Junia claims her husband only knew her that one time. He says she is not a girl to prevaricate, so while she is no longer a virgin, she is yet inexperienced, and could be taught to please."

William le Clare said, "So what it all boils down to, cousin, is that I find her suitable, and she be willing."

Lord Mortimer nodded with a small smile. "Aye," he agreed.

Merin Pendragon returned home the following day.

"You remained longer than I thought you would," Argel said. "I would have sent Brynn to seek you had you not returned today."

"William le Clare came to visit," he replied.

"Tell us!" Gorawen said. "What think you, my lord?"

"I like him," Merin Pendragon said. "I think him most suitable, but he must see Junia, and be assured she is willing to marry him. He will come to Dragon's Lair in a few days' time."

"Will you speak with our daughter before he comes?" Ysbail wanted to know.

"I think it best I do," the Dragon Lord told the three women. "Where is she? She is usually at her loom this time of day."

"She and Brynn and several of our men went riding," Argel replied. "The day is pleasant, and she has been cooped up all winter."

"Is this William le Clare a man of property, my lord, and where does he live?" Ysbail wanted to know.

"Near Hereford," the Dragon Lord answered her.

"Is he a man of means?" Ysbail prodded.

"He has lands, and stock, and since he had a wife I will assume he has a goodly hall. I do not know," Merin responded honestly.

"Should you not know?" Now it was Argel who spoke up before Ysbail annoyed her husband with her determined probing.

"He is Edmund Mortimer's cousin," the Dragon Lord said. "What more is there to know? Mortimer would not recommend him were he not suitable. Junia is not a princess, Ysbail, and considering the misbehavior that led to such tragic events, I am relieved that William le Clare would consider our daughter at all."

"An older man is a good thing. It would be difficult for Junia to accept a younger man. She would be always making comparisons," Gorawen spoke up. "We must hope, Ysbail, that Junia will please William le Clare."

"I dare not speak with her," Ysbail said. "She will only listen to Argel."

Argel chuckled. "She is angry, but she never forgets her manners. I credit you with that, Ysbail."

Junia returned with her brother in mid-afternoon. They had missed the main meal of the day, but were back in time for the evening meal. Junia went immediately to her loom. She was weaving a wall tapestry depicting Christ's crucifixion. It suited her mood of late.

Argel came and stood by her side, a hand resting lightly on Junia's shoulder. "Your father may have found you a husband, Junia." She felt the girl stiffen. "His name is William le Clare," she continued in a low, calm voice. "He is Lord Mortimer's cousin, and a widower. There were no children of his first union, and he hopes for a child with a young wife. He is coming with Lord Mortimer to visit us in a few days."

"Simon is not gone a year," Junia responded.

"No, but we could not wait until the year was up to seek out eligible prospects. William le Clare's arrival on the scene is most providential, my child. If he would have you it would be an excellent match for you. Every bit as good as Averil's."

Junia laughed bitterly. "Do you believe I care about such things? Those are things my foolish mother cares about. Not I, lady."

"Ysbail is what she is, Junia," Argel said reasonably. "Even as you are what you are. You cannot change her now. But your father and I would have you happy again. Will you promise me to greet William le Clare fairly, and give this a chance?" She moved around to take the girl's face in her hands, and looked into her eyes.

Junia sighed deeply. "I still hurt," she said softly.

Argel nodded, and bending, kissed the girl. "I know, my child, I know," she said.

"I will greet this man fairly, lady," she promised. "Even if he does not suit me, or I him, I would not have him think me ill bred."

"Then I am content," Argel said, smiling at Junia.

"Lady, what does he know of me?" Junia asked nervously.

"All, my child. Your father felt he must know all from the outset," Argel said.

Junia nodded. "It is better," she agreed.

"I will tell your father, then, that you look forward to William le Clare's arrival," Argel responded to the girl, smiling again. "He will be pleased, Junia."

"My mother knows?"

"Aye," Argel said, and then unable to help herself, she giggled.

For the first time since Simon de Bohun's death Junia began to laugh, and she laughed until the tears were rolling down her face, and she was gasping with the delicious knowledge that the kindly Argel, whom she had never heard say an unkind word about anyone, had no more respect for Ysbail than Junia did. But, by the rood, she hid it well! "Oh, lady," Junia said as she finally managed to control her laughter.

"We are very bad, my child," Argel replied, but her lips were twitching.

"Thank you," Junia said, and she took Argel's hands up in hers and kissed them.

"Oh, dearest one, I do want you happy!" Argel said, and then turning, she hurried back to where her husband and the others were anxiously waiting. The smile upon her face told them what they needed to know.

Eight days later a messenger arrived from

Lord Mortimer to say that he and his cousin would be coming to Dragon's Lair in two days' time. A flurry of excitement ran through the household as the Dragon Lord's women bustled about to see that all would be in readiness to receive their guests. Junia, however, sat in the hall at her loom, ignoring the busy action around her.

She knew that she would have to marry despite her lack of enthusiasm. A woman of her class had but two choices: marriage or the veil. She had no calling for the church, and she knew it. Besides, she was much too independent a soul. The dull routine of a convent day would render her mad in short order. And the vow of obedience was not one Junia thought she could accept. Yet under the law a woman must also be obedient to her husband and lord. Still, she knew a man might be manipulated a bit now and again. No. Being a wife would be far easier than being a nun.

What was William le Clare like, she wondered? Well, she knew that he was old. More than twice her age. And he wanted an heir. She shuddered remembering that to get an heir one must couple with one's husband. She knew Simon had tried to be gentle with her, but it had all been so distasteful and crude when he had mounted her. And yet her mother, Gorawen and

Argel seemed to enjoy their time with her father. There must be more to a husband's relationship with his wife than what had happened between her and Simon that awful day. And it should be a private thing. Yet the thought of coupling her body with another man both revolted and frightened her.

But if he was pleasant, and she thought she might be able to live with him, Junia made up her mind that she would accept a proposal of marriage from this man. She would be sixteen in a few weeks, and she didn't want to have to endure the prospective husband parade that Maia had been forced to accept. She would not love him, but she would be a good wife to him, and she would, despite her distaste, do her best to give him the children he desired. But best of all she would be away from Dragon's Lair, and the Dragon Lord, her father, who had killed the man she loved.

She took care with her garb the day their guests were suppose to arrive. Her undergown had a high round neck, and tight long sleeves. It was of fine lightweight silk, deep green in color. Over it Junia wore a sleeveless overgown with open sides. It was made of a pale gold-colored brocade. A girdle of enameled green links was fastened about her waist. Her black hair was carefully part in the center, and she wore two thick braids. The three older women nodded at each other, pleased. It was obvious that Junia was making an effort. Still, she did not ask for their approval when she came into the hall, and she went immediately to her loom, sitting down, and beginning her work again.

The guests arrived, and were welcomed. The women eyed William le Clare with interest. He was a tall, well-made man who did not look at all as if he were in his middle thirties. His hair was a rich, dark chestnut brown. It was thick, and curled slightly at the nape of his neck. His eyes were neither green nor brown, but rather a deep hazel color. His head was nicely rounded, but he had a long face with a long aristocratic nose, high cheekbones, deep-set oval eyes, and a large narrow mouth that was in perfect proportion with the rest of his face. His voice when he spoke was low and well modulated.

"I would call him handsome," Gorawen said to the other two women, who nodded in agreement.

"Pray God and his angels that my daughter finds him suitable," Ysbail said.

"Pray God and his angels that this suitor finds Junia suitable," Gorawen said.

"Fetch your daughter, woman," the Dragon Lord called to Ysbail, and she immediately arose, moving quickly across the hall to where Junia sat at her loom. When she reached the girl she said in a voice devoid of any emotion, "Daughter, your father calls you to come to him. Will you obey him now?"

Junia arose, and without a word moved back across the hall to where her father stood with his guests. She smiled, and curtsied to the three men. "Da, you wish my presence?" she asked him.

He did not answer her, saying instead, "William le Clare, this is my daughter Junia. Turn about, girl, and let the man see you. He cannot buy a pig in a poke."

"I was not aware that I was being sold," Junia replied pertly.

William le Clare laughed. He had been afraid the girl would be some poor beaten-down creature. He had only agreed to come to Dragon's Lair that he not offend his cousin, Lord Mortimer. But the girl had spirit. She might prove a pleasant companion, and a lively lover. He needed to know more. "I am not offended, Merin. I find your daughter amusing." He looked directly at Junia. "Lady," he said, reaching out to take her hand. "You will walk with me."

Not will you, Junia thought, *but rather, you will.* He was a man who took charge. "I will walk with you, sir," she said, and she took his hand.

They moved away from the others, walking slowly down the length of the hall.

"I am seeking a wife only for the purpose of siring an heir," he began. "I would tell you immediately that I loved my late wife with every fiber of my being. What love I believe I have left is for my child."

"In that I will concur," Junia said. "If I am able to give you a child I will love that child, but I will have no love for you, my lord. I will love and mourn my late husband, Simon, the rest of my days."

He nodded. "Then we are of one mind, lady," he told her.

"If you find that I suit you, my lord, I will come prepared to oversee your household as a good chatelaine should do. I will obey and respect you," Junia said.

"Always?" he asked, his hazel eyes twinkling.

Startled by the teasing tone in his voice Junia look up into William le Clare's face.

"You do not strike me, Junia, as a very obedient girl," he told her softly.

She blushed. She actually blushed, and she was angry for a moment that this man could have elicited such a reaction from her. "My lord, I can only promise you that I will do my best by and for you," she responded stiffly.

"Speak freely, lady," he said low. "We must be completely honest with one another. Are you willing to be my wife or no?"

"I am willing," Junia replied.

"Why?" he demanded, the hazel eyes searching her face for the truth.

"Because there are only two choices open to me, my lord. You know them both. Because I do not want to be put on display for a parade of men seeking my hand in marriage. Because I am anxious to leave my father's house since I can never forgive him for killing my husband, Simon de Bohun. I could have lived without my honor, my lord, but living without Simon is proving difficult. I choose to accept your offer of marriage because you seem a good man who would treat me fairly, though God and his angels know my choices to date have not been successful. I am not suited to the church. I must marry. You need a wife to give you a child. Our families know each other. If you will have me, I will accept you as my husband, and do my best to be a good wife to you," Junia said quietly. "I suppose I shock you with my frankness."

"Nay, your honesty pleases me, Junia," he told her. "If you thought to drive me off, then you have failed in your attempt. Now, I will be as candid with you. I loved my wife, Adele. We knew each other since childhood, and we married when she was fourteen and I was eighteen. Our greatest sorrow was in not having a child. Then Adele developed a great canker in her belly. When we had to face the fact that she was dying my wife made me promise that I would wed again that I might have the heir she had not been able to give me. I swore to her that I would do her bidding, but I told her then that I should not love another wife. I remember her smiling at me when I said it. She told me that I should not cheat another woman so cruelly, but I cannot love another, Junia, and you must know that before you agree to wed me. I will treat you well, and I will respect your position in my household as my wife, and as the mother of my children. But I can never love you. Can you live with that knowledge, Junia?"

"If you can comprehend that I will mourn Simon de Bohun forever, my lord, aye. We will be friends. I think being friends is better than falling in love," Junia replied.

"When will you wed me, then?" he asked her.

"Simon has not been dead a year yet, but I will marry you immediately, my lord," she told him. "There was no joy and feasting when I wed Simon. I do not want any now. I hope that you will understand."

He nodded. "I do, Junia. Come, then,

and let us speak with your father on the matter."

The Dragon Lord protested weakly when his youngest daughter said there would be no festivities for her marriage to William le Clare, but Argel overruled him, and Gorawen and Ysbail both soothed him. "But your sisters will be hurt," Merin Pendragon said. "You were at their weddings."

"I am but a widow remarrying," Junia said sharply. "I do not want a great deal of fuss or to-do. I would wed on the morrow, and leave immediately afterwards for my new home." Then she turned to William le Clare. "Where is our home, sir?"

"Hereford," he told her. "A three days' journey from here. My house sits atop a hill looking west into Wales. I have fields, and meadows. A small forest. A village with a mill and a church. My serfs are industrious and not given to rebellion. You will be happy there, Junia."

"Aye," she agreed, "I believe I will. Why would you object, my lord?" she asked her father.

"I don't," he grumbled, "but why can you not be wed in a proper fashion like your two sisters?"

"Now if I recall, Averil dragged you, Rhys FitzHugh, and a party of men across the country to Aberffraw for a judgment from the prince because Rhys had bride-napped her thinking she was your heiress. Honor demanded he wed Averil, or that someone else be willing to take her. And then at the last minute Averil decided she would marry Rhys so the prince saw them joined that same day. It was a simple wedding.

"As for Maia, she sat meek as fresh milk while every eligible man in the March tried to court her. Then said she would wed no one but the Lord of the Lake, and locked herself away until you agreed. That, I will admit, was a nice wedding.

"Now, my lord, we come to me, the youngest of your daughters. Because you and the de Bohuns couldn't put aside a hundred-year-old feud, Hugo and Simon de Bohun are now dead, and their castle of Agramant lies a burned-out ruin. Hugo, I will agree, deserved to die, and it did give me particular satisfaction to see his head upon a pike, but Simon was as innocent of what had happened as I was. Yet you still killed him.

"William le Clare loved his late wife. He seeks a second wife for the purpose of having a child. I am pleased that despite my adventures he will have me to wife. But there is, will be, no love between us. This is a practical arrangement. Let us not make it more than it is. With my good lord's permission we will wed early on the morrow, and then depart for Hereford. Surely you will cease your objections, my lord sire."

"But we will have a small breakfast after you are joined," Argel said quietly. "You cannot begin your long journey without something in your bellies."

"Agreed, lady!" William le Clare said, and he looked to Junia who bowed her dark head in acceptance.

So in the same gown in which she had greeted him the day before, for it was her best gown, Junia married William le Clare early the next morning. Argel had arranged a pleasant meal for them all, and after they had eaten, the bridal couple, and Lord Mortimer, prepared to depart. Junia's few personal possessions and dower chest had been packed and stored in a cart for transport. She refused her father's offer of a serving girl.

"William will provide me with a servant," she said. "Farewell, my lord."

"Junia, will you ever forgive me?" he asked her.

She gave him a bleak look, turning away without answering him. Dutifully she hugged and kissed her mother. Ysbail, her usual sharp temper cowed by her daughter's recent fury, whispered low, "God bless and protect you, my daughter. I think you have done the wise thing."

"What, Mother," Junia said, half teasing,

"you do not wish to come with me?"

"I will not come to you until you ask me," Ysbail replied proudly.

Junia turned away from her, and bid first Gorawen, and lastly Argel good-bye.

"You can always come home," Argel told her softly.

"Never again, Lady Mother," Junia replied.

They departed Dragon's Lair, and riding across the fields before the keep Junia thought of that long ago day when Rhys FitzHugh and young Roger Mortimer had surprised them all by the brook, and stolen Averil away. They had all been so young. Now Junia felt as if she were a hundred years old. The man she loved was dead. She was married to a man she could never love, and who could never love her. So much for girlish daydreams.

They reached Lord Mortimer's house in the late afternoon, their journey slowed slightly by the cart carrying Junia's possessions. After the evening meal Junia found herself alone in a small guest chamber. She undressed herself and climbing into bed fell asleep. A maidservant awakened her early, bringing water with which she washed. She dressed and went down to the hall where she found her husband and Lord Mortimer already at table. Junia joined them, eating heartily.

"We are a two-day journey from here to my home," William le Clare told his bride. "I have arranged for us to spend the night at the monastery of St. Wulfstan. It is a long day's ride, Junia, and I would have you prepared for it."

Thanking Lord Mortimer they departed for Hereford. William le Clare had not lied. The day's ride was very long, and they reached their destination as the sun was beginning to slip beneath the hills behind them. They were welcomed, and shown to separate guest quarters. As there were no other women traveling through that night Junia found herself quite alone. A meal was brought to her, for the monastery had no place where women guests might eat. She was awakened in the early morning by a most ancient monk who brought her a small trencher filled with oat stirabout, and a small cup of cider. She giggled to herself thinking the abbot probably considered the old fellow safe from her feminine wiles. She had slept in her gown, and so after relieving herself she ate quickly, assuming her husband would want to get started early.

William le Clare smiled when he found her already awaiting him in the courtyard. "The ride will not be quite so long today," he promised her. "I am pleased to see you are a woman who understands the value of time."

Her little cart rumbling behind them, they set out again. They traveled with a dozen men-at-arms, one of whom was driving the vehicle so it would not be necessary to return a serf. Junia began to pay attention to the countryside about her. It was different from her mountainous and rugged Welsh homeland. The land rolled gently. There were fields and meadows and orchards. Hereford had a most prosperous and green look about it. It was mid-May she realized. *Married in May. She'll rue the day.* The old saying popped into her mind. She wondered if her father had given her husband sixteen silver pennies or if because she had not yet celebrated her birthday, had he given William only fifteen. Her curiosity piqued, she asked him.

"He counted out sixteen pennies," William told her.

Junia smiled. The Dragon Lord had felt guilty. Good! "When did he say he would see the rest of my dower paid?" she asked her husband.

"Within the month," he told her.

Junia nodded, satisfied.

It was in the middle of the afternoon that he pointed as he said to her, "There is your new home, Junia. There is Landor."

She looked, and felt an odd sense of

pleasure. The house was stone, two storied on one end, with a slate roof. They turned off the main track, and followed a tree-lined path up a long and gentle incline until they finally reached the house. Almost at once several servants came forth to greet their master.

"This is your new mistress," William le Clare told them. "I have taken another wife. You will obey her, for the house and all in it are now hers." He lifted Junia from her horse, but rather than putting her on her feet carried her through the front door of the house saying, " 'Tis an old custom in this part of the country to carry the bride into her new home the first time." He set her down on the floor of the front hallway.

Junia found herself rosy with her blushes, especially as the house servants who had been already informed of a new mistress had gathered to meet her with smiling faces, and were winking and poking at each other.

William le Clare looked about, and then he signaled a pleasant-faced young woman forward. "This is Susan, my lady wife. She will serve you. Take your new mistress upstairs, Susan, and see she is settled," he ordered the girl.

Susan led Junia up the staircase and down a hall into a lovely bedchamber.

"This was the old mistress's room, lady. It is clean, but we were not expecting a new mistress. Master said he was going to visit Lord Mortimer."

"Lord Mortimer is my da's friend," Junia explained. "The chamber is fine, Susan, but I am used to regular bathing, and we have been on the road for three days. Will you arrange a bath for me?"

Susan nodded. "Where is your family home, my lady?" she asked, and going to a wall cupboard she opened it, and pulled out a round oak tub. Setting it by the fireplace she said, "I'll have the lads bring up the hot water." Going to the door of the chamber she called out, "Water for my lady's bath!"

"My father is called the Dragon Lord. We are descended from the great King Arthur, Susan. Pendragon is our family name," Junia explained.

"Then you be Welsh," Susan answered, nodding. This was a piece of information to tell the others, she thought. They had all been very surprised when Wat came running into the house crying that the master had brought home a new bride. This girl was much younger than Lady Adele, God assoil her good soul. The master had taken her to get an heir on for certain, Susan thought. He should have no trouble since she was fair enough.

The bath water came, and the tub was filled. Junia bathed, and then put on an orange tawny undergown, and a sleeveless gold and orange brocade overgown that Susan admired greatly as she led her new mistress down to the hall of the house where William le Clare was awaiting his bride.

"The meal is ready," he told her. "You must be hungry after our long journey today. Come." He brought her to the high board and seated her in the mistress's chair.

After the meal Junia asked to be excused from the hall as she was weary.

He nodded his consent, adding low, "But you will recall, Junia, it is our wedding night." His handsome face was serious.

"Of course, my lord," Junia answered him. "I will await you." How odd she thought as she hurried up the stairs. Her wedding night. She had never had a wedding night with Simon. Just a cruel coupling before his father and his father's rough men. She thought back, and decided that she had not really enjoyed her coupling with Simon. The process had been rather unpleasant, and it had hurt. It was only supposed to hurt once, but that was only what she had heard. She did not know if it was true.

Susan was awaiting her. The serving woman helped her young mistress from her garments, leaving her with only her lawn chemise with its ruffles at neck and sleeves. Carefully she put everything away as Junia washed her face, hands and teeth. She had unpacked Junia's belongings. Now she handed Junia her ash-wood brush.

"You may go now, Susan. I will not need you again tonight," she told the woman.

"Yes, lady," Susan answered, curtseying.

"And, Susan, I am a widow," Junia informed the servant lest the other servants look for any evidence of her virginity on the morrow, and not finding it, gossip.

Susan blushed, and Junia knew she had been correct to bring up this point.

Junia sat down on the large oak bed. The linens smelled of lavender, and the heavy dark green velvet bed curtains were not musty. Unplaiting her hair she began to brush it out. She had worn a veil on their journey and so her tresses were not too dusty. *Still,* she thought, *I must wash my hair tomorrow.* Slowly she drew the brush bristles from the very top of her head to the tips of her dark locks. This was a pleasant room, and she felt strangely comfortable in it. It was the same feeling as when she had first seen the house from a distance, sitting on its hillock.

The door to her chamber opened quietly, and William le Clare entered. He smiled at her as he began to undress, and said, "You may change the room to suit yourself, Junia. Adele said it was an easeful chamber."

"God assoil the lady Adele's good soul, my lord, she was right about that. It is an easeful place, and while I may put my own possessions about the chamber, I am content to live in it as it is." She was careful to avoid looking at him now. She did not know what the protocol was with a man for a wedding night. For any night, she considered, almost laughing aloud.

Walking over to her he took the brush from her hand. "Let me," he said, sitting beside her, and brushing her long hair. "What lovely hair you have, Junia. It is thick and soft to my touch. Has it ever been cut?"

"Nay, my lord, only trimmed," she answered him.

"It has the sheen of a raven's wing, wife," he told her. She felt him pull the curtain of her hair aside, and then his lips kissed her neck.

Junia sat very still. She had absolutely no idea of what she should do, or indeed if she should do anything.

"Would you remove your chemise?" he asked politely.

Obediently Junia stood up, undid the ribbons at the neckline of her garment, and drew the chemise off over her head, laying it on the settle by the hearth.

"Turn about so I may see you better," he said.

Junia turned, her head turned from his gaze. Her heart was beating very quickly.

He was silent for a long time, and then he said, "You are very beautiful, wife."

It grew silent again, and finally Junia burst out, "I do not know what you want of me, my lord. You must guide me, for I have no real knowledge of what I must do."

"Ah," he said, and then, "tell me exactly what happened, Junia, when you were robbed of your virtue." Reaching out he drew her down into his lap.

It was the first time since that day that Junia had allowed herself to think on it. She was not certain she could, but then she said, "I was forced to disrobe. I would show no fear before Hugo de Bohun and his men, for I knew that was what they wanted. They wanted to gain their first pleasure from my shame at being naked before them. I gave them no satisfaction, however. When I was naked I was pulled down upon the ground, on my back. Two men knelt by my head, holding my arms down. Two men took my legs, and held them wide apart. Then Simon was forced down upon me. He tried very hard to be gentle, but his father took a leather strap, and beat his bottom to make him perform well before them. He whispered to me to scream when my maidenhead was shattered or his father would be dissatisfied. He did not have to tell me. The pain was hurtful, and the men surrounding us cheered my deflowering while many of them took their own manhoods in hand, and spilled their seed upon the ground. After that I would not let Simon have me, for I was ashamed, my lord."

William le Clare realized as he listened with horror to Junia's monotone recital that he was glad that both of the de Bohuns were slain by his young wife's father. He had himself never known such cruelty, and that it had been done against a virtuous maid of good family was criminal. Now, if he was to have an heir of his young wife he must contend with the damage done her. "I am sorry, Junia," he told her quietly. "But now you must tell me of the kissing and petting games you and Simon played before this event occurred. Can you do that?"

"We played no such games, my lord," she said, and he heard the truth in her speech. "We sat and we talked," Junia explained. "When we first met we spoke of all manner of things that we knew, or wished we knew; we spoke of the dreams we had for our futures; and finally we spoke of marriage only to discover the feud between our families. We met that unfortunate day because as we discovered afterwards, each of us hoped that the other's family was willing to make peace that we might marry. Instead, Hugo de Bohun followed Simon, and you know the rest," Junia finished.

William nodded. Now he understood it all. "Ideally, Junia, when a man and a woman make love," he began, "there is pleasure in the act."

"I found no pleasure in what Simon did that day," she answered him honestly.

"Of course not," he agreed. "You were raped, Junia. Hugo de Bohun wished to impress upon you and his son his dominant will over you both. He did that by forcing Simon to you as a stallion is brought to a mare. Your body was not properly prepared for a man, my wife."

"But Simon was aroused," Junia said. "I am not so foolish that I don't know a man must be aroused to take a woman."

"Aye, and men are easily aroused as a general rule," William agreed. "But you were not aroused, Junia. And believe me it is a far more pleasurable experience for a man and a woman when both are properly prepared for passion."

"I can already feel your arousal beneath

my buttocks," Junia told him frankly.

He found himself chuckling. This penchant Junia had for the absolute truth could prove her undoing one day. "Aye, Junia, I find you very desirable," he admitted. "But you are nowhere near ready to be mounted by me."

"How do I make myself ready?" she asked him innocently.

"You don't, wife. I ready you," he told her. Then his big hand began to caress her small round breasts with a delicate touch.

Junia started. "Why are you doing that?" she demanded to know.

"Because a woman's breasts have two functions. The most important of which is to nourish her children, but the more delightful role of the breasts is to be caressed by a lover so the lady may be brought to arousal herself. Kissing at the same time helps," he explained. "Lift your lips to mine, Junia," he commanded gently, and she obeyed.

His big mouth pressed strongly against hers. His big hands stroked the firm globes of her bosom. She attempted to concentrate upon both of his actions that she might understand better, but her head was beginning to spin, and she was really beginning to feel quite weak. She pulled her head away from his. "My lord . . ." she began, but he found her mouth again, and continued to kiss her. His palms cupped her breasts one at a time. Then his thick thumb and his forefinger gently pinched a nipple. Junia shivered as a bolt of sensation pierced her.

"Are you beginning to feel the pleasure?" he asked her, and she nodded. "Good," he said. "Now, Junia, let us lie together in this bed that was built for a man and wife." And when they were side by side he began to caress her body with a tender touch. His fingers moved from her breasts back up to her face. He touched her cheekbones, ran a finger down her nose, and across her lips. His fingers trailed across her torso, and her belly. They moved leisurely over her mons, and she trembled.

"Why do you have no body hair?" he asked her, remembering the golden down on Adele's legs, and the tufts beneath her arms. He was fascinated and not just a little stirred by Junia's smooth skin.

"Gorawen says a woman is more delectable when she is not covered in fur like some animal," Junia explained. "She taught my sisters and me how to make a paste that removes our body hair. If it displeases you I will not use it." The touch of his hands moving with such sure skill over her body was exciting, Junia thought to herself. Simon had never touched her in such a thrilling manner.

"Nay, I find your silken skin kindles my desires greatly," he told her, and then he kissed her a slow kiss that left Junia breathless. "Now, wife, I mean to touch you in a secret place, and you must not be afraid," he told her.

Junia felt a single finger press insistently through her two nether lips. To her surprise she seemed wet, for his finger seemed to swirl about in that hidden cavern of her body. Then he touched her in a place she hadn't even realized was there, or that would respond in such a heated manner to his touch. She tensed.

Feeling it he murmured softly in her ear, "It's all right, Junia. I am going to give you your first taste of the pleasure a man and a woman can have together. I don't want you to be fearful. Trust me, wife." The finger grazed and glossed over that sentient little nub of flesh he seemed to have discovered. It chafed and it fretted at her, and it was with great surprise that Junia began to feel that bit of her begin to tingle. And the tingling grew until she was moaning and straining against that finger. She felt as if that piece of her flesh was swelling and swelling, and the tingling increased in intensity. Junia suddenly gave a surprised cry as the pleasure burst, and drowned her in sweet sensation.

"Oh, William!" she said, using his name

for the first time. Her eyes, which had been open were now shut as she experienced the feeling he had given her as it drained away.

"Now, Junia," he told her, "your body is well prepared for a husband." He mounted her, and gently pushed himself forward. She was tight, but wet, and his manhood slipped easily within her. He had, to his surprise, been aching to possess her.

She felt him filling her gently, and for a moment she was surprised, for when Simon had had her it had hurt. Now she was very aware of her husband's tender lust as he began to fill her completely, and then his pubic bone pressed against hers. She was fully impaled on his firm manhood. She was so aware of the length of him. Of how hard he was, and yet he was not hurting her. It had not been this way the last time. She had considered that she might not be able to bear him taking her, yet now as he began to gently move on her Junia realized that she was eager for his passion. She could feel him trembling in his great effort not to harm or frighten her. And he wasn't harming or frightening her. Indeed, she had enjoyed every moment of their congress so far.

"William," she whispered into his ear, "it is all right. Make love to me now, and show me the rest of the sweetness, for having had a foretaste, I am eager for it all!"

"I will not be able to cease until we are both well satisfied," he groaned.

"I do not think I will ask it of you, my lord," she murmured back at him. "Oh! I can feel you throbbing within me!"

Her speech aroused him to passionate action. He began to move on her, within her, and he could indeed not stop. Her little cries of excitement drove him onward.

"Wrap your legs about me, Junia!" he cried out to her, and when she did he slid deeper into her, and he felt her fingernails clawing down his back in the heat of her desire. He didn't think he could hold back much longer. He so desperately wanted her to be completely fulfilled, and then he felt the tremors within her sweet body beginning, growing in intensity until she was crying out with her pleasure. He released his love juices at that same moment.

"Ohhh, William!" she sighed gustily.

"Ohhh, Junia!" he replied.

And nine months later in the midst of a howling February blizzard, Junia gave birth to twins, a son and a daughter. Both babies were sound, and strong of limb. The boy was baptized Simon. The girl, Adele. And looking down at his children, cradled in their mother's arms, William le Clare knew why his first wife had smiled when he had said he would never love again, for he had fallen deeply in love with his second wife, even as she was in love with him.

"When did you know?" he asked her as he admired their sleeping offspring.

"From that first night," she answered him, "but I dared not admit it to you." And he understood. "When did you know?" she queried him.

"I think from the first moment I saw you," he replied, "though I dared not admit it even to myself. It seemed so disloyal."

"I know," Junia said. "I felt the same way."

"You promised always to be truthful to me," he teased her with a loving smile.

"I did, but I did not promise to tell you all, William," she responded pertly, and he laughed softly.

"You have given me the greatest gift a woman can give her husband. Our children," he said.

"Nay, William, you have given me a far greater gift," Junia told him.

He looked puzzled. "What was that?" he said.

"You have taught me to love," she said, and then Junia smiled a radiant smile at her husband, and William le Clare smiled happily back at her. The world was theirs now, and as far as he was concerned it always would be.

Epilogue

The summer that Brynn Pendragon turned eighteen he was married to the granddaughter of the Prince of the Welsh, by one of Llywelyn's illegitimate daughters. She was fourteen, and her name was Enit.

For the first time in many years the Dragon Lord's children were all under the same roof. Averil at twenty-four was still beautiful. She had given Rhys three sons and two daughters. Maia, now twenty-three, was the mother of three — two daughters and a son. Her husband, Emrys, was content with his mortality. And Junia, now twenty, came with her husband, William le Clare. They had two sons, and a daughter. The love that they had finally been able to admit to had but grown over the last four years. And Junia had finally made peace with her father.

"I am forgiven, then," he said.

"Aye, I forgive you, Da, but I still believe that you were wrong to slay poor Simon de Bohun," she told him.

The Dragon Lord was wise enough to be

content with her forgiveness, and speak nothing of the rest. He looked about his hall that night, satisfied with what he saw. His family burgeoned. He had his women, his children and his grandchildren. They were far from the constant strife that seemed to plague their prince in his never-ending struggle with the English for the autonomy of Wales. The line of descent from Arthur Pendragon, the once and future king of the British, was safe, was assured now, and would continue on. It was more than enough.

About the Author

BERTRICE SMALL is the author of thirty-three novels of Historical Romance, and four erotic novellas. She lives in the oldest English-speaking town in the State of New York with her husband of forty years, George. She is the mother of Thomas, mother-in-law of Megan, and grandmother to Chandler, Cora and Sophia. Longtime readers will be happy to learn that her dearest feline companions, Pookie, Honeybun and Finnegan are still keeping her company as is Nicky the cockatiel.

Readers are invited to write her at: P.O. Box 765, Southold, NY 11971-0765, or at: bertricesmall@hotmail.com. I also hope that you will visit my Web site at: BertriceSmall.com.

God bless and good reading from your most faithful author,

Bertrice Small